H.E.A.L.

ABBY AND THE RELICS

ASHWIKA BALLEPU

ADHIRA MEENAKSHISANKAR

Published by Hemingway Publishers

Cover design by Hemingway Publishers

ISBN: Printed in the United States

For all those kids who want something a bit more magical in their life

—Ashwika

For our parents

—Adhira

TABLE OF CONTENTS

Prologue
Escape from H.E.A.L

Melissa had never been more terrified in her life.

She was scared just looking at Lizzie. Her hands trembled, and she took in shaky breaths. Tendrils of fear snaked through her body, threatening to burst out of her. She was aware that Lizzie was talking to her, but the fear drowned out all the background noise.

Melissa had short blond hair and hazel eyes. Her skin was pale, almost unblemished, except for the dark circles under her eyes and a tiny scratch on her cheek. She wore an oversized outfit with a black cloak tied loosely around her waist.

Lizzie was a couple of years older than Melissa. Her long, black hair streaked with purple flowed past her shoulders. Her hazel eyes mirrored Melissa's, but there was a hardness in them that Melissa couldn't quite place. Lizzie also had pale skin—almost as if they were two halves of the same whole.

Lizzie's clothes were in much better condition than Melissa's: she wore a purple satin dress paired with earrings and jewelry carved from amethyst, each piece shining with a quiet elegance.

Melissa was inside Lizzie's hideout, a metallic dome cloaked by invisibility, hidden from the world. Melissa was the only one who could see it because, whether she liked it or not, she was Lizzie's sister.

Melissa shut her eyes and tried to block the world out.

'Take it step by step,' her mother used to say whenever Melissa was going through something frustrating.

Step 1: Convince Lizzie to go into hiding with her.

Step 2: Go into hiding.

Step 3: …Actually, there was no step three. But the best things came in threes, right?

The sisters were the two most wanted people in Happily Ever After Land. Lizzie had done things that Melissa did not want to speak about or hear about. But that did not erase them. It was entirely fair that Lizzie was wanted.

Melissa's situation was more complicated. She was not evil, or at least she tried not to be. But she had cursed Sleeping Beauty. She had a horrible temper. She supposed all the stress and worry about Lizzie had boiled over, and in a moment of weakness, she had taken it out on Sleeping Beauty. She had apologized several times, but no one listened. And perhaps, rightfully so.

For the most part, being wanted was fine with Melissa. She knew she couldn't redeem herself or Lizzie. They were too far gone. Best to just lay low.

But then, last week, an angry mob had tried to kill Lizzie. And it wasn't a small group. Hundreds of citizens, holding blazing torches in the air, chanting, "Begone once and for all   !"

Knowing that every day could be turned into a battlefield felt like she was really awake and aware for the first time. They needed to get away fast, before they both got killed.

"MELISSA, ANSWER ME WHEN I'M SPEAKING TO YOU!"

Melissa flinched, snapping back to reality. "Um, uh, what?"

"Are you even listening?" Lizzie snapped, crossing her arms.

"Y-yeah," Melissa stammered.

She hesitated. How could she convince Lizzie to hide? Lizzie hated hiding.

Lizzie always wanted to stand out…and whenever she did, nothing good happened.

Melissa took a deep breath. In. Out. Just get it over with. "Lizzie—" She hesitated. Because the truth was, she was scared. And Melissa had a million reasons, and then some, to be afraid of Lizzie.

Once, back in elementary school, there had been a girl—Jessica Davidson. And Jessica was one of the best singers in the entire school.

Except for Lizzie. Lizzie was the best at singing. Both had auditioned for the lead role in the school musical. Melissa hadn't dared—she sounded like a frog with a head cold when she sang.

Everyone was surprised when Jessica got the part. Lizzie, strangely, hadn't seemed mad. "Whatever. Jessica was good," she had said with a shrug.

But the next morning, Jessica didn't utter a word. Melissa had asked her what was wrong.

Melissa still remembered the terror in Jessica's eyes when she opened her mouth and her tongue was missing.

The teachers had panicked. The entire school was flung into chaos. In the commotion, Melissa was the only one who'd heard Lizzie cackle.

She had known, without a doubt, that Lizzie had done it. Jessica never spoke again. Never sang. Never again would she fill the world with her enchanting melodies.

Lizzie had taken her place in the musical. Everyone had raved that the musical was awesome. *Lizzie was awesome. Lizzie had saved the show. Lizzie was perfect…* Except for Melissa. Melissa knew the truth. The harsh, bitter, cold truth.

"Melissa, what is your problem?" Lizzie demanded, snapping Melissa out of the memory.

Melissa's fists clenched. "My problem? My problem is that you're taking over my life!" Melissa blurted out, her fear not controlling her for a tiny second.

"Oh, I don't care what you do!" Lizzie exclaimed, throwing her hands up in the air. "Feel free to go hide under a rock!"

Melissa sighed. She had pleaded with Lizzie over and over again to come into hiding with her. But Lizzie had refused. Melissa had come up with different tactics to get Lizzie to come with her—first, she had gone for fierce and sure of herself, then she had used scare tactics, which only flared Lizzie up. When she had cooled down, Melissa didn't try to act scary or confident. She acted like herself. Scared. Sad. Lonely. And most of all, wishing that her sister wouldn't be so evil. Then they wouldn't have to go through any of this.

Melissa hated to admit it, but she needed Lizzie. No way could Melissa face danger on her own…and that was a big problem for a woman on the run.

Melissa was breathing hard. She tucked her hair behind her ears and glared at Lizzie. A bead of sweat dripped down her forehead. She hoped that Lizzie couldn't sense her fear.

"You have to understand! I'll get caught if you don't come with me!" Melissa protested.

Lizzie smirked and twirled a strand of her purple hair like she didn't really care. "H.E.A.L will always hate us, whether we are hiding or not."

In that instant, she let go of her fear and unleashed her fury. "YOU'RE EVIL!"

"You're just realizing that now?" Lizzie cackled. "I *am* the *Evil Queen*, after all."

"But Lizzie, please!" Melissa pleaded. "We have to leave, or we'll get hurt!"

"You're such a coward, Melissa."

"But if we don't go, we'll get killed!" Melissa protested, her voice cracking like it used to when she was younger. It still did.

"Oh, silly Melissa." Lizzie smiled menacingly. At that moment, she looked more evil than ever before. She leaned toward Melissa. "I'll let you in on a little secret." She paused and lowered her voice a little more. *"That will happen anyway, hiding or not."*

"But Lizzie, I can't go without you! I need you!" Melissa was crying at this point.

"Don't 'but, Lizzie!' me!" Lizzie growled. "I won't help you. Go grovel at someone else's feet."

"I wish Mother and Father were still here," Melissa sobbed.

All of a sudden, her legs weren't strong enough to hold her up. She wobbled and crumbled to the floor. Tears streamed down her cheeks, leaving tear marks behind. She almost never cried, but when it came to her sister, she always became the soft Melissa.

Usually, Melissa carried a hard shell to protect herself from the cruel world. Over the years, she'd learned (the hard way!) that if you're soft, you won't survive. It was as simple as that. And Lizzie was the only one who could break through.

"Crybaby," Lizzie scoffed, rolling her eyes. "You're such a whiner."

"Why do you have to be so mean to me? You're supposed to be my sister! Act like it!" Melissa shrieked. For a moment, she let herself believe that Lizzie would apologize and they would truly love each other again like they used to.

"You know, Melissa, you'd be much more agreeable if you didn't speak." Lizzie smiled cruelly. "Maybe if I controlled you…"

Melissa knew what her sister was talking about. Lizzie wanted to bewitch her. "WHAT?! Y-you can't d-do that!"

Melissa curled her fingers into fists. Her stomach hurt with anguish. She loved Lizzie, who, even if she was evil, was her sister. Melissa's anger only rose for a moment and then fizzled away. Now, she just felt miserable.

"I can and I will." Lizzie's eyes were turning green, a hideous neon green.

"I *am* the Evil *Queen*." Her voice was soft, but it echoed as if it were many.

Melissa's insides turned cold with fear. She knew what this meant. This meant she was going to get bewitched.

Melissa could *not* let that happen. She turned and ran faster than she ever had before.

"You can't get away, you crybaby!" Lizzie taunted. "You can hide all you want, but in the end, I *will* find you."

Melissa opened the door and slipped out just as the enchanted laser was about to pierce her. It wasn't an easy task. The door was made of steel, and it was heavy. But Melissa was strong, and she managed to do it.

As she ran, her hair whipped around wildly, and the wind caused her eyes to sting with tears. Her lungs screamed in pain, but she kept going. She collapsed once she was far enough from Lizzie. Melissa sank to her knees, panting..

Why did this have to happen? Melissa thought mournfully.

She knew she had to get away and fast before Lizzie tracked her down. There was only one place she could escape for good...***the Unknown***.

Chapter 1
Something Magical

"Mom, I'm home!"

Twelve-year-old Abby Palmer hurried through the doorway and slipped off her pale pink raincoat. Raindrops dripped onto the hardwood floor, so Abby hastily hung it up. She tucked a lock of her short blonde hair behind her ears. Abby's eyes were bright blue, like the clear summer sky. She had fair skin, which had gotten slightly tanned in the sun.

It didn't rain much in July, but today, the skies were mourning, gray and heavy with despair. Abby was glad to be inside, enjoying the cozy warmth of her house.

"Hi, sweetie," her mother greeted her with a welcoming smile. "Did you have a good time?"

Abby had just returned from the Jenkins' house. She regularly went to her neighbors' houses to babysit their little kids (All of her neighbors had either little kids or high schoolers. She wished there was someone her age on the street) whenever she was free to make money.

Her mom, assuming Abby wanted to make money for college, had reminded her that it was six years away and that Abby didn't need to worry about it. Yet, Abby had seen the FINAL NOTICE stamp on the bills, which seemed to stare back at her in bold red ink. College? Abby was just trying to make sure they had enough for dinner.

Today, she had babysat for the Jenkins' family, who had an adorable 2-year-old named Calista. But the minute her parents left, she became a whirlwind. Juice on the carpet, crayons on the walls, and screams that could shatter glass.

Abby sighed as she kicked off her matching pink boots. "I guess so." Abby placed the boots on the shoe rack next to her turquoise Skechers.

Abby's mom must have noticed Abby was feeling down. She said, "Hold on. I have the perfect thing!"

Her mother strode into the kitchen, and Abby followed her. She plopped down in a wooden chair. A few minutes later, her mother returned to the dinner table, holding a freshly made Caprese sandwich—Abby's all-time favorite snack!

Abby smiled. Caprese sandwiches were special—her dad used to make them all the time, humming songs from the 1950s while layering the mozzarella cheese. 'Cooking is an art,' her dad always used to say.

A Caprese sandwich is an Italian sandwich made of tomatoes, mozzarella cheese, and basil. To Abby, it was the most delicious thing in the world.

When she was little, Abby went through phases of obsessively researching things until she had memorized every little detail. She'd done this for video games, TikTok, fashion trends—and, of course, Caprese sandwiches!

Did you know that Caprese sandwiches were first made in the 1950s when King Farouk asked his chef for a snack and was served a Caprese sandwich?

"Thanks, Mom!" Abby exclaimed, grabbing the sandwich and sinking her teeth into the soft bread. A juicy tomato exploded in her mouth.

Her mother smiled. "Just remember, you're in control of your life, Abby. Don't let anything bring you down."

For a moment, a shadow passed over her mother's face, but it vanished in the blink of an eye. Abby wondered if she had imagined it.

"You always say that," Abby replied, her voice light as she grinned. She scarfed down the rest of the sandwich, hugged her mom, and then left the kitchen.

Abby went to her room to study. There was a mountain of worksheets stacked on her desk. Her mom liked to keep her busy with them whenever Abby didn't have anything else to do. She also promised that if Abby finished them, they could go to Dunkin' Donuts, and Abby was definitely a fan of Dunkin' Donuts.

Abby loved her room. It was painted a warm shade called 'Sunset Orange,' and her window faced the east, so her room was always the brightest and coziest in the house. Her mom liked to say that Abby's room had positive energy.

A desk sat nestled in the corner. Against the walls were numerous boxes and storage containers, because Abby liked things neat and organized.

Her drawers were filled with clothes and mementos from her younger years. She treasured the shiny medals and awards displayed on an achievement rack above her drawer. Honestly, whenever Abby wanted to reminisce, she would visit those drawers.

Abby enjoyed listening to music as she worked. She grabbed her gray headphones, slipped them over her ears, and turned them on. "What Makes You Beautiful" by One Direction streamed through, and she hummed along, drumming her fingers on the table as she filled out the worksheets.

When she finished filling out the last of her worksheets, Abby leaned back in her chair, her eyes growing heavy. The warm glow of her lamp flickered…then disappeared entirely. Abby started to snore softly.

Abby was standing in a forest. Even though she lived in the suburbs, she recognized this place. It was the one from her mom's stories, with towering, brave pine trees blocking out the sun and a worn dirt path winding through the forest.

Though familiar, it didn't make the forest any less intimidating. Abby looked around, her heartbeat quickening as she realized she was all alone. She seemed brave, but that was only when others surrounded her Alone, she felt like a chicken.

She walked down the path for some time. Sunlight filtered through the canopy, illuminating the forest floor. Sparrows perched in the trees, singing their sweet melodies.

Suddenly, a rustling sound came from behind her. She whipped around, but there was no one there.

The rustling came again, louder this time, but she kept walking, glancing over her shoulder. A chill ran down her spine. To calm herself, Abby began humming "Firework" by Katy Perry, but the nervous feeling lingered.

After several minutes of tense walking, a cottage came into view. At first, she hesitated, but then she rushed up to the door and knocked. The rustling stopped as soon as she knocked, much to her relief.

The door creaked open to reveal an elderly woman who looked warm and inviting. She had stormy gray eyes and was slightly hunched over. The woman smiled, her eyes twinkling as though she was about to share a secret. She wore an emerald green cloak, which looked elegant but still comfortable.

"Hello, dear. I've been expecting you," the woman said. "What's your name?"

"My name's Abby," Abby replied. She didn't know what this all was, but she somehow knew she could trust this woman despite the oddness of her statement. How could the woman have been expecting her?

"Nice to meet you, Abby," the woman said warmly. "I'm Eleanor Queen. Come in!" Abby nervously followed Eleanor inside.

Eleanor sat down in a cozy armchair by the fireplace, patting the chair next to her. Abby hesitated, biting her fingernails before taking a seat.

"What brings you here?" Eleanor asked, her voice soft but curious.

"I don't know," Abby admitted, her voice tinged with uncertainty. "Honestly, I don't even know where I am."

The old woman smiled knowingly. "You are in H.E.A.L, my dear."

Abby's brow furrowed in confusion. "Huh? What's that?"

"Happily Ever After Land," Eleanor explained, her eyes twinkling. "You might know it better as the fairy tale world."

"The fairy tale world?" Abby repeated, still trying to process the information.

"Yes, my dear…" Eleanor's voice trailed off as her words slurred together, and her eyelids drooped.

Abby's heart skipped a beat as she watched Eleanor's eyes shift to black and white—spiraling like she was in a trance. Eleanor slumped forward in her chair, and a low, soft chant began to escape her lips. Abby had to strain to hear the words.

"When darkness has fallen, a girl from the Unknown…"

Abby froze, a wave of fear washing over her. She instinctively jumped out of the chair and backed away, her pulse quickening.

"Eleanor?" Abby asked weakly, her voice trembling. "What's happening?"

Eleanor's eyes flickered back to their normal gray, and her body relaxed.

"Eleanor!" Abby cried out, panic rising in her chest. She rushed to Eleanor's side, checking her pulse. It was steady, thankfully, but Eleanor wouldn't wake up.

"Wake up! Wake up!" Abby screamed, shaking the woman's shoulders, her desperation evident.

But Eleanor didn't stir. Abby's heart raced faster, and the weight of what just happened started to sink in. What had she witnessed?

Abby bolted outside, desperate for help. But as soon as her foot hit the cobblestone path, the forest began to fade around her.

"No, no, no, no!" she screamed, her voice echoing in the space. She searched for an escape, but the trees, the ground, everything began to dissolve before her eyes.

Soon, nothing but emptiness remained. The last thing Abby could do before everything vanished was yell a desperate, final cry.

"HELP!"

Abby snapped out of her dream. Her eyes flickered open, and she looked around, eyes wide.

"Was that all just a dream?" she asked herself.

Her mom was hovering over her, worry in her eyes. "I was so worried! You were kicking and swatting at the air, and then you screamed, 'HELP!'"

"Uh, I had a dream. Well, it was a mix between a nightmare and a dream," Abby replied, still shaken.

Abby didn't know how to explain her dream. It felt so... real. She realized she had genuinely believed the dream was real, even though it was just that, a dream.

Her mother cocked her head, concern deepening in her eyes. "A nightmare?"

"Yeah..." Abby nodded slowly. "I'm sorry I scared you. It was a pretty scary nightmare."

"Sweetie, you can tell me anything," her mom reassured her.

Abby didn't want to explain everything to her mom. She knew her mom would probably start analyzing what caused the nightmare, and Abby dreaded those talks. It had just been a dream—or a nightmare! Just a figment of her imagination, right?

"Well, I was asleep, even though it was in the middle of the day. I was just tired," Abby explained, trying to downplay it.

"OK," her mom said, clearly still concerned. "Tell me more."

"So, basically, I was in this forest, walking through it. Then, I found a hut, and a lady opened the door. She said her name was Eleanor Queen. She mentioned something about a fairy tale world. Then, she started chanting something and just collapsed. I was scared, so I ran outside to get help. And that's when the forest started disappearing!" Abby finished.

"What was the chant?" Abby's mom asked, her breath shallow as she tried to understand.

"Like this: *When darkness has fallen, a girl from the Unknown...* that's where she stopped and went unconscious," Abby explained.

"Really...?" her mom asked, worry clear in her voice.

"Yeah!" Abby wondered why her mom was so worried. It was just a dream, right?

"And...did she say what the fairy tale world was called?" Abby's mom asked, biting her lip.

"Happily Ever After Land." Abby frowned. "Why?

Her mom's eyes widened, and her face turned grim. Any trace of her previous worry was now replaced with fear.

"Lizzie..." her mom murmured.

"Mom? Who's Lizzie?" Abby asked, genuinely confused.

"Lizzie, the Evil Queen..." her mom continued, slowly backing away.

"The Evil Queen?! Like Snow White's stepmom in the fairy tale? You've got to be kidding me!" Abby laughed, trying to lighten the mood.

"My sister…she's rising…" her mom whispered, her voice trembling.

Abby's worry grew. "Hey, hey! Mom, are you okay?" she asked, concerned.

Her mom stared at Abby, clutching her purple gem necklace tightly. What was happening? Nobody could ever make her mom this nervous!

"I'm scared, Mom. Please, what's wrong?" Abby begged. "Please, talk to me!"

Abby stood up and leaned in closer, noticing her mom's eyes glistening with... tears? She never cried! Not even when Abby's dad went missing two years ago and was declared dead.

Abby gave herself a pep talk.

"Okay! She's alright, just scared about me. She's absolutely, a hundred percent fine!" Abby whispered to herself, trying to believe it.

That's when her mom decided to speak, much to Abby's relief.

"Abby, I'm going to tell you something I've never told anyone before." Abby's mom said. "It's going to sound crazy."

"Okay, Mom. What is it?" Abby asked, holding her breath.

"I…I'm from the fairy tale world, Abby," her mom whispered.

Abby just stared at her mom. Her expression shifted from curious to concerned in an instant. Was her mother going crazy? The fairy tale world wasn't real! Sure, sometimes she *wished* it was, but that was just daydreaming! She's either gone crazy, or this is some late April Fools' prank, Abby thought.

"You're kidding, right?" Abby laughed nervously.

"Do I look like I'm kidding? Here, I'll—I'll show you!" her mom yelped frantically.

Abby sighed and partially leaned on her desk. Her elbow nudged a pile of papers, and a probability worksheet fluttered to the ground.

Her mom glanced at the sheet as Abby stared at it, already dreading what was to come. Abby sighed again, fully expecting her mom to blow on it and say, "Tada, it's magic!"—just like she had once done to amuse three-year-old Abby at her birthday party.

Except, she didn't.

Instead, her mom bent toward the paper but didn't pick it up. A purple arc flowed from her mom's hand to the paper and lit it up. It floated upward as her mom stood. Abby's mind raced, searching for a rational explanation, but none came to her.

"So…magic's real!" her mom exclaimed, placing the glowing worksheet back onto Abby's desk.

Abby stared at the paper, still faintly glowing. *Am I still asleep?* She thought. She pinched herself and yelped in pain. She wasn't asleep! It had to be real!

Abby let out a high-pitched squeal, and her mom immediately covered her ears.

"Magic's real, it's real, really, really, real!" Abby jumped up and down, squealing. "Wait. What is The Unknown?"

"It's…" Abby's mom seemed to be at war with her tongue. "Earth. The girl in the prophecy? It's…it's you, but—"

"ME?!" Abby screeched, shocked. "Go to the fairy tale world?! That's amazing! Let's go!"

"But, I can't let you," her mom continued.

"What? Why not?" Abby asked, dismayed.

"The Evil Queen, Lizzie, she's my sister. She's on the loose in the fairy tale world, and my highest priority is keeping you safe," her mom explained. She leaned forward and looked Abby in the eye. "Please, Abby, I need you to listen to me. Prophecy girl or not, you're staying here."

Abby's eyes widened. Her mother's hazel eyes were filled with tears—again! Twice in one hour! Abby took a deep breath. She knew that her mom only cried when she really, really felt strongly about something.

Abby wanted to listen to her mother, but she also really wanted to find the fairy tale world! She always felt like something was missing in her life. Well, something was—or rather, someone—as her dad had been for two years. But something more! Something not as obvious.

Something…magical.

Abby folded her arms and looked outside. It was nighttime already. A couple of lone stars twinkled, along with about two planes and a lone helicopter.

Abby's mom sighed and left the room. She glanced one more time back at Abby with a desperate look on her face. "Please, stay home. It's for your own good. Now, dinner's ready. Come downstairs."

Abby stuffed her papers in her desk drawer. She went downstairs to the dinner table. Two steaming plates of Alfredo pasta were arranged neatly on the table.

Abby loved pasta almost as much as she loved Caprese sandwiches. She gobbled up the pasta and raced upstairs to brush her teeth. Her mom entered her room and smiled as Abby tucked herself into bed.

"Good night, my sandwich!" her mom leaned in and kissed Abby on the forehead. It was a little embarrassing, but sweet.

"Good night, Mom," Abby replied.

"Remember, You'r—"

"You're in control of your life, Abby. Don't let anything bring you down," Abby repeated. "I know, Mom."

"Sleep sweet, my child. Don't let the bedbugs bite!" Abby's mom walked away.

Abby closed her eyes and tried to get to sleep, but it was just so hard! She had so many questions. After an hour, she finally fell asleep, dreaming of magic and fairies.

In Abby's dream, she was admiring a bubbling stream that sparkled with magic. Abby kicked off her sandals and dipped her toes into the cool water. Suddenly, she heard a gasp. Abby looked up and saw a woman with purple hair and hazel eyes. A blast of purple light shot forth from the woman's hand, heading straight for Abby. When the light hit her, Abby screamed.

She snapped out of her dream. Her eyes flew open. Abby glanced at the window and saw the moon still high in the sky, casting a silver glow across her room. She heard a strange noise from outside her door, a soft popping sound like bubbles bursting. She glanced at her rainbow clock—it was 12:14 a.m., way past midnight.

Abby was still tired, but her curiosity had already gotten the best of her. Abby crawled slowly out of bed, following the sound until she stopped in front of her mother's door. She peered inside and had to bite her lip to keep from gasping. There was a portal on the floor... and then her mom jumped in!

Panic surged through Abby's mind. *Is she coming back? Where did she go?* Abby considered that maybe her mom had gone to a late-night party and didn't want Abby to know she'd be home alone. But that didn't seem like her. And where could she have gone so late at night? There could only be one other place: *H.E.A.L!* But still… why had she gone?

Abby's gaze flickered back to the portal, still open on the floor. *Maybe I can go in!* She cautiously stepped closer… and closer…

Her foot hovered over the swirling light. Just as she was about to step in, the portal disappeared with a whoosh!

Abby gasped. Her heart dropped into her shoes. The portal was gone.

Still in shock, Abby walked back to her room. She was dazed, trying to process what had just happened. In a matter of seconds, her mom had vanished, and Abby had seen magic up close.

Abby knew she had to find her mom. *What if she can't get back?* But then she reassured herself. She was probably overthinking it.

She'll be back soon, Abby thought. *It'll only take a few minutes. Maybe an hour at most. When it's light out, she'll be back.*

She slipped back under the sheets, trying to get some sleep. Everything would be fixed by sunrise. It just had to be. It had to.

Chapter 2
The Bad Fairy's Return

Picture this: a close-knit town where the streets sparkle with magic and the air hums with warmth. The cinnamon-sweet scent of enchantment drifts through the breeze, and the trees bear glimmering, magical fruit that hums with quiet energy… yet a whisper of fear slithers through the cobblestone paths.

Goldilocks has been stirring up trouble again, spreading a rumor that the Evil Queen had been wreaking havoc everywhere she went. Even though the Evil Queen is supposedly in jail.

Of course, no one takes it seriously at first. Goldie is known for spreading rumors and drama.

But then the whispers grow louder. Reports start trickling in—from far more reliable sources. And soon, even the skeptics begin to wonder: what if it's true?

But as more reports from more believable sources came in, no one could deny that this might be…*real*.

But something else is astray. This, no one knows about…for now.

"Pinocchio!"

"Yes, Father?"

"Could you fetch some raspberries from the bucket, please?"

Melissa had just landed in the village where she grew up. It looked so different now, yet so familiar. The problem was that she had landed in the middle of the busy square, where anyone could see her. *Ugh.*

People were shouting from behind their carts, hawking everything from enchanted brooms to glowing vials of healing potion. The air buzzed with magic and murmured with gossip. Not ideal for someone trying to stay under the radar.

She had come because she wanted to catch up on what had happened since she left. If Abby was getting a prophecy in her sleep, there was no doubt something new was stirring.

She also wanted to make sure Lizzie was not more powerful than she was 13 years ago— because if she was, that could only mean one thing: the end of the world was inching closer. Melissa's plan was simple—slink through shadows, eavesdrop on gossiping villagers, gather intel on H.E.A.L., and be gone before Abby stirred from her dreams.

As she gazed around the familiar square, a wave of memories washed over her like a warm tide meeting cold sand. She remembered when she was too tired to walk and her dad perched her up on his shoulders. The memories of her mom teaching Melissa and Lizzie how to sell things in the village square. And how Melissa had been scammed by a villager who promised her magic beans. Melissa had been just seven, so she hadn't yet learned not to trust everything she saw. She had now...*the hard way*, she thought ruefully. *All right, Melissa, stop reminiscing and do what you came to do. You need to get back to Abby quickly, before she wakes up.*

Melissa tucked her chin, pulled her cloak tighter, and began to retreat into the shadows of the woods just a few paces away. If anyone recognized her…

Too late.

A little boy with a long nose looked at her, and a hint of recognition showed on his face. His brow furrowed. Pinocchio. He stared at her so hard that the bucket in his hands slipped. Fresh, juicy raspberries tumbled across the cobblestones, bouncing like tiny red jewels.

Please, please, PLEASE don't recognize me, Melissa thought, going farther back into the shadows of the woods.

Pinocchio had come from another world—one that Lizzie had destroyed. He and his father had found refuge in H.E.A.L. after their homeland was reduced to ruins.

"Father!" Pinocchio said loudly. "I-isn't that the Enchantress? From your stories?"

Pinocchio's father, Geppetto, looked up. He squinted at her, then shrieked. "My boy, it's her! Run!"

"No, we'll kill her now!" Pinocchio declared, standing his ground. Melissa's blood ran cold, and she froze. Then, to get people's attention, Pinocchio screamed, "It's Melissa! The Enchantress! HELP!" Pinocchio screamed. She was pretty sure she heard glass shatter somewhere.

"Shut up, Pinocchio," Melissa warned, her voice low.

For twelve years, Melissa had clung to the light Abby gave her. A second chance. A clean slate. A sliver of hope when the world had offered her none. Abby had been her only brightness after Jay vanished—disappeared, and later declared dead.

But now that she was back in H.E.A.L. Melissa could feel something shift inside her. Anger crept towards her mind.

Fairness, they said. *Magic*, they said. *We'll solve your problems*, they say. Well, if that was true, how come Melissa had grown up in a dirty, run-down neighborhood?

Their parents hadn't always been poor. They were solidly middle class—comfortable, if not extravagant. They'd lived in a humble but well-kept home that always smelled faintly of fresh paint, a scent that lingered no matter how many times the walls chipped and were repainted. The porch was lined with baskets of flowers, always freshly watered and blooming, like little acts of defiance against the chaos of life.

But just after Melissa turned four, life threw them a curveball.

Melissa's father worked at a lumber mill. She was too young to grasp the danger back then—the heavy machinery, the screaming saws, the ever-present threat of injury. To her, it was just another part of grown-up life.

Dangerous or not, the job paid well enough to keep food on the table, joy in the home, and even a few small luxuries—dolls, picture books, and warm winter boots.

Then came the snowstorm. Eight inches fell overnight, coating the village in a thick, powdery blanket. Melissa and Lizzie attended different schools—Melissa in preschool (yes, even the fairy tale world had preschool), Lizzie in elementary. Melissa's school was canceled. Lizzie's wasn't.

That created a problem. Unlike most of Melissa's classmates, her mother couldn't stay home. She was a hospital healer—committed, reliable, and unable to call in, especially during a storm where many people could get sick or hurt. And she didn't want Melissa being exposed to germs at her workplace either.

After a heated round of arguing and problem-solving, a reluctant plan was made. That day, Melissa would accompany her father to the lumber mill.

When they walked in, her father leaned close and whispered, "Mel, baby, I have to work. Sit right here on this bench, and don't touch anything. Be as quiet as a church mouse, okay?"

With that, he left. Melissa, wide-eyed and excited, looked around in awe. She had no idea that bringing a four-year-old to a lumber mill was not only dangerous—it was illegal.

Melissa bounced in her seat, swinging her legs, waiting for her father to come back and show her the machines. But he never did. She'd later learn that everyone was working in another part of the mill that day—far away from where she sat.

After a while, boredom crept in. Curiosity followed. Melissa slipped off the bench and wandered over to the biggest machine in sight. She started poking at the levers and wheels, mesmerized by their size. She didn't know that one wrong move could lead to serious injury—or worse.

A glint of metal caught her eye at the machine's base. It was a lever—just the right size for her tiny hand. With innocent curiosity, she reached down and pulled.

WHIRR! The machine roared to life.

Melissa shrieked and stumbled backward, her heart hammering. The sight of razor-sharp spinning gears sent tears streaming down her cheeks.

Within seconds, the thundering sound brought a crowd. Her father, his boss, and several coworkers came rushing in.

"Melissa!" her father gasped, grabbing her shoulders and pulling her back from the machine.

"Papa!" Melissa wailed. In her tiny mind, she wondered, *Why did the machine try to eat me?*

The boss's face turned red with rage. "Is this your child?" he demanded, rounding on Melissa's father.

"Y-yes," her father admitted, voice shaking.

"What were you thinking? This is a lumber mill, not a daycare!"

Her father looked like he might cry. "Please…I can explain. Just give me another chance—"

"No!" the boss snapped. "I'll decide your punishment later!"

Later, her father announced at dinner that he no longer had a job. "Girls," he softly said. "I…my boss fired me."

"WHAT?! WHY?" their mother screamed. "This can't be!"

"M—Melissa—it's not her fault—my boss—she touched the machine—" her dad stammered.

"Oh, Mel, baby. It's not your fault, it was the weather's fault," Melissa's mom gave a weak smile. Melissa looked at Lizzie to see what she would say, but she just looked shocked...and angry. She didn't look like herself.

"You idiot!" Lizzie had screamed at her later, when their parents were whispering behind a closed door. "Why'd you have to touch it? You ruined everything!"

From there, everything went downhill. Melissa's father ended up working as a plumber with barely any pay. They moved to a lousy house with a hole in the living room! Lizzie never forgave Melissa.

But when Melissa was in 6th grade and Lizzie was in 8th grade, they hit rock bottom.

Melissa's mother caught a deadly fever. They could not afford to visit a doctor.

"Lizzie, you need to quit school to get a job," Melissa remembered her father saying. "You need to support the family."

"What?" Lizzie gasped. "No! My teacher says I'm so smart, one day I can be famous or something! I can't drop out!"

"Your mother is going to die, Lizzie!"

"Why can't Melissa do it? It's her fault we don't have any money!"

Their father's eyes flashed with anger. His hand moved so fast, Melissa barely saw it. He slapped Lizzie so hard her head jerked sideways. Lizzie's hand flew to her face.

"You will obey," their father rasped. "End of conversation."

Melissa's mother was past help, though. She died a week later. A small funeral had been held. Melissa had run out of tears that day.

The family moved again, to the slums. Lizzie wasn't able to get back into school. Not that it was a great school—it was a horrible neighborhood with horrible people.

Later, Melissa found out that the man who fired her father was Geppeto—Pinocchio's father. And guess what? Geppeto had reconsidered firing her dad. He had wanted to give him a second chance. But it was Pinocchio who convinced him otherwise, insisting that firing Melissa's father was the right thing to do.

Pinocchio hadn't aged a day since. Even though he was made of flesh and bone now, he still aged at the same pace as wood—agonizingly slow.

Rage surged through Melissa's chest. Her fists clenched as she opened her eyes. She hadn't even realized she'd closed them.

Suddenly, her senses sharpened. Screams filled the square. Townsfolk were panicking, running in all directions. They grabbed whatever they could find—tree branches, pitchforks, garden tools. One teenager even waved a plastic sword like he was about to charge into battle. Melissa blinked. *Seriously? Plastic?*

But the absurdity didn't calm her. Instead, it stoked the fire burning inside her. Pinocchio had destroyed her life. He didn't deserve comfort. He didn't deserve a happy ending.

He didn't even deserve a life.

She took a step forward, her voice rising into a cold chant, sharp with fury.

"Turn back into what he was before, A piece of tree, sold at the store! Back isolated, all alone— Turn into a tree with a gravestone!"

With a sharp *pop*, Pinocchio vanished. In his place stood a withered tree, gnarled and gray. A gravestone appeared in front of it with one chilling inscription:

'Pinocchio Wood.'

"NOOOOOOOOOO! MY SON! WHAT HAVE YOU DONE TO HIM?!" Geppeto's scream tore through the square.

He collapsed near the gravestone and sobbed. Tears dripped down his face fast, then faster. Melissa felt a flare of anger roar inside of her at the sight of the man who had caused all her misfortune.

It was Melissa's first instinct to curse him too, but then she realized it was much more satisfying to watch him cry.

He wiped away his tears and slowly rose to his feet. A small crowd had gathered around them by now, their expressions a mix of shock, fear, and disbelief.

A little girl nearby burst into tears. "MOMMY! WILL I BECOME A TREE TOO?"

The girl's mother didn't hesitate. She scooped her daughter into her arms and bolted from the square.

"STOP!" the guy with the fake sword shouted, raising his flimsy weapon like it would do any good.

Melissa laughed darkly. "Stop? *You* dare to tell *the Enchantress* to stop? No, young man. I will not."

She could feel it—magic crawling down her arms, pooling in her fingertips, hot and electric. It pulsed, begging to be unleashed.

Stay in, she thought. Not yet.

But the magic had its own will.

It raced from her hands like lightning, shooting across the square, and struck a house at the edge of the village. *BOOM.*

In an instant, the house crumbled into a fine, gray dust, collapsing in on itself like a sandcastle in the wind. Melissa's eyes widened at the destruction… then her lips curled into a smirk.

Victory tasted sweet.

"That was our home!" a woman wailed, clutching a baby boy to her chest. The child cried with her.

Geppeto stepped forward, trembling—whether from grief, fear, or both, Melissa couldn't tell.

"W-why… why must you do this?" he whispered, his voice barely audible over the stunned murmurs of the crowd.

Melissa raised her chin, her eyes glowing. "Because I'm the Enchantress." She flipped her hair with a wicked smile.

She didn't say the words that clawed at her throat: Because of you.

"You're evil!" Geppeto roared, the grief gone, replaced by rage. His face was flushed, fists clenched, eyes burning.

"You're *just* realizing that now? I'm the *bad fairy*," Melissa said with a twisted laugh, hearing Lizzie's voice echo in her own. The irony stung.

A nervous murmur swept through the crowd. People clutched their loved ones. Someone dropped a basket of apples. No one dared to move first.

Right on cue, Jack and Jill stepped out from the crowd, creeping toward her with pitchforks gripped tightly in their shaking hands.

Seriously? Melissa rolled her eyes. *What is this, a scene from The Boy Who Cried Wolf?*

She flicked her wrist casually, and the grass at their feet shriveled into ash. Flowers nearby crumpled into dust, turning an eerie shade of gray.

"Nobody likes you, Melissa!" Jack barked, voice cracking.

"No one ever will!" Jill added, fire in her eyes.

Melissa just smirked. "That's where you're wrong. My daughter will *always* stand by me. Abby."

She started to cackle—but the sound caught in her throat and died.

The moment she said Abby's name, it was like everything inside her shifted. The rage, the pride, the thirst for vengeance—they all flickered and dimmed.

Abby.

Her light. Her hope. Her only anchor in a world that had long since betrayed her. *Oh no. Oh no. I have to get back—before Abby wakes up!*

With panic gripping her heart, Melissa turned and bolted into the woods. Behind her, the villagers shouted and whispered in a blur of confusion and relief.

She ran as fast as her legs would carry her, branches snapping beneath her feet, heart thudding in her ears. She reached the portal clearing—and stopped cold.

When the name Abby was mentioned, all the hate and need for revenge vanished. Abby was love and hope. Her light in the dark. Suddenly, she remembered.

Oh, shoot! I need to get back before Abby wakes up!

Melissa dashed into the woods, leaving all the villagers confused and relieved. She raced back to the spot where the portal was, only to realize it was gone.

The potion only worked if no one discovered it. Abby must have seen it. That innocent discovery had severed Melissa's way back. *No. No, no, no. This can't be happening.*

Her breath came in ragged gasps. She needed another portal potion. But gathering the ingredients would take time—*too* much time.

Melissa ran deeper into the woods, foolishly hoping it might be somewhere there. Then she heard a growl.

She whipped around to see a wolf pack facing her. They all looked shocked and terrified when they saw her infamous face.

Melissa wasn't evil, but she'd done evil things, things Abby should never know about. She'd let anger control her, always! She really was just heartbroken inside.

"Hey, wolf. What's up?" Melissa greeted the leader of the pack. She smiled at him, like they were old friends.

"CHARGE ON THE ENCHANTRESS!" the wolf bellowed. He ran forward a bit before stopping in his tracks.

Turning around, he realized his pack was too afraid. Melissa watched with amusement as the wolves cowered, their ears flat, tails tucked.

Cowards. Just to test their fear, she sent one sharp swipe of dark magic skimming through the air, sizzling as it passed inches from their paws. The wolves yelped and bolted.

Pathetic, Melissa thought with a smirk.

She turned and resumed walking, but a voice called out from behind—one that definitely didn't belong to any wolf.

"Melissa? Melissa, is that you?"

She froze. No one in H.E.A.L. called her Melissa. Abby called her *Mom*, and Abby wasn't here. Not unless…

No. It couldn't be. She slowly turned around, heart thudding.

At first, her breath caught in relief—it *wasn't* the Fairy Godfather. But that relief was crushed a second later when she saw who it *really* was.

Lizzie. The Evil Queen. Her sister.

Of all the people she expected to run into, Lizzie had been dead last on the list.

Melissa screamed—loud, raw, and visceral.

Lizzie winced and covered her ears. "Geez, what's with the banshee routine?" she huffed. She tried to sound annoyed, but Melissa could see the smirk tugging at her lips.

Melissa tried to make her face appear neutral, hiding the panic curling in her chest like smoke. But her heart was pounding so loudly, she was certain Lizzie could hear it.

"L-L-Lizzie! Hey, sis," Melissa stammered. "How's it going, Liz? 'Sup? On the real!" (Melissa always started to speak weirdly when she got scared.)

Melissa had grown a little braver since she had last seen Lizzie. Lizzie hadn't expected that Melissa wouldn't run away, and she was annoyed that Melissa didn't entertain her by acting as scared as she had been a long time ago. But then her face brightened.

"Melissa, I haven't seen you in a long time." Lizzie smiled coyly. "I think I saw your beloved daughter Abby in these regions," she informed Melissa.

"Yeah, right, and I'm from a far-off galaxy," Melissa scoffed.

"Melissa, please quit being sarcastic. Anyways, I didn't come here to chat," Lizzie sighed.

Lizzie reached behind a tree and dragged out a net—large enough to hold a person.

And inside it was…someone who looked exactly like Abby. But something was off.

Melissa squinted, her breath catching. Then it hit her.

The girl in the net wasn't *acting* like Abby. She wasn't scared. She wasn't thrashing. She wasn't even crying. Her expression was blank, like a puppet without strings. Abby would've been screaming her lungs out by now.

Melissa quickly summoned her magic and looked through the veil, back to Earth.

Abby was still in bed, safe and sound.

This girl? Not Abby.

Lizzie's triumphant smirk faded when Melissa didn't react. "…Well?" Lizzie asked, raising a brow. She was clearly waiting for her sister to scream, cry, or fall apart.

"That's not Abby!" Melissa exclaimed. She couldn't believe Lizzie expected her to believe that was Abby. She bent over, laughing.

When Melissa straightened up, she saw something she hadn't seen in years—and never wanted to see again. Lizzie's eyes were glowing that same hideous neon green, and her voice began to shift, as if it belonged to not one person, but many.

"Yes. It. Is," Lizzie hissed, her voice dangerously low and echoing—as if the trees themselves were whispering her words.

There were no walls, no cave—yet the sound reverberated all around them. Melissa shivered. A chill wrapped around her spine.

And then she felt it. The pull.

The dark bewitchment, invisible but powerful, yanked at her soul. It tugged her toward Lizzie, and it took everything Melissa had not to give in.

She turned and ran—bolting toward the town like her life depended on it.

Because it did.

The force tried to drag her back, clawing at her limbs, her mind, her will. She could almost taste freedom. Just a little farther…

She thought of Abby. If Melissa didn't make it back, what would happen to her? She'd be alone. An orphan.

Melissa's lungs burned. Her legs screamed with every step. But stopping wasn't an option.

She ran like she never had before.

But it wasn't enough. She needed more. She needed to fly.

It had been years since she last flew, but desperation had a way of awakening old magic.

She pushed harder. Her feet left the ground, just barely—her body lifted into the air—Then, a sharp jolt.

Something yanked her back mid-flight. With a cry, she was pulled backward—back into the woods, back into Lizzie's grasp.

"Do what I say… or else," Lizzie growled, her voice venomous.

Melissa wanted to resist, to scream, to fight. But her body betrayed her. Every fiber of her being caved to Lizzie's will.

She collapsed to her knees, sobbing.

All she could think about was Abby—and the miserable life that might await her now.

"Y-yes… Queen Lizzie… f-fairest of them all… I will o-obey," Melissa choked out, her voice breaking.

Lizzie smiled. "Good. You most certainly will."

Chapter 3
What In Both Worlds Is Happening?

Abby couldn't sleep that night. She kept tossing and turning, thinking about how her mother had vanished. The feeling inside her was like the rush she'd felt after drinking a strawberry Frappuccino from Starbucks—her body buzzing with a kind of electricity that wouldn't turn off.

Abby finally gave up on sleep. She got out of bed, her hair sticking up in all directions like wild grass, and trudged to the bathroom to brush her teeth. She tried combing her hair, but it refused to settle down.

She walked into the kitchen, flicking on the light. The glow of the bulb made her squint and blink until her eyes adjusted to the light. The kitchen smelled faintly of coffee and old toast.

Abby hoped her mom would suddenly appear, stepping out from her secret trip to the fairy tale world. She had so many questions about magic and wanted to hear more stories.

But the kitchen was empty. No footsteps, no humming from her mom, not even the clink of a coffee mug.

A shiver ran down Abby's spine. The silence felt heavy, pressing against her ears. But…her mom had to be home by now, right?

Abby squeezed her eyes shut for a moment and mentally facepalmed herself. *Mom's home,* she told herself firmly. Maybe her mom was just extra tired from her magical adventure and was still sleeping. Abby thought about waking her up, but decided that would probably be rude.

She glanced around the kitchen and spotted a plate sitting on the dinner table. Crumbs dotted the plate like tiny specks of dust—it was the remains of the sandwich she hadn't finished yesterday.

"Blech! Gross," Abby muttered to herself.

She picked up the plate and walked to the trash can. When she dumped the sandwich inside, she peeked in to make sure none of the crust had fallen out. The trash was overflowing with onion peels curling like ribbons, crumpled milk cartons, and empty CLIF bar wrappers that smelled faintly of chocolate and nuts.

Abby put the plate in the dirty dish rack. She sighed, hoping her mom would come down soon. She leaned against the counter, her fingers tracing the cool surface, and stared at the dish racks, letting memories drift over her like waves.

Back when Abby was four years old, it was total dish chaos. Abby's mom had to sort through clean plates that Abby had helped wash the day before and put them away in the cabinet.

Her mom was always too tired from working at a busy restaurant and didn't have time to put them in the cabinet. Sometimes, by accident, the dirty dishes would go in the cabinet when her mom's brain was sluggish from work. It was exhausting to keep sorting them out, and food crumbs sometimes ended up stuck to the clean plates.

But then one day, Abby remembered her dad standing in the kitchen, talking to Abby's mom.

"Hey, what if we make separate dish racks?" he asked.

"How would that help?" Abby's mom said, looking puzzled.

"After you clean a plate, put it in another rack. Tomorrow it'll be easy to tell which ones are clean and ready for the cabinet. No confusion!" her dad explained.

Abby's mom smiled and sighed. "You're a genius, Jay."

After that, they bought another rack, and Abby made little signs out of construction paper that said "Clean" or "Dirty."

Her mom used to smile at the racks and run her hands over the "Clean" and "Dirty" signs as if they were something precious. But Abby's mom hardly ever looked at the racks anymore—not after her dad went missing and was declared dead.

"MOM? Are you here?" Abby yelled into the quiet house. No answer.

Abby's stomach clenched. She ran to the bedroom, knocking hard. The door creaked slightly—but still, no answer. The silence was thick, as if the house were holding its breath.

"Mom? Are you here?" Abby shouted again, louder this time.

No sound came from the room. The portal had closed when Abby last saw it. What if…what if she's trapped? Abby thought, panic creeping in.

Abby shook her head. Her mom would know how to make another one, right? She cautiously opened the door. The sheets were neatly smoothed on the bed. Everything was exactly as her mom had left it. And the floor was sealed tight.

A horrible feeling washed over Abby. She was home alone. She wrapped her arms around herself and took a deep breath. At least there are no robbers like in the movies, she thought, trying to comfort herself.

"Mom? Mom, please, where are you?" Abby shouted, just to make sure, in case her mom was still here and hadn't heard her. The silence was too much. She started singing. "I got the eye of the tiger, a fighter, dancing through the fire, 'cause I am a champion and you're gonna hear me roar. Louder, louder than a lion, 'cause I am a champion and you're gonna hear me roar."

After some silence, Abby sighed. Her mom hadn't come back, that much was certain. She took a few shaky breaths, trying to steady the strange tightness in her chest.

She sat for a moment, thinking hard about how her mother had disappeared into the fairy tale world. Her memory of that night was fuzzy—a blur of light, fear, and wonder. Then she remembered the perfume. The little glass bottle her mom had sprayed into the air, shimmering like a thousand tiny stars, before the portal opened. Maybe she could find that bottle!

Abby slid onto her knees and checked under the bed. She lifted the edge of the quilt and squinted into the darkness. A stale smell of dust drifted out. Her eyes swept over an old TIME magazine with a curled cover, a few dust bunnies drifting like little ghosts, and a lone striped sock. Then she froze.

There, half-hidden beneath the magazine, was a photograph. She pulled it out carefully.

Abby stared at the glossy photo. She had never seen this woman before. The woman was standing behind a bush filled with peculiar fruit and was holding a vial full of liquid. She was smiling, her pearly white teeth on display. Her purple, slightly wavy hair was half standing up on its own, and her almost-purple eyes sparkled. She was beautiful. No, she was *stunning*.

Abby turned the photo over. On the back, in her mom's neat, looping handwriting, it said:

May 9th, 2012.

So many questions filled her brain. Who was the woman? Why did her mom have a picture of her, taken over a decade ago? And why was the photo under the bed?

But Abby didn't have time to worry about this right now. She stuck the photo in her forest green backpack (Abby always carried a backpack with her) and went over to a box in the corner.

Inside, there were some documents and bills. There were also several one-dollar bills and an Eiffel Tower model marked, 'Abby's b-day'. Abby laughed a little before continuing her search.

Abby was getting agitated. She was starting to feel panicky. Where was that perfume bottle?!

She walked over to the desk and started pulling out drawers.

First drawer—stationery: pens, pencils, sticky notes, and a ruler.

Second drawer—junk: old batteries, paperclips, random bits and bobs.

Third drawer—books: some paperbacks, a small dictionary, and a few notebooks.

Fourth drawer—Abby paused. A thick photo album sat there, its cover soft and worn at the edges.

A yellow Post-it note was stuck on top. It said, *"Give when Abby is 15."*

Abby grabbed the album and started flipping through the pages quickly, her fingers trembling. At first, there was her mom as a baby, tiny and bundled in a pink blanket. Then, as a kid, laughing with two missing front teeth. Then her high school prom, dressed in a shimmering gown with flowers in her hair. Then Abby's mom and Abby's dad's wedding day, standing under an arch of white roses, smiling at each other like they held the whole world. Then she held baby Abby, cradling her close, her eyes shining with love. Then a bunch of pictures of Abby and her mom and her dad, playing in parks, blowing out birthday candles, hugging tight in holiday sweaters.

The pictures stopped after that. But the weird thing about them was that in some of the earlier ones, part of the photo had been ripped out, leaving jagged white edges like puzzle pieces missing.

Abby thought it was probably the same woman from the photo under the bed, judging by the glimpses of purple hair or the edge of a flowing sleeve that remained. Abby put the album in her backpack as well. Then she sank onto the bed, the mattress squeaking under her weight.

"Where could the perfume be?" Abby wailed out loud, her voice echoing in the silent room.

What if she never found it? What if her mom was trapped forever? She'd be an orphan. These thoughts brought tears to Abby's eyes. For the first time in two years, she cried, big, hot tears rolling down her cheeks.

She rubbed her eyes furiously, then grabbed a Kleenex and blew her nose. Abby took a deep breath, trying to calm the thudding of her heart.

When she regained her composure, she had an idea. What if it was in her mom's lockbox? Her mom had always kept it in the highest cabinet, so Abby couldn't reach it. She also always stood in front of it whenever Abby came into the room, which was definitely suspicious.

Abby dragged a chair over and climbed on it to reach the cabinet on the wall. Her fingers stretched as high as they could go. Jackpot! The lockbox was there.

She grabbed the box and started entering the code. She had seen her mom enter it before, so she knew three letters out of four. "Okay… H… E… A…"

What was the code? HEAT? HEAR? HEAP?

Suddenly, Abby remembered her dream. Eleanor Queen had called the land H.E.A.L! As in the fairy tale world! That had to be it.

Abby put in the L, and the box clicked open. Her breath caught in her throat. YES! The perfume bottle was inside, nestled in a bed of soft velvet.

She snatched it and took a deep breath. Abby sprayed the perfume in a circle, the sweet, floral scent filling the room.

POP! The outline of the circle glowed purple, and the floor inside the circle turned into a shade of blue that looked like the sky, rippling gently like water. Abby stepped closer.

She stuck a foot in experimentally. WHOOSH! Something grabbed her foot and pulled her in! Her eyes widened, hair whipping around her face as wind roared in her ears.

Abby screamed as the world swirled around her. She had three thoughts:

WHEEEEEEE!

I hope I can save Mom!

I'm going to the fairy tale world S QUEE!

She had absolutely no idea what she was getting into.

Abby landed hard on her back in a thick, springy bed of moss. She groaned, wincing as she sat up and rubbed her aching shoulder. *Thank goodness for the moss,* she thought, grateful for the soft landing that had spared her from worse.

A gentle sound caught her attention—the faint trickle of water. She turned to her right and spotted a small stone fountain nestled between two trees. At its center stood a statue of The Little Mermaid, her mouth open in a frozen expression, spitting a steady stream of water into the basin below.

Inside the fountain, coins shimmered beneath the rippling surface—pennies, nickels, dimes, quarters, even a lone dollar bill floating near the edge. But what made Abby's heart skip a beat was the sight of her backpack bobbing gently in the water. *How did it get there?!*

Abby jumped up and grabbed her bag. *Oh, thank goodness.* The photo of the woman was fine, and so was the photo album, even if it was a little soggy.

Abby felt a tap on her shoulder. She turned around to find a boy about 10 years old, wearing farmer's clothes. He had dark brown eyes, shaggy brown hair in desperate need of a haircut, and…shoes with *glue* on his shoes? Huh?

The boy noticed her staring. "After I fell off the hill, I decided to glue my shoes to the ground so I would never fall again."

"What?" Abby blurted out. "That's the worst idea ever! Your shoes won't even stick, they'll just…"

Abby trailed off as she realized what the boy had said. "Wait, did you say you fell off a hill? Like Jack and Jill? You're Jack?!"

The boy nodded seriously. He waved his hand toward a girl standing under an apple tree nearby. "That's my sister, Jill."

Jill came bouncing over. She had dark hair in two messy braids, dark brown eyes, and wore farmer's clothes just like Jack. She had a mischievous smile and looked to be about Abby's age.

"Hi, I'm Jill!" Jill chirped with a big grin.

Then, without another word, Jill turned and walked away as if she hadn't just introduced herself. Abby blinked in surprise. That seemed kind of rude. Who just said their name and left? Abby certainly wouldn't!

Jack's eyes suddenly widened. He started jerking his head behind Abby and moving his mouth silently, trying to warn her of something.

Abby wasn't great at lip-reading. What was he saying? She's bong to Lush, who in the down hen? She's going to rush blue in the mountains? Or…she's going to push you in the fountain?!

Abby whirled around just in time to catch Jill's outstretched hands reaching for her. Abby wobbled a bit but managed to stay upright. Then, determined to get even, she shoved Jill as hard as she could. Jill let out a yelp and tumbled into the fountain with a huge splash.

Jack's jaw dropped open. Then he broke into a huge grin. "My sister has been pushing people for a long time now! No one has ever been able to push Jill into the fountain!"

All the people in the square stopped what they were doing and started clapping. Abby felt her cheeks grow warm with pride.

She grinned back at them. "It was nothing."

Jill climbed out of the fountain, dripping wet and sputtering. She wiped water out of her eyes and stared at Abby with newfound respect. "Wow…that was amazing!"

"What's your name?" Jack asked Abby.

"Abby," Abby replied. "Abby Palmer."

The mood in the square shifted instantly. A hush fell over the crowd as everyone stared at her with wide eyes.

"Abby Palmer?" a man cried.

"Uh, yeah?" Abby squeaked. "What's wrong?"

"The bad fairy said you were her daughter and only supporter!" a woman blurted, clutching her little girl closer as if shielding her from danger.

Abby gasped. That must have been her mom! But… no. Her mom wasn't a bad fairy. That didn't make any sense. Why would anyone call her that?

"What do you mean?" Abby asked the crowd, her voice trembling with confusion.

"She's the fairy who cursed Sleeping Beauty!" Jill answered, arms crossed. "How could you not know that?!"

"No!" Abby took a step forward, her fists clenched. "My mom isn't the bad fairy! She's the best mom ever! She…"

Her voice faltered. Abby's eyes stung with sudden tears. Why was she sad? She had no reason to be sad! But…

What if she never found her mom? What if… what if her mom really was the bad fairy? The thought hit her like a wave. Abby, suddenly drained, sank to the ground, her knees folding beneath her.

She felt a gentle tug on her sleeve.

"Sweetheart, don't you know? Never sit on the cold ground, or you won't have children. Come with me!"

Abby looked up, startled. Eleanor Queen! The same woman from her dream—standing there in the flesh, just as regal and mysterious as before. But… how? Was that even possible?

* Of course it is, Abby,

* she reminded herself.

* This is the fairy tale world.

* She scrambled to her feet, brushing moss from her blue jeans.

Without a word, Abby slung her backpack over her shoulders. Numbly, she followed Eleanor. What else could she do?

Eleanor led her through a narrow path into the woods. The trees arched overhead like a tunnel, their leaves whispering in the breeze.

Soon, they arrived at a small, ivy-covered cottage nestled between two ancient oaks—the same one from Abby's dream. Of course it was. Eleanor had been there too.

Eleanor stepped up to the door and pushed it open with ease.

"You don't lock it?" Abby asked, blinking in surprise.

"No," Eleanor replied. "It's far enough from civilization that we only need to worry about animals."

"What about the animals, then?" Abby asked, leaning forward.

"Ah, well, this old lady has got some tricks up her sleeve," Eleanor explained with a wink.

Abby giggled as Eleanor suddenly spun and demonstrated a quick kick and a playful karate chop. "Sweet."

Eleanor chuckled and walked over to the stove, starting to make tea. "Go sit by the fire, honey."

Abby sank into a cozy armchair by the fireplace. She watched the crackling flames and the orange glow they cast all around the cottage, filling the room with gentle warmth. Her mind whirled with questions.

Who was the mystery girl from all the photos? And was her mother really the bad fairy?

Eleanor sat across from Abby, holding two steaming cups. "Are you OK now?"

Abby nodded shakily. "Eh-le-wor?" She realized she hadn't swallowed her tea yet, so she gulped it down. "Eleanor?"

"Sorry, what were you saying?" Eleanor asked gently.

"Um, so…Eleanor…" Abby shifted in her seat, twisting her fingers together.

"Mm?"

"I had a dream that you gave me a prophecy…"

Eleanor smiled, her eyes twinkling. "Yes, dear! That really happened!"

"But that was a dream." Abby furrowed her brow, confusion creasing her face.

"Who says dreams aren't real?" Eleanor said softly, tilting her head.

Abby stared at Eleanor like she'd grown an extra head. "What?"

Eleanor sighed. "You have a lot to learn, honey."

"What do you mean?" Abby cried, frustration bubbling up inside her. She was tired of everyone speaking in riddles and keeping secrets.

Eleanor pressed her lips together, thinking. "It's a long story…"

"I don't care!" Abby exploded. "Just tell me what you mean!"

Eleanor's eyes widened. Then she patted Abby's hand gently. "I think it's time you learned."

Abby leaned forward, her breath caught in her throat. "Learned what?" she whispered. And somewhere deep in Abby's chest, a strange, powerful feeling stirred…as if she was about to discover a secret that could change everything.

Chapter 4
Lizzie's Story (The Past)

Before Lizzie became the most feared and powerful queen, she was a nobody. Her family was poor, and they lived in a crumbling, forgotten neighborhood with questionable activities taking place in the back alleys.

Lizzie had always done great in school—better than her little sister anyway—but could she go to the college of her dreams, The Prestigious College For Non-magicals and Magicals, and get the awards she'd always dreamed of? No, because they were too poor!

It was ridiculously unfair. They lived in a world named Happily Ever After Land, for heaven's sake. Shouldn't everyone be able to get a happily ever after in life?

Apparently not. The Fairy Godfather and all the other rulers were too busy with insignificant, vain distractions that they never even bothered to try to help everyone else, though they claimed they were kind and generous. As if!

This had always bothered Lizzie, even when her family hadn't been living on the poverty line. The rulers had wands they could wave and make everything better. Why didn't they?

Lizzie would make a much better ruler, she always told herself. She knew how to do magic, after all.

Some people would call the kind of magic she had dark, black, forbidden, or even evil magic. But it wasn't, not really! She was going to help people with it.

Then why do you practice in secret? the little voice in her head whined.

Because I was a commoner! Lizzie argued.

But you're not anymore. Lizzie, stop hiding it! You are a queen.

She smiled, as it was true. She was married to King Ferdinand. She *was* a queen. Lizzie had her eyes set on the throne ever since she had become poor, and marrying King Ferdinand had been the perfect way to earn the status. But of course, King Ferdinand wouldn't marry a woman living in a poor neighborhood, so she had brewed up a small potion to make him marry her. Lizzie had reassured herself it wasn't evil or bad to do that, just necessary.

Many people found it rather odd that she had married King Ferdinand at the tender age of 19. But it was the way it was in H.E.A.L. After all, hadn't Cinderella married Prince Charming at 19 years old as well?

"Mother!" a voice came. "Mother! It's time for the ceremony!"

The power is at your fingertips—unleash it! This is your LAST CHANCE! the voice in her head continued.

Lizzie's life was not perfect. She had to get rid of King Ferdinand's daughter, that way too nice Snow White, who called her 'Mother.' As if! Snow White loved giving their precious jewels away to the orphanages. Why couldn't they let the civilians do that, huh? And she treated all their servants *nicely.* They were *servants,* for heaven's sake! But if Snow White became the queen, Lizzie wouldn't *be* a queen anymore.

The worst part was that they were only eight years apart in age. 8! It was just embarrassing. Lizzie could easily be Snow White's older sister. King Ferdinand was not Lizzie's age—rather, about 11 years older than her. But he had taken a youth potion a long time ago, so technically, he was Lizzie's age.

She couldn't think of anything worse than not being a queen. Even her sister, her crybaby sister, the worst sister in the world, ranked slightly above not being a queen.

Lizzie rose. A princess's 15th birthday was marked by a coming-of-age ceremony. And Snow White turned 15 today.

The most important part of the ceremony is when the Fairy Godfather comes and puts the enchantment on the princess, binding her to the queendom. Lizzie could not let that happen.

"I'm coming, sweetie!" Lizzie called, faking sugary sweetness. "I'll just put on my dress!"

"OK!" Snow White chirped.

She had no idea what Lizzie was going to do.

WHOOSH! The doors burst open, and the Fairy Godfather strode in. "Hello, Snow White!"

Snow White squealed and then clamped a hand over her mouth. Squealing was not very ladylike.

It was traditional to do prayers before the enchantment, but it was not necessary for anyone but the princess to pray. Lizzie rose. "I'll be back in a second, sweetie!"

Lizzie walked out of the ballroom and whispered her plan to the Hunter. He nodded grimly.

Lizzie stood outside and watched as the Hunter quietly strung his bow. He shot at Snow White, missing by an inch.

Snow White screamed. "RUN!" King Ferdinand cried.

Snow White ran into the woods, the Hunter on her heels. Lizzie smiled. The Hunter would surely finish her off.

Days passed. Then, one morning, the Hunter came running back. "Your Majesty! She is not dead!"

"WHAT?!" Lizzie roared. She ran into the woods herself, disguised as an old woman with a basket of apples.

She found Snow White's cottage. She pretended to be an old woman, and that foolish girl actually ate a poison apple! Didn't it occur to her that this "old lady" was pretty shady?

But everyone knows what happened next. Snow White awoke. After she returned to the palace, King Ferdinand decided to throw a party, and everyone got emotional. She married Prince Charming and had a grand wedding. It was too embarrassing for Lizzie to think about that.

Anyway, after Snow White was awoken, she alerted the other queens and kings that Lizzie had tried to kill her.

A year later, a small, magic group came and challenged her. Her sister, Melissa, came crying at her feet. 'We should go into hiding, Lizzie!'. From then, she lay low, planning her revenge. The last she had heard from the outside world was that Snow White was going to have a baby.

They tried to imprison her. Ha! That would never work! Lizzie escaped, obviously.

Crybaby. Lizzie tried to banish her, but Melissa ran away to the Unknown. Somehow, she survived—even had a baby.

Lizzie had done horrible things to the magic group. One by one, she had picked them off. They weren't a problem anymore.

For now, Lizzie could relax. No one else was brave—or foolish—enough to oppose her.

Chapter 5
The Adventure Begins

Abby's stomach dropped. Her fingers curled into fists. No. No way. This had to be a joke. "Wait…Lizzie's my AUNT?!" Abby cried, utterly aghast.

Eleanor winced. "Yes."

"But my mom's not evil, right?" Abby leaned closer, her heart pounding. "Tell me she's not!"

"Well, it's complicated," Eleanor replied. "Your mother, Melissa, isn't evil at heart. But she has one heck of a temper."

"A temper?" Abby asked, raising an eyebrow. Her mother never raised her voice at Abby at home, not even once.

"I don't think you want to know…" Eleanor trailed off. Abby gave Eleanor a look that said, 'I'm not leaving until you tell me,' and she gave in. "Your mom cursed Sleeping Beauty," Eleanor admitted.

"WAIT, *WHAT?!*" Abby exclaimed, her mouth falling open. "Is that what everyone meant when they called her the *bad fairy?* But— my mom isn't bad. She's good! Better than a lot of people! Lizzie, for starters! She's the Evil Queen!"

"Like I said, it's complicated. She loves her sister, but she doesn't like what Lizzie has become," Eleanor clarified.

"So, just to be clear—my aunt is an evil queen who wants to take over the world?" Abby realized, her voice dripping with disgust. "That's fantastic news. I can't believe it. "

"Yes," Eleanor confirmed with a weak grin.

"If Lizzie is this powerful, why isn't she ruling already? Why hasn't she won?" Abby asked.

"Because she underestimated us," Eleanor said with a slight smirk.

"Us?"

"The resistance."

Abby's eyes widened with each name Eleanor listed. "Me, Snow White, Sleeping Beauty, Cinderella, Rapunzel, Jack—the one who killed the giant—the Hunter, the Fairy Godfather and a few other citizens whose names I don't know."

"Wait, did you say Fairy God*father*?"

"Yes. You'd be surprised how many people think all fairies are women. That's why the name 'Fairy Godfather' always throws people off."

"What happened to the rest of the group?"

"Some died. The 3 Little Pigs ran off the moment they faced real danger. The majority disappeared, becoming spies and *secretly* stopping evil, like Little Red Riding Hood. Though she's not very little anymore."

Abby digested this. It was all a lot to process. "So, a long time ago, Lizzie tried to kill Snow White, but then she failed."

Eleanor nodded. "She wants to wipe them all out—the queens, the king—until she's the only ruler left." Eleanor's voice dropped. "And she's close."

"How close?" Abby asked, her spine tingling with chills.

Eleanor hesitated. "Closer than we'd like to admit."

"Wait," Abby interrupted, thinking back to what Eleanor had said. "You said *the* king before. Like, there's only one?"

"Yes, darling. Prince Charming is the only king."

Abby frowned. "Is he married to all of the queens at once?"

"No. He's been divorced a lot."

"Wha—"

"Let's not go there."

"Right. So, then a year later, the magic group—"

"We call ourselves the Dreamwalkers."

"Dreamwalkers?"

"We can visit people in their dreams."

"So, the Dreamwalkers challenged Lizzie, and my mother tried to convince her to come into hiding. Lizzie tried to banish Mom, but Mom ran away to my world, married my dad, and had me. Lizzie killed most of the Dreamwalkers?"

"Yeah."

Abby leaned back in her chair. "Oh…wow. Wow."

Eleanor nodded. "It's a lot."

Abby suddenly had an idea. She rummaged in her backpack and pulled out the photo of the woman. She showed it to Eleanor. "Who is this? I found it under my mom's bed."

"That's Lizzie!" Eleanor gasped. "Oh dear. We have less time than I thought…"

"Less time for what?" Abby asked, concerned.

Eleanor rubbed her temples. "Abby…you need to go. Now."

"Wait, I don't even know how to defeat Lizzie!" Abby cried.

Eleanor groaned, rubbing her forehead. "Hold it…wait. I'll tell you the prophecy in a minute…" Suddenly, her eyes started spiraling black and white like they had in Abby's dream. She chanted in a soft, low voice:

"When darkness has fallen,

A girl from the Unknown,

Will bring down the Evil Queen's throne.

Collect five relics and wield them with might,

You will need to find the Book of Light.

You will discover your true inner power,

As you defeat Lizzie at the witching hour.

Save our world once and for all,

Your name we will forever recall."

"But I can't defeat Lizzie!" Abby countered. "I'm just twelve—"

Eleanor reached forward and entwined her fingers with Abby's. "Abby, are you brave?"

"I…try to be?"

"Say yes or no."

"Um, well…"

"I need an answer."

"Yes."

"Are you kind?"

"Yes."

"Are you honest?"

"Yes."

"Then I think you'll be fine."

Eleanor hurried over to her cabinet and shoved dented cans of tomato soup and some water canteens into Abby's lap.

"Abby, you have to go now. Your best bet to find a clue is in the forest," Eleanor ordered.

"But what do I find?" Abby asked.

"A relic. There are five of the relics. You'll know when you see it," Eleanor reassured her. "And bring friends with you! Oh, and you have to find the Book!"

"But—I need to find my mom!" Abby protested.

"You'll probably cross paths with her on your quest. Good luck!" Eleanor exclaimed.

Eleanor practically shoved Abby out the door and waved her to the town square.

Abby followed the trail and ran into the town square. She shoved the tomato soup and water into her backpack. As she walked along the trail, she thought about how a mission to find her mom had turned into all of this. *Maybe I could just not do it at all?* Abby thought. But there was a prophecy about her. And Abby knew from various fantasy books that if there is a prophecy, you could not avoid it. Besides, she might find her mom on the way!

Jack and Jill walked up to Abby. Jill was still slightly wet and had a towel wrapped over her head.

Abby took a deep breath. "Hey, guys."

"What was that all about?" Jack asked.

"Eleanor says I should defeat the Evil Queen, and I need help to do it. We have to collect relics—there are five of them. And the Book of Light. I was going to just go find my mom, but…"

"*We*? Wait, are you asking us?" Jill squealed.

Abby blinked. "I…sure?" *There's no avoiding it now. Oh, what have I gotten myself into?*

Jill gasped excitedly and unwrapped the towel, dropping it to the ground. Her dark braids fell to her shoulders, dripping water. "OMG!"

Jack snorted. "Jill, are you trying to be a hero again? We've all seen you try, and we all know how it works out."

"Well, I didn't know how to carry Elijah down the hill! Why do you blame me?!" Jill huffed, her cheeks getting red.

"What are you guys talking about? Who's Elijah?" Abby asked, scrunching her forehead.

"Oh, this story is SO ridiculous. You'll love it." Jack grinned.

"No, she won't! And it's not ridiculous!" Jill protested.

"It is. It all happened on a bright sunny morning. The village thought it would be fun to hold a magical scavenger hunt, which meant there were magical items hidden around for all the kids. Jill and

I went our separate ways when she headed up the hill while I checked out the tall grass. She saw Elijah, my friend's brother, lying on his back and trying to get up. It turns out he was chasing a flying clue, stumbled, and fell down. I think he had a broken leg or arm or something. Anyway, Jill offered to carry him down, even though Elijah insisted that the adults would come. Jill ignored him. She attempted to get him down. Let's just say, in the end, Elijah had to get help from the sap fairies." Jack smirked.

"Sap fairies? Huh?" Abby asked.

"You don't know? Sap fairies are the most powerful healing fairies, but they're only ever needed if someone has a fatal injury. Like, when people almost die," Jack explained. "That's how bad her attempt to be a hero went. People stayed away from her for a week. No, a month. Actually, people are still wary of her when he offers to help them."

"So you almost killed this Elijah guy by trying to help him?" Abby didn't feel so safe around Jill anymore.

"It was an accident! I was just trying to help," Jill protested, throwing her hands up in the air.

"And be a hero and finally be the talk of the town? More like the laughingstock," Jack snorted. "She *never* gets noticed, and when she does, it's because she's done something embarrassing or bad."

Abby felt like she could hear Jill's thoughts. She kind of felt sorry for Jill, but Abby guessed that Jill only wanted to be a hero for once and have everyone notice her. Not because she wanted to help Abby, but to help herself. That stung. But Abby needed all the help she could get.

"First, what's the Book?" Abby asked.

"Didn't your mom teach you anything? It's called the Book of Light, and it is said to contain a lot of powerful, good magic. And a lot of light. Obviously," Jack explained.

"Good to know," Abby said. "So, let's go and defeat the Evil Queen, guys!" She tried to sound brave. As if it were that easy.

"Great!" Jill forced a big smile, throwing the towel to the ground. "Where do we start?"

"We need to go into the forest. Off the trail," Abby replied.

Jack's eyes went wide. "I changed my mind! I'm not coming!" Jack squirmed.

"Come on! We'll be heroes! Nothing bad will happen to us, right?" Jill asked.

"If there's glory and defeating villains involved, I'm in!" Jack exclaimed. "But… there are wolves, bears, and you never know if a goblin is waiting in the forest, eager to kidnap something. Someone."

Jack gulped, and his face turned pale. Abby watched as Jack stared into the deep, dark forest. The trees seemed to whisper warnings.

Abby didn't want to pressure him. She was about to say he didn't have to do it, but she really wanted company.

"Jack, I *promise* we won't let anything happen to you," Abby promised. "And if something does happen to you, we'll make sure you get better."

"F-fine, but if anything happens to me…" Jack whimpered.

Abby put on a peppy attitude. "Don't worry. Nothing will happen to you. Now let's go find a clue!"

"This is a terrible idea," he said, staring at the tangled darkness ahead.

Lizzie was on top of the world. She had her little sister and the Big Bad Wolf eating out of her hand.

Oh, Melissa. Melissa was always stubborn. Didn't know when to leave a subject alone. But Melissa was under a curse for now. She wouldn't get in the way.

And that wolf. If brains were leather, he wouldn't have enough to saddle a junebug. But he did what Lizzie asked without complaining. That was good enough.

Lizzie smiled. She was going to get the relics. She was going to be all powerful. Abby couldn't stop her from building a portal to the Unknown.

"My queen?" the wolf asked hesitantly.

"Yes, wolfie?"

"What about the girl?"

Lizzie curled her lip. "What did I say about her?"

That useless niece is trying to collect the relics to stop me. Ha! She is just a girl. Not even a teenager. She has no magic, no strength, no weapons, no power—unlike me, Lizzie thought with a smirk.

Before the wolf could answer, Lizzie went on. "She doesn't even know where the first relic is!"

"Neither do we."

Lizzie glared at him. "Shut up."

He did.

"Okay." Lizzie clapped her hands together. "Hmm…first step. Where did that daughter of yours go, Mel?"

"Where? Where is Abby?" Melissa blankly asked.

Lizzie rolled her eyes. She held her hand palm up and focused. *Show me, Abby Palmer.*

A bubble appeared. Melissa's daughter was there, in the forest. She was with two villagers—Jack and Jill.

She had friends. *No worries. The more the merrier,* Lizzie thought.

Lizzie stood and gathered her purple-streaked black hair into a messy bun, like she always did when she was thinking hard.

In her view, they had two options. One: get rid of Abby Palmer. Two: Forget her and go after the relic.

The relic *was* somewhere in the forest, where Abby and her friends were. So they could just multitask.

Decided. Lizzie beckoned to the wolf and Melissa. She went to click off the magic bubble. Oh, haha—Abby and her friends were tired already. They'd only been walking for seven minutes!

When Lizzie laughed, Melissa's head snapped up. "Abby?"

"No," Lizzie told her bluntly. "You're never getting her back." She wrinkled her nose at her sister, her foolish sister, and then spun on her heel. "Come on, wolfie."

The Big Bad Wolf rose from where he had curled up next to a tree. Lizzie always found that nickname ironic. There was nothing big or bad about him when he was around her; in truth, he was a coward.

Lizzie only kept him around because of his strength, claws, speed, and general hugeness. He intimidated people. And she supposed he was useful in battle. He only acted this way around Lizzie. Oh, and woodcutters, because of the Red Riding Hood story that everyone knew.

Lizzie started walking, the wolf right behind her, before she realized Melissa hadn't gotten up yet. "Melissa?"

Melissa looked up at Lizzie. "Abby," was all she said.

"We're going to find Abby," Lizzie informed her. It technically was not a lie. She just left out the small detail of planning to kill Abby when they found her. Very small detail. Totally.

"Abby," Melissa repeated.

"Yes, Abby! Now get a move on, you fool!"

Melissa stood. She followed Lizzie stiffly, her eyes blank.

That was much better. She smirked. Satisfied, Lizzie marched ahead of the wolf and Melissa.

At the moment, they were in the fields just outside the forest. The three crossed over to the cobblestone path to avoid making footprints in the dirt.

They entered the shady cover of the woods, and Lizzie sighed with relief. She was glad to be out of the sunlight. She hated sunshine because, in her opinion, why did the world have to be so sunny all the time? There were plenty of people suffering. It was like the sky was ignoring them.

It'd been beautiful and bright and sunny the day Lizzie's mom had died.

Lizzie snapped out of her memories when a mosquito bit her on the arm. She swatted it away. OK, maybe she didn't like *everything* about the woods.

They were five minutes in when it happened.

She heard a noise–a bird's cheep. Nothing out of the ordinary. The sound of birds was all one heard in this forest.

But for some reason, Lizzie wanted to know where that sound was coming from. She looked around and saw a robin sitting on the ground a few feet away.

At first, Lizzie didn't notice anything wrong, but then she realized the robin's feathers were streaked with red. Blood. It was injured.

"Abby," Melissa piped up. Lizzie ignored her. It was just a robin. It didn't matter. Lizzie peeled her eyes away from the robin and took a shaky step forward.

Then the robin made a sound, a helpless tweet. Lizzie froze.

It gave another feeble chirp. Lizzie was instantly taken back to her childhood. She remembered feeling that impotent when she was 14 and all the bad things started.

She edged closer to the bird. One of its wings sagged.

"My queen?" the wolf called.

"What?" Lizzie snapped. She took a step closer to the robin.

"We really should be going. It's getting late."

"Shut up."

"But your majesty—"

"Do not speak when I tell you not to." Lizzie squatted next to the robin.

The little bird flapped its good wing vigorously in an effort to fly. It rose about two inches off the ground before spiraling back down.

Lizzie wanted to tell the bird it was going to be okay, but she hated that. People didn't know that, not always.

Behind her, Melissa gasped, staring at the ground. The wolf cleared his throat. "My queen, there's a…"

"What?" Lizzie asked, transfixed on the bird. It hopped forward, and Lizzie cupped her hands. "Come here, birdie."

"Your Majesty!" the wolf cried. "Look out!"

Suddenly, a stick lying on the ground a couple of inches away became…not a stick. A snake! It was a snake!

Lizzie yelped and tumbled backward, landing on her butt in the dirt. The snake glared at her with beady eyes and turned toward the bird before striking.

A minute later, all that was left of the robin was a feather.

"The bird," Lizzie whispered.

"My queen?" The Big Bad Wolf asked. Lizzie didn't reply.

The Big Bad Wolf came forward and sat down, folding his long legs underneath him. Lizzie stared at the remains of the powerless bird that hadn't deserved to die like that.

Chapter 6
Real Talk: This Forest
Is A Death Trap

The forest pressed in around them—twisted vines and gnarly roots and shadows shifted with every gust of wind. It wasn't cold, refreshing wind, but rather the sweltering wind that you only experience in the middle of a heat wave.

Jill groaned and collapsed onto a fallen tree. She stretched out her legs. "We've been walking for *hours*."

"It's only been 7 minutes," Jack informed her, checking his analog watch.

"Yeah, but I've been through a lot!" Abby protested. "In the past couple of days, I discovered magic was real, my mom disappeared, I went to find her through a *magic portal,* I almost got pushed into a fountain, and a bunch of other weird stuff happened!"

"Plus, this forest is creepy!" Jill added.

"Ok, I guess we can rest," Jack agreed reluctantly.

"Don't blame me when we're getting chased by a wolf."

They sat down beside the tree. Abby took a deep breath and collected her thoughts. After a few minutes of resting, they could keep walking to find the first relic. If they didn't, they should probably ask around (subtly!) to see if anyone knew where it was. Abby nodded to herself, satisfied with her plan.

Suddenly, a cold gust of wind blew in their faces. They all looked at each other with surprise. It had felt like a desert a minute ago—how could it be cold?

A low growl echoed through the trees. Jack froze. "Uh…please tell me that was your stomach."

Abby's face paled. "I don't think so."

"It's…a wolf!" Jack shivered, eyes wide, "See?! I told you a wolf would come! I told you!"

"She's coming!" Jill yelled. "Quick, hide!"

"Who's coming?!" Abby yelped, looking around nervously.

"The Evil Queen always has an aura of cold wind near her," Jill replied. "Ugh! Where should we hide?!"

"Look!" Jack pointed to a log covered with moss. "That log is hollow! Get inside!"

Abby really didn't want to—what kind of bugs would be in there? But she climbed in after the others anyway. It was tight, but they fit. Abby held her breath. *Stay quiet.*

After a few moments that felt like eternity, Jill whispered, "Guys…look outside. Don't scream."

Abby peered out the side of the log and had to bite the inside of her cheek to keep from shrieking like a toddler. An enormous wolf paced outside, its red eyes glowing in the dim light. It licked its lips, flashing sharp teeth stained with…red stuff. Abby really hoped it was ketchup.

Abby heard footsteps. She ducked back into the log, her heart racing. Who was coming?

"Ah, my sister," a voice came. "You have done well. Leading me right to the child. Perhaps I will not punish you after all."

"Yes, my queen," another voice recited. Abby stifled a gasp. It was her mom! So if this other woman was calling her mother her sister, then there was only one person she could be—Lizzie.

The wolf inhaled. "I smell children—three." *AIEEE!* Abby's face turned pale, and she gripped the log tightly. The wolf talked?! Although after everything else that had happened today, Abby supposed she shouldn't be surprised.

Abby risked a glance outside. Her mother looked as if she were in a trance. *Oh no, what happened to her?* Abby wondered, fear knotting in her stomach. *Lizzie must've cursed her.*

What if...what if it never wore off? What if there is no way to fix the curse?

Abby's mind filled with rage. She forgot all about staying hidden. She crawled out of the fallen tree, jumped to her feet, and screamed at Lizzie, "LET MY MOTHER GO!"

Lizzie smirked and pressed her fingers together. And—wow. Abby, horrifyingly, could see the resemblance between herself and Lizzie.

Jack and Jill crawled out of the log, too. Jill tugged on Abby's sleeve. "Um, Ab? We should probably run."

Abby snapped out of it. "OMG, I'm so sorry!"

"No time!" Jack yelped, sprinting off. Abby and Jill followed.

I really should have listened to Mr. Samson in PE, Abby thought as she ran. Jack and Jill were way in front of her.

Abby risked a glance over her shoulder. The wolf snarled. He was running after them! Thankfully, Lizzie was not chasing them. But the wolf was still pretty terrifying!

"WE'RE GOING TO DIE!" Jack screamed. "ABBY, COME ON!"

Abby turned and dashed after the others. But then, Jack tripped on a tree root! He went down hard, screaming. The part of his head that already had a scar (from falling down the hill, Abby presumed) received the most impact.

"Jack? Jack!" Jill yelled. "Get up, get up!" She knelt next to her brother.

Abby silently urged Jack to say he was fine and get up, but he stayed on the ground, motionless. *Get up, get up!* Abby urged him in her mind. The wolf got closer, closer still.

Abby took a couple of steps backward, wanting to run, but not wanting to abandon Jack and Jill. The wolf crouched and prepared to pounce. They were going to die! Abby closed her eyes, waiting for the fatal blow. But…it never came.

Abby peered through one eye. The wolf was frozen in midair, its teeth bared. Abby looked around. A woman stood by the trees, holding out a staff with a giant green gem at its tip. She had cast a spell on the wolf!

The woman was pretty, with curly black hair tied in a messy braid, green eyes, and dark brown skin. She was dressed in a green cloak and looked to be in her mid-twenties.

Jill ran over to Abby. She was carrying Jack, who was unconscious, on her back. "I think he broke his arm," Jill reported, then looked at the stranger. "Who's that weird lady?"

"Weird lady?" The said weird lady looked a little offended. "I am a Dreamwalker!"

"Oh! Do you know Eleanor?" Abby asked, hopeful.

The lady tilted her head. "Eleanor? Everyone knows Eleanor! She's the one who gave the prophecy all those years ago." She studied Abby. "Is that why you are wandering in the woods? The prophecy?"

Abby wondered if she should lie. This was a random woman, after all. They didn't even know her name! She decided to change the subject. "Um…could we come to your house? We're kind of lost."

"Of course," the lady agreed. "We can discuss this further, and I can give you directions." She turned and started walking. Abby and Jill followed.

A few minutes later, they came to a—whoa. Was it a castle? It was huge, made of marble, with towering—well, towers. And was that a *drawbridge?* Abby thought that was only in fairy tales. Oh, wait! This *was* a fairytale!

Abby started to laugh maniacally. Jill shot her a strange look. Abby stopped.

"AMELIA!" the woman yelled. "OPEN THE DRAWBRIDGE!"

A girl dressed in servant clothes—she looked a couple of years younger than Abby and Jill—dutifully hit a button on the wall of the castle. The drawbridge unfolded and hit the grass with a thud.

"Why do you need a drawbridge if there's no moat?" Jill wondered. Abby thought that was a very good question.

The lady shrugged. "Hey, I didn't build it."

They walked across the drawbridge and into the castle. And, wow, it was impressive.

It was beautiful, yet kind of dark. The entire space was black—black walls, black decor, black floors, and a black ceiling. A dim light was on. It felt empty and lonely. Abby couldn't help thinking how different this was from Eleanor's place.

"Well," the woman started. "First things first. AMELIA!"

Amelia, the servant girl, came running. "Yes, ma'am?"

"Take the injured boy to the infirmary," the woman instructed.

Amelia curtsied and took Jack from Jill. She staggered under his weight, as he probably weighed the same as her, but she dutifully left.

"Now." The woman smiled. "Let's talk."

"Who are you?" Jill blurted.

"I am Jadeine, keeper of jewels," the woman explained. "I have a jewel room somewhere around here." Abby thought that if she had enough jewels to fill a jewel room, she would know exactly where it was.

Jadeine continued, "You were running from the Evil Queen, yes? And the Big Bad Wolf?"

Abby noticed Jadeine hadn't answered her question, but she let it go. "Yes. Uh, I got a prophecy that said to defeat Lizzie." She chewed her lip, wondering what Jadeine would say.

Jadeine's jaw dropped. "You—you want to defeat The Evil Queen? Don't you know about the sisters?"

Jill dropped her gaze. But Abby was confused. "What sisters?"

Jadeine sighed. "Five years ago, two sisters lived in a little cottage. Everyone in their village loved them—they were kind and loved helping people. When the Evil Queen started to threaten the king and queens and started a war, they decided they should stop her and save the world by finding the relics, like you're doing now. The way you save the world is by collecting the relics and a special book. Each relic is guarded by a keeper who is not affiliated with either side of the war. They simply give the relics to people deemed worthy. The sisters went after the first relic, but the Evil Queen heard of this and sent her pet wolf after them. The older sister was badly injured and went back to the village to heal, and she survived. The younger sister kept searching after her sister got better, but the Evil Queen cursed her never to leave these woods again."

Jill gasped. "Wait—you're the younger sister?"

Jadeine grunted. "Yes."

"So, did you get the first relic?" Abby asked.

"Well…" Jadeine started. "It's a long story."

"We have time," Abby told her, which wasn't really true, but she was curious. "Tell us about the relics. We didn't know much about how to defeat Lizzie before we came here."

Jadeine sighed again. "Well, I tried. So, five relics were enchanted by the Fairy Godfather to cause the Evil Queen's downfall. He picked five keepers to guard them. The keepers weren't on either side of the war. When my sister and I went after the first relic—this staff—we killed the keeper, mistakenly thinking she was on the Evil Queen's side. After the Evil Queen cursed me, the Fairy Godfather asked me to be the keeper of the staff, the first relic. It was a punishment, but also a chance at redemption."

Abby tried to wrap her brain around this. It was quite a lot of new knowledge at once. But she didn't have time to worry about that right now because Jadeine was raising her staff!

"Get out!" she screamed at the girls. Abby didn't understand the sudden change in Jadeine's behavior.

"Wait!" Jill yelled. "We need the staff!"

"Well, I'm not going to give it to you," Jadeine growled. "Now get out!"

The staff glowed a brilliant green color. Jill tried to drag Abby back to the entrance, but Abby, shocked, stayed frozen in place.

A bright beam of light shot toward her. She ducked just in time, and it hit a gold-framed mirror on the wall. The mirror fell to the floor and smashed into pieces.

Jadeine began to shoot magic all over the place. Mirrors, vases and vials of strange liquid fell to the ground and shattered. Finally, she dropped the staff and took a deep breath.

Jadeine wobbled. She grabbed the wall to steady herself. "I'm so sorry about that."

"What was that?!" Jill cried. "You can't just shoot magic at us and then *apologize!*"

Jadeine sighed. "I didn't mention it before. You're both so young—I didn't want to scare you. The staff will control you sometimes, even if you want to give it up."

"So…" Abby looked up hopefully. "Will you give it to us, then?"

Jadeine shook her head. "I won't kill you, but no. You should leave. Go home and relax. Stay out of all this!"

"Don't you want the Evil Queen to be overthrown?" Jill sounded disgusted.

Jadeine shrugged. "Keepers are not on either side, remember?"

Abby groaned inwardly. She felt all the weight of the past couple of hours descend on her at once. Where was her mom? Where were the other four relics?

Abby lunged for the staff on impulse. Jadeine cried out and jumped back, shoving Abby into a table. She clutched her side and groaned. Jadeine grabbed the staff and darted away.

She tried to make a break for it, but Jill was standing by the door. She kicked Jadeine in the shin, forcing her to the floor. The staff fell out of Jadeine's hands.

Abby grabbed the staff and stepped over Jadeine. She grabbed the door handle. Jill followed her to the door and was about to exit with Abby, but froze. "Abby, we can't leave yet."

"Why?!" Abby cried. "We got the relic! Let's go!"

"We have to get the permission of the keeper before we leave with the relic," Jill explained.

Abby kicked a nearby cabinet and then hopped around holding her toe. "I hate that rule! It's the worst rule I've ever heard!"

Jill shrugged. "I didn't make it. The Fairy Godfather did."

Jadeine rose. "I *can't* let you leave. I'm so, so, sorry."

Suddenly, it clicked in Abby's mind. Jadeine wasn't the enemy. She was a kind woman who had been hurt by the Evil Queen, same like many other people in H.E.A.L. She just didn't want Abby and Jill to get hurt, too.

Abby reached out and grabbed Jadeine's arm. "Look, the Evil Queen hurt you and your sister, too. Don't you want to see her overthrown?"

Jadeine stared at her shoes, her eyes brimming with tears. Finally, she whispered so softly Abby almost missed it, "Yes."

Abby stepped back. "I thought so. Will you give us the staff?"

Jadeine hesitated. Then she nodded. "I, Jadeine, give you permission to leave with the jade staff, the first relic."

Abby had kind of expected a Lord of the Rings type of moment, with heavy smoke and strange whispering. But nope. The staff just sat there, being regular staff.

Jill straightened. "So. What do we do now?"

Abby stared at her. "What do you think?!"

She sighed. "No, I mean, which relic do we go after? And what about Jack?"

Just then, Jadeine's servant, Amelia, came running. "Miss Jadeine!"

"Yes, Amelia?" Jadeine replied, turning to face her with calm curiosity.

"The injured boy has broken his arm, and he should rest and heal." Amelia looked at Jill. "He's your brother, right?"

Jill nodded. "Abby, what will we do with only two people? It'll be hard!"

Jadeine smiled. "Don't worry. Amelia, go check on Jack."

She frowned. "I just did."

"Well, go again!"

Amelia scampered off. Jadeine leaned forward as soon as she was out of earshot. "I'll come with you."

"I thought you were cursed?" Abby asked.

"Yes," Jadeine confirmed. "There is a way around it, however. The Evil Queen told me that if I made a sacrifice, she would let me go."

"What kind of sacrifice?" Jill's eyes got big. "Like with a pyre and all?"

Jadeine laughed. "No. I would just have to send someone to be her servant."

"Not it!" Jill cried immediately. Abby elbowed her.

"Amelia will do it," Jadeine decided.

Abby frowned. "That's kind of mean. I mean, she's already your servant."

Jadeine shrugged. "Amelia is my only servant. It's for the better." Jadeine shook her head and closed her eyes. "In the third cabinet on the left, there's a bottle of golden liquid. Bring it here."

Abby rummaged through the cabinet contents and found a small glass vial filled with what looked like liquid gold. She started to hand it to Jadeine, but then pulled back. "Why didn't you do this before, if it was so easy?"

Jadeine pressed her lips together. Only then did Abby see the look in her eyes—pain and regret. "I didn't want to curse anyone, but now I suppose if we defeat the Evil Queen, Amelia will be freed."

Abby began to see Jadeine in a whole new way. She could have gotten out anytime she wanted, but instead, she stayed in the woods, all so nobody else would have to suffer.

Jadeine grabbed the liquid and poured some water into it. The golden elixir dissolved, and it just looked like normal water, if a little sparkly.

"It's ready. AMELI—!" Jadeine yelled, but got cut off by Jill.

"Wait! Shouldn't it be someone you care about?" Jill asked. "It's a *sacrifice* after all."

"I do care about Amelia. So much," Jadeine said. Only then did Abby see the tears in her eyes.

"I think Jadeine really does care about her, she just doesn't show it," Abby realized. "Am I right?"

Jadeine nodded. "I do care, of course. She could've left any time she wanted to, but she didn't. Always stayed...for me. Brought me food and newspapers and everything. I love her." Jadeine wiped her eyes. "AMELIA!" she yelled again.

Amelia came running down the hall and screeched to a stop in front of Jadeine.

"Yes?" Amelia asked.

"Are you prepared to do something that will help us defeat the Evil Queen?" Jadeine asked.

"I—I guess?" Amelia stammered.

"Drink the water then," Jadeine instructed, holding out the glass of "water". Amelia looked confused, but she took it and drank it cautiously. She disappeared as soon as she swallowed the water.

"Is she OK?" Jill asked.

"Let's see," Jadeine replied.

She snapped her fingers, and green mist appeared in front of them, creating an image. The hazy figures of Lizzie, the Big Bad Wolf and Abby's mom could be seen. They were arguing about something. Lizzie threw her hands up in the air and sat down on a rock. Just then, Amelia suddenly popped out of thin air.

"Wh–what?" Amelia asked, eyes wide. She scanned her surroundings in fear.

"Who is she and what is she doing here?" Lizzie asked, standing up.

"Excuse me, my queen, but I believe Jadeine has finally sent us a servant," The Big Bad Wolf said.

Lizzie considered this. "That makes sense. What's your name, girl?"

Amelia looked petrified, but when the Evil Queen asks you something, you answer. "A–amelia, ma'am."

"Oh! You're that man's daughter, aren't you? You are going to be very useful. Very, very useful indeed." Lizzie smiled, her voice dripping with satisfaction.

Amelia gulped. The image vanished.

"Poor Amelia," Jill sympathized. "But we'll save her!"

"Yeah!" Abby tried to be peppy. "We will!"

Jadeine's eyes brightened. She looked happy, but Abby could see a twinge of sadness on her face. "My other servant will look after Jack. Let's—let's go!"

They left the creepy palace and began walking through the woods. As Abby started walking, she realized it was getting dark out. The sun had been barely past its zenith when they had been saved by Jadeine.

In the dark, the once noisy and bright forest was almost silent, except for a few owls' hoots now and then. The tall trees blocked out most of the moonlight. They had to rely on the glowing staff to see.

The staff reminded Abby of another question. "Jadeine?"

"Mm?"

"You said the staff will control you."

Jadeine laughed. "That's part of the curse the Evil Queen put on me. It's off! We're good!"

Abby sighed with relief. Phew. Finally, something was going right.

Suddenly, they heard voices. Jadeine froze. She grabbed one of Abby's and Jill's arms each and pulled them behind a thick tree.

Abby didn't dare peek, but she listened.

"What did I say about that?" The first voice came. It was low and harsh. Abby knew that voice—the wolf!

Another voice huffed. Lizzie! "I suppose he hasn't harmed anyone. We will keep him."

"But, my queen!" the wolf pleaded. "He disobeyed!"

Lizzie sighed. "Yes, but considering who she is and how little the number of my pure followers there are these days, we can't get rid of her. But, boy, understand that this is your one chance."

"Y-y-yes," the third voice stammered. Amelia. "I understand, ma'am."

"Shall we go, then?" Abby bit her tongue to keep from gasping. That was the voice of her favorite person in the world. Her mom. Melissa.

"Yes." Four pairs of footsteps walked away. Well, the wolf didn't really have a pair of feet, he had two pairs, but that didn't really matter.

As soon as the evildoers were out of earshot, Jadeine whispered, "I hope he's okay. Please, let him be okay."

They started walking again. Luckily, they were going in the opposite direction from Lizzie and her crew.

A while later, they reached the town square. Abby realized there were no streetlights—only torches flickering in the dusk. She guessed it was because streetlights didn't exist in the fairy tale world.

Jadeine started laughing like a crazy person. Abby understood— she had done it herself today. Jadeine ran to the fountain and splashed.

Then her expression grew serious. She walked back to Jill and Abby. "Girls, before we look for the second relic, I need a favor."

"Yes?" Abby prompted.

"I need to see Jocelyn," Jadeine replied.

"Who's Jocelyn?" Jill wanted to know.

Jadeine smiled. Her eyes seemed to be a mix of orange and green in the dim glow of the torches. "My sister."

Chapter 7
The Sisters' Reunion

Jocelyn used to care.

She used to smile and knit colorful scarves, and bake cookies. She used to run barefoot in the soft sand of the beach as long as the summer sun lit up the sky with its smile. But now her feet never touched the shore. The ocean only reminded her of what she'd lost.

A few years ago, she had gone on a quest with her sister, Jadeine, to defeat the Evil Queen. Jocelyn got attacked by the Big Bad Wolf and had to stay at the village to rest and heal. Jadeine kept searching, though. One particularly gloomy night, Jadeine had left the cottage and said she'd be back in a few days. Except she never came back. Ever.

Jocelyn had healed now…on the outside. Her heart was broken, though. Jadeine was one of her only family members left—*Well, she used to be,* Jocelyn thought—and it was safe to say Jadeine was dead. Jadeine hadn't returned in five years.

She was the one who had been her ray of sunshine through the Evil Queen's clouds. Now she was gone. But the part that hurt the most was that she didn't remember Jadeine's face, only the green cloak she always wore–*had worn,* Jocelyn corrected herself.

Now, Jocelyn didn't think anything mattered. She hadn't left her house in five years, and why should she? The villagers didn't care for her much anymore, and she didn't care for, well, anything really. Not anymore. She was just waiting until she could join her sister in heaven.

Jocelyn grabbed a book with a dark blue cover and started to tear out the pages absentmindedly. Suddenly, there was a knock at the door. Jocelyn glanced out the window and noticed the sky was dark and the stars were twinkling. *Is it really night already? Who would be visiting so late?* Jocelyn thought.

"Come in," Jocelyn called wearily. It was probably one of those so-called "caring" villagers who came by every few weeks, dropping off food and trying to get Jocelyn out of her house. They needed to mind their own beeswax, but Jocelyn couldn't really complain. They kept her fed, after all.

A girl came in. She had short, messy black hair and mischievous brown eyes. She was wearing farmer's clothes. She was about twelve. Jocelyn knew her very well—everyone in the village did—it was Jill. Jill was famous after she and Jack had fallen down the hill. But Jill had never met Jocelyn, so why would she be visiting?

After her came another girl around the same age. This girl, Jocelyn, didn't recognize. She was dressed very oddly. Her shoes had strange strings attached. Her hair was dirty blond, and her eyes were bright blue. Jocelyn didn't yet know that this girl was Abby.

"Why are you here? Came to drop off food?" Jocelyn snapped.

Jill smiled like she knew a secret. Abby stepped out of the way, and a woman came forward. She was wearing a green cloak and was holding a staff. *That green cloak. The very same one,* Jocelyn thought. She couldn't see the person's face, much to her dismay.

Jocelyn's heart leaped into her throat. She didn't want to get her hopes up, but it was impossible not to hope. *Is it...could it be...*

The woman smiled and lifted the hood, revealing herself. Jadeine. "Jocelyn. My sister. It's been a long time."

Jocelyn froze for a moment, not believing her eyes. Not wanting to believe that her sister was alive and home, because she was afraid that if she did, Jadeine would disappear, and she would wake up from a dream. Like how all her dreams went. But Jadeine didn't disappear.

"JADEINE!" Jocelyn shrieked with glee.

The grief she had experienced for five years suddenly vanished and was replaced with joy. Jocelyn jumped up so fast, her chair fell over. She ran to Jadeine and they hugged in a tight embrace. Jocelyn started laughing, and then her laughter turned to tears.

When the sisters were done laughing and crying, they pulled apart. "What—where were you?" Jocelyn asked. She almost started to cry again, but collected herself. "I thought you were dead!"

"I've missed you so much, and I'm so sorry I left," Jadeine apologized.

"It's fine. But why did you not come back?" Jocelyn queried.

Jadeine slipped out of her cloak and placed it on a chair nearby. Jadeine explained that she had been cursed by the Evil Queen and had only broken the curse today. Jocelyn listened in shock.

"That's just like her!" Jocelyn spat when Jadeine was finished. "I should have known…"

Suddenly, Jocelyn snapped out of her trance. *I missed out on five years of my life! Oh, wow. What has happened to the world outside?* she thought.

Abby stepped forward. "Hello, Jocelyn. I'm Abby."

"Nice to meet you, Abby," Jocelyn said.

"Nice to meet you too." Abby smiled.

Jadeine put a hand on her back. "Abby, here is the prophecy girl."

"Really?" Jocelyn asked. "So you're from the prophecy!"

"Yeah!" Abby replied. "I'm surprised you know about that if you've been locked in your house for five years."

Jadeine laughed. "Abby, the prophecy has been around much longer than five years. When was it made? I can't quite remember…"

"Twenty years ago," Jocelyn answered. "Right after the bad fairy vanished."

"Stop calling her the bad fairy!" Abby snapped. "She's my mom! And her name is Melissa!"

"I'm sorry," Jocelyn apologized. "Be warned, though: she did some horrible things back in the day."

Abby looked upset, so Jocelyn changed the subject. "How long will you be staying?"

Jill looked at Jadeine. "We really should get going."

Jadeine sighed, but nodded. "Yeah. We're collecting the relics."

Jocelyn's heart felt heavy. Jadeine had just come back, and now she wanted to leave again?! "No. You just came back home, and if you actually die, I don't know how I would—"

Jadeine stopped her. "Yes, of course. But otherwise, the Evil Queen will never be overthrown."

Jocelyn pressed her lips together, worried, but didn't argue. She supposed she should just be thankful her sister was alive—and she was! So why did she have a bad feeling about all this?

"Do you guys want some tea and jam-filled biscuits before you go?" Jocelyn asked in an attempt to get her sister to stay longer. "You know, you can't do much relic-collecting on an empty stomach!"

"All right," Abby agreed. "I am hungry. And biscuits sound delicious."

Jocelyn busied herself with the tea so she wouldn't think about the Evil Queen. The tea bag had slightly expired, but Jocelyn supposed it was fine. What's a couple of weeks? After that, she reached into a bag filled with biscuits that the villagers had given her and took out one each for Abby, Jill and Jadeine.

Jocelyn handed a cup of steaming ginger tea and jam-filled biscuits to Abby, Jill, and Jadeine each. "None for yourself, Jo?" Jadeine asked.

Jocelyn smiled and waved a hand. "I'm not in the mood for tea."

Jadeine sipped politely. Abby slurped up half the cup in one go. When Jill was done, she licked the inside of the cup clean. They also scarfed down their biscuits in only two bites.

"The tea is so good!" Jill marveled. "What did you put in it?"

Jocelyn shrugged. "I added some pepper."

"Pepper in tea?" Abby wondered. "That's not a normal combination."

Jadeine laughed. "Jo's always been a great cook. I remember all the toddlers would come sit on our porch when they were tired from playing and beg for cookies."

Jocelyn was surprised Jadeine remembered that. She hadn't done that for a long time…she wondered where the village children got their cookies from now.

"Should we go now?" Jill asked.

Jadeine nodded. "The clock is ticking."

Jocelyn looked out the window. "It's still night. Are you absolutely sure you don't want to stay the night and leave in the morning?"

"I'm tempted," Abby admitted. "But I agree with Jadeine—the clock is ticking."

Something snapped inside of Jocelyn. "No! I can't let you go! I don't want to spend all my time worrying about you—again! No, you just came home, please!"

"Jocelyn. I'm doing this so no one has to go through what you went through," Jadeine said.

Jocelyn calmed down. "I'm sorry. I'll pray for your safe return. Goodbye for now."

Jadeine grabbed her emerald cloak off a chair and wiggled into it. "Goodbye—we'll meet you as soon as we defeat the Evil Queen!"

Jocelyn could sense that Jadeine was trying to convince herself as much as anyone. Jadeine liked to keep a calm and confident composure, even around Jocelyn.

"Wait!" Jill cried, frowning. "What *is* the second relic?"

"Oh!" Jocelyn was glad to be helpful. "My memories are hazy, but I believe it is near the hill you fell off, Jill."

"OK!" Abby walked to the door. "Best be going, then. Bye, Jocelyn."

Jill waved and followed Abby out the door. Jadeine paused. "I really will come back for you, you know."

Jocelyn tried to smile. "I know."

They hugged one last time. Jocelyn felt a sense of responsibility for her younger sister, but Jadeine had always been the faster one. The braver one.

"JADEINE!" Jill called from outside. "You coming?"

Jadeine squeezed Jocelyn and then left. Jocelyn righted the chair that she had knocked over. She hoped Jadeine would be safe and overthrow the Evil Queen eventually.

Until then, Jocelyn would start fixing her life.

Chapter 8
The Secret Deal

KNOCK. KNOCK.

Eleanor stood up from where she was knitting by the fireplace. Her scarf was coming along nicely—it was blue and silver and almost done. The loud knocks shook Eleanor's cottage door. She set her knitting aside, heart pounding. Only bad news came this late at night.

Eleanor opened the door. Standing outside was Geppeto—Pinocchio's father. He was with one of the Little Pigs.

The oldest Little Pig was a girl, and her name was Victoria, usually called Vicki. After her were the twins, christened Nicholas and Richard, or Nicky and Ricky. Nicky was standing beside Geppeto.

Eleanor noticed that Geppeto's eyes were rimmed red and puffy, like he had been crying. His beard needed to be shaved, and his clothes were dirty and disheveled.

"What's wrong?" Eleanor asked, concerned. "Did something happen?"

Geppeto burst into tears.

"Why, come inside!" Eleanor cried. She pulled Geppeto inside. Nicky followed.

Geppeto, wiping his eyes, sat down in one of the armchairs. Eleanor sat across from him and handed him a handwoven handkerchief. "Thank you," he whispered, blowing his nose.

Since Geppeto didn't look well enough to talk, Eleanor looked at Nicky. "What happened?"

Nicky gulped, and his voice faltered. "The bad fairy paid us a visit yesterday morning."

"As all of us know," Eleanor said solemnly.

Geppeto took a deep breath. "S-she arrived in the town square and she—she—"

Nicky, in a low voice, explained, "She turned Pinocchio into a tree."

"Oh, poor Pinocchio!" Eleanor gasped. "That's terrible."

Nicky nodded. "She's horrible."

"I'm so sorry, Geppeto," Eleanor whispered. "He had a good life, though."

"He's not dead!" Geppeto exploded. "He's just—a tree! Temporarily! We'll turn him back!"

Nicky leaned towards Eleanor. "He's in denial," he whispered.

"What happened after she cursed Pinocchio?" Eleanor asked.

"Then she ran off into the forest. Supposedly, she was put under a spell by the Evil Queen to obey her."

"How did it happen?" Eleanor asked.

Nicky counted on his fingers. "Well, let's see. A forest sprite who saw the whole thing told Goldilocks, and of course, Goldilocks told everyone. So now the whole town knows."

Eleanor bit her lip. Lizzie had promised her that she wouldn't harm anyone else, or let her sister harm anyone else. *But Lizzie might not know, right?* Eleanor thought hopefully.

"Oh, don't worry, Eleanor," Nicky said. "We all know to stay away from *them*."

"Who else is with them?" Eleanor asked, though she already knew.

"The Big Bad Wolf," Nicky replied. "Obviously. Her sister, if the rumors are true. And…I don't know, she might have picked up a few others on the way. You know how convincing she can be."

There was silence as they all thought about how evil Lizzie was.

Eleanor broke the silence. "Is there anything else?"

"Yes, actually," Nicky answered. "Supposedly, Jack and Jill left with that strange girl from the Unknown. The bad fairy's daughter, right?"

"Yes," Eleanor confirmed. So at least one part of the plan was going as it was supposed to.

"That's it. Becky is really worried," Nicky sighed.

Becky was Jack and Jill's mother. No wonder she was worried. Her children were going on a dangerous quest to defeat the Evil Queen. "I'm sure they're OK," Eleanor reassured Nicky.

"I hope so," Nicky said.

Eleanor nodded. "Do you need anything, or did you just want to give me the news?"

Nicky lowered his voice. "Well, Geppeto was crying a lot, and I figured you would understand, because, you know, the Cyrus thing?"

Eleanor's eyes widened. So *that's* what this was about! Unfortunately for Nicky and Geppeto, she wasn't in the mood to talk about Cyrus right now. She never was.

Eleanor kept her calm, though. "Um…yeah. I'm sure we can turn him back into a boy, Gep! All is not lost!"

She managed a twisted smile. Geppeto did too. There was an awkward silence. Eleanor looked at Nicky, waiting for more news. Nicky glanced at Geppeto.

"Uh, that's all." Nicky stood up hurriedly. "Let's go, Geppeto."

Geppeto followed Nicky out the door. As soon as they were gone, Eleanor jumped to her feet. She needed to talk to Lizzie and make sure that Lizzie hadn't known about what her sister had done, and hadn't *let* her sister do it.

You see, Eleanor knew magic. Her specialty was in portal potions. She had a bunch of them in her cabinet right now! She grabbed one and gulped it down, thinking: *I want to see Lizzie.*

Swoosh! Swirling mist appeared in front of Eleanor. She could see Lizzie, who was sitting on a rock and kept fidgeting with her dress as if she was nervous about something. Melissa was kneeling on the ground, and the Big Bad Wolf was pacing nearby. Amelia, whom Eleanor didn't recognize, was kneeling next to Melissa.

"Lizzie!" Eleanor exclaimed a little too loudly.

Amelia jumped. Melissa looked around. The wolf snarled and prepared to pounce. If Lizzie was shocked, she hid it well.

"Eleanor." It was a statement, not a question.

"Lizzie, did you know about this?" Eleanor cried.

"Did I know about what?" Lizzie asked.

"About what your sister did! By turning Pinocchio into a tree! We had a deal!" Eleanor said.

"She did? Serves him right," Lizzie said. "But Ellie, I don't seem to remember what that deal was."

"You know full well what it was!"

"No, actually, I don't. Please enlighten me."

Eleanor explained. "Our deal was that if I told Abby Palmer the prophecy and if I performed magic and took the relics from her, I would give them to you. In exchange, you would let Cyrus go. And we ALSO agreed you wouldn't harm anybody else, or let Melissa harm anybody else."

Lizzie smiled. "Ah, yes! That *was* the deal. Forgive me, Ellie, I didn't know about what she had done. Why don't you step through this portal now, and we can continue with our deal."

Eleanor didn't believe that Lizzie hadn't known about what Melissa had done, and she wanted to pry it out of her. But more than that, Eleanor wanted Cyrus back. And she knew that pressuring an evil queen and possibly making her mad was probably not the best idea.

"All right," Eleanor replied. She sighed and stepped through the portal into the forest.

It took her eyes a second to adjust to the darkness. But once they did, she recognized this particular part of the forest! This part of the woods was nice and calm, with no tree roots looking to trip you. She used to go picking for herbs all the time here—until the Cyrus thing.

Long ago, Eleanor had been living all by herself. Cyrus had been an orphan, and by luck, they crossed paths. Cyrus had been adopted by Eleanor. They had lived happily in Eleanor's hut until The Evil Queen grew at large and took Cyrus away. Eleanor didn't know what Lizzie had done to Cyrus, but Cyrus never came back.

Eleanor snapped back to the present. Amelia was in front of her, playing with her auburn braids. Eleanor noticed that she was wearing a servant uniform, but it wasn't disheveled or dirty or torn, so Eleanor guessed that Amelia hadn't been part of Lizzie's crew for very long.

"Who's this?" Eleanor asked, pointing at Amelia.

"That's Amelia!" Lizzie's face lit up. "My new servant! Amelia, this is Eleanor. She's going to be *very* helpful to us.

Amelia smiled and awkwardly waved. "Hi."

The wolf rose. "Come on. We've been resting long enough."

As they walked, Lizzie leaned in to Eleanor. "Very, very, helpful indeed."

Chapter 9
The Hill

Invisible paint brushes streaked the sky orange and red. The air was crisp, filled with birdsong, and the warmth of the rising sun melted away the chill. Abby realized they had been walking for the whole night. Sparrows sang their sweet songs in the treetops above.

They were not in the forest anymore, but rather a sort of valley. That meant they had to go up all the way to get a better vantage point. Abby hated climbing up steep hills. It was too much effort.

"How much farther?" Jill asked for the umpteenth time.

"We're almost there," Jadeine replied, also for the umpteenth time. Only this time, she was right.

They were finally at the top of the hill! Abby looked over the edge and was instantly stunned. There was a huge, crystal clear lake down in the valley, with wildflowers and tiger lilies dotting the grass. A lone swan floated in the middle of the lake.

"It's beautiful," Abby whispered. The sight took her breath away—like a postcard from a dream.

Jill nodded. "It's more beautiful than the last time I came here."

Jadeine nodded in agreement. "Right. Didn't Jocelyn say this was the hill you fell down?"

"Yeah, uh…" Obviously, Jill didn't want to talk about it.

"The whole village was laughing about that for a month and a half!" Jadeine barked a laugh.

"How'd you even fall?" Abby wondered.

Jill's ears turned pink, and she crossed her arms defensively. "Do we have to talk about that?" The memory was still humiliating.

"Yeah."

"Ugh, fine. Jack and I were arguing, and I got angry. I pushed him. I had too much momentum, and I fell down too."

"Oh, what were you arguing about?"

"Oh, uh, nothing interesting," Jill said that in a way that made it sound like it was very interesting.

"Come on! Tell me!" Abby exclaimed.

"Er, well…we were arguing about who had to carry the water down?" It was a question, not a statement.

"Um…sorry, but that's kind of childish," Abby pointed out.

"That was 6 years ago!" Jill exclaimed. "We weren't mature 6 years ago!"

"Wait." Abby furrowed her brow. "You were six, Jack was four. And you were hauling water down hills? Which is basically child labor?"

Jadeine chuckled again. "I keep forgetting you're not from here. Everyone sends their kids out alone. Red Riding Hood's mom did it, too."

"And she almost got eaten by a wolf!" Abby retorted. "Irresponsible."

"We should look around now," Jadeine decided, changing the subject.

"Yeah…" Abby studied the hill. "I have an idea! Maybe the relic is underground."

"How exactly do we get down?" Jill asked. "We don't have a shovel."

Abby punched her lightly in the arm. "Of course we don't."

Jill laughed. With a start, Abby realized by now they were better friends than she had thought. Even though she hadn't known Jill that long, it already felt like they had years of shared memories. Maybe that's what fairy tale adventures did—turned strangers into friends faster than you could say "happily ever after".

Jadeine shook her head. "No need. I have a better idea." She held out her hand. "Abby, the staff?"

Abby gave it to her. Jadeine took a deep breath, planted her feet, and then whispered something under her breath.

The huge jade at the top of the staff glowed brightly. Then the staff turned into a spear. Abby gasped in delight.

Jill squealed. "WOW!"

"Staff, dig!" Jadeine commanded it. The staff dug into the ground, dragging Jadeine.

"Ooh," Abby whispered. "Cool."

"ABBY, JADEINE IS BEING DRAGGED DOWN BY A SPEAR!" Jill sounded ecstatic, for some reason.

Five seconds later, the staff had disappeared from their view and was zipping back for Jill. She grabbed the end, and it flew down the hole it had made. "WHEEEE!" Jill yelled.

Then it was Abby's turn. Before grabbing the staff, Abby hesitated. *Would I be stuck underground forever? No, the staff is there to help us. It has dug a large hole in the ground. Ugh, Abby, get a grip.*

The staff poked Abby in the shoulder, as if impatient. "All right, all right," she told the staff, and grabbed it as well.

The staff reared into the air and started flying in circles. "AIEEE!" Abby screamed. "UNDERGROUND! TAKE ME UNDERGROUND!"

The staff vibrated, as if laughing. It made a couple of loop-de-loops in the air, as if it were fun to watch Abby scream and kick. Then, the staff did a free fall. Abby screamed so loud that her throat went dry.

"Underground!" Abby begged. The staff finally obeyed.

Abby dropped to her knees as soon as the staff set her down. "Oh, sweet ground. I missed you."

"Thanks, staff," Jill said. "Uh…do you have a name?"

"Nope," the staff answered.

Jadeine shrieked. Abby fell backward onto her bottom. Jill's jaw dropped.

"Are y'all surprised I can talk?" the staff asked in a definitely male voice. "You shouldn't be."

"How—why—what?!" Jadeine managed. "You never talked before!"

"You never asked me any questions," the staff reasoned. "So I didn't talk."

"So, you don't have a name?" Jill queried.

"No, but I'd like one!" The staff sounded hopeful. Could the staff be hopeful?

"Uh, what should we name you?" Abby wondered, getting to her feet.

"What's your name?"

"Abby."

"That's a nice name! Call me Abby."

"You can't be Abby. I'm Abby."

"What's her name, then?" The staff pointed at Jill.

"Jill. You can't be Jill, either. It would get too confusing."

"So what do you suggest?"

Abby considered this. "Well…do you like the name Jay?"

"Jay?" The staff tilted in the air. "Sure! I'll be Jay! Call me Jay!"

"Guys!" Jadeine interrupted. "Come on!"

"Oh, right!" Abby had lost track of time. "So, where would the relic be?"

"I don't know, honestly," Jadeine replied. "I don't see any direct tunnels."

"Hey, staff! Can you scan the hill?" Jill asked.

"Underground?" the staff clarified.

"Of course, underground!" Jill exclaimed.

The staff made a tunnel with its surprisingly sharp emerald. Soon, the staff was gone. Abby found an earthworm in the ground beneath her and kicked it away in disgust. She hated earthworms. No matter how many times she watched videos about how earthworms help the planet, she still thought earthworms were gross.

Jill picked the earthworm up and cradled it in her arms like it was her baby. Abby made a gagging motion.

"Jill, ew!" Abby exclaimed. "You're cradling *A WORM!*"

"You hurt it," Jill noted, frowning.

"Why do you care?" Abby asked.

"Earthworms help the environment, Abby," Jill explained.

"I know, but it feels so GROSS!" Abby exclaimed.

"They're just living beings, poor wittle beings," Jill cooed. "You're so cute! Yes, you wittle bittle baby! I'm talking to you, you cutie pie!"

Abby was confused, thinking Jill was calling her cute, but realized she was cooing to the earthworm. *Blech!* The staff returned, dirt flying all over them. Abby wiped the dirt off her sleeve.

"Hi, Jay. Jill was acting like she was an earthworm's mom," Abby groaned.

"That's because I am! Hey, what do you think earthworms like to eat? Tell me!" Jill demanded.

"You've gone delusional," Abby concluded, shaking her head. She hoped that Jill was joking.

Jill lowered the earthworm to the floor, and the terrified earthworm slinked away. Probably because Jill wanted to be its mom, it probably had a mom already. Abby snickered at the thought. The poor widdle earthworm crawling to its mommy and crying about a giant who had said she was its mommy. Abby returned to real life and stopped daydreaming. They looked at the staff expectantly.

"I didn't find anything except a stick and a mushroom. Neither was of any interest, " the staff reported.

"Ugh." Jadeine rolled her eyes.

Abby thought for a second about where it might be, until she got an idea. "Did you guys notice the lake?"

"Yeah!" Jadeine exclaimed.

"So, does anything important live in a lake? Or anyone?" Abby asked.

Jadeine slapped her cheek, then her other cheek, then both her cheeks, and finally her forehead. Jill and Abby gave her strange looks.

"Oh, shoot! I totally forgot!" Jadeine exclaimed.

"Who?" Jill and Abby pressed. "And why did you do the cheek slapping?"

"Royal sea anemone cushion shop! The owners live on a lake!" Jadeine said, ignoring the second question.

"Um. Are they important?" Abby asked.

"Oh yes! They make about a million gold leaves per hour!" Jadeine gushed.

"WHOA. We should totally check that lake out!" Jill exclaimed.

"What are gold leaves?" Abby asked. No one answered her question. She figured it was probably some kind of fairy tale currency.

They let the staff get them out of the hole in the hill and fly down towards the lake. They got to their feet when they reached the edge of the lake.

"The shop is underwater," Jadeine replied. "And we can only go in with the owners' permission."

Abby rolled up her pant cuffs. "What do we do?"

"Just wade into the center of the lake!" Jadeine explained. "It's not that deep—four feet five at the most."

Jill started into the lake, picking her way through pebbles. Abby followed and then looked at Jadeine. "Aren't you and your staff—I mean, Jay—coming?"

Jadeine shook her head. "No…I can get kind of weird around millionaires. I'd better not."

Abby shrugged. Soon, she and Jill were standing in the middle of the lake. "What now?" Jill asked.

The swan floated toward them and honked loudly. "BETTER MOVE BEFORE IT BITES YOU!" Jadeine yelled from the shore.

"*That*?" Jill queried. "It doesn't look ferocious."

The swan didn't like that. It nipped Jill's leg.

Jill yelped and hopped on her good leg. "Ow! Ow, ow, ow! That hurt!"

The swan honked excessively like it was laughing. But then, something strange happened. Slowly, the swan transformed. It grew taller until it was a woman who towered over Abby and Jill. She was wearing a blue dress that matched perfectly with her sky blue hair.

The lady kept on laughing. She fell into the water, laughing. But, to Abby's surprise, she kept on laughing underwater, bubbles forming at the surface. Then, the lady surfaced with a serious expression.

"What do you want?" the lady hissed. "Who dares disturb me?"

"Um—uh—" Abby stuttered. She glanced at Jill for support, but she was just staring in awe at the woman. "Um. Jill, are you okay?"

"I—I apologize for disturbing you, Your Highness," Jill said.

"Huh? Your Highness? Is she royalty or something?" Abby asked.

"She's the Merqueen!" Jill exclaimed. "Hi, I'm Jill and this is Abby!"

"Look, I don't care about two random girls named Jill and Abby," the Merqueen scoffed.

"Abby's no random girl! She's the prophecy girl!" Jill exclaimed.

"The prophecy girl?! This changes everything!" the Merqueen squealed.

This is my chance! Abby thought. *We need to go with her. Maybe she'll have information about the relic!*

"Can we see your palace?" Abby asked.

"Sure!" The Merqueen produced a key out of thin air. She bent down and started fiddling with something underwater. "I'm Nadine."

Abby heard a click. Suddenly, Abby and Jill both plunged forward into the water. But instead of getting a faceful of lake water, they were standing in a beautiful palace. The couches were made out of sea anemones, and the walls were lined with coral. Abby wondered if the Merqueen bought the couches from the sea anemone company.

"Wow!" Jill cried. "You've got a beautiful palace!"

Nadine blushed with pride. "Well, I am the Merqueen."

"Are you a mermaid?" Abby wanted to know.

Nadine nodded. "Yes, but when I talk to humans, I cast a spell that makes me look human. Otherwise, they tend to get uncomfortable."

Abby studied Nadine's legs, but they seemed normal to her.

"So," Jill said. "Do you have a relic?"

"Well, yeah. I do." Nadine looked confused.

"Well, we need your relic," Abby deadpanned.

Nadine gasped. "I can't give that to you! Out, now!"

"No!" Abby cried, desperate to bargain. "Please? We need to defeat the Evil Queen!"

Nadine shrugged. "What has she ever done to me?"

So she couldn't use the same words she used with Jadeine. "Uh…"

Jill had a plan, though. "Would you give it to us if we did you a favor?"

Nadine considered this. "Actually…there is something you could do."

"What is it?" Abby asked, leaning forward.

Nadine shot them a diabolical grin. "You need to find the Sea Witch and bring her here."

Whatever Abby had been expecting, it wasn't that. "Excuse me?!"

Nadine grunted. "I need revenge!"

"Wait, slow down!" Abby yelped. "What did she do?"

"You know who my sister was, right?"

Abby looked at Jill. "Am I supposed to?"

Jill nodded vigorously. "Abby, Nadine's sister is the Little Mermaid!"

Abby's eyes grew huge. "Oh."

"So, anyway, that evil Sea Witch is going to pay for what she did to my little sister!" Nadine narrowed her eyes. "Bring her here, dead or alive. Actually, alive would be better, because it's my fight, not yours."

Abby turned to Jill. "Um…"

"Can we talk for a minute?" Jill asked. "We need to decide."

Nadine waved a hand. "Sure. Go ahead."

Abby pulled Jill away from the Merqueen. "Should we do it?"

Jill shrugged. "Well, the Sea Witch is one of the most famous villains. But we need the relic."

"So…what do you think?"

"It's your prophecy, Ab. It's your call."

Abby thought about it, long and hard. In the end, she decided, "We'll do it." She figured there was no other way to convince Nadine to give them the relic.

Jill nodded. She stood up and told Nadine, "We accept."

Nadine squealed. "Yay! OK, off you go!" She snapped her fingers, and suddenly Abby and Jill were standing in front of Jadeine and the staff.

"How'd it go?" Jadeine wanted to know.

Abby groaned. "Ugh! Horrible!"

Chapter 10
Aeryn

"So where does the Sea Witch live?"

"I don't know!" Abby threw her hands in the air, exasperated. "Jill, stop asking. None of us knows!"

Jill rolled her eyes. "I only asked twice! And we need to find her!"

Abby sighed. "Sorry. I know it's not your fault—but we're short on time."

"I'm sorry too. I mean, the Sea Witch is known for making deals that are always in her favor. She can lure you into a bad deal. She's dangerous and I'm nervous."

"She *is* dangerous." Jadeine bit her lip. "I think Goldilocks once said the Sea Witch lived in the Liquid Sunlight Ocean. Of course, you can't always trust Goldilocks, but I think that's our best bet."

"Liquid Sunlight?" Abby mused. "That doesn't sound like a witchy ocean."

"What is even liquid sunlight?" Jill wondered.

Jadeine shrugged. "No one really knows. Probably something sunshiny."

"Where is it?" Abby asked.

"I don't know." Jadeine's shoulders slumped. "I can't remember exactly what Goldie said—this was six years ago."

"I know where it is."

Abby's eyes widened, and she whirled around. A boy was standing behind them. His caramel colored hair caught the light in a way that made it glow. Not quite blond, not quite brown—just like in the in-between shimmer of twilight. His eyes were light blue. He looked about 11 years old.

"Who are you?!" Abby yelped. "And have you been following us?"

"I'm Aeryn!" he chirped, not answering her second question. "Who are you?"

"Aaron? Like A-A-R-O-N? " Jill asked.

"A-E-R-Y-N," the boy spelled. "I know, it's a weird name. Blame my mom."

Abby shook her head. "What do you want?"

He shrugged. "Well, I heard you talking about where the Sea Witch is, and I know, so I thought I would help you." Then, to their utter shock, he began to rise off the ground.

For the first time, Abby noticed two almost transparent wings sticking out of his back, fluttering like dragonfly silk. She screamed.

He screamed, too. "Why are we screaming?"

"You-you—are you, like, a fairy?" she sputtered.

He nodded, his eyes growing huge. "Are you?"

"Uh...no."

"Back to the point," Jadeine interrupted. "We were talking about the Liquid Sunlight Ocean…"

"Oh, yeah!" Aeryn rose even higher in the air. "So, uh, last week I was on trial—"

"On trial?" Abby asked at the same time that Jill asked, "Why?"

"Um, well, it's a long story. So, anyway, this fairy was making a complaint. She told the Fairy Godfather that the Sea Witch was making the water off the coast angry, and it was high tide all the time. She wanted him to finally prosecute the Sea Witch for everything, and he said, 'It is too expensive to go all the way past Mermaid Lake.'"

Jadeine snapped her fingers. "Of course! Now I remember! There's a river that connects Mermaid Lake to the Liquid Sunlight Ocean—that's how the Little Mermaid met the Sea Witch in the first place."

Abby smiled. "Great! Let's go, then!"

"I don't actually know where it is, though." Jadeine frowned.

"Want me to take you?" Aeryn offered.

Abby looked at her friends. "One second. We need to talk."

Abby pulled Jill and Jadeine behind a tree. Jill whispered, "Should we trust him?"

Jadeine lifted a shoulder. "We don't know if he's working with the Evil Queen."

Abby nodded, but Aeryn didn't seem evil to her. He reminded her of fizzy soda—too many energetic bubbles at once. "On the other hand…we need help."

"I think we should accept," Jill decided. "He seems nice enough. But we'll keep an eye on him."

"All right," Abby agreed. She called to Aeryn, "OK. Take us to the Liquid Sunlight Ocean."

Aeryn beamed. He fluttered back down to the ground and started walking. Abby and the others followed him.

Abby asked Aeryn, "How long is the walk?"

"Oh, well, it's off the southern coast of the mainland. I'd say we can get there in about a day or two."

Abby nodded. "Oh! I'm Abby, by the way. And this is Jill and Jadeine."

"OK."

They walked in silence for a couple of minutes until Jill piped up, "Say, how did your trial go?"

Aeryn slumped. "Horrible. I got banished."

"What did you do?" Jadeine gasped.

"It's a long—" Aeryn started.

"We've got time," Abby interrupted.

Aeryn sighed. "There's this fairy. His name is Ben. And he is a bully. So last week, he was being really mean to this girl, Gracie. He was playing mean pranks on her and calling her names."

Abby covered her mouth. "That's horrible."

Aeryn nodded. "So I may have tangled him in the scratchiest vines on H.E.A.L. He itched for *hours*."

Jill snickered. Aeryn stared at her. She regained control of herself. "I'm sorry, it's just that he deserves that."

Aeryn cracked a smile. "Yeah. But then he turned me in, and the Fairy Godfather banished me for not being peaceful, blah, blah, blah."

Jadeine's mouth fell open. "Wait, why isn't Ben on trial?!"

"'Cause his mom is one of the 12." Aeryn rolled his eyes.

"The 12 what?" Abby asked.

"The original twelve fairies who gave gifts to Sleeping Beauty," Aeryn explained. "And Ben's mom is one of them, so he gets an 'out' card."

Abby shook her head. "That's not fair!"

Aeryn shrugged. "I know."

"I'm hungry," Jill put in. "Have we got any food?"

Abby dug in her backpack. She pulled out a can of tomato soup. "Let's sit and eat."

So the four of them ate. The tomato can was squished and was probably days old, so it did *not* taste good.

"Abby, what *is* this?" Jill made a face.

"Tomato soup, obviously," Abby replied, trying not to gag.

"It tastes like garbage," Jill complained. "Ugh. But I'm too hungry to care."

After they had drunk all the remnants of tomato soup, Aeryn started to walk in the opposite direction from Mermaid Lake. Soon, they were in a dense forest, where sunlight could barely squeeze through the canopy.

"I have a really bad feeling about this," the staff whimpered.

"Wait, the staff talks?!" Aeryn yelped.

Abby nodded.

"Ok. So the answer to the staff's question: It's because we're getting closer to the Sea Witch. It's getting dark. Wanna find a spot to sleep for the night?" Aeryn asked.

"Um…sure?" Abby replied nervously.

"I really have a bad feeling about this," Jill said, picking at her fingernails, which were filled with dirt.

"Me too," Jadeine agreed.

"Relax, guys. Let's see…here! This is perfect to get some shut-eye!" Aeryn exclaimed, pointing to a tiny clearing.

Abby felt happy to have sunlight on her face again. She lay down, and fallen leaves crunched beneath her. Abby watched as the sky turned darker, until eventually, the night stars came into view. The stars twinkled, and shooting stars shot across the sky. She kind of doubted that Aeryn wasn't on Lizzie's side, but after all, he had helped them find a great spot to rest.

"Doesn't this feel so…magical?" Abby whispered to Jill.

"No, not when I'm worrying about a bug getting in my hair!" Jill huffed.

"Oh. Yeah, right, bugs! Ahhh!" Abby mocked her.

"Hey, did you see your face when you went inside the log? Your expression when you looked at a bug was like this," Jill replied, crossing her eyes and holding her mouth open like she would scream.

Abby laughed. Her eyelids grew heavy until finally, she closed her eyes and went into her Dreamworld.

Chapter 11
The Sea Witch

"WAKE UP, ABBY!" Jill screamed into Abby's ear.

"I'm deaf now," Abby grumbled.

"Come on, if you want to capture the Sea Witch, we better get a move on!" Aeryn called.

"Nooo, please." Abby yawned. "It's like, 5 in the morning!"

Suddenly, a howl erupted through the forest. That definitely woke Abby up. She scrambled to her feet and turned around to see Jadeine running into the clearing with apples in her palm.

"She's here!" Jadeine exclaimed. "I was collecting apples, since the tomato soup tasted horrible, and she's here! RUN WHAT ARE YOU WAITING FOR?!"

"Who's here?!" Aeryn yelped.

"The Evil Queen, let's go! Come on!" Jadeine shrieked.

The foursome dashed into the trees beyond. When the ear-splitting howls dissipated, they slowed down. Jadeine gave everyone an apple. Abby studied the apple to make sure it was safe to eat, then bit into it.

Her eyes widened. "It's so good!" The apple was sweet with just the right amount of crunch.

"Shh!" Jadeine whispered. "Be quiet, she's still close."

"Hey, why are you all huffy?" Jill asked.

Jadeine rolled her eyes. They walked for a couple of hours without talking much. Soon, Abby heard the roar of waves. They turned the corner and saw an ocean. It had to be the Liquid Sunlight Ocean. But it didn't look sunny, like Abby had expected. Instead, the waters were gray and murky.

"So…this isn't sunny," Jadeine noticed. "Why is it named Liquid Sunlight Ocean if it's not sunny?"

"Uh, don't ask me," Jill said.

"I *wasn't* asking you. I was asking *everyone*," Jadeine clarified with an annoyed look.

Abby sighed at their bickering. "Who's the best at holding their breath?" Abby asked, changing the subject.

"I can do spells so we can breathe underwater for an hour," Aeryn suggested.

"That's great!" Jadeine exclaimed.

"Ok, give me a second." Aeryn closed his eyes.

Aeryn floated slowly into the air. Magic swirled around him. Bright beams of light hit all of them. The sparkles slowly vanished, and Aeryn was on the ground again.

"That was so cool! It was like a light show. But I don't feel any different," Abby said.

"Just get into the water," Aeryn said, gesturing to the waves.

At first, they were hesitant that his spell wouldn't work. Then Jadeine ran up to the shore. She slowly sank beneath the waves.

Abby went next. She was hesitant. The water rose to her ankles, then her knees, then her waist. *What if I die?* Abby thought. Visions of her being trapped underwater forever filled her mind. She shook her head to clear it. Abby slowly swam out deeper, then let herself sink under the water.

Aeryn flitted above the water, teasing the waves as they lapped at his feet, then plunged into the depths.

Jill was last. She dashed into the waves.

"Remember me when I die!" Jill screamed.

After Jill went in, everyone swam towards each other. Aeryn opened his mouth to show they could breathe underwater. Cautiously, everyone followed Aeryn.

"Ooga. Blooga looga. Testing. Testing." Jill tested it out. "Hey, I can talk!"

"Come on, try it, Jadeine and Abby!" Aeryn persuaded.

"Ah. Ah. AH! Wow. Now, where would the Sea Witch live?" Abby wondered.

"Maybe down there, in those jagged rocks, with sharks circling it," Jill suggested, pointing downwards.

Everyone looked down. Jagged rocks stuck out on the ocean floor. Great white sharks snapped their jaws at Abby, but didn't move.

"I say we use someone as bait to lure the sharks away," Aeryn announced.

"OOGA BLARG! I mean, no! No way!" Jadeine exclaimed. "You can be bait, if you want to."

"That's just weird! I mean, you're a fairy, you're supposed to be peaceful, albeit the Ben thing!" Jill reprimanded him.

Aeryn just shrugged. "Well, not always."

"How about this?" Abby pointed at a gap between the smallest sharks. "On the count of three, we dive."

"OK," Jill agreed. Aeryn and Jadeine nodded their agreement.

"We go down in 3,2,1!" Abby counted.

They dove towards the cave as quickly as they could. Abby felt the water pressure fighting her—she had never been a good diver. When she neared the rocks, a shark lashed out at her. Somehow, she managed to dodge it, but she was just met by another shark.

Abby spied a small opening in the rocks. Could she fit? Abby made herself as small as she could and squeezed in. On the other side, the waters felt angrier somehow. The sharks that had been fighting her stopped and floated away.

"Anyone home?" Abby whispered.

"The Sea Witch is," a voice rang out.

"Abby! Omigosh, hi, you're safe!" Jill cried, appearing in front of her. Abby hadn't seen her come in, and she wondered how Jill got away from the sharks.

"Jill! I'm so glad you're safe!" Abby exclaimed.

Abby hugged Jill. But when she did, Jill felt…scaly like a fish. And her hair was…greenish?!

Abby glanced outside and was startled to see Jill kick a shark in the nose. But if Jill was there…who was she hugging? Abby let go and backed away, eyes wide. She looked like Jill, but the girl she was hugging wasn't Jill. *The Sea Witch,* Abby thought.

The Sea Witch's face began to melt, which was creepy. Her face looked like the Sea Witch's after a second. She slithered towards her. The Sea Witch cleared her throat, which sounded like a person being strangled. Abby hated that sound.

"I think you know who I am, Abby," The Sea Witch informed her.

"I think I do," Abby replied. "You're the Sea Witch. How do you know who I am?"

"The fairy. He is my nephew," The Sea Witch cackled.

Abby stared at her. "What? No! He's a fairy! You're a witch. How can you be related?"

The Sea Witch smiled. Her teeth were yellow. "I'm not lying."

"How do I know you're telling the truth?" Abby asked.

"Because I am her nephew!"

Abby whirled around to see Aeryn. Waiting in the doorway. Her blood ran cold.

A rope lay in his hands. Suddenly, Aeryn threw the rope around Abby and tied her to a marble column. Abby squirmed, but the rope was too tight.

"Sorry!" Aeryn chirped. "I tied the Devil's Knot. You'll never get out!" Aeryn told her all this with the same cheery attitude he had had back in the forest. Abby didn't get how a bad guy could be so…cheerful.

"And your backstory? Were those all lies?" Abby asked.

"Yes and no," Aeryn answered.

Abby felt her eyes become watery. She had trusted Aeryn. *I'm so gullible! He showed up in the middle of nowhere!* Abby thought. The Sea Witch let Aeryn leave.

"YOU'RE A TRAITOR!" Abby shouted at the top of her lungs.

Aeryn yelled back, "I KNOW! BYE AUNTIE!"

Jill swam into the entrance of the cave, Jadeine right behind her. Jadeine's eyes widened. "Wha—where is Aeryn going? Why are you tied up?"

Abby just shook her head.

They put two and two together. "Oh no," Jill whispered. "It was a trap?"

The Sea Witch laughed. "I can't believe you trusted him! Dumb humans!"

Two octopi lunged out from the ground and tied up Jill and Jadeine with some spiky coral. Abby felt tears start rolling down her cheeks. Her eyes burned. This was all her fault.

"I'm sorry, guys," she whispered. "I shouldn't have trusted him."

Jadeine shook her head. "No, Abby. It wasn't your fault."

Jill agreed, nodding her head. "Yeah! We trusted him, too!"

Abby looked at the Sea Witch. "What do you want with us?"

"You shall be my servants!" the Sea Witch replied. "Oh, this is my lucky day!"

She started to swim off. "Wait!" Jadeine cried. "Where are you going?"

"I'm going to collect some sea glass!" the Sea Witch called over her shoulder. "It makes the best knives!" And then she was gone, the two octopi on her tail.

Jill groaned. "Now what?"

They were silent until Jadeine gasped. "Oh no!"

"What?" Abby asked sullenly.

"Aeryn only enchanted us to breathe underwater for an hour. How long has it been?"

Abby tried to check her watch, but it was dead. "I don't know. Fifteen minutes, maybe?"

"How do we know he was telling the truth about that?" Jill pointed out. "He lied about everything else."

True. The three went a few minutes without talking. Then Jill piped up. "What do you think we'll have to do as servants?"

Abby shrugged. "Collect her sea glass for her, probably."

Jadeine sighed. "I really thought we had a chance of defeating Lizzie…but we still have four more relics to go."

"What about my mom?" A horrible thought struck Abby. "What if she stays under the curse forever? Or what if Lizzie gets tired of her and…"

"We can't think about that!" Jill cried. "Come on, Abby. Think positive. Maybe your mom got free and ran away. Maybe she's coming to save us."

Save them…that gave Abby an idea. "We're not in that deep, right?"

"Yeah," Jadeine replied. "In fact, we're still in the shallows. See?" She pointed up, and Abby could see the sun and the sky up there.

Jill frowned. "Wait, but there were sharks! Sharks don't live in the shallows."

"The Sea Witch probably enchanted them to live here," Jadeine suggested. "She's a witch, after all."

"Guys," Abby interrupted. "What if we yell for help?"

"Help?" Jill seemed dubious. "Who would be here to hear us?"

Abby ignored her. She took a deep breath and yelled, "HELP! SOMEONE! THE SEA WITCH TRAPPED US!"

No answer. Abby sighed.

Jadeine bumped her shoulder against Abby's. Abby assumed that was meant to be reassuring. "It's OK," Jadeine soothed. "We'll try again later."

Ten seconds passed. Then ten minutes.

Jill burst into tears. Abby looked at her, surprised. "What's wrong?!"

Jill wiped her eyes. "I—MY MOTHER WILL BE SO UPSET! AND JACK! WE'RE GOING TO DIE DOWN HERE, AND I NEVER GOT TO SAY GOODBYE! WE'RE SCREWED! SO SCREWED!" Jill wailed.

Abby opened her mouth to calm her down, but then a voice came from above: "Did you hear that?"

"Hear what? I didn't hear anything," another voice replied.

Jadeine squealed. "We're not screwed! HELP! WE'RE DOWN HERE!"

"Did you hear it this time?" the first voice asked.

"Yeah…are some other mermaids in the ocean? But they sound different."

"They couldn't be humans, could they?"

"Maybe…they sound like they're near the Sea Witch's lair!"

"Let's go check it out! Maybe someone needs help."

"YES! DOWN HERE!" Jill screamed.

Two mermaids splashed into the water. The first had dark hair and green eyes, along with a silver tail. The second had a gold tail and auburn hair.

"Wow, cool beans," Abby breathed.

"I told you there was someone down here! Hello, I'm Camilla, and she's Bethany," the golden tail mermaid said.

"You can call me Beth, and call her Cam!" Bethany exclaimed.

"No! My nickname is NOT Cam," Camilla huffed. "Camilla is fine."

"I'm Abby, and this is Jill and Jadeine," Abby told the mermaids. "Can you cut us out?"

Bethany took a mirror out of her handbag. "Sure can."

"How will you cut us out with a mirror?" Jill wanted to know.

Bethany pressed a button on the mirror, and spikes sprang out. Abby gasped. She thought those things were only in ninja movies, and they weren't in a ninja movie. Beth started sawing at the ropes, and in a minute, all three were free.

How those mermaids had a knife mirror at that time, Abby didn't know. Who carried a knife mirror around? But she was too relieved to worry about it.

"Thank you, Beth and Camilla," Jadeine told the mermaids.

Camilla smiled. "Oh, no, sweetie. No problem!"

"Now, come on." Bethany started swimming upwards. "Let's get you out."

Bethany and Camilla helped the three onto the shore. The mermaids themselves stayed in the water, however. Obviously.

Abby gasped in the air—she had never realized air tasted so good.

"Were you trapped by the Sea Witch?" Camilla asked knowingly.

"Yeah," Jill replied.

Camilla *tsk*ed. "Ugh. She's always causing trouble."

"Is there anything we can do for you in return?" Jadeine asked.

"No!" Bethany cried. "Oh, honey, you don't have to do that."

"No, seriously!" Abby looked at the mermaids. "We would've had to be servants of the Sea Witch forever. We're in your debt."

"Well…" Camilla considered. "There is one thing."

Bethany turned to her friend. "Not the water quality thing."

"Water quality thing?" Jill asked.

"The Sea Witch didn't use to live here," Camilla explained. "When she moved in, she started messing up the water—now it's all dirty. I submitted a complaint to Cinderella, but I'm not sure if she received it. Could you be a sweetheart and tell her about it?"

"No," Bethany chastised. "They've been through enough—"

"We would love to do that," Abby cut in. "Where does Cinderella live?"

"She lives pretty far south," Jadeine replied. "But I think she's holding a ball in her summer palace?"

"Cinderella has a summer palace?" Jill asked.

Camilla nodded. "She loves to hold balls—all the queens will be there, and so will King Charming."

"King Charming's the one who got divorced a lot?" Abby tried to recall what Eleanor had told her.

Bethany snorted. "Mm-hmm."

"So, you want us to go to the ball?" Jadeine asked.

"Yes," Camilla clarified. "She'll be there."

Jill looked at her friends. "That sounds easy enough."

Abby lowered her voice. "Yeah, but don't you think we're going off the road here?"

"What road?" Jill looked around.

Abby rolled her eyes. "It's an expression. We didn't even manage to kidnap the Sea Witch like we were supposed to—we lost so much time. Now you want to do this?"

"Oh, come on!" Jadeine exclaimed. "They saved our lives, Jill. We have to repay them."

Jill sighed, but she gave in. "Fine." Then Jill told the mermaids, "We'll do it."

Camilla squealed. "Yay!"

Jadeine, Jill, and Abby said goodbye to the mermaids and started trekking through the forest. They were silent for a while, until Jill spoke up.

"I'm soaked," Jill complained. "I didn't realize before, but I'm soaked."

Abby shrugged as if she was saying 'so what?' "Jill, we're going to meet *Cinderella*! And all the other queens! And King Charming!"

"So?" Jill asked.

"Aren't you excited?!" Abby's smile faded a bit.

"Not really," Jill answered. "Royalty can get kind of snooty. Once a duke was passing through town, and when he saw me covered with dirt, he kept saying all these mean things."

Jadeine laughed. "I think I met Cinderella once before…she was just passing through town. She's really nice."

"Well, that's good, I guess," Jill said. "Well, Abby? How excited are you? We've already covered a lot of ground. About 1 hour more if we manage to hitch a ride."

Abby squealed in response. They were going to meet people she'd always dreamed of meeting.

Chapter 12
The Ball

"HEY! OVER HERE!"

Jill waved her arms at an oxcart filled with pears. Jadeine had thought that Cinderella's summer home was south of the Liquid Sunlight Ocean, so that's the direction they went in. Soon, their feet were sore and thirsty. Then, the oxcart appeared, like a miracle.

The driver pulled over. "Need anything?"

"Could you give us a lift?" Jadeine pleaded. "We're going to Cinderella's Ball."

He looked them up and down. "Cinderella's Ball in *those* clothes?" he asked.

"Umm…" Jill trailed off. "We just ran away from—" Abby elbowed her hard, and Jill winced in pain.

"Running away? Why?" the driver inquired suspiciously.

"Um…our babysitter was really mean—" Abby got cut off by the driver.

"Wait, she babysat *all* of you? Including the young woman there?" the driver pointed at Jadeine.

"Um…yeah…? Anyways, we were invited and she wasn't, and she was really jealous and tried to lock us away," Abby fibbed.

"This is starting to sound like Cinderella's story," Jill whispered.

"Oh." Abby turned back to the driver. "Please, can you take us?"

The driver sized them up. Finally, he gave in, probably because they were drenched and dirty. "Fine, since I'm going in that direction. Get in—I'm Bert, by the way."

"Thanks!" Abby exclaimed, climbing in. They had to sit in the back with the pears, but she didn't mind.

As they traveled, Abby took in the scenery. She realized she hadn't really gotten a chance to rest and see the world since arriving in H.E.A.L.

The houses by the side of the road were picturesque. Abby wished she could live in a world like this. No litter, no pollution, friendly people, and magic was in the air. But then again, on Earth, they didn't have Evil Queens or Big Bad Wolves.

H.E.A.L was like a sweet melody, like the music at a carnival. Sometimes, though, it was like the creepy Halloween sounds that made her sleep with the lights on.

The next thing Abby knew, Jadeine was shaking her gently. "Wake up," she said. "We're here."

Abby sat up and gasped. In front of them was the most picturesque palace she had ever seen. It was made of a material almost like glass, and it sparkled when the sun hit it. It was also gigantic and loomed over the tiny houses surrounding it. Abby had always dreamed of seeing a fairy tale castle, especially Cinderella's castle.

A small prick of sadness poked her as she remembered her dad once saying, 'If I could go anywhere, it'd be Cinderella's palace. A true beauty.' She felt like he should be the one seeing it, not her. Abby set her thoughts aside and tried to wake Jill up.

"Jill…take a look," Abby breathed, shaking Jill gently.

Jill stirred awake next to Abby. "Mmm…what? Oh, wow!"

"Beautiful, isn't it?" Jadeine asked softly, her voice filled with awe.

Bert stopped the cart. "You guys can get off here, right?"

Abby stretched her stiff legs and hopped off the cart. "Yeah, thanks."

Jadeine dug in her pocket and placed two gold coins in Bert's hands. "Here you go."

Jill tripped over the side of the cart and lay on the ground, groaning. "Ugh…I was dreaming about pears. Every single one of them had a bite taken out of it."

Abby pulled her up and looked at the palace. "Do we just…go in?"

Jadeine shrugged. "Well, there will be a guard checking if you look suspicious. But, yeah, we pretty much just walk in there. And the doors are open."

"That's pretty loose security," Abby said.

On the stairs, a bored-looking guard was sitting, just as Jadeine had predicted. "State your name and occupation," he drawled, looking down at the floor.

"Abby Palmer," Abby told him. "And…uh…I don't have a job?"

The guard looked up. "Children?" He turned to Jadeine. "These yours?"

"Uh…yes," Jadeine lied. "I am Jadeine. I'm a Dreamwalker."

The guard sat up straighter with interest. "Dreamwalker, mm?" His eyes flitted to the staff, then to their clothes. "I would allow you in, but...," The guard looked distastefully at their clothes.

"Please! We didn't mean to come like this, it's just that there was this—" Abby got cut off by the guard.

"No. If you wish to go in, you must have an invitation and appropriate clothes," the guard said.

Abby turned away, defeated. But Jadeine wasn't ready to give up. She pointed the staff at the guard, and an eerie green mist surrounded him. When the mist cleared, the guard was leaning against the palace wall, eyes closed, and snoring gently.

"Thanks, Jadeine!" Abby and Jill exclaimed.

Abby squeezed the excess water out of her clothes and stepped inside. The inside was beautiful, but a little...

"Lonely," Jadeine noted.

"Now, where would Cinderella be?" Jill wondered.

Jadeine bit her lip. "Probably in the main ballroom. But I don't know which way it is...let's try that hallway." She pointed to the left.

Abby nodded. "If it's not, we can ask someone for directions. Sure, let's try that hallway."

They started walking down the hallway.

"Guys...do you think we should get a change of clothes?" Jadeine asked.

"Yeah! Jadeine, you can conjure up some fancy ball gowns!" Jill exclaimed. "With sequins…"

"Okay…" Jadeine trailed off. In the blink of an eye, their regular clothes had changed into dresses. They weren't gowns, but they were pretty. Abby wore a pale blue dress with flowers going down the sleeves and skirt. Abby had gold earrings and a gold necklace. Jill wore a chartreuse sleeveless gown with her hair tied up in a bun. Jadeine wore a simple yet beautiful pale green gown.

"Oh. My. God!!!" Jill shrieked. "This is a-ma-zing!!!"

"I've always wanted something like this! Thanks, Jadeine!" Abby thanked her.

"It was nothing." Jadeine smiled. "Now let's go."

Soon, they came to a halt. The hallway branched off into two other hallways and a staircase in the middle of the two. Jill groaned. "Which way? This castle is like a maze."

"Are you guys lost?"

Abby whirled around. A boy and a girl were standing behind them. They looked about thirteen. They both had black hair. The girl's skin was dark brown, and the boy's was a couple of shades lighter. The girl had blue eyes, and the boy's eyes were one blue and one gold— what was the scientific name for that?—heterochromia. The girl was wearing a pale blue dress with flowers near the collar and a flower crown with baby's breath and lavender. The boy wore, surprisingly, only a white dress shirt and red pants.

Jadeine nodded. "Very much, yes. We're looking for the ballroom."

The girl smiled. "It's up that staircase."

"Oh!" Abby exclaimed. "Thank you. We would've been lost forever! It's really big."

The girl laughed. "Yeah, it is. I'm Cherry, and this is my brother Apple."

Abby stared at them. "Your names are…Cherry and Apple."

Next to Abby, Jill made a weird sound, like a duck being strangled. Abby turned to her. "Are you OK?"

"Abby!" Jill hissed. "These are Snow White's kids!"

A million answers flashed through Abby's mind, ranging from *Oh! Sorry if I offended you! to Wow, you're her kids?* to *Nice to meet you, I'm Abby*. But the one that came out on top was: "Snow White named her children Cherry and Apple?!"

"Our mom's a foodie," Apple explained.

This just keeps getting weirder and weirder, Abby thought. "Isn't Apple a girl's name? Like this character on Ever After High—ow, Jill! Stop!" Jill was grinding her heel into Abby's foot.

"It's ok!" Apple smiled. "Mom wanted to name her firstborn Apple, to make a point, and then when I turned out to be a boy, she did it anyway 'cause she didn't wanna wait for another."

"Oh," Abby said. "Uh…I'm Abby. This is Jill, and Jadeine."

Jadeine looked around and saw a stairway that had a sign hanging on the wall on top of it, which stated 'Ballroom'.

"So the ballroom's upstairs…" Jadeine said.

"Want us to take you?" Cherry offered.

"Thank you!" Jill squeaked. "I mean, we would love that!"

Cherry and Apple turned and started walking. Abby caught up to them. "I'm twelve. How about you guys?"

"I'm twelve, too!" Cherry chirped. "And Apple's fourteen."

"Oh, OK."

Cherry and Apple led them up the stairs to a door marked MAIN BALLROOM. "This is it," Cherry told them.

Jill went in first. "I see Cinderella!" she reported.

Jadeine followed her, but Abby hung back. "Aren't you guys coming?"

Apple shook his head. "Cinderella asked us to babysit her son, but he ran off. We need to find him."

Cherry frowned. "Hey…are you the prophecy girl?"

"Yeah," Abby replied. Then she wondered if she could trust them. She had a right to be suspicious, after Aeryn.

"Well, bye," Apple told her. "Come on, Cherry. Let's find Cinderella's kid."

Abby watched them rush off. As she stared at the hallway, she felt like she was forgetting something. Then, she remembered. They would have to go back and get the second relic…maybe ask Nadine if they could do another favor. Then, Abby rushed inside the ballroom. The flashing lights and laughter immediately dazed her. Jill ran up to her.

"WHAT TOOK YOU SO LONG?!" Jill yelled over the music.

"I WAS JUST TALKING TO CHERRY AND APPLE!" Abby replied.

"WELL, YOU WERE TALKING FOR A LONG TIME!" Jill shouted. "JADEINE AND I ALREADY TALKED TO

CINDERELLA." Jadeine squeezed through the crowd and appeared next to Abby.

"WHAT DID SHE SAY?" Abby asked.

"SHE SAID YES."

"C'MON, LET'S GO!" Jadeine piped up.

"NO!" Jill complained. "I WANT TO DANCE!"

"YOU WERE THE ONE WHO SAID WE'RE RUNNING OUT OF TIME!"

"YEAH, BUT THAT WAS BEFORE! THIS IS NOW!"

Jadeine looked at Abby for support, but Abby agreed with Jill. "IT'S FINE, JADEINE. WE'LL JUST DANCE FOR A FEW MINUTES AND THEN LEAVE…"

Jadeine sighed, but then she was swept away in the crowd. Jill ran off, leaving Abby alone.

Abby danced for a while, but then she got tired. So she walked off in search of a quiet place.

Surprisingly, one of the window seats was unoccupied. Abby sat down and closed her eyes.

Tap. Tap. Tap.

Abby turned around to find the face of Lizzie right outside the window. Abby screamed, but no one heard her over the music. "What are you doing here?" Abby cried.

Lizzie had been tapping with a knife, and she just kept tapping. The threat was clear. Let me in, Lizzie mouthed. Abby backed away while Lizzie kept tapping harder and harder. Lizzie's cheeks heated, and her eyes narrowed.

She pulled her arm back, preparing to break the window. *If I open it for her, then she won't get in and hurt everyone, and I can still shut the window if she wants to harm me,* Abby thought. Nervously, she opened the window. "What do you want?"

Lizzie smiled. "Give me the first relic, Abby. I know you have one, as Amelia told me."

"I would never give you the first relic," Abby said. She began to close the window, but Lizzie kept it up.

"If you don't, then I *will* hurt one of your friends," Lizzie threatened. "Come to think of it, didn't I see you talking to Prince Apple and Princess Cherry? It seems to me like you were getting a lot of information out of them…"

"I wasn't," Abby said, her throat as dry as sandpaper.

"Hmm…I don't believe you." Lizzie smirked. "Oh! It's time for the Big Bad Wolf to feast on some royalty…I'm thinking he'd enjoy two kids named Apple and Cherry."

Abby gasped. "No! You can't!" She tried even harder to shut the window, but Lizzie was just too strong.

Lizzie cackled. "I ca—"

A kick to the back of the head cut her off. Lizzie crumpled. The person standing behind her was Eleanor Queen!

"Eleanor!" Abby cried.

Eleanor smiled. "Abby! Are you doing well with the relics?"

Abby shrugged. "We have one, and we're on our way to the second. Does that count?"

"Well, the plan is working," Eleanor muttered.

"Huh? What plan?" Abby asked.

"Oh, sweetie, it's nothing," Eleanor leaned in. "As much as I want to stay, Lizzie won't be out for long. Go find Snow White's kids and run with them—she won't rest until she's killed them and you."

Before Abby knew it, she was being pushed back through the window by Eleanor. "Wait!" Abby yelped, but before she knew it, Eleanor was gone.

Someone tapped her on the shoulder. Abby whirled around, her breath catching in her throat. *Did Lizzie manage to get in somehow?* She thought. Her breath slowed when she realized it was Jill and Jadeine.

"GUYS!" Abby yelled. "WE NEED TO LEAVE!"

"WHY?" Jill asked.

Abby filled them in. Jadeine frowned. "OH NO. WHERE ARE CHERRY AND APPLE? DO YOU KNOW?"

"THEY WENT TO LOOK FOR SOMEBODY!" Abby replied. "C'MON."

Abby, Jill and Jadeine looked around. Abby caught sight of Cherry and Apple a couple of yards away. She made her way through the crowd over to them. "CHERRY! APPLE!"

They turned. "WHAT'S WRONG?" Cherry yelled.

"YOU'RE IN DANGER!"

Abby didn't know what she had expected, but it wasn't the actual reaction she got. Apple looked at her weird. "ARE YOU FEELING OK?"

Abby groaned. "UGH…JUST LISTEN! THE EVIL QUEEN WAS HERE! COME WITH ME, PLEASE! SHE THREATENED TO FEED YOU TO THE BIG BAD WOLF!!!"

Cherry shook her head, not believing it, but Apple nudged her. "CHERRY! REMEMBER THE DEATH THREAT MAMA GOT?"

Cherry's eyes widened. "OH…ALL RIGHT! SHOULD WE, UH, STAY HERE OR…"

"WE CAN'T! SHE'LL COME IN AND FIND US!" Abby exclaimed.

"ISN'T THERE A GUARD?" Cherry asked.

"UH…HE'S ASLEEP? C'MON!" Abby said.

Abby grabbed one of their arms each and tugged them out the door of the ballroom. Jill and Jadeine were on their heels.

"Come on," Abby hissed, shutting the door. "Where's the nearest exit?"

"Where everyone came in," Apple replied.

Abby didn't waste a moment. She ran down the stairs. "Come on!" she called over her shoulder.

Two minutes later, they were standing on the steps. The guard was still asleep, snoring peacefully.

Abby blinked in the bright sunlight. "You guys need to run."

"Oh, can't we help you?" Apple pleaded. "You're collecting the relics, right?"

"I know where the third one is," Cherry offered.

Abby opened her mouth, then closed it. She thought about Aeryn and how he had betrayed them. Then she looked back at Cherry and Apple. "Well…one sec."

Abby pulled Jill and Jadeine away. "Should we trust them?"

"It's not like they're random people," Jill pointed out. "We know exactly who they are—besides, Lizzie said she wants to kill them."

"So?" Abby asked.

"*So,* they're not working with her!"

"They could still be evil," Jadeine put in. "I mean, Aeryn never said he was working with Lizzie."

Jill started to argue, but she was interrupted by a howl close by.

Abby looked up. Cherry looked terrified. "Was that the Big Bad Wolf?!"

Apple opened his mouth, but Cherry got her answer. The Big Bad Wolf stepped out from behind the palace and snarled at them.

Abby got an idea and turned to the guard. "WAKE UP, WAKE UP!!!"

The guard did not wake up. He just kept sleeping.

"Oh no," Jadeine whispered.

The wolf laughed. "Wonderful. The queen will be so happy."

Cherry screamed, "Will you kill us?"

The wolf laughed. "Maybe. But first...I have some other prey to catch."

"That prey is me, isn't it?" Abby whispered to Jill. Jill nodded.

The wolf growled and pounced, claws extended. Abby shrieked, frozen. In the movies, people's lives always flashed in front of their eyes when they were about to die, but that didn't happen to her. All she could think was, *I failed Mom...and the whole world.*

But...she didn't die. Apple launched himself at her and pushed her out of the way, so the wolf missed Abby and slashed Apple's cheek. It didn't look like that bad of an injury, but Apple fell to the ground, his eyes fluttering shut.

The wolf screamed with frustration. "Argh! These dumb people...always protecting each other."

"What do we do?" Abby screamed.

"We run!" Jill exclaimed.

The wolf looked at Abby, then at Apple, who was still unconscious. The wolf threw his head back, and suddenly he was about twenty feet tall. The wolf grabbed Apple's collar in his mouth and then bounded over to Cherry.

Cherry shrieked, "GIVE MY BROTHER BACK!"

The wolf just laughed and grabbed her collar in his mouth, too. Cherry screamed, but the wolf sprinted into the horizon.

"Well...they're gone." Abby let out her breath.

"OH NO! WE HAVE TO DO SOMETHING!" Jill screamed.

"Jill, calm down!" Jadeine pleaded.

"What's the matter with you?" Abby asked.

"THE MATTER IS THAT SNOW WHITE'S KIDS ARE IN A WOLF'S MOUTH!" Jill shrieked.

"Let's hope they're OK," Abby said.

"How can you be so calm?" Jill wailed. Then she took a deep breath. "Sorry, sorry, but until a few days ago, the most exciting thing that happened in my life was the bakery adding a new item to the menu. Now, wolves are kidnapping royalty, and the Evil Queens are after us. I'm sorry. I'm overwhelmed."

Jadeine patted Jill's arm. "It's fine."

"Okay, guys. Let's focus. We need to get back to getting the second relic," Abby said. "We should try capturing the Sea Witch again."

"But Apple and Cherry are kidnapped!" Jill wailed.

"Jill, what if Lizzie is using them as bait? What if she wants us to go back and look for them so she can get the second relic? We have to get there before her!" Abby exclaimed.

"That's a good point. I agree. We should go and try to capture the Sea Witch again," Jadeine agreed.

"We almost became prisoners! It's too risky. What if we stole the relic from her?" Jill suggested.

"NO!" Abby and Jadeine gasped in horror.

"I'm just saying. You're okay with royalty going to Lizzie." Jill shrugged.

"Well, they'll be fine!" Abby protested.

"Will they?" Jill raised her eyebrows.

"All right, we'll steal the relic," Jadeine agreed. "But remember, we have to be careful and hope we don't get killed."

Jill and Abby argued as they walked to the lake.

"Abby, they're royalty! Even if your theory is right, and they're bait, we still have to save them!" Jill moaned.

Abby threw her hands in the air. "So?! They're still human!"

"Exactly! They're human! They don't deserve this!"

"Jill, we just met them."

"Abby, Apple saved your life!"

"Not necessarily…"

"What the heck is wrong with you? If he hadn't pushed you out of the way, you'd be wolf chow! Like he is going to be! They are *nice people*!"

"What about stealing the relic? Nadine's a nice person."

Jill turned away. "I'm tired of arguing with you. Abby, do you seriously not care?"

Abby bit her lip. She *did* care, but she was pretending not to, so she wouldn't cry. Jill was right. He had saved her life, and they didn't deserve to be taken to Lizzie, who showed no mercy. But she wanted to get the relics.

Soon, the trio arrived at the lake. Jill pointed at the middle. "Is everyone clear on the plan?"

Abby nodded. "Come on."

A swan was floating around in the lake. "Nadine?" Jill asked. "That you?"

"That's not her," Jadeine told her. "That's just a guard."

Jadeine gave Abby a thumbs-up. Abby nodded, and Jadeine yelled, "TWINKLE, TWINKLE LITTLE STAR!"

The swan honked at her. Abby slipped behind the swan and rummaged in her backpack. She grabbed a sleeping potion Jadeine had given her earlier. She tapped the swan. When it turned, she spritzed the potion in its face. Its head lolled to the side, and it slept.

"Now what?" Jill asked.

Jadeine jerked her head at the swan. "Wait for it."

Slowly, the swan transformed into a middle-aged guy. The keys to Nadine's palace were hanging around his neck. Careful not to wake him, Abby slipped them off. "Now…what do I unlock?"

Jadeine held out her hand. "Give them to me."

Abby dropped the keys into Jadeine's palm. Jadeine twisted her hand like she was unlocking an invisible door, and suddenly they were in Nadine's palace.

"Where will the relic be?" Jill asked.

"Best bet is it's in her room," Jadeine answered.

They cracked open each door, hoping to find the relic and the queen, but found nothing. That's when Abby noticed a trapdoor beneath her feet.

"Guys! A trapdoor!" Abby exclaimed.

They opened it and found a long, winding staircase leading into darkness. It was for sure where the relic would be kept…because that's a relic–y location. *Was relic–y a word?* Abby wondered. It should be.

They carefully descended the stairs. With each step, when they saw no bottom, they became dismayed.

Finally, a floor appeared. In the center of the room, lay a tiara on a platform. Abby carefully lifted it and snatched the tiara. They listened for alarms, but heard none. They were about to go back up when they heard footsteps rushing down the stairs. They had been too deep underground to hear the alarm!

Abby tried to think about how they would escape. But her mind was too scared to do anything. They would probably get captured and die… Maybe she wasn't even the prophecy girl. Perhaps she was just another ordinary girl who happened to have a fairy for a mother.

These thoughts kept Abby from thinking positive. *Why did I think I was the girl with the prophecy? Did I even need to come here? Am I just…another normal, meaningless girl?* Abby thought. Abby's heartbeat pounded so hard she could hear it. Her eyes glazed over. The noise of the now very loud alarm and the guards' shouts all felt like they were far away. Abby was hyperventilating.

"What do we do?" Jadeine asked, clearly unfazed.

"Quick, on the ceiling! There's a ladder here! You just can't see it because it's dark!" Jill exclaimed.

Jill and Jadeine clambered up the ladder as fast as they could. But Abby was motionless. She just knelt on the ground.

"Abby! Come on! COME ON!" Jill exclaimed.

"I'm not the prophecy girl, I'm not going to save anybody, not even my mom, I can't save anybody, and I just can't do it," Abby said.

"Abby, please, hurry!" Jadeine urged.

Jadeine climbed down and motioned for Jill to go ahead. She knelt next to Abby and shook her, uttering calming thoughts in her ear. Abby remembered what her dad used to say when she felt like this. 'Whether or not you succeed, there will always be people who love you. They will never, EVER make you feel bad about not succeeding. Her senses came back as she repeated her dad's words in her head over and over again. She unfroze and leaped to her feet.

Abby and Jadeine swung to the top, just as guards filled the room. Apparently, humans also lived here.

The doors were still open, and Abby almost took off with the others before remembering that they couldn't just steal it. She turned around and dashed to a door marked 'Queen's Chambers' on it. Abby pounded on the door, and Nadine came out in full battle armor. This time, she had a long, silvery tail instead of legs.

"YOU!!!" Nadine shrieked.

"Please, please, give us permission, please, I beg you!" Abby begged. She dropped onto her knees, and tears burst out of her eyes like a dam. She didn't know why she was crying, but as she thought about it, she realized it was because if the Merqueen didn't give her permission, H.E.A.L would be doomed.

Nadine softened, but only for a moment. She screamed, "ATTACK HER!!!"

"Please! Listen to me!" Abby pleaded. "I know Lizzie's never done a thing to you, but have you seen what she's done to the world? We *need* your relic!"

Guards grabbed Abby's arms, and she screamed, tears streaking down her face. She struggled to free herself from the strong grasp of the guards. Abby kicked one of the guards in the shin, but the guard just kicked right back. Abby felt the grip loosen a bit and sprinted forward as hard as she could. She couldn't change Nadine's mind, not now anyway. *Later,* she thought. *We'll get permission later.*

Abby ran towards the doors, which were slowly closing. *Almost*...and then the doors slammed shut right in front of Abby. Suddenly, she felt an excruciating pain throughout her arm and realized it was jammed in the doors. She used her other arm to pry the doors open and slipped through it, clutching the tiara.

Jadeine grabbed her hand and pulled her up towards the surface. Abby gasped for breath. She shook her wet hair around and tried to dry it. It didn't work. They trudged out of the water and onto land. Abby brandished the tiara in the air, but she felt a pang of guilt and all of a sudden felt like something was karate chopping her inside.

"I can't believe I did that," Abby moaned. "I feel so guilty."

"Nadine is a nice woman, and we should never have done that," Jadeine declared.

"Apple and Cherry belonged to a nice woman, too, and they got taken to Lizzie!" Jill exclaimed.

"They didn't *belong* to Snow White," Abby protested. "But yes, I do see your point now."

"Abby, I totally forgot we needed to ask for permission!" Jill exclaimed.

"I tried, but it didn't work. We have already upset her. We have to do a huge favor for Nadine. Maybe…we could bring the Little Mermaid back to life!" Abby suggested.

"That's impossible," Jadeine said, her face clouding over.

"We can't go back there now. The guards will arrest all of us. We should move on to the third relic and get permission later. Jadeine…you know where the third relic is?" Abby asked, shoving the tiara in her backpack.

"No," Jadeine sighed.

"But I know who does…" Jill smirked. "C'mon! Let's go find Apple and Cherry!"

Chapter 13
The Magic Within

It was a miracle.

A miracle that Abby, Jill, and Jadeine found Apple and Cherry. They were searching fruitlessly (no pun intended) in the nearby forest when they just happened to see Apple and Cherry. The wolf was going in the opposite direction they were heading.

They had been searching for about an hour. Abby's knees were aching, and Jill had been complaining the whole time. Abby felt her heart lift at the sight of them, the way it used to when her dad used to surprise her with a cup of hot cocoa filled with jumbo marshmallows on a stormy day.

Apple caught sight of them and frantically pointed to the woods. He mouthed, *Run! Leave us!* Abby shook her head, but Jadeine was backing away already. Abby stepped forward stealthily and—crunch! She stepped on a dry leaf. Too late to run now.

"You! Abby Palmer!" the wolf snarled, whipping around.

The wolf dropped Apple and Cherry on the ground and ran in Abby's direction. The siblings stood up. Apple's wounds had healed, and Cherry looked much better, too. They looked very relieved, but as the wolf dashed towards Abby, their expressions grew panicked.

Abby had planned their rescue a hundred times in her head, but she hadn't thought it would go like this. She had been imagining that the wolf would be…too fazed to react.

But Jadeine had a plan. She threw the staff at the wolf, the end of the staff pointed towards him. Unfortunately, Jadeine had a horrible aim, and the staff hit Cherry in the forehead instead.

"OWWW! THAT HURT!" Cherry yowled. She massaged her forehead.

"Sorry!" Jadeine apologized.

Apple grabbed the staff and threw with all might. The staff spun towards the wolf and hit him square in the eye. He howled and collapsed.

"Thanks, Apple! You're good at saving people from wolves! Now would be a perfect time for a magic rope to appear…" Abby trailed off.

"What for?" Cherry asked.

"To tie the wolf up before he gets back up," Abby replied.

Suddenly, Abby felt a heavy weight in her backpack. She opened it and found a shimmering rope lying at the bottom. Abby gasped and smiled triumphantly. Abby pulled it out and threw it at the wolf because she had a gut instinct that it would work.

It magically constricted the wolf to a tree. Abby just stared at the rope in amazement. *How did a rope just appear when I needed it?* Abby thought. Then again, this *was* the fairy tale world. The wolf scratched at the rope, furious.

"Let's go, guys," Jill said. "We don't want to be here if the wolf becomes free."

As they ran away, the wolf's howls faded and were drowned out by the sound of chirping birds and the rustle of leaves. They stopped to catch their breath in the middle of the forest.

"Well, that was close." Apple let out his breath.

"It really was scary," Abby agreed. "Anyways, Cherry, you said you knew where the third relic was, and we were hoping you could tell us."

"Right. It was with the Sky Queen, but she'd never give it to you." Cherry frowned.

"And she lives in the sky," Jill pointed out. "None of us can fly…"

"But I can," came a voice from behind them.

Abby froze. She knew that voice. They whirled around to see Aeryn with a cheerful look on his face. Abby didn't know how he'd found them, but she suspected that he had been spying on them from above. Her blood ran cold.

"IT'S AERYN, RUN!" Abby screamed. Apple and Cherry were probably confused by that, since they had never met him, but they listened anyway.

They took off, but since Aeryn could fly, he was easily right behind them.

"Wait!" Aeryn called out. He flew in front of them with the same cheerful face, but desperation in his eyes. "I'm sorry! I'm really, really sorry. My aunt ordered me to tie you up."

Abby felt a rush of anger fill her mind, and she felt it take her over—but only for a second. She unclenched her fists and jaw, and the thoughts that bombarded her for a second faded.

"The Sea Witch ordered you to do that?" Abby asked. "Well, I don't think you're telling the truth."

"But I am," Aeryn protested. He sounded like a lost puppy.

"You fool me once, shame on you. You fool me twice, shame on me," Abby recited, then tried to go around him.

"The Sea Witch *tricked* me in order for me to trick you," Aeryn explained.

"I won't be gullible this time. Come on, guys, let's go," Abby ordered.

But her group stayed in place. Jill looked at her boots and bit her lip. Jadeine's lips were pursed, and her face was in a state of confusion. Apple and Cherry were looking around awkwardly.

"Come on! Guys!" Abby said and clapped her hands to get their attention.

"Abby… I think we can trust him this time," Jill announced. 'And he's the only one of us who can fly."

"He's not 'one of us, '" Abby snapped bitterly. "No. He's just a stranger who tried to trap us with the Sea Witch." She crossed her arms.

"Abby…he's our only chance at getting to the third relic," Jill said, trying to convince Abby.

"Ugh…" Abby glared at Aeryn. "Well, fine, I guess. But I am going to keep an eye on you." Abby made the 'I'm watching you sign with her fingers.

"Thanks, Abby! So you have Jill and Jadeine on your team and…SNOW WHITE'S KIDS?!" Aeryn exclaimed.

"Hello to you, too," Cherry huffed.

"Yeah, they're with us," Abby told him.

"Oh…um…sorry," Aeryn said, looking embarrassed. "I guess I was kind of shocked.

"Anyways, you said you can help us?" Abby asked.

"Oh yeah! I can give you wings for an hour. You should be able to get the relic by then," Aeryn replied.

"I'm going to try to believe that you won't let us fall to our deaths," Abby grumbled.

"I have a feeling Aeryn's sorry about what he did, Abby," Jadeine told them. "Stop giving him a hard time."

"Me too, me too!" the staff chirped. Abby felt like Aeryn and the staff were the same person.

"Fine, *sorry,* fairy boy who got banished and tried to imprison us," Abby said sarcastically.

"Abby. Actually, apologize." Jadeine frowned.

"Fine. Sorry, Aeryn, for giving you a hard time," Abby apologized.

"It's okay. I'm going to do the wing spell now," Aeryn said. "And then I'll go, because clearly you don't like me one bit."

Aeryn chanted a spell, and wings just like Aeryn's popped on their backs. Aeryn started to walk away. She was relieved, but as she stared up into the clear sky, Abby wasn't so sure about flying on her own…

"Aeryn, can you help us?"Abby asked. "I'm kind of not sure about this."

Aeryn walked back to the group. "Oh, okay. I'll make sure you're flying correctly."

"Wait!" Cherry cried. "The palace could be anywhere in the sky."

"Well, we're in luck. The palace is actually right above us. What's the saying?-right place at the right time," Aeryn announced with a gleeful grin.

They rose into the sky, wings flapping. The wind tickled Abby's cheeks. Soon, a palace made of fluffy white clouds and frosty winds came into sight. As Abby and the group reached the large double doors, an angel with a bushy mustache swooped down and blocked their way.

"Angels? Seriously?" Abby asked.

"Don't mock me, lowly human," the angel huffed. "I am a guardian of the Sky Queen."

"That's kind of mean coming from an angel. We only want to consult with the Sky Queen," Abby said.

"Why should I let you come in?" The angel challenged them.

"Royalty should have the right to come in," Apple piped up.

"Oh! Princess Cherry and Prince Apple! Welcome!" the angel chirped nervously. "I didn't see you. Just so you know, your bodyguards can't enter."

"They're not our bodyguards, they're our friends, and they saved us from Lizzie's wolf! They have a right to come in," Cherry protested.

The angel sighed, but waved them in. As they entered the palace, they were stunned by crystal chandeliers and exotic art. There were mirrors on all the walls.

"Who is she—Vanity Queen?" Jill asked.

"Shush, she's here," Jadeine hissed.

"You're right, I am," The Sky Queen said, descending from the ceiling.

A messenger hurried into the room, carrying a scroll.

"Your Majesty! The Evil Queen is coming! She sent us a letter!" the messenger announced, shaking with fear.

"Tell her she'll have to wait," The Sky Queen told him with a frosty tone.

"But she's…right here!" the messenger wailed.

Lizzie, Abby's mom, and Amelia strode into the room. Abby hadn't been expecting them to arrive right now. Her face was filled with terror, and so were the faces of her friends. Lizzie looked at Abby with wide, angry eyes.

"You," Lizzie rasped.

"Nice t-t-to see you," Abby sputtered, wearing a sarcastic grin.

"Oh, please, quit the dramatics. I haven't come for you…Although now you're here," Lizzie thought it over.

Lizzie prepared to charge at her when the Sky Queen's face twisted, "STOP!" she roared. "I WILL NOT HAVE A FIGHT IN MY CASTLE!"

Lizzie froze in her tracks, a sword raised above her head. "Ugh, fine. Yes, *your highness?*"

"I just recently heard you kidnapped one of my people and stole a lot of food," The Sky Queen snarled, ignoring Lizzie's sarcasm. "You have no right to be in my realm."

"I KNOW I DON'T! " Lizzie yelled. "BUT I WANT TO ASK YOU SOMETHING! YOU DON'T HAVE TO BE SO RUDE!"

"You…yelled at…ME. ME. And *you* talk about being rude?" The Sky Queen said, her voice sounding like it was ready to scream.

"*Sorry*. I talk in a loud tone usually, to herd my supporters to go the way I want them to, so they don't run away. Besides, I've come for your relic," Lizzie said.

"You can't have it. No one can have it. Ever," The Sky Queen's voice teetered on the edge of a full-out tantrum.

"Well, look at poor, poor Abby in fright. You must be scaring her," Lizzie cooed with a syrupy tone.

"Well, I'll deal with you first. Then that Addy girl," The Sky Queen declared.

"My name is Abby. Not Addy," Abby squeaked. Of course, Lizzie and the Sky Queen were too busy having a glaring contest.

"*You must.* You must give it to me. You don't remember when we used to be best buddies, I assume," Lizzie growled.

"I remember that very, very well. I want to forget it for a reason, you know," The Sky Queen said.

"THE WORLD WILL BE UNDER BETTER RULE WITH ME AS THE ONLY QUEEN, SKYLER!" Lizzie roared.

"How dare you utter my actual name in front of these children! HOW DARE YOU OPENLY SPEAK OF OVERTHROWING ME! I'll never give it to you!" The Sky Queen exclaimed.

Abby didn't know why The Sky Queen wouldn't like her name. In school, Abby had learned that your name is basically your identity. They had done a lot of projects in their names, and she always played Name Game on the first day of school. Abby wished she was in school now…

"Your Highness, we really need the relic too and for a much better reason," Abby put in.

"So, you're probably the prophecy girl, I suppose. You're Adrienne, right?" The Sky Queen asked, but not without a harsh tone.

"Abby Palmer," Abby answered, her voice quavering. "We really need the relic."

"WELL, I CAN'T GIVE IT TO YOU! INSOLENT CHILD!" The Sky Queen yelled.

Abby didn't know anyone with a temper like the Sky Queen's. The Sky Queen instantly scared people. She appeared to be a kind and just person, but if you set her off, she would erupt into a ball of anger.

"Please!" Abby exclaimed.

"Never in the name of Frost Mountain!" The Sky Queen exclaimed.

"Frost Mountain…"Abby muttered.

Abby scanned the room until her eyes fell upon an oversized mirror. Oversized things *always* hid in fairy tales. She ran to it and checked for hinges. Sure enough, there were.

"No! Guards, hold Adrienne—no Abby—no what's-that-girl's name, Alicia? Yes, it was Alicia! No…ARGH! The girl's name…Arishia? Aybella? Ali*zia*? Argh, you know what?! Hold Alicia back, and I don't care if that's not her name!" The Sky Queen ordered.

While the Sky Queen fumbled with Abby's name, Abby swung the mirror open. On the inside, she read jumbled letters that were probably an anagram. Abby's friends formed a protective circle around her. Lizzie's group just stood there, unsure of what to do. It read:

Fosmuti Retonan

Abby slowly tried to solve the anagram. Fit Umso Tona REN? No…maybe it was retina nos…ARGH!!! THINK ABBY, THINK! WHAT ABOUT…Frost…yes, the word frost is in there…and the second word should be mountain! Frost Mountain!

Why would anyone hide the name of a mountain in a mirror? Maybe because that was where the relic was!

"Let's go, guys," Abby told the group. Then she whispered in their ears, "I know where the relic is."

"What is it?" Jill asked eagerly.

"I'll tell you later," Abby said. "I don't know where exactly." A mountain was a pretty big landform, and knowing that it was near Frost mountain didn't narrow it down much."

"Wait!" The Sky Queen suddenly cried. "You can find the relic on top of the mountain! It's with someone!"

"Why are you telling us this?" Abby asked, realizing that it was on top of Frost Mountain.

"I…Lizzie has offended me, so I will allow you to take my relic!" The Sky Queen reasoned.

They ran for the exit, but Lizzie stopped them.

"Not yet. You see, I have the Merqueen relic," Lizzie announced. "And don't you want to get it?"

Lizzie twirled a tiara identical to the one Abby had, smirking. She twirled it on her fingers. Abby checked her bag and found the tiara still lying at the bottom, well concealed.

"Wrong. We already have it," Abby informed her.

"NO. YOU. DON'T!" Lizzie screamed.

Lizzie's eyes turned green, and her voice echoed. The Sky Queen screamed in anger and began to charge at Abby and Lizzie, but her guards rushed in and took off running with The Sky Queen. Abby clutched her bag tightly. The bewitchment grasped Abby's shoulders, but she resisted.

"YOU CAN'T DO ANYTHING TO ANYONE ELSE!" Abby yelled.

Abby's mind flooded with anger. Lizzie had already destroyed so many people's lives, like Jadeine's and Jocelyn's and Abby's. She didn't want that to happen to anyone else. She WOULDN'T let it happen.

A purple burst of light formed a shield around the group from Abby's hand. A streak of purple light hit Lizzie's group. Lizzie,

Melissa, Amelia and the wolf disappeared. The purple shield faded away, and Abby gasped for breath.

"ABBY, OMG! YOU CAN DO MAGIC! THAT WAS AWESOME!!!" Jill exclaimed.

"Amazing indeed," Cherry breathed.

"I can't!" Abby protested.

"Then what do you call that?" Cherry cried. "You saved our lives!"

Abby laughed. "I guess…I can. Maybe I got it from my mom!"

Abby's eyes widened as she had a thought. Was she…a fairy?!

Chapter 14
The Courage

There was good news, bad news and awesome news.

The good news: The curse Lizzie had put on Melissa was finally wearing off. She could finally think for herself!

The bad news: The curse hadn't worn off completely. She still had to do whatever Lizzie told her.

The awesome news: Abby could do magic! Go Abby!

Lizzie was fuming right now. She was pacing and talking to herself:

"She can do magic?! No one told me that! Well, it's fine, I suppose, she's not that experienced. She just caught me by surprise! But ugh! Eleanor's gone, too. I thought we had a deal! And we're no closer to getting the third relic, no thanks to that useless wolf! I told him to get Snow White and her children, and he's not back yet! And it looks like they ran off with *your daughter*!"

That last part was addressed to Melissa. Melissa looked up.

"It's because of your daughter we're in this mess!" Lizzie spat. "Why'd you have to go and have a daughter?"

"You were the one who made me *want* to go," Melissa informed her, then immediately regretted it.

Lizzie hissed. She opened her mouth, then closed it. She took a deep breath. "Arguing isn't doing us any good right now. We can get the third relic later."

That was classic Lizzie. Going from raging to enthusiastic in the blink of an eye.

So the three of them went off. "Who has the fourth relic?" Amelia wanted to know.

"What makes you think we're going to find the fourth relic?" Lizzie purred. "No, my dear. We're going to find the Big Bad Wolf. Even if he's useless, people are scared of him, and that's something."

"Do you know where he is?" Melissa piped up.

Lizzie shook her head. "No, but it can't be hard to find him. He would've been pretty close to the palace, right?"

"How did he let them get away?" Amelia wondered. "He's really big and scary."

"His bark is worse than his bite," Lizzie laughed.

"They're still kids," Melissa pointed out. "And doesn't he have that power of his where he grows to be twenty feet tall?"

Lizzie considered that. "Oh! I know! It's because of their crazy desire to save each other. If it had been me, I would've run away the moment he looked at someone else."

Melissa knew that was true. She also knew that the 'someone else' he would look at would most likely be her.

They walked in silence for a while, and then Melissa heard a distant howl. She wondered if she was hallucinating, but then Lizzie yelled, "It's the wolf!"

She took off running. Melissa and Amelia ran behind her. In ten seconds, they were standing in front of a tree.

The tree looked normal. But there was something on it that you don't see every day. It had green leaves and a brown bark, of course. It also had The Big Bad Wolf with a swollen eye tied to it with a shimmering rope.

Lizzie burst out laughing as soon as she saw the wolf all tied up. "Oh, wolfie!"

He growled. "Don't laugh."

"How did you get all tied up?" Amelia asked the wolf with concern.

"It's a long story," he answered.

"We've got time," Lizzie told him as she sawed at the rope with a knife.

He grunted. "When they exited the palace with Snow White's kids, I was waiting for them. I pounced on Abby, but that prince shoved her out of the way. So then I grabbed him and his sister and took off, because I figured Abby would come for them eventually. But when they did, they threw a staff at me and it stabbed my eye. Then they tied me up."

Lizzie laughed even harder. "Who threw the staff?"

"The keeper threw the first time, but she missed by a mile. Then Prince Apple picked it up, and he actually has good aim, so it hit me."

"I've always found it ironic that Snow White named her firstborn Apple," Melissa commented. "You would think she would be traumatized after the poison apple incident."

After a couple of minutes, the wolf was free. He stretched his hind legs and gave a growl for good measure.

"You know, Abby is going after the relics in order. We could start with the last relic, and then Abby won't be there to stop us!" Lizzie exclaimed.

"Great idea," Melissa muttered sarcastically.

"What? What did you say?" Lizzie asked, threateningly.

"I said, um…late iota?" Melissa hazarded. Melissa didn't want to flare Lizzie's anger, so she decided that she wouldn't tell Lizzie what she actually had said.

"Mm-hmm. Right," Lizzie scoffed.

Suddenly, the ground shook. Amelia clutched Melissa's arm. A noise that sounded like a herd of elephants grew near. Lizzie listened carefully, then scrambled up the tree. Melissa and Amelia followed.

"What is it?" Melissa asked.

"It's a pack of wild wernshrue!" Lizzie cried.

"What? A pack of When Shoes?" Amelia asked.

Lizzie didn't reply. The pack of wernshrue came into view. They were taller than a giraffe, had the head of a boar, the body of an elephant, and arms and legs of a giant.

"That's terrifying!" Amelia yelped.

"I know, right?" Lizzie grinned.

"Wow…massive," Melissa breathed.

After the pack passed, they climbed down from the tree. A couple of bugs had settled in Melissa's hair, but when she tried to remove them, Lizzie held out her hand. "Place the bugs in my hand."

"Ew!" Melissa wailed. Lizzie narrowed her eyes, and Melissa quickly adjusted her attitude. "But I'll do it."

Melissa picked out a ladybug, 2 beetles, and a glowing cockroach. She placed them in Lizzie's hand, who put them inside her pockets, probably for an experiment.

"Now that that's done, I'm thinking we should pay a visit to the swamp! Immediately!" Lizzie clapped her hands together.

"Why?" Amelia asked.

"We need to strike a deal with Eleanor again…by bringing back Cyrus."

It had been an hour since they went into the swamp, and no signs of Cyrus were there. Melissa had begun sweating, Lizzie's hair was wet and frizzy, Amelia's hair was perfect, but she had many rashes, and the Big Bad Wolf claimed he couldn't see well.

"This is torture!" Amelia groaned.

"Let's look deeper then," Lizzie suggested sharply. "Maybe you won't complain so much."

"NO!" Melissa and Amelia screeched at the same time. "I mean, no. Sorry."

"I'm going to fetch the children," the wolf informed her. "I'm going blind here!"

"You had better return with someone," Lizzie warned.

The wolf gleefully bounded away from the swamp. Melissa looked at the wolf, wishing she was him in the moment.

A croak interrupted Melissa's thoughts. Melissa looked down to see a frog. Cyrus! Lizzie had cursed Cyrus to be a frog a long time ago. Cyrus the frog always had 2 bright green and 4 bright red dots on him, so he could always be picked out from the rest of the frogs.

"You're Lizzie's sister, right? Nice to meet you," Cyrus croaked in displeasure.

"Nice to meet you too. Today's your lucky day." Melissa scooped Cyrus up, as Cyrus croaked in protest.

Melissa handed Cyrus to Lizzie. Lizzie waved her arms around, muttering a spell. Suddenly, the whole swamp was lit up in a dazzling white light. Melissa was entranced as it faded away. In the center stood Cyrus. He had slick, black hair, tanned skin, and a torn outfit. He was a boy who was about 15 years old, older than Abby.

"Am I totally free to do what I want? With no additional favors?" Cyrus breathed in awe.

"Yes. You also don't have to do any favors, lucky you," Lizzie told him.

"Good," Cyrus said. "I can't believe I'm free!"

Melissa didn't get how Cyrus wasn't totally petrified of Lizzie. Cyrus had even been cursed by Lizzie! Melissa would have been horrified if she had been turned into a frog.

Lizzie snapped her fingers, and all of them were in the town square. All the villagers stopped what they were doing, dropped what they were holding, and ran for their lives, screaming like little girls.

"I love how they're so terrified of me," Lizzie laughed.

"They're also terrified of me." Melissa jutted her chin out. She sort of hated being hated, but for some reason, she was a little proud of it.

And Melissa was *never* proud of it. Maybe Lizzie's behavior had rubbed off on Melissa.

"Not more than me," Lizzie countered.

"Liar! People screamed so loud when I visited them." Melissa huffed. *ARGH! I don't want anybody to hate me, so why am I arguing? And Lizzie wouldn't have wanted me to do this. Maybe the curse wore off!*

Melissa tested it out. She tried running. She was snapped back, though. Melissa sighed with exhaustion.

"Stop trying to run! And quiet, Melissa! You're a baby!" Lizzie yelled.

Her cheeks heated, and she curled her hand into fists. Melissa was done with accepting her fate. Cyrus wasn't scared of Lizzie, so why should Melissa be? Enough was enough. She wasn't scared of Lizzie anymore! She was a brave woman. *The bravest woman in the world.*

"I DON'T CARE WHAT YOU SAY!" Melissa screamed. "AND I'M NOT A BABY! I AM A GROWN WOMAN WHO KNOWS HER STUFF! I AM A PERSON AND IT'S TIME YOU START TREATING ME LIKE ONE!"

"I AM THE EVIL QUEEN, MELISSA!" Lizzie shrieked back, her eyes turning neon green. "I CAN DO WHATEVER I WANT!"

"YOU CAN'T EVEN STOP A LITTLE GIRL FROM TAKING WHAT YOU WANT!" Melissa roared.

"Silly Melissa. YOU DON'T REALIZE WHAT TROUBLE YOU'RE GETTING INTO!"

"I! AM NOT! SCARED OF YOU!"

Lizzie quieted down, humiliated that Melissa wasn't scared of her. Melissa lifted her hands in the air and pointed at Lizzie, her finger shaking. The anger coming from Melissa had overwhelmed Lizzie and broken the curse.

"Mellie," Lizzie tried to soften Melissa, so she could catch Melissa by surprise and then send Melissa to starve on a deserted island. "Mellie, I'm doing this for revenge, for Father and Mother. You know I get mad sometimes. I care for you so much. I'm sorry if I hadn't acted like it."

Hearing this made Melissa want to become soft again, but she didn't let herself. "You don't give a fig about them. Unlike me," Melissa said, her voice cracking. But Melissa was acting. Her magic was ready to attack.

"Mellie…YOU'LL BE SORRY!" Lizzie cackled. "You'll always never rise above me, and you'll spend your life regretting yelling at me!"

"No, I WON'T! YOU! ARE! CURSED!" Melissa shouted. Lizzie's eyes widened with surprise.

As a blinding purple light shot from Melissa's fingertips, Lizzie dashed away. Now, Lizzie was the coward. She had never seen her sister so defiant, so brave. Lizzie hid behind a tree. She watched as Amelia thanked Melissa repeatedly, and the wolf wandered off. Cyrus ran to Eleanor's house. And Lizzie was all alone.

"I'll get you, Melissa. And when I do, it'll be nasty," Lizzie vowed.

Chapter 15
Negative 20 Degrees

Abby couldn't believe she had defeated Lizzie. Sure, only temporarily, but she could do magic! And now, Abby knew that the third relic was at the top of Frost Mountain.

The others probably viewed Abby as the most perfect person on the planet. But the truth was, she wasn't. For example, she wasn't great at accepting defeat. Her handwriting was awful. And…a lot of other stuff.

She shook it off. Abby was excited. She couldn't wait to hike Frost Mountain, despite the fact that she normally hated climbing up steep hills. She just hoped it wouldn't be really cold. She hated the cold.

"Abby, you never told us where the relic was in the Sky Queen's palace. Can you tell us now?" Jill asked.

"On top of Frost Mountain," Abby replied with a smile. "I'm excited."

"Frost Mountain?!" everyone shrieked. Apparently, no one else was excited about this.

"What? What's wrong?" Abby asked nervously.

"That's the mountain the Snow Queen rules over," Cherry informed her. "The Snow Queen is the most terrifying queen in the world. The Snow Queen is actually pretty diplomatic, and she doesn't want to be evil. But if you do one tiny thing to upset her, like having stiff hair— which by the way, The Snow Queen hates stiff hair—she will freeze you and never let you out of her icy prison. That's why she's commonly mistaken for a villain."

"It's in our kingdom," Apple explained. "There's a lot of tension between Mama and the Snow Queen, because the Snow Queen only has control over the winter in our kingdom, and the Snow Queen wants to have more power."

"Not ours yet. It's still Mama's," Cherry corrected.

"Right," Apple sighed.

"She…wow. That's intense." Abby brushed her hair back to make sure it wasn't stiff.

"How exactly are we going to climb it if we don't have any gear?" Jadeine asked.

"Wait! Aeryn can give us wings again, right?" Abby suggested.

"No, it's too much magic to hold the spell up through the cold and icy conditions up there. Only I can fly, because I was born with wings," Aeryn explained sadly.

"Oh. Well, if that's the case, there are many shops we can get gear from." Cherry said.

"I'm excited," Aeryn called from the back.

Jadeine had made him stand in the back of the group, in between her and Jill, because he hadn't been deemed wholly trustworthy yet.

"Right," Abby muttered sarcastically. "To push us down."

"Abby! What did I say about being nice to Aeryn?" Jill reprimanded her.

Apple looked at the path ahead and looked delighted when he saw it came to an end a few yards away.

"Hey, guys, we're almost to our—I mean, my mom's—kingdom," Apple announced. "Only a minute to get there."

Soon, a beautiful village came into view. In the center was a big, blue and white palace with many windows. The village was vibrant, with much activity going on. The villagers stared at Apple and Cherry as they passed by.

"Why are they staring at you?" Abby asked.

"We're royalty, remember? We're famous," Cherry explained.

"Right. So…do you know where we can get gear?" Abby asked.

"No." Apple shook his head. "We should ask around."

Abby strode over to a girl who was selling cupcakes. Chocolate cupcakes. *Yum.* Abby's stomach rumbled at the sight of the cupcakes, and Abby realized they hadn't eaten good food in a long time.

"Hi," Abby greeted her. "I'm Abby."

"Oh! You're the prophecy girl! I'm Tiger!" the girl exclaimed cheerily. The girl had wavy black hair and eyes that were so dark brown they looked black.

The girl also had tanned skin with a couple of freckles. She was wearing a white dress with a pin that stated 'Tiger, The Cupcake Girl.'

"Your name is…Tiger." Abby stared at her the same way she had stared at Apple and Cherry when she had first met them.

"I know, everyone in the village has weird names," Tiger laughed.

"I'm Apple," Apple told her.

She smiled. "I'm Tiger. You must be Prince Apple. Of course."

"You said that already," Jill informed her.

Tiger blushed. "Oh! Uh…"

"Do you know where we can get gear for mountain climbing?" Abby interrupted.

"Oh, sure! Let me show you. My dad sells stuff." Tiger turned and walked off. She seemed relieved.

Tiger showed them the way. At last, they stood in front of an old shop with peeling paint. A friendly man waved them over.

"Hello! I see you have met my daughter, Tiger. I'm Cricket Canterwood," the man told them.

"Pleasure to meet you. Have you got any gear?" Jadeine asked.

"Sure do!" Mr. Canterwood exclaimed.

Mr. Canterwood showed them hiking poles, snow boots, travel backpacks, jackets, hats, gloves and maps.

"This hiking pole is durable and costs 14 marigolds. And *this* jacket can keep you warm at the top of any mountain! Costs only 20 marigolds! And with these snow boots, snow will never touch your socks again! It costs only 5 marigolds!" Mr. Canterwood advertised.

Abby ordered the climbing gear. In return, Mr. Canterwood requested 5 denze. Abby had no clue what denze were, but when she looked at Tiger, Tiger was astonished. *What's with all the flowers?*

"Wow! That's very expensive. But we're royalty, so, yeah." Cherry smiled.

Apple fished out 5 strange-looking flowers from his pocket and handed them to Mr. Canterwood, who smiled with glee. Everyone took their gear and left the shop.

"Why did you give him flowers?" Abby asked.

"Those are denze flowers. Flowers are currency here," Apple explained.

"Anyway, onto finding relics." Abby tried to sound peppy, but she really was terrified.

They had only walked a couple of yards ahead when they were stopped by the cupcake girl, Tiger. Abby smiled at Tiger and walked around her. But Tiger blocked their way again.

"Um…can you move?" Abby requested.

"Sorry," Tiger mumbled. Then, Tiger put on a soapy smile. "Uh, hey! Good luck on your journey! Well, uh, I know I won't be useful, but I want to help you!" Tiger told them.

"It's too dangerous. You'll get hurt!" Abby protested. "The Snow Queen is nasty."

"Let her come. The more the merrier!" Aeryn exclaimed, which reminded Abby of when Lizzie had said 'the more the merrier,'. It hadn't ended well. "Besides, have any of you hiked before?"

No one had, except Tiger. Abby saw Aeryn's point. "All right."

Tiger, Abby, Jill, Jadeine, Cherry, Apple and Aeryn went to the base of Frost Mountain. Abby started to climb up. It wasn't too difficult. *Hey, this isn't so bad. I can do this!* Abby thought.

She had no idea how wrong she was.

The group had only been hiking for an hour, yet conditions were barely survivable. Snow rained down on them, winds blew at them, hail poured down on them, and the snow was knee-deep.

Aeryn had apparently done some sort of fairy magic to keep himself warm. He was floating eight feet in the air. Tiger, despite being human, seemed completely fine as well.

Jay, the staff was annoyingly bubbly. "Isn't this fun?!"

"Lucky you," Jadeine muttered. "You don't have a body."

"And lucky me!" Aeryn called from above.

"Aeryn, I'm f-f-freezing. Can you help?" Jill pleaded.

"I already tried, what, a million heat spells? It doesn't work near the Snow Queen," Aeryn sighed.

They all plopped down in the snow with a sigh. Apple immediately closed his eyes, and his head lolled to the side.

"I'm COLD!" Cherry moaned. "And Apple fell unconscious!"

"He's just sleeping," Jadeine blearily mumbled.

Aeryn chanted something, and Abby instantly felt warm, but she still wasn't content—the wind stung her face. The hail hit with astonishing force. "How much more do we have left to hike?" she groaned.

"Only a bit more. You can do it!" Aeryn chirped.

They all got to their feet and trudged through the snow, the unforgiving wind blasting in their face. Abby shivered and wrapped her arms around herself.

"It's a castle," Jill observed. "Over there, look!"

In the distance, the hazy silhouette of a castle could be seen. On closer inspection, they realized it was the Snow Queen's palace.

"Should we…go in?" Apple asked hesitantly.

Jadeine shrugged. "Might as well."

They went inside cautiously—the door wasn't locked. The inside of the palace was very warm. Abby could feel her cheeks again. She patted them softly until Jill snickered.

"Where is the Snow Queen?" Abby wondered.

"I feel her," Aeryn informed them. "She's near!"

"That's just you being cold," Abby told him dismissively.

They turned the corner…bumping into the Snow Queen. She was a tall woman, with frosty white hair and blue skin. She wore a sheepskin cloak and held an icy scepter. Abby realized that the scepter was probably the third relic. She felt like the scepter was special, in a way.

"What are you doing here?! Leave or freeze," The Snow Queen ordered.

"Your Majesty! I'm so sorry!" Jadeine squeaked. "We need to speak to you!"

"Hmph. Very well. Why have you brought the fruit kids here?" The Snow Queen inquired.

"Hey! We're not the fruit…oh. I guess we are," Apple said, apparently awake.

"We need to talk about the relic, Your Majesty," Cherry said.

"It's a dire situation," Abby added.

The Snow Queen walked away. The group followed, and they found a cozy-looking room with soft chairs and a fireplace with a fire made out of ice. An ice chandelier hung on the ceiling.

"W-Wow, this is n-n-nice. Er, a-actually, it's i-i-impressive," Jill said, trying to flatter The Snow Queen.

"Thank you, child," The Snow Queen answered.

"We're here to talk about…your relic," Jadeine said cautiously.

The Snow Queen's calm face became one of fury. "SKYLAR HAS TOLD YOU THE RELIC IS HERE?! OR HAVE YOU SIMPLY BEEN ASKING DOOR TO DOOR?!"

"Madam, I-I-Skylar-The Sky Queen…she—," Jill got cut off by The Snow Queen.

"JUST! ANSWER!" The Snow Queen roared.

"We snooped in The Sky Queen's palace, and I'm so sorry we upset you," Abby quickly said.

"BE TRAPPED IN ICE FOREVER MORE, UNGRATEFUL, PATHETIC COWARDS!" The Snow Queen screamed.

In the blink of an eye, ice covered their bodies. "Ta-ta." The Snow Queen cackled and left.

Abby's eyes grew wide as she tried to squirm, but stayed still.

I let down H.E.A.L again. I hate ice! I hate snow! I hate winter! I never want to see them again! Abby thought.

Abby tried to use her newfound magic to break free of the ice. She pressed her head against the ice, but it didn't budge. *I! NEED! TO! GET! OUT!!!* Abby furiously thought. Abby didn't know it, but her emotions had channeled her magic, and it shot from her head to the ice, and ricocheted to Jill, Jadeine, Apple, Cherry and Tiger. Then the ice slipped from them, melting into puddles. Abby gasped.

"We're free!" Jill cheered.

I'm so glad that's off!" Jadeine exclaimed.

"Remarkable!" Tiger breathed.

Apple and Cherry began chattering happily. Abby dashed forward and looked around. The scepter was left unattended (wow, these keepers are loose on security). Abby snatched it.

"Run, before she comes back!" Cherry yelled and dashed for the exit.

When everyone got out, Abby didn't see Aeryn. "Where is Aeryn?" she asked. "He didn't come out."

"I don't—" Apple started. But then something happened to Abby.

Her eyes turned a deep blue, and she spoke. She seemed hypnotized.

"One who does not have a pure heart shall not melt. If a true one emits warmth, they shall be free from a forever icy curse." Abby chanted.

Abby slumped, then stood up straight again.

"What did I do?" Abby cried.

"You became all weird and said…a warning? You sounded like the Snow Queen." Jadeine answered.

"But…Aeryn didn't do anything bad. He helped us!" Jill exclaimed, confused.

"Maybe…maybe he was planning to do something bad. Maybe he was just trying to be good for longer, then turn on us!" Abby realized. "See, Jill? I knew he was up to something!"

"Wait. We never got permission to take the relic," Jadeine realized.

"Yeah… guess we'll have to go back," Abby sighed.

Just then, the snow in front of them swirled faster and faster. Mounds of snow rose up, slowly shaping into the figure of a tall woman with a flowy dress and a tiara. The Snow Queen!

"Hello, mortals. I, the Snow Queen, have come to say that I may have…overreacted. I willingly give you the relic. Keep it," the Snow Queen's aniform said.

"Thanks, Snow Queen!" Abby exclaimed.

The Snow Queen's aniform smiled, then the snow fell back to the ground. Jadeine let out a squeal that sounded so unlike her. They all smiled in relief. Then, their cheeks got cold.

They let the staff fly them down. When they reached the ground, Abby was glad.

"I was so c-c-cold!" Cherry shivered. "Even after Aeryn put that warmth spell on us."

"You were? It was rather toasty!" Tiger cried.

"HOW?!" everyone yelled.

"I accidentally paid a visit to Greenland once, through a random portal. I was stranded for a week on an iceberg," Tiger explained.

"Wait. You've seen Earth-I mean, the Unknown?" Abby asked.

"Yes! Rather horrible if you ask me," Tiger shuddered. " No offense."

"None taken," Abby said. She held the scepter up in triumph as everyone clapped.

"Also, you think we can pay my mother a visit?" Apple asked.

"Yes, of course!" Abby squealed. "I've always wanted to meet Snow White!"

Chapter 16
Chaos Everywhere

Snow White was worried sick about her children. After the ball at Cinderella's summer house, they had disappeared! A day later, a wolf had snuck into her palace and had attempted to kidnap her!

She had dreamed about the wolf giving her an apple. Not her son, Apple, but the food apple. And she had eaten it! And died! And she was cold and hungry when she had become a ghost, and the wolf tormented her every single day! Snow White didn't think it was even possible to torment a ghost! Then the wolf had eaten her children!

Snow White shook her head. She wouldn't let her dream get to her head. Even though it quite literally had. Because everyone in H.E.A.L knew that dreams could sometimes be real, or a prophecy, Snow White gazed out the window and tugged on her lacy dress.

She leaned forward and saw a group approaching the castle. There was the famed Jill, Jadeine, Abby, Tiger and…

She rubbed her eyes. Could it be? Cherry and Apple! Snow White leaped out of her chair and ran outside. She rushed forward and hugged Cherry and Apple.

"Hi, Mama. I'm sorry, Apple and I left without telling you," Cherry told Snow White.

"I'm so glad you're safe. Where have you been?" Snow White cried.

"Lizzie sent her wolf after us. It tried to eat us, and it almost did, but those other people saved us!" Cherry exclaimed.

"Well, I'll forever be grateful to them. Now what have you two been doing?" Snow White asked.

"We got the third relic!" Apple exclaimed.

"What?!" Snow White cried, flustered. Whatever she was expecting to hear, that was *not* it.

"We're helping Abby, the prophecy girl!" Cherry added.

"That's very brave of you, but that's so…dangerous! Stay here! I won't let you do that!" Snow White yelped.

"It's not that dangerous!" Cherry protested.

"I simply can't let you out of my sight again!" Snow White pulled her children towards her, hugging them tight. "I can't believe you escaped *again*! You will be staying home until the prophecy girl defeats Lizzie!"

"Again?" Tiger queried.

"They're always running away," Snow White explained. "This is, like, the eighth time it's happened!"

"Apple's the one who runs away!" Cherry protested. "Not me. I'm a good daughter, unlike him."

Apple elbowed her. Tiger laughed.

Abby walked closer to Snow White in awe.

"You're…Snow White! A legend!" Abby exclaimed.

Her eyes lit up and she rubbed her hands together. Soon, she was squealing. Jill tapped her shoulder.

"Um, Abby? You're being awkward," Jill told her.

"Sorry, sorryyyyy!" Abby squealed.

As Abby looked at Snow White fussing over her children, though, Abby's awe wore off and was replaced with longing. Longing to be with her mom again. Longing to be pulled into a tight hug, and to hear her mom call her 'my sandwich'. Cherry snapped her back to attention.

"Sorry, Abby. We're staying here. Queen's orders," Cherry groaned.

"That's all right," Abby told her. "It's not your fault. Bye, then!"

Apple pressed his lips together as the group walked away. No one heard him whisper, "Mama's crazy if she thinks I won't run away again."

"What's the fourth relic?" Abby wondered.

"It's with Mrs. Arunis," Jadeine smiled. "I crossed paths with her once, and it was, um, awkward. But it was when I was a little girl. Apparently, she already knew she was destined to be a keeper, and she told me. She was a teenager at that time, so she wasn't careful about who she told that she would be a keeper too. "

"Great! Where does she live?" Abby asked.

"Cinderella Town," Jadeine told the group.

"Cinderella Town? I can take you there!" someone chirped.

They turned to see a guy with an oxcart with pears in it. Bert!

"Are you Bert?" Abby asked.

"No! I'm his son!" the man corrected.

So…not Bert.

"Can we have a ride?" Jadeine asked.

"I just offered!" the man exclaimed. "Get in!"

They climbed in. Abby was eager to ask the man some questions she had always wondered about H.E.A.L.

"So, what's your name?" Abby asked.

"Calisto, but people call me Cal."

"Who's your favorite queen?"

"Sleeping Beauty. She's awesome."

"Have you ever seen the Evil Queen?"

"Yes, I have."

"When?"

"Last month. She visited my town once and cursed our award-winning gardener."

"Do you know anyone with magic powers?"

"No."

"And also, where do you live?"

"What is this, an interview?"

Abby blushed. She didn't mean to sound annoying. She was just so excited! Could you blame her?

"Abby," Tiger said. "Do you think the keeper of the fourth relic will be willing to give the relic to us?"

"I'm not sure. But we'll have to hope," Abby replied. "Hope for the best."

The oxcart jolted to a sudden stop. Abby leaned over to see what had stopped them. She choked when she realized Lizzie was standing in front of them. Lizzie didn't look evil, like she usually did. She looked surprised. Abby noticed that Lizzie didn't have her evil team (well, only the Big Bad Wolf was really evil. Abby's mom and Amelia had been forced) unlike she usually did.

"Back off," Abby warned. "And slowly."

Lizzie actually *listened* to Abby, which caught her by surprise. Lizzie took a deep breath, then rammed into the cart. After she did, Lizzie let out a shriek. Not one that signified her evilness, but a scared one, like a puppy lost in a thunderstorm. Now Abby was really stunned. Lizzie was scared.

"I'm j-just warming up, Abby. I never expected this," Lizzie said. Lizzie crouched down, muttering something about how to expect the unexpected.

Abby needed to get the cart away from Lizzie before she 'warmed up' and hurt them. Abby tried to use her magic and get the oxcart to fly. She tensed her muscles and put her focus into making the oxcart fly. Unfortunately, Calisto started throwing his lunch at Lizzie, which distracted Abby. For a second, the cart vibrated, but it didn't move.

Lizzie muttered a soothing chant to herself and straightened herself. "I. Am. Not. A coward. Melissa has gotten it all wrong."

"Melissa, as in…my mom?" Abby asked. Then she narrowed her eyes. "Have you hurt her?"

"Not yet," Lizzie smirked at Abby. "For now, she's all well. But we'll see about that. For her comment about me being a coward, I'll destroy everything she lives for. That's a worse fate than death."

"Don't you dare touch her!" Abby shrieked.

Lizzie cackled. An angry spark of light lashed out at Abby. Abby screamed and ducked. "Abby, Abby, Abby. When will you ever get this? I can do anything I want. I will have my reve—"

Eleanor was standing behind her. She punched Lizzie, and Lizzie crumpled.

"Eleanor, thank god you're here!" Abby exclaimed. Eleanor was at the right place at the right time.

"Hello. You've been progressing!" Eleanor told Abby, looking at the relics that the group was holding.

"Wait…how are you here?" Abby asked, suspiciously.

Lizzie rose. She grinned at Abby, showing missing teeth. Gross!

"Your *dearest Eleanor* has agreed to turn you in if I give her Cyrus," Lizzie tattled.

"I don't believe you!" Abby cried. "And who's Cyrus?"

Eleanor punched Lizzie again. Lizzie just laughed. "You can run, but you can't hide…"

"It's true." Eleanor lowered her gaze. "Long ago, I snuck into a castle. I wanted to sneak a peek at a princess, because I was a poor young woman. I found an empty room. I put on a beautiful dress and did my hair all fancy. I was in the garden when a young frog swam up to me in the pond and talked! He asked if I could free him from a curse. I agreed. No later than that, he turned into a boy! The boy then told me his name was Cyrus. I was years older than him, so I adopted him. He was my sunshine, my only sunshine. Then Lizzie came and turned him into a frog yet again! Cyrus was bewitched and hopped far away to a swamp. I told Lizzie that if she could undo the spell, I would betray you in return. And I deeply regret it." Eleanor bit her lip, her eyes brimming with tears.

"So trust no one, is what you're saying." Abby had a lump in her throat.

"Maybe," Eleanor whispered.

Lizzie rose slowly and started to run towards them. Abby stayed frozen, stung by Eleanor's betrayal. Well, she had only done it to get the Cyrus guy back, but still, Abby felt heartbroken.

"Run, Abby!" Jadeine yelled, tugging at her arm.

Oops. Abby dashed away with Jadeine, Jill and Tiger. Lizzie ran after them. Abby clutched the ice scepter and mermaid tiara tightly. After a while, Abby started to feel fatigued. Her adrenaline wore off, and she started to fall behind.

Jadeine glanced over her shoulder. "Abby! She's right behind you!"

Abby's eyes widened. She looked behind her.

Lizzie laughed and grabbed Abby's arm. "Finally, I caught you!"

Chapter 17
Unexpected Meet

Apple was already plotting an escape.

He and Cherry were in the castle library. Apple was sitting by the window, staring at the setting sun. Cherry was reading a book. Their mom was in the next room, already asleep. Apple could hear her snores through the supposedly soundproof wall.

Really, his mom was making this too easy for him.

Apple considered going out the front door, but a servant would probably see him and alert Snow White. The window was easier. And more fun. "Cherry," Apple said.

"What?" She didn't take her eyes off her book. She loved books.

"Come on. Let's go find Abby."

Now she looked up. "We're escaping?! Mama said not to! It's dangerous!"

Apple rolled his eyes. "Whatever. I'm going. If you're a chicken…"

Cherry grunted. "Fine."

Apple turned the latch on the window and slipped out. One thing he had always found super annoying—he was super short. Apple was a full 4 inches shorter than Cherry, so she was a lot taller than him even though he was older.

Apple climbed out of the window and jumped down to the ground. The library was on the first floor, so Apple didn't die a painful death. Cherry wanted to make sure she looked regal and beautiful, so she took some time fixing her clothes and hair.

While he was waiting for her, he heard a weird noise. He whirled around, but only saw a bush with blue flowers.

Then the bush…*blinked.*

Apple screamed and lurched backward. A woman climbed out of the bush. She had sky blue hair and was wearing a dress that was the same shade as her hair.

She scowled at him. "I'm looking for Abby Palmer—the prophecy girl!"

She sounded pretty mad, which told Apple she probably wasn't a friend of Abby's. "Who are you?" he asked.

"I'm the Merqueen!" the lady replied. "My name is Nadine. Abby and her friends stole my relic from me. Do you know where she is?"

Apple wondered if he should tell her where Abby was or not. Abby had told him about their deal with Nadine and how they had ended up breaking their promise. "Uh…what do you want with her?"

"I want my relic back, obviously! She didn't hold up her end of the deal. Why should I hold up mine?"

Apple opened his mouth, but just then Cherry hopped out of the window. "Apple! I—who's this?"

Apple quickly filled her in. Cherry frowned. "They stole it?"

"Yes!" Nadine sounded impatient. "They stole it, and I want it back! Where are they? Tell me, or I will turn you into a fish!"

Apple and Cherry looked at each other. Neither of them wanted to help Nadine, but they especially didn't want to become fish. "I think they went to find the fourth relic," Cherry finally told Nadine.

Nadine's face lit up. "Great! I know where that is! She'll pay." She turned and started walking.

"Wait!" Apple cried. He couldn't let her get revenge on Abby. "Can my sister and I come with you?"

Nadine considered this. "Well…"

"Please? We're small, and we have the advantage of being children," Cherry pleaded.

Nadine sighed. "All right. C'mon."

Apple and Cherry followed Nadine as they walked. Soon, they found themselves in a small town square with a fountain at its center. One of the Three Little Pigs ran up to them. "Did you hear what happened?"

"What?" Apple asked her.

"An hour ago, the Evil Queen, the bad fairy, a servant girl, and the Big Bad Wolf were here! But then the bad fairy turned on her sister and cursed her! The Evil Queen ran away."

Nadine opened her mouth, but then they heard a commotion by the road. Nadine, Apple, Cherry, and the pig ran to the side of the road to see what was going on.

It was Abby, Jill, Jadeine, and Tiger! An oxcart lay abandoned behind them. They were all running, and the Evil Queen was right behind them. She caught Abby's arm and yelled, "Finally! I caught you!"

"Not so fast!" Apple shouted and ran onto the road. Cherry followed him.

Tiger screamed, "What do we do?!"

The Evil Queen placed her hand on Abby's head and began to chant something. Abby's eyes turned black and then started to flutter closed.

So Apple did what was both the bravest and most foolish thing he had ever done in his life. He ran to the Evil Queen and punched her in the face.

She cried out and stumbled backwards, letting go of Abby. Abby's eyes turned blue again. "What? Where—"

"No time!" Apple yelped, tugging her away. Then the group ran for it.

They finally collapsed in a heap in the middle of the forest. "I can't believe you punched the Evil Queen, Apple," Jill panted. "That's the craziest thing I've seen anyone do before."

Apple snorted. Then Jadeine sat up. "Why is Nadine here?"

Nadine sprang to her feet. "Yes! I want my relic back!"

"What?" Abby pushed the tiara behind a tree, like that would hide it. "Why?!"

"Why do you think so? You stole it! You didn't hold up on your end of the deal!"

Nadine started towards Abby, but then Cherry tugged on her arm. "Wait! What if we make a new deal with you?"

Nadine scowled at him. "You all already broke one promise. You can break another."

"Yeah, but that was only Abby, Jill, and Jadeine," Apple pointed out. "What if Cherry, Tiger, and I make a new deal with you? Would you agree to that?"

Nadine considered. "Well…yes. And I know the perfect thing! I'll give you the relic if you…relocate the geese in my lake!"

"Excuse me?" the group yelled in unison.

Nadine laughed. "The geese are all so loud when I try to sleep. You can catch them all and release them somewhere else! There are only twenty."

Apple, Cherry, and Tiger looked at each other. "OK?" Tiger decided finally.

"Great!" Nadine clasped her hands together. "Chop, chop! Off you go!"

Chapter 18
Finding Ms. Arunis

They were no closer to finding the fourth relic than they had been the day before.

When it had grown dark out, they lay down to sleep. Now, they couldn't remember which direction they had been heading.

In other words, they were absolutely, hopelessly, lost.

Abby was starting to think this was a wild goose chase. Plus, their group was down to only three people now, since Apple, Cherry, and Tiger were off on a literal wild goose chase.

At least Jadeine knew where the fourth relic was. It was with this person named Ms. Arunis. That was something! But it was of no use if they couldn't find her.

"Abby? Are you awake?" Jill whispered, nudging Abby.

"Yes," Abby answered, sitting up. "I didn't sleep all night."

"Me neither! But when I finally fell asleep, I dreamed we used the staff to fly us out of here."

"So…we're going to do what you dreamed?"

"Yep! Jadeine's coming too!"

"Why are you so…happy?" Abby asked, squinting her eyes. "I mean, it's literally 2:30 a.m."

"Because we won't be lost!" Jill replied happily.

Jadeine moaned and yawned. She turned away from Abby and Jill.

"If you two want to talk, do it away from me," Jadeine yawned.

"Jadeine, I found a way to make travel easier," Jill said.

"I just want to sleep," Jadeine grumbled.

"You can do that later. C'mon!" Jill exclaimed, pulling Abby and Jadeine to their feet. "Staff, take us to Cinderella Town."

They grabbed onto the staff, and the staff soared up into the inky black night sky. Soon, they were flying out of the forest. The stars twinkled above them and the wind gently blew at Abby.

"It's so pretty," Abby sighed dreamily.

Abby looked down and noticed a town that was so charming, she was sure she was still dreaming. Cinderella Town! Except…they flew right past it.

"Staff! Go down!" Abby cried.

"Nope," the staff replied.

Abby figured he was being ornery. "Fine, *Jay*. Now go to Cinderella Town. Please," Abby demanded.

"I can't. I'm under orders from Lizzie," the staff informed her.

"Wait, Lizzie?!" Abby shrieked. "I hope this is a very early April Fool's joke!"

"I don't think so, whatever April Fools is! I think he'll take us right to her!" Jill realized.

"We have to jump!" Abby cried. The staff tilted upwards and whacked Abby on the head. Hard.

"Ow!" Abby exclaimed.

She looked down at the field of wheat beneath. It would be an easy fall…right? Jill easily dove down without hesitation, and Jadeine followed.

Should I leave the staff? The staff was the first relic, and they needed it to defeat Lizzie. But she had to jump or she'd be taken to Lizzie. *I'm not the only scared person. I'm not alone in this. I have friends who support me,* Abby thought. Abby nervously let go of the staff and plunged through the night sky. She instantly screamed, her heart dropping to her feet. Her hair wildly flapped in her face. Abby landed with a THUMP on the ground.

"Ow… I think I broke a bone," Abby groaned, rubbing her back.

"You're fine," Jadeine soothed. "Let's go."

Abby sat up and jumped to her feet. They trekked through the thick wheat. It didn't take long to reach Cinderella Town. Abby walked on the cobblestone and glanced at the multicolored shops. There were pictures of glass slippers everywhere!

"Where's Ms. Arunis's house?" Abby wondered.

"We can search or ask a post guard," Jadeine replied.

"Post guard? What's that?" Abby asked.

"Like a mailman," Jadeine explained.

"I say we ask the mailman," Abby decided.

"Good choice," Jadeine told her. "Post guards know everything, for their routes."

They asked around, and a kind old lady directed them to a post office. They walked in, and a merry tune rang out. A post guard looked up and frowned.

"Who are you?" he asked.

"Hi! We want to know where—" Abby began.

"WHO ARE YOU?!" he yelled.

"Short-tempered guy," Jill muttered.

"And I have excellent hearing, too," he huffed, glaring at Jill.

"Sorry, I'm Abby, and this is Jill and Jadeine," Abby told the post guard.

"What's your business here, eh?" he asked.

"We want to know where Ms. Arunis's house is?" Abby looked at him hopefully.

"She specifically asked me not to tell anyone her address," the post guard sniffed.

"Please?" Abby tried. "We really need to find her or—"

"Or what?" the post guard taunted.

"Or we're all going to die!" Abby huffed, getting angry. "Give us her address or I'll—I'll fire you!" she spitballed.

"You can't fire me! Army guards! We have some very un-Cinderellian-like citizens here!" the post guard called.

"You wouldn't dare. We're not even citizens!" Abby cried.

"Prove it," a thick voice came.

A burly-looking man stood in the doorway. He had a ring that had the image of a slipper on it. So did the post guard. Another lady came in. She also had the same symbol. Abby noticed that everyone had it. She held up her hands.

"I don't have a slipper symbol," Abby told him.

"Smart girl," growled the burly man.

"Arrest her, now!" the post guard exclaimed.

Abby and Jill sprinted to the doorway, while Jadeine stood frozen.

"I hate kids!" the burly man erupted.

"What's going on here?" the lady asked, walking towards them.

The lady had silky, light brown hair tied up into a loose bun. She had gray eyes and chapped lips. She had smooth, tan skin and pearl earrings with a ruby and jade necklace. Her shirt looked expensive. It was lilac and she wore a long, bright red skirt. She wore elevated high heels that echoed when she walked.

"Ah, just arresting some trouble-makers." The post guard chuckled nervously.

"No! We just wanted to know Ms. Arunis's address!" Abby exclaimed.

"We want to meet her, but we don't know where she lives," Jadeine explained.

"The post guard resisted telling us, and Abby got angry," Jill continued.

"The guard called us un-Cinderellian citizens and wanted to arrest us," Abby added.

"We told him we weren't citizens, and he had no right to arrest us." Jadeine sighed.

"Then we proved it. The guard was angry that he was wrong, so he chased us!" Jill cried.

"Ah, I see. Manuel? You're a post guard, not the police," the woman sighed.

"Uh, but they lied, you see! Stole some letters," Manuel lied.

"But I have magic. And I can see they're innocent," the woman retorted.

"Miss, please get out and don't come back!" the burly man yelled.

"And Diego. You've been arrested twice, and Cinderella lets you roam free. Be grateful," the woman chided him.

"Want to wrestle? Rather have you in one piece," Diego growled.

"I bet you'll be a fly to me." The woman smirked.

Diego clenched his fists and charged. The woman leaped into the air and floated just above his head. He jumped for her feet, and she suddenly appeared behind him. When he whirled around, she threw a quick flurry of punches, and he crumpled to the ground.

"Now you wanna bet?" the woman asked.

"I… I'm sorry, Ms. Arunis," Diego half-heartedly apologized, getting to his feet limply.

Abby gasped. This was Ms. Arunis?

Ms. Arunis ran out the door. Abby chased after her, and Ms. Arunis rounded a corner. When Abby peeked around the corner, she saw nobody there. Abby walked back sulking.

"You catch her, Ab?" Jill asked.

"No." Abby sighed.

"Let's go back. Maybe Ms. Arunis hid somewhere!" Jadeine suggested.

Abby sat down on a bench, chin resting on her hands. *What if I never finish this?* Abby thought. *I might die…or someone else will. I can't risk that!*

Abby tried not to let tears flow, but one escaped, rolling down her cheek. It fell off and landed on the cuff of her pants. Abby sniffled and rubbed her eyes. Then she stood.

"Ok, let's go check it out." Abby's voice was scratchy.

They turned the corner and found a trash can. Abby peered inside while the others searched around the alley. It was filled to the brim with garbage. Maybe Ms. Arunis had hidden in there!

Abby tossed out a banana peel. Then a Cinderella Milkshake. (What was a Cinderella Milkshake?) And a half-eaten hamburger. Gross. Then Abby noticed a crumpled-up paper. She picked it up and realized it was a letter.

Dear Melissa,

I hope you're doing all right. I know I left on short notice, but I wanted to let you know I found the magic perfume. I'll be back in a week. I have to spend some time on Dragon Island. I know it's dangerous there, but I'll be careful.

Always,

Jay Palmer

Abby couldn't believe her eyes. Jay Palmer was her dad's name!

Breathlessly, she reread the letter. *I'll be back in a week.* But…her dad had never come back. Why?

Maybe…maybe he was trapped there. At Dragon Island! Abby's heart soared like a bright kite in the sky. If they could get to Dragon Island, maybe her dad would be there!

How lucky was it that Abby had pulled this letter out of a trash can? If she hadn't…Abby's eyes brimmed with tears again, and she wiped them with the back of her hand.

Jill wandered over. "Bad news, Abby. I didn't find her," Jill told Abby.

"That's okay. Look!" Abby squealed, her eyes sparkly. She thrust the letter into Jill's hands. "My dad went missing two years ago. But I think I know where he is!"

Jill read it and looked at Abby, just as excited. Abby looked up and saw Jadeine walking towards them.

Jadeine shook her head. "Sorry, Abby, she wasn't there."

"It's fine. My dad was here! I know where he is!" Abby exclaimed.

Jadeine also read the letter. She smiled at Abby.

"Great. I know it feels like a huge victory to know where someone you didn't think you would see again is." Jadeine smiled again.

"We have to sleep. It's getting late," Jill observed.

"Sure, I'll book a floating room," Jadeine replied. "We're in a town now, so it'll be easy."

"Floating room? What's that?" Abby asked. She imagined a floating Airbnb.

"The windows are hyper realistic and the bed is made of enchanted clouds," Jill explained.

Abby frowned. "What about my dad?"

Jadeine squeezed Abby's hand. "We can't go to Dragon Island right now—it's too dark out and the dragons will be hungry. We can sleep and go in the morning, after we're rested."

Abby chewed her lip, but nodded. She *was* sleepy.

A few minutes later, they were in a beautiful room. It was exactly how Jill had described it.

"Let's sleep. I haven't had a good bed in days," Jill sighed.

"How are we going to get the relic from Ms. Arunis if she doesn't want us to?" Abby wondered.

"We'll have to try," Jill replied. "Remember what we did with Nadine's relic?"

"Yeah, and she got mad at us and wanted revenge," Jadeine pointed out.

Abby spied a TV and a remote. She picked it up and switched the channels a couple of times before settling on a fantasy show.

In the episode she was watching, Abby saw a girl chasing another girl whom she suspected had done magical graffiti art. When they turned a corner, the graffiti girl was missing like Ms. Arunis.

Abby glanced at the screen. The girl on the screen touched the wall…and went into it.

Abby jumped from the bed. Ms. Arunis had gone into the wall! She looked around, but saw that Jadeine and Jill were already sleeping. Abby quietly turned off the TV and slinked under the covers, too. She could tell them in the morning.

Abby could hardly sleep, though. She was so excited that they might be able to get the fourth relic by tomorrow, she couldn't sleep! She wriggled all night. Abby was awake until the first cracks of light seeped through the curtains. Abby jumped up, glanced at the clock, and slumped in disappointment as she realized it was only 5:00 a.m.

Jadeine had her eyes open, though, staring at the ceiling.

"Jadeine! I know where Ms. Arunis went!" Abby cried.

"Shouldn't you be asleep?" Jadeine mumbled, blinking blearily.

"I couldn't sleep! Ms. Arunis went inside the wall!" Abby shrieked.

"Who's she? What are we doing now?" Jadeine grumbled.

"Are you still sleepy?" Abby smirked.

"Yes! Now, can you be quiet? We're not awake yet," Jadeine told her, throwing the covers over her head.

"Ugh, fine! We'll go when you wake up!" Abby rolled her eyes.

Abby pranced towards the curtains and pulled them open. Sunlight hit her face. Abby closed her eyes to block the sun, and she suddenly felt groggy. She felt her eyes become heavy…then drifted off to sleep.

She fell to the ground with a THUMP! Abby lay there for quite some time.

"WAKE UP, SLEEPYHEAD!" Jill yelled in Abby's face.

"Stop it. I was awake all night," Abby groaned.

"You slept, though, right? Jadeine told me your plan!" Jill chirped.

"She did? That's wonderful. Now stop bothering me." Abby yawned.

"It's 11 a.m. and it's really late in the day," Jill singsonged.

Abby sat up and jumped to her feet. She got ready, and they checked out of the hotel. They walked to the same spot, and Abby put her palm against the wall, waiting for it to go through. But the wall was solid. Abby sighed in disappointment. She slumped against it.

"Guys, I was wrong." Abby sighed.

"It's okay. We could go to the post office and see if she comes there again," Jill suggested.

"She won't. She knows we're here." Abby leaned against the wall and let out her breath.

Abby suddenly didn't feel the wall. She rocked backwards and fell on her back. Abby sat up and looked around. She was in a lovely house that was well-lit and had vibrant flora.

"I did it!" Abby cheered.

Right on cue, Jill and Jadeine tumbled in. They looked around. Then they panicked. Footsteps were just around the corner! Ms. Arunis. Abby dove behind a couch, Jill behind a thick lamp, and Jadeine under the couch pillows.

Ms. Arunis entered the room. Abby remembered they couldn't steal the relic, so she stood up. Ms. Arunis noticed Abby and screamed.

"Sorry for barging in," Abby apologized.

"You—you found me," Ms. Arunis gasped. "How...?"

"Well, duh. I'm right here," Abby said.

"I assume you're here for a reason," Ms. Arunis guessed.

"Well, yes. I hope you're alright with me…borrowing your relic," Abby carefully chose her words.

"I can't give it to you. I'm sorry, but I have a reputation to keep," Ms. Arunis sniffed.

Abby scowled. She hated people who were obsessed with reputations. "*Sorry,* but we might all die if you don't give it to us," Abby replied hotly.

"How do I know you're good?" Ms. Arunis asked, flipping her hair. "What if you're with Lizzie?"

Abby was stunned. She didn't know how to respond.

"You're right. But what about you? Are your intentions on saving the world?" Abby finally replied.

"No, it's being a good keeper, unlike your friend Jadeine," Ms. Arunis huffed.

Jadeine erupted from the pillows.

"How dare you! I'm right here, you know!" Jadeine exclaimed. Jill also got out behind the lamp and crossed her arms.

"Yes, but where's the rest of your crew? Abandoned you?" Ms. Arunis inquired.

"No, they're doing a favor for the Merqueen," Abby replied.

"Ah, I see. So Nadine did keep her word after all." Ms. Arunis grinned.

"What? She made a deal with you?" Abby asked.

"She said she would disguise a guard as a goose and imprison them," Ms. Arunis answered.

"No! That's so unfair!" Abby exclaimed.

"Life's unfair, my child," Ms. Arunis told her.

Jadeine sighed. "I hope they're okay."

Then, they heard the sound of someone screaming.

Chapter 19
Geese Poop

Cherry was *not* okay. The moment she set foot in Nadine's pond, she heard the squelch of geese poop and gagged. It stank! And besides, Cherry was royalty. She wasn't built to do these kinds of things, although Apple seemed to be doing alright.

"I don't suppose this is the most pleasant job in the world," Cherry groaned.

"It isn't," Tiger replied with a firm nod. "Also, you don't have to speak like you're giving a royal announcement. We're your friends."

"Well, Apple is my brother, and you're more like an... acquaintance," Cherry corrected.

"Ugh, enough with the big, fancy words like acquaintance," Tiger groaned. "You're a teenage girl, not a queen who gives inspiring speeches 24/7."

"Well, soon I'll *be* a queen who gives inspiring speeches 24/7," Cherry pointed out.

Tiger lunged for a goose, who nipped her ankle and swam away. Tiger fell into the water, lifting her head just in time to avoid getting poop on her face. She wiped the water from her face.

"Hahaha! That's hilarious!" Cherry laughed so hard she had to grab Apple to steady herself.

"*Your Majesty*, maybe do some actual work?" Tiger suggested bluntly.

"Yeah, Cherry," Apple chimed in.

Tiger lunged for the same goose and caught it this time. She ran out of the water and threw it into the woods far away, so the geese wouldn't come back. Cherry touched the feather of a goose and recoiled in disgust.

"How do you pick up these things?" Cherry asked.

"Easy," Apple told her. He picked up a goose and ran off in the direction Tiger had gone.

Cherry sighed. She sat down in the water. As soon as she did, she heard a squelching sound. She checked her pants and realized it was covered in goose poop. Cherry had forgotten all about the concealed goose poop hidden beneath the water.

"EW EW EW EW EW!" Cherry shrieked.

Tiger came back to see Cherry running around like a maniac. When she saw the geese poop on Cherry's pants, Tiger doubled over in laughter. Tears squeezed from her eyes. When Apple arrived, he saw Tiger laughing. And then he started laughing!

Then Cherry laughed hard because Apple and Tiger looked like they were dying of laughter. Nadine suddenly entered the pond. She crossed her arms. A little giggle escaped. Then a snort.

Then everyone, including Nadine, was laughing. Even the geese were honking abnormally! And…one of the geese slowly morphed into a man! A guard!

"What's going on here?" the guard asked.

"HAHAHAHAHA!" was Nadine's response.

"Someone has the laughing sickness!" he declared.

"HAHA—what's the—HAHAHA—laughing sickness?" Cherry asked.

"You never stop laughing!" the guard answered.

The guard suddenly sneezed. Then he made some throat-clearing sounds. The guard chuckled a bit. Then he started laughing too! *Abby can probably hear us from miles away!* Cherry thought. Cherry staggered over to the pond and fell in. The splash shocked her out of laughing. But her splash only caused the others to laugh harder.

Cherry shook her head, and water droplets flew from her hair. What would she do?

"Nadine!" she cried. "You can do magic, right? Help!"

Nadine was too busy laughing to do anything. So Cherry ran up to her and slapped her hard.

"NADINE!" Cherry yelled.

Nadine stopped laughing. "What? Oh, thank you! I think we've found the antidote!"

Nadine and Cherry slapped the guard, Tiger, and Apple. (Cherry had the most satisfaction in slapping her brother.) They all finally stopped laughing.

"Now." The guard straightened. "I shall do my job!"

"Which is?" Tiger prompted.

"To make you Queen Nadine's prisoners forever," He lunged at Cherry, who shrieked and ran behind her brother, trying to hide, which was ridiculous, since she was four inches taller than him.

"RUN!" Tiger yelled. The trio turned and dashed into the forest. The guard followed.

"Uh, um, we didn't finish the favor!" Apple panted, pulling the others behind some trees.

"Oh, so what?" Cherry asked. "We're going to be prisoners!"

"No, we won't," Tiger soothed.

Tiger stopped and whirled around twice. An orange necklace around her neck glowed. Tiger disappeared, and an actual tiger appeared!

She surveyed the area. The guard came dashing around the corner, bumped into Tiger/tiger, and screamed, running away.

Tiger returned to her normal shape.

"Did you see the guard's face?!" Apple exclaimed gleefully.

"I know, it was so funny! Hahahahahahahahahahaha!" Tiger laughed. But she didn't stop laughing. Cherry felt the urge to laugh all of a sudden.

"Oh no…" Cherry said.

They all burst into laughter. The guard returned and started laughing as soon as he saw them. Cherry was laughing so hard she could barely stand. She fell and hit her head, snapping out of it. She slapped Tiger.

Then, she turned to her brother and slapped him as hard as she could. He stopped laughing and winced, looking at Cherry's gleeful face.

"Did you enjoy slapping me?" Apple asked.

"Very much," Cherry told him joyously.

"This calls for revenge!" Apple shrieked.

Apple smiled and slapped Cherry back. Cherry screamed and started laughing again.

"Oops." Apple slapped Cherry again, harder this time. Cherry narrowed her eyes at her brother.

"You little rat," Cherry spat.

"I'm older than you, so you have to do what I say," Apple smirked.

"I'm taller than you, so you are a brat," Cherry retorted.

"That makes no sense." Apple scrunched his face up.

"Let's just go find Abby," Tiger sighed.

"Wait! What about the deal?" Apple cried.

"It's a trap, right?" Tiger said. "We'll figure out something else."

They walked deeper into the forest, farther away from the lake and the guard whom they had left to succumb to the laughing sickness. Cherry's cheek still hurt. She wanted to go home. The guard had wanted to make her a prisoner! She would probably have been treated like an animal, despite the fact that Cherry was royalty!

The trees covered the sky. A howl erupted through the forest. Cherry snapped her head sideways to realize a wolf—*the* wolf—was running straight towards them! Everything happened so fast. Cherry pushed Apple and Tiger out of the way and tried to run, but the wolf caught her collar and grabbed her in his mouth again.

"Help! Apple! Tiger!" Cherry cried out.

Tiger and Apple ran after the wolf, but the wolf was too fast. Cherry shrieked.

As the wolf ran, Apple and Tiger became dots on the horizon. Cherry was on the verge of tears. Thoughts of never seeing Apple again made tears run down her cheeks.

Then, saliva dripped on her hair, her beautifully styled hair that had been twisted into curls by her hairstylist.

"EW EW EW!" Cherry screamed.

"Ugh, can you stop being annoying?" the wolf growled.

"I live on annoying!" Cherry replied.

"Well, you might die soon then," the wolf informed her.

Cherry closed her mouth and tried to think of a clever comeback.

"You know, you don't have to obey the Evil Queen's wishes," Cherry piped up.

"I can't betray my mom now, can I?" the wolf asked.

"Mom?! But how?" Cherry cried. *How can a wolf be the son of a human?* Cherry thought, confused.

"She magically created me. I wasn't actually ever born," the wolf explained.

"So…you're practically her, except different," Cherry realized, fear lodging in her stomach.

The wolf just laughed wildly and sped up.

Cherry sighed. When would she get out?

When would she see Apple again?

Would she see anything ever again?

Or would she die?

Chapter 20
Deal with Darya

Apple regretted not being able to rescue Cherry. *But what's the worst that could happen? Nothing much, right?* He hoped there was still time to rescue her.

Tiger and Apple had gone searching for Cherry after the wolf took her away, but a bear assaulted them, probably thinking they were going to hurt its cubs. Yes, Tiger had tried to scare the bear by turning into a tiger. But the bear had swiped off her orange necklace, and Tiger became powerless. They were left slightly limping and in no position to save Cherry. They had decided to get some rest before trying to find Cherry again.

"How much longer to the nearest town?" Apple asked.

"2 miles at the most. We're in the fields now," Tiger replied.

"I wish we had saved Cherry," Apple said mournfully. His face darkened, and he wilted like a dehydrated flower.

"At that moment, I felt like she wasn't living up to being your sister," Tiger admitted.

"Ugh, Tiger, she's MY SISTER! It's a life instinct to save her," Apple said. "And I failed."

"You pretty much messed up," Tiger said with a small grin.

"Are you trying to make me feel bad?" Apple asked.

"Maybe," Tiger replied, grinning. Then she looked up. "Oh, we're here!"

Apple looked at the town. It was amazing. Cinderella Town! The sidewalks were carved from marble, and the rooftops were decorated with rainbow tiles. The sun reflected off the windows, making them appear tinted orange and red. *Splendorous,* Apple thought.

They walked for a while in the streets before turning a corner. The moment Apple stepped around, he gasped. A trash bin had been knocked over, its contents littering the ground. *Ew, this is even worse than goose poop.*

Apple heard muffled voices from behind the wall. He was never one to eavesdrop, but then, he heard a familiar voice and pressed his ear against the wall. Suddenly, the wall wasn't solid anymore! Apple flailed, screaming, and fell into the wall. He looked around. He was in someone's house…and there was Abby! And Jill! And Jadeine!

Jadeine and the others whirled around to face Apple. He got to his feet.

"Hey, you guys!" Apple cried.

"Apple! You're safe!" Abby exclaimed.

"I'm glad I'm safe, too. That guard was annoyingly persistent," Apple said.

"Prince Apple? Is he an offering for the relic?" Ms. Arunis asked.

"NO!" Abby shrieked.

"Hmm, I don't see any other way," Ms. Arunis huffed.

I can't give Apple up. What else do I have? Abby thought of all the things in her backpack. She got an idea. Abby pulled out all of the cans of tomato soup and held them up. Ms. Arunis stared at them for a couple of seconds before bursting into laughter.

"Is that all you have?" Ms. Arunis laughed. "Ridiculous."

Abby's voice wavered. "It's good, fresh, yummy tomato soup."

"Do you not think I have *money,* Abby?" Ms. Arunis asked. "This insults me. You're treating me as if I'm a beggar."

"You're not treating us very nicely either," Abby pointed out.

"I will never accept a measly meal! Something more…valuable," Ms. Arunis's eyes flicked to Apple, and he gulped.

Abby slumped her shoulders. She slowly nodded. Abby didn't want to do it. But she couldn't really steal it. Although she had stolen the second relic, Abby had decided she would make amends later. But that seemed impossible now. They had to make a real trade.

"Ok, you can have Apple," Abby gave in.

"Yeah, sur—wait, WHAT?!" Apple shrieked.

"I'm sorry, Apple. Sometimes you have to make sacrifices," Abby said, looking down at her shoes.

"But—but, Cherry!" Apple sputtered.

"Cherry?" Abby asked. "What about her?"

"I need to save her!" Apple exclaimed. "From the Big Bad Wolf!"

"Yes, we'll rescue her for you. And we'll rescue you too, as soon as we can. I promise." Abby whispered the second part so Ms. Arunis wouldn't hear.

"But—!" Apple protested.

Ms. Arunis grabbed Apple. But she didn't give the relic to them. She turned and walked away.

"No! What about our deal? Where are you going?" Abby asked.

"A deal? I don't remember anything of the sort." Ms. Arunis waved a hand dismissively.

Ms. Arunis snapped her fingers, and all of a sudden, the house was gone. Instead, she and Apple were standing in a room with crystals on the wall and ceiling.

"Where are we?" Apple asked.

"On Dragon Island, of course," Ms. Arunis replied.

"Um… are there actual dragons here?" Apple asked.

"We're inside a dragon-proof prison building," Ms. Arunis told him. "Outside, there are dragons."

"What kind of dragons?"

"What do you think? *Dragon* dragons!"

"How many?"

"About fifty."

"A big island then?"

Ms. Arunis sighed. "Why do you ask so many questions?"

Apple put his hands up. "I'm just curious. Who are you?"

Ms. Arunis smiled. Then her teeth turned…yellow?

Apple screamed and lurched backward. Ms. Arunis's beautiful face slowly transformed until she was a witch!

"Who are you?!" Apple screamed again.

The witch laughed. "Not Ms. Arunis. My name is Darya, sweetie."

Apple choked. Darya was Rapunzel's captor. He had thought she was dead! "Why did you pretend to be Ms. Arunis?" Apple asked.

Darya shrugged. "Not much entertainment for a witch like me. When I came to pick up my mail, I heard Abby and her friends arguing and thought they'd make good entertainment for me."

"Witches get mail?" Apple asked.

"The Sea Witch always sends me mail. It's annoying, but I collect them anyway," Darya explained.

Apple realized he was being too friendly with the witch. "Well, that's just EVIL of you!"

"Not really. No one wants to give me entertainment, so I create my own. Simple."

"Do you have the relic or not?"

"What do you think?! Ms. Arunis does."

"Where is she?!"

"Dead."

"Then how does she have the relic?"

"It's buried with her."

Apple retched. "Ugh! Gross!"

Darya laughed. "I know, right? Splendidly scary, I must say."

Apple sighed. He had so many questions! Where was Tiger? Where was Cherry? Was Aeryn still frozen? Where was the Evil Queen?

A door opened. Apple whirled around. A man walked into the room. He had longish salt-and-pepper hair, and his beard was unshaven, but it looked cool on him. Roguish.

"Who's this?" the man asked, nodding at Apple.

"He's Prince Apple!" Darya crowed. "Snow White's son!"

The man raised his eyebrows. "Interesting…very interesting."

"Who are you?" Apple asked. Wow, he was asking that question a lot today.

"My name is Jay," the man replied. "Jay Palmer."

"Palmer…" Apple trailed off. "By any chance, do you know Abby Palmer?"

Jay's eyes widened. "She's my daughter! You know her? Is she here?"

Apple opened his mouth, but a loud slam cut him off. Darya had left the room.

"Is she here?" Jay asked again.

"No," Apple answered, and then caught himself. "Well, she's here in H.E.A.L. Not here on the island."

Jay frowned. "Oh, no. Don't tell me she's collecting the relics!"

"We are."

Jay paced, muttering to himself. Apple looked around. "Is there a way out?"

Jay shook his head. "The doors to this room are magically locked."

"Then how did you get in?"

"That was the bathroom."

Apple tried the door Darya had gone through. Sure enough, it was locked. "Ugh!"

"Yeah, that always gets on my nerves," Jay said.

"Mm-hm. Well, how did you end up here?" Apple asked.

"Well…" Jay frowned. "I was just touring this island, and Darya disguised herself as a sweet old lady and invited me in. After I was pretty sure Darya meant no harm, she locked me in."

"Did she explain why?" Apple queried.

"She said that she wanted company." Jay shrugged. "And I was like 'Well, at least you could be honest,' and Darya was like 'You'd never come in then,' and then I was like 'Why lock me up then?'. And she just left the room."

"Ah. OK." Apple nodded.

"Tell me about Abby," Jay requested. "What happened so far?"

Apple thought about it. "Well, my sister Cherry and I were at Cinderella's summer home for the ball. Abby told us that the Evil Queen wanted to kill us, so we left. Then the Big Bad Wolf came along and kidnapped me and Cherry, but Abby saved us. Then we went to retrieve the third relic, followed by the fourth. But something weird happened…the Evil Queen also had the first three relics, same as us."

Jay gasped. "Oh no! No, no, no!"

"What?" Apple asked.

Jay groaned. "One set of relics is fake."

"But…is it ours or the Evil Queen's?"

"No way to be sure."

Apple's eyes widened. Were their relics…fake?

Chapter 21
Dragon Island

"Tiger!"

Abby stepped out of the wall and found Tiger by the garbage can. Tiger shoved a banana peel back in the knocked-over garbage can, an expression of pure disgust on her face.

"Abby!" Tiger exclaimed.

Jill and Jadeine stepped out after Abby. "You found Tiger!" Jadeine cried.

"Well, I didn't really find her," Abby said. "She was just here. Tiger, where's Cherry? Apple was saying he had to rescue her or something."

"Well, Apple, Cherry, and I were doing Nadine's deal," Tiger started.

"That was a trick!" Jill told Tiger.

Tiger sighed. "A little late for the warning. Anyway, the Big Bad Wolf came and took Cherry away. We tried to go after her, but, um, we had a run-in with a bear. Then Apple and I decided to find you guys. We came here, and then Apple fell into the wall? I was trying to figure out where he went when you all showed up."

Abby quickly recapped what had happened in the past couple of minutes. "So now Apple's gone," she finished gloomily.

Tiger sighed. "That's…ugh. Well, does anyone know where he is?"

Everyone looked at Jadeine. She put her hands up. "Why is everyone looking at me? How should I know?"

"You know stuff like that," Jill stated.

"No, I don't," Jadeine huffed.

"Well, does anyone have any ideas where Apple might have gone?" Abby looked at Tiger.

"How should I know?" Tiger asked. "I'm just a girl who likes selling cupcakes."

Abby noticed that Tiger smiled a knowing smile. Abby wondered why Tiger was smiling. It was kind of creepy, so Abby pushed the thought out of her mind.

"Never mind," Abby sighed.

Abby started to pace around in a circle. Was it hopeless? Maybe they could find Apple, but that would take a long time. He could be anywhere. She realized, so could the fourth relic and Ms. Arunis. She suddenly felt very tired.

"I need a nap," Abby announced.

"That's for babies!" Jill informed her. "Babies. Like the worm. I wonder what happened to Icapella."

"You *named* it?" Jadeine sounded disgusted. "Oh my gosh, Jill, you're so gross."

Jill simply shrugged. "Icapella's really sweet. And intelligent. And cute! And, hey, let me tell you a couple of reasons why…"

"Not now," Jadeine groaned. She slapped her cheek, her other cheek, both cheeks and then her forehead, like she had done at the hill. Abby and Jill traded looks of confusion.

"Yeah...that's weird. Back to the topic, people always get ideas when they're sleeping," Abby replied.

Abby walked around and found a bench. There was a brown paper bag on it, so Abby shoved it aside. She lay down on it and squeezed her eyes shut. She hadn't realized how tired she was. Abby instantly fell asleep.

She looked around. Abby was in a crystal room. She saw Apple in the center, and a woman who looked like The Sea Witch, but a little different. The woman left the room, and a man entered, that Abby had only ever seen in her dreams in the past 2 years, a person she thought she'd never see again.

Her father.

Apple and Abby's dad started talking.

"Dragon Island...I...prisoner..." Abby could only hear bits of what he was saying.

"Escape," Apple said.

Abby snapped awake. She gasped and struggled to catch her breath. When she did, she looked her friends in the eye.

"Guys," Abby breathed. "Who says dreams can't be real?"

Abby and everyone else looked at Jadeine, since she was a Dreamwalker. This time, Jadeine did know the answer.

"Well, some dreams aren't real, just figments of our imaginations. But, yes, some dreams are real," Jadeine said.

"Oh. My gosh," Abby said. "Would you say, if I wanted to see where Apple was and found out where he is in my dream, would the dream have actually happened in real life?"

Jadeine's eyes widened, and she nodded. "Those kinds of dreams are 100% real. Did you see him…?"

"OH MY GOSH, YES! I had a dream where I saw Apple in a place called Dragon Island. He's a prisoner, though, but still! I know where he is. And my dad, too!" Abby enthusiastically exclaimed.

"Yay!" Jill cheered. "We know where her dad is and where Apple is!"

"Don't cheer yet. We have to save them," Abby declared.

"But… how?" Tiger asked. "How can we get there?"

"I would start with the staff, but…" Abby trailed off.

"It's okay. We can find a transporter!" Jadeine suggested.

"What's that?" Abby asked.

"They're like magic airlines!" Jill exclaimed. "I met this one transporter once, she was super nice!"

"How do you find them?" Abby asked.

"Honestly? You just shout for them," Jadeine replied.

Abby looked around and closed her eyes. "TRANSPORTER! UH, WE NEED YOU!" Abby yelled.

Abby felt people staring at her and blushed. Had Jadeine and Jill pranked her? Because now was not the time for pranks. No person walked up to them and said they were a transporter. Abby sighed miserably.

"Don't be so sad. Transporters are always late. Personal experience," Jadeine said.

"Oh my gosh, Jadeine, that's so true." Tiger nodded. "When I was lost once, I called for this transporter and she arrived, like, 10 minutes late."

"I don't see anyone. Let's go around. Maybe she landed somewhere else," Abby frowned.

They turned around. All of a sudden, a woman was standing in front of them. She had the same color hair as Jadeine. She had feathers stuck in her hair and dozens of rainbow necklaces around her neck. The woman wore a blue toga and sandals. Abby squinted her eyes. This lady looked insane and like she came from a Greek history book.

"Oh, for heaven's sake, not her," Jadeine muttered, averting eye contact with the lady. She shuffled behind Abby and kept her head down.

"What's wrong, Jadeine?" Abby asked.

Jadeine shot her stink eye. Abby clicked the information together: Obviously, Jadeine didn't want to see this strange woman.

"Jadeine? Is that you? You're alive!" the woman gasped.

"Uhhhhhhh. Yes, Auntie," Jadeine answered, blushing, giving Abby the stink eye once more.

"She's your *aunt*?" Abby asked.

"Yeah…*she's crazy! I describe her as The Formidable Toga Lady, and you're in so much trouble*," Jadeine whispered. Abby just stared at Jadeine with a look of innocence.

"Don't try to hide anything, sweetie!" her aunt exclaimed.

"Um, anyway, I'm Abby, and we need to go to Dragon Island." Abby changed the subject.

"Well, that costs some gold coins! 7 to be exact," her aunt told them.

"Thanks for agreeing to take us! What's your name?" Abby asked.

"Ms. Everly Holdstein!" the woman replied.

Jadeine fished out 7 gold coins from her pocket and placed them in her aunt's palm. Her aunt closed her palm and then opened it. The coins were gone.

Ms. Everly asked them to place their hands in hers. All of them obliged. Abby squeezed her eyes closed as she felt her feet lift off the ground as they spiraled in circles. When the wind stopped, Abby opened her eyes. She was on a small beach with a lot of grass.

Ms. Everly squeezed Jadeine and planted a kiss on her cheek. "Goodbye, my little jade! Stay far away from dragons!" Then, she vanished.

"Well, let's find Apple!" Abby cried.

"She might be the cringiest aunt ever," Jadeine declared.

"Hey! I didn't know you hate her! Besides, your aunt seems pretty nice and she cares about you a lot!" Abby protested.

"I don't hate her!" Jadeine exclaimed, a hint of hurt in her voice. "She's just…really cringy."

They started walking. The sand was soft on Abby's feet. She squished her toes in it. The breeze tickled Abby's cheeks.

Jill whooped and ran into the waves. She splashed Abby.

"Hey!" Abby cried, but she was happy. She knew they were on a mission, but this felt like a vacation!

Jill laughed and walked back onto the sand. Her footprints stood out now because her feet were wet.

Then the group came to a big rock blocking the path. Abby was about to go around it, but then the rock…twitched?

Then, the "rock" shifted, and Abby could see scales gleaming on it. It wasn't a big rock…it was actually a dragon! She looked at the others, terrified.

Run, Jadeine mouthed silently. They all gladly complied.

Finally, they stopped at a large metal building. Abby searched for a door, but found none.

"There's no door," Abby glumly reported.

"Maybe there's a secret code?" Jadeine wondered.

"Um…open sesame!" Abby tried.

Nothing happened.

"Well, my dad said the most magical words are 'Thank You!'" Abby went on, undeterred.

The metal didn't budge an inch. Abby sighed.

"Great," Jill muttered sarcastically.

Tiger whirled on her. "Don't be like that!"

"Like what?"

"All sarcastic and negative!"

Jill huffed, opening her mouth to complain, but then they heard a roar and a scream. "Did you…hear that?" Jadeine asked.

Abby's first instinct was to run away, but then she realized it might be her father or Apple. She dashed in the direction of the sounds, the other on her heels.

Apple was standing there, holding a knife out in front of him.

There was also a dragon there…and it was prepared to open fire.

Chapter 22
Dragon Prisoner

20 minutes before Abby and the group arrived...

"Stop asking. I already told you."

"Are you sure?" Apple asked again.

Jay groaned. "I already told you! The doors are locked by magic. The dragons will kill us even if we find a way out! What more do you want?"

Apple sighed. "I want to go save my sister. Don't you want to get out?"

"Of course!" Jay moaned.

"How long have you been stuck here?" Apple asked.

"Two years!" Jay cried. "Two years of trying to find a secret exit and failing!"

"Pardon me."

Apple and Jay both whirled around. Darya was standing at the door. She had returned. "I heard you talking...if you really want a way out, Prince Apple, there is one way."

Jay groaned. "Not that! Don't ask him that!"

"What do I do?" Apple asked immediately.

Darya laughed gleefully. "I will let both of you leave if you..." She paused for suspense.

"What? Tell me!" Apple was impatient.

"On the other side of the island, by the caves, there is a dragon. Fifty-one of the fifty-two dragons on the island obey me, but that one doesn't. I hate it!"

"What do you want me to do?" Apple asked nervously.

"Kill it! Obviously!"

Apple frowned. He didn't like killing animals…when his father asked him to go hunting for deer, he always declined. (So did Cherry, but Apple suspected she just didn't want to get dirty.) On the other hand… "What if I can't kill it?"

Darya smiled. "Then my fifty-one obeying dragons kill you—and Jay."

"Don't do it!" Jay pleaded. "It's impossible. She told me that, too…"

"You're not dead," Apple noted.

"Her terms were different then. My sentence was ten years. She told me she would free me right away if I killed it, but she would never let me leave if I failed…and I did!"

Apple bit his lip. "Uh…how much time do I get?"

Darya considered. "How about…two hours?"

Apple thought it over. It was extremely risky. But he raised his chin in determination. "I'll do it."

"No!" Jay groaned.

Darya clasped her hands together. "Great! Off you go!"

"Wait!" Apple yelped. "Don't I get weapons?"

Darya sighed. Then she snapped her fingers together, and a knife appeared in Apple's hand. "Here you go. That can bring down a dragon if stabbed right."

Apple took a deep breath. He could do this!

Apple couldn't do this.

He was standing in front of the most beautiful creature he had ever seen in his life. He looked at the knife, and then back at the dragon.

The disobedient dragon was lying on her side, fast asleep. There were no scales on her belly—it was her weak spot. Apple could easily do it, physically. He could jab the knife into her stomach and end her life forever.

Mentally? He couldn't do this. The dragon was beautiful. Her scales were white and sparkled dazzlingly when the sun hit them. She hadn't done anything wrong. Why should he kill her?

Apple could easily imagine killing a human. He had done it before.

Apple's eyes brimmed with tears as he remembered the day he met Elyse. He was eleven years old.

Elyse was the child-eating witch who almost ate Hansel and Gretel. She had shown up at the palace, wanting to kill Apple's mother.

Apple's mother had cowered in the space behind the stairs. She had motioned for Cherry and Apple to come with her.

But Apple had known Elyse would find them eventually—she had only been in the next room. So he had smashed a staff that had been resting against the wall through the display box that held a beautiful knife.

That knife was only meant for decoration. Not for actual fighting, but Apple's mom had said it worked perfectly fine.

When Elyse stormed in, it was as if Apple's hand had moved without him meaning to. A moment later, Elyse was dead on the floor.

Apple had dropped the knife and stared at her, stunned. Had he done that?

When the police asked questions, Snow White had lied and said she had done it herself. Apple knew why she had lied. Even if Apple had killed a villain, Snow White thought that some people may speak bad of him if they knew he had murdered Elyse. He murdered a villain, but that still defined him as a murderer. And everyone would be wary of a child being a murderer, because all the adults had it stuck in their heads that kids below 19 were irresponsible and not trustworthy enough. Murderer. That's what I am, Apple thought. But he didn't want to be one. So he wasn't going to be one.

Apple dropped the knife. "I can't do it. I won't do it," he whispered out loud.

"You are an honorable young man, Prince Apple."

Apple whirled around. A woman was standing there. She had dark skin and dark hair, which was woven into many beaded braids. Her eyes were dark green. She was beautiful. "Who are you?" Apple yelled.

The woman smiled. "I have many names. The one you may most likely know is Sleeping Beauty."

Apple's eyes widened. She was dead…wasn't she? "You can't be. You died five years ago."

She smiled. "Did I? You can call me Crystal."

Apple couldn't believe his eyes. "I…why did you call me honorable?" She wouldn't say that if she knew what I did to Elyse, he thought.

"You refused to kill the dragon," she explained. "Although you knew your life was at stake."

"That's the problem!" Apple exploded. Something about Crystal made him want to spill everything to her. "I can't kill her, but if I don't by—" he glanced at his watch—"7:25, I die! So does Jay Palmer!"

Crystal sighed. "Such is life. Decisions between yourself and someone else…or two other people."

Apple dropped his gaze. "What do I do?"

"That's up to you," Crystal told him. "You kill the dragon, you and Jay go free, but a life is lost. If you don't kill the dragon, you and Jay will die. If you escape and swim away, then, well, you don't know what might happen."

Apple blinked. "Swim away?" He turned his head, and sure enough, he could see land in the distance.

"That is Rapunzel's kingdom," Crystal went on. "Darya was exiled here as a punishment. This way, Rapunzel could keep an eye on her, but Darya wouldn't be too close. She cannot leave unless it's mail. Honestly, I don't think she should even be allowed to go and get mail. But, I suppose Rapunzel prioritizes mail. Ever since she was stuck in that tower and not able to write a letter to the outside world."

Apple sighed heavily and sat down in the sand next to the knife. When he looked up again, Crystal was gone. Apple wondered if he had been hallucinating. But no, her footprints were in the sand.

Apple stared at the dragon for about ten minutes. No brainwave came to him. He closed his eyes, wishing he had never met Abby, so he wouldn't have to do this. Wishing that he had stayed put in the castle and never left.

No. Apple didn't wish that, not in his heart. He realized he truly wanted to defeat Lizzie. But he couldn't because he was going to die here. With Abby's father! He had failed them all.

Just then, Apple heard a roar. His eyes flew open, and he screamed, pointing his knife at the source of the sound.

The dragon was awake.

Chapter 23
All Confusion and No Privacy

Apple had blown it.

He was going to die! And then Darya would kill Jay. He had failed Abby, Cherry, and everyone!

Then Abby came running. Jill, Jadeine, and Tiger were right behind her.

"Abby!" Apple yelled.

"Apple! Hi!" Abby exclaimed. "Are you still a prisoner or something?"

"Uh…how did you know that? Uh, but we've got bigger problems right now," Apple muttered, eyeing the dragon. "Like, literally."

They all noticed the dragon and looked at it in terror. "What do we do?" Tiger cried.

"Kill it!" Jill suggested.

"No!" Apple screamed. "You can't kill her! And she's not an it!"

Jill looked at Abby like, *Can you believe this guy?*

"You had no problem killing Elyse," Tiger blurted, then immediately clapped a hand over her mouth.

Apple choked and almost dropped his knife. "Wha—how do you know that?"

"Uhh…" Tiger squeaked. "Well. It's complicated."

"Who's Elyse?" Abby wanted to know.

"I thought Snow White killed Elyse!" Jill looked back and forth between Apple and Tiger.

"Guys?" Jadeine shouted. "Apple was right! We have bigger problems!"

The dragon opened its mouth wide. Apple closed his eyes, knowing it was about to burn him to a crisp.

Only…the fire never came. Then he felt a weird tickling sensation.

Apple opened his eyes. Everyone was gaping at him. And the dragon was *licking his face!*

Darya appeared next to the dragon. "Well done, all of you!"

"I thought I was supposed to kill her!" Apple cried. He was really confused.

Darya shook her head. "No." Then something happened to her. She transformed into Crystal!

"Crystal!" Apple gasped. "You're Darya? I mean, Darya is you? I mean…what?"

Crystal smiled. The others looked even more confused than Apple. "Darya was never here—she got eaten by a dragon a year ago. Then I came along. I never really wanted you to kill Lumi—that's the dragon. I was testing you to see if you are ready for the circumstances ahead. Then I could give you my gift."

"Um. You can't just randomly snatch me and imprison me!" Apple exclaimed. "You didn't need to do that!"

"I was also testing you on other things," Crystal explained. "Maybe I could have been a little gentler."

"Um, thanks, I guess," Apple muttered.

"What's the gift?" Tiger asked.

"Wait!" Abby cried. "What about my father?"

"He was imprisoned by Darya two years ago, before I got here," Crystal explained. "He made a bad deal with her. She never plays fair—she loves blackmail. She made a deal with Rapunzel's parents, too, remember? Unfortunately, I can't break that spell—only someone really powerful can."

Abby's shoulders slumped.

"Now, come on, y'all! Let's go!" Crystal spun on her heel and started walking towards the safe room. Lumi the dragon bounded beside Apple—she kind of reminded him of an eager puppy.

As they walked, Apple filled Abby and the others in on what had happened on the island.

"Were you disguised as Ms. Arunis, too, Crystal?" Jadeine called.

Crystal nodded. "Yes, I was!"

"There's something I still don't get…" Abby walked up to Crystal. Apple followed her.

"Yes, my dear?" Crystal asked.

"Are you a keeper?"

Crystal shook her head. "No. Lizzie killed Ms. Arunis, so I took the relic to my fairy godmother for safekeeping. But I have some things I think you'll want."

Abby leaned in to Apple. "What do you think she has?"

He shrugged. "Who knows?"

By now, the others had caught up to them, too. "How did you know about the Elyse thing?" Apple asked Tiger.

"I know many things," Tiger said ominously.

"Like what?" Apple pressed his lips together. "You're just a village girl! How could you know that?"

"Am I a village girl?"

Apple scowled. "What did you do to Elyse?" Jill asked curiously.

Apple crossed his arms. "Not important."

"It's *very* important," Tiger informed him. Then, Tiger proceeded to tell everyone about what happened. Apple grew angrier with every word.

"HOW DO YOU KNOW THAT?!" he exploded when she finished. "YOU COULDN'T! THERE WERE ONLY FOUR PEOPLE IN THE ROOM WHEN THAT HAPPENED, AND YOU WEREN'T ONE OF THEM!"

"There's no need for yelling," Crystal chastised him gently.

"THERE IS A NEED FOR YELLING! WHAT IN THE WORLD, TIGER?!"

"You're right, there were only four people in the room when that happened."

"Then how do you know?"

"I...I read your thoughts."

Apple opened his mouth and then stopped. "Wait, what?!"

Tiger sighed. "Once upon a time, there was a witch. She had two daughters, Isabella and Liliana. They could all do magic. Then the witch's husband died, so she remarried. Her new husband had a daughter—Cinderella. After the whole ball incident, the Fairy Godfather punished Isabella and Liliana to stay young forever. Isabella ran away to Snow White's kingdom and changed her name to Tiger."

Jill gasped. "You're one of Cinderella's stepsisters!"

"And you can do magic!" Abby realized. "That's how you read Apple's thoughts."

Apple was fuming. "I don't care how she did it! She did it willingly, without permission!" He marched in front of the group, followed by Lumi. He marched forward without a backward glance.

"I'm sorry! I really am!" Tiger yelped.

"Then why did you do it?" Apple asked.

"A lot of people think Cinderella's stepsisters are evil. I… I wanted to know if you hated me, too, even though you didn't know who I am. I wanted you to be my friend. And…sometimes I have a problem with blurting things out. I didn't think you would mind that I told them that–I think killing Elyse was a brave thing to do. "

Apple slowed. Now he felt bad!

Tiger looked at Apple with tears in her eyes. "I hope you can forgive me…"

"I can't!" Apple snapped.

Apple was never going to talk to Tiger again.

Chapter 24
Reunion

Abby wanted to see her father so badly that she felt like every second she didn't see him was like being pulled into a black hole—being stretched like spaghetti. But a part of her felt uneasy.

A little voice in her head whispered, *What if he's super different?*

So when they reached the safe room, Abby hung back as the others filed in. She listened to them talk:

"Who are you guys?" Jay wanted to know.

"I'm Jill, and she's Jadeine and she's Tiger," Jill chirped. "You know Apple already."

"And…where did Abby go?" Apple peeked his head around the door. "Abby, c'mon."

Abby stepped into the room. Her heart threatened to burst, like bubbles floating up into the sky.

"Is that really you, Abby?" Jay gasped.

"Dad…" Abby breathed.

Jay ran to the center of the room and swooped Abby up in a big hug. Abby willed herself not to get too emotional.

"Are you alright?" Jay asked.

"Yes, but are *you* okay?" Abby asked.

"I mean, I'm not cuffed," Jay joked.

"Also, have you been properly introduced to my friends?" Abby inquired.

"I know their names," Jay replied. "And I met Apple before you all came."

They pulled apart, and Jay rested his hands on his daughters' shoulders.

"And how's your mom?" Jay asked.

"Um…bewitched, but she got free and spoke up to Lizzie," Abby told him.

"That's awesome! Is she here too?"

"No, I couldn't find her."

"Well, how do we leave? Are we free?"

"I'm sorry, you can't just leave." Crystal appeared.

"Um, why?" Apple asked. "I did what you asked!"

Crystal sighed. "You all don't understand. You can't just defeat Lizzie by collecting the relics. There's more."

"Like what?"

"Like the prophecy. You can't just collect the relics. You need to get the Book of Light. Then you need to use their powers. I don't know how, but…you just do. Oh, and you have to sacrifice someone."

"I know who'll be sacrificed," Apple muttered, glaring at Tiger.

Tiger whimpered and moved farther away into a corner.

Abby stared hard at Apple. Suddenly, it felt like she was falling into a pit. Apple's voice whispered into her mind.

I really, really hate Tiger. I mean, what made her tell? There wasn't any reason! Couldn't she have, at the very least, just kept quiet? Apple thought.

Abby snapped out of it. Apple was mad, really mad, but *Abby could read MINDS!* Just like Tiger. She didn't know if it was a bad thing or a good thing. Abby decided not to try and read Apple's mind, or anyone's. It was an invasion of privacy.

Abby decided to see if Tiger could hear her thoughts.

Uh. Tiger, can you hear me? Abby directed her thoughts at Tiger.

ABBY?! Abby heard Tiger's startled voice, except it wasn't really Tiger's voice, it was her thoughts. *Since when do you have my abilities?*

Uhhhh. Since a long time ago? Maybe. I don't know. I just discovered it.

Oh. Huh, it's like our own secret way of talking!

Yeah! Abby smiled.

"Crystal, do you have the relic?" Abby asked.

"No, not now," she answered. "I'd have to ask my fairy godmother. But, I can retrieve it for you."

"Thanks, Crystal. So, Dad, we'll go get the relics and come back when we get them!" Abby announced.

"At least stay a day!" Jay pleaded.

"Sorry, but H.E.A.L is on the line," Abby declared. She really didn't want to leave her father, but if she hesitated at all, she would have a total meltdown. Better to pretend she didn't care. *Be valiant, Abby!*

Abby stayed behind as the others filed out of the room. She looked at her dad one final time.

"Abby?" Jadeine called from outside. "You coming?"

Abby started to leave, but then Crystal yelled, "WAIT! ALL OF YOU! THERE'S SOMETHING ELSE!"

She ran outside with them. "Come on back with me," she told them.

They followed Crystal around the building. At the back was a tree, and chained to the tree was…Aeryn!

Abby screamed and backed away.

"No!" Aeryn yelled. "Come back! I need to talk to you!"

"No, traitor!" Jill shouted.

"Don't worry," Crystal soothed. "He's tied to the tree; he can't hurt you."

Abby saw it was true; Aeryn's hands were tied down and all. "How did you get out of the curse? Since you betrayed us once, and you were about to betray us twice?"

"After you guys left, Lizzie came by. She un-enchanted me and ordered me to go and find y'all. I tried, but then Crystal caught me."

Apple sighed. "We should have known."

They should have. That meddling Lizzie!

"So?" Jadeine asked. "Is that all?"

Aeryn shook his head. "I found out something important!"

"Yes?" Jill prompted.

"A lot of people want revenge."

"Like who?" Abby asked.

"The Merqueen, for stealing her relic. Then there's Pinocchio's father, because your mom turned his kid into a tree."

Abby frowned. "She turned Pinocchio into a tree?"

"He was already made of a tree," Tiger pointed out.

"Yeah, but like a *tree* tree," Apple explained.

"A *tree* tree?" Abby asked.

"Can we just get a move on?" Apple pleaded.

Jadeine nodded. "Yeah. He's right, come on."

The group started walking, and then Abby realized something. "Wait. How will we get off the island? And didn't you say you had the relic?"

"Lumi knows where it is! She'll fly you!" Crystal suggested.

"Lumi the dragon?" Apple gasped.

"Of course! Is there another Lumi?" Crystal asked.

"How do we do that?" Jill asked. She looked at Apple. So did everyone else.

"Why is everyone looking at me?" he protested.

"She's *your* dragon," Abby reasoned.

Apple sighed. "How should I know?"

"Maybe we just climb on her?" Jill suggested. She gingerly placed one foot on Lumi's back.

Lumi didn't like that at all. She screeched, shoving Jill off of her. Lumi curled her wing around Apple instead.

"See? Your dragon!" Jadeine told him.

Apple groaned. "Uh…what do we do, though?"

Crystal, laughing, came over. "It's easy." She showed them how to climb on the dragon without hurting her.

"Now, off!" Crystal told Lumi.

Abby screamed as Lumi took off at a slanted angle. The wind whipped her face as they went up and up and up…Apple, sitting behind her, gripped her shoulders so tightly she knew it would bruise when they got off.

Just when she thought it couldn't get worse, Lumi dived *down.* Apple's face snapped forward into Abby's back, and this time she was the one clutching Jill's shoulders.

Right before Lumi was about to crash land in the water, she pulled out of her nosedive and landed gracefully on the shore. With her tail, she picked Apple off and placed him gently on the ground. Then she reared back, causing everyone else to slide off her back.

Abby groaned and rolled over to her friends. Lumi was licking Apple's face now.

"Is this Rapunzel's kingdom?" Jadeine wondered.

"I think so," Apple replied, wiping dragon slobber off his face. "There's Rapunzel's tower in the distance."

"Is *this* where the relic is?" Abby asked.

"I don't think so," Apple said. "I think Lumi just needs some rest."

"And how do you know?" Tiger asked quietly.

Apple didn't want to answer her question, but the rest of them looked like they wanted the answer, so he gave in. "I think I have a special connection with Lumi."

"Oh! That's neat," Jill said.

Abby looked, and sure enough, a tower loomed above everything else. With a start, she realized it was getting dark out. "Wanna sleep here, guys?"

The grass was pretty soft. "Sure," Jadeine replied, curling up.

Abby lay awake for a while, wondering if they could ever defeat Lizzie. And hoping, with all her heart, she would defeat Lizzie and get her dad out of the Dragon Island prison.

Chapter 25
Ismelda

"WAKE UP, SLEEPYHEADS!"

Abby screamed and sat up. Jill was laughing hysterically next to her.

"Do you always wake people up like that?" Tiger groaned.

Jill nodded. "Every time."

Apple got to his feet. "Ugh, no thanks, Jill. I was having a great dream…"

"Where to next?" Tiger asked.

Jadeine ticked everything off on her fingers. "Let's see…we need the first relic back from wherever it is, the fourth relic and the fifth relic. We also need to figure out which sets of relics are the fake ones."

"And we need to find Cherry," Apple reminded her.

Jadeine nodded. "That too."

"What about Nadine?" Tiger put in. "She's out for blood."

"We'll defeat her if she gets here," Jill suggested. "She's evil."

"Not entirely!" Apple countered. "You three betrayed her first."

Before she could stop herself, Abby muttered, "You're one to talk."

"What?" Apple whirled on her.

"Nothing!" Abby cried.

Apple shook his head, scowling. "You said, 'You're one to talk.' Look, if this is about the Elyse thing—"

She couldn't stop herself. Right now, all she saw was a murderer in front of her. "You're a killer! How do we know we can trust you?"

Something in Apple's eyes changed. "What? Why are you calling me a murderer? I was defending myself then!"

"I can't trust you anymore! I don't care!" Abby shot back. She might have kept yelling, but then she realized Apple was crying.

"I can't stay around here," he wailed. He looked at Tiger. "I trusted you too…I was wrong. I'm sorry."

"Wrong about what?" Jadeine asked.

"When Crystal told us someone had to be sacrificed, I said it should be Tiger…" Apple wiped his eyes. "I was wrong. It should be me…you're right, Abby. I'm a murderer…"

"What?" Abby cried. "No! That's not what I…"

Apple shook his head. "I'm sorry. I can't stay here anymore. Goodbye!" Then, he ran off into the forest.

"Wait!" Tiger cried. "Apple, you're not a murderer! You're a great friend! Come back!"

There was no answer. Abby sank to the ground. "Omigosh…"

"Omigosh is right!" Jill spun and looked at Abby. "Did you just offend Prince Apple?"

"I just…" Abby started, but Jill wouldn't let her finish her sentence.

"You're such a Snoopy McSnoop face! How come you get all the cool stuff? You get a prophecy, and you just act so rude all the time! Ugh! Bye, Abby! See you in millennia!" Jill exclaimed.

With that, she turned and marched off in the direction Apple had gone.

"I won't be mean anymore, I was just scared, and I'm sorry!" Abby was desperate. " I don't like getting mad at people!"

"Yeah, and you're just being mean in front of Apple when we're not even talking about the Elyse thing? And it's not on purpose? Ha!" Jill called over her shoulder. "You *always* want to!"

Abby groaned. She half-expected Jadeine to run off, too, but she stayed next to Abby and Tiger, massaging her forehead wearily.

"What next?" Tiger asked halfheartedly.

Jadeine shrugged. "We go after one of the other relics?"

"Which one?" Abby wondered. "The staff is working with Lizzie. We have the tiara and the scepter. The fourth relic wasn't with Crystal at the moment. The fifth…we don't know where that is either."

"I don't know," Jadeine admitted.

"Why don't we ask around?" Tiger suggested. "See if anyone else knows."

"Okay," Abby agreed. Jadeine nodded too, so they set off in the direction of town.

When they reached there, Abby noticed the same thing as in Cinderella Town—everyone had a symbol. The only thing different was that instead of a slipper, these people's symbol was a tower identical to the one in the distance.

"Hey!" Tiger called to a man walking down the street. "Do you know where any of the relics are?"

He stared at them. "What?!"

"There's a prophecy!" Abby informed him.

His confusion turned to concern. "Did you hit your head?"

Jadeine sighed. "Come on, guys."

"How does he not know?" Abby wondered. "I thought everyone knew about the prophecy."

"Rapunzel's kingdom is pretty cut off from the others," Jadeine explained. "He might not have heard about the prophecy."

"Um. 20 years since the prophecy was first out in the world, and they *still* don't know?" Abby asked.

Next, they approached an old lady sitting outside a giant shoe.

She, Abby, figured, was the Old Lady Who Lived in a Shoe.

"Hello," Jadeine greeted the old lady.

"Hello, sweetheart," the lady replied. "May I help you?"

"Yes, actually," Abby told her. "We're looking for the relics. Do you…"

The old lady's scream cut her off. Abby jumped back, startled.

"THESE GIRLS ARE WORKING WITH LIZZIE!" the old lady shrieked. "RUN!"

"What? No, ma'am, that's not…" Abby got cut off by Tiger.

"RUN, ABBY, RUN!!!" Tiger yelled.

The man from earlier bravely ran after Abby, Tiger, and Jadeine. They ran as fast as they could and finally shook him off.

Abby stopped. They were in the same forest Apple and Jill had run into, she realized. "Well, that was a big fail."

Jadeine laughed. "Yeah, we didn't think that through."

"Why does Lizzie want the relics?" Tiger asked. "They're supposed to defeat her, right?"

"They weren't made specifically for that purpose," Jadeine explained. "The Book of Light was made to be more powerful than the most powerful thing in the two worlds. And Lizzie already knows where that is…so if she gets her hands on the Book of Light…she'll be undefeatable."

Abby shivered. "Yikes. Who will Lizzie sacrifice?"

Jadeine smiled. "That's the cool part. The person who gets sacrificed must do so willingly, with no blackmail or bribery involved. So whoever she sacrifices will have to truly believe in Lizzie."

Abby wondered who would do that. Not the Big Bad Wolf, surely…so who?

Abby opened her mouth, but she was interrupted by a crash from behind. She spun around.

Nadine was standing there.

Abby was gaping. Jadeine held up her right arm, then realized she had no staff, and set it down.

"Chop, chop! Come on, let's go!" Nadine exclaimed in a hurried tone.

"Why?" Abby asked.

"Because the Merqueen says so," Nadine replied, raising her chin.

"Well, you can't control us, so bye," Abby shot back.

"I. Order. You!" Nadine shrieked.

Jadeine grabbed Abby and Tiger's hands and ran. Jadeine looked over her shoulder and gasped.

"That's no Merqueen! That's Lizzie!" Jadeine exclaimed.

Abby looked back, but didn't see Lizzie/Nadine. She slowed a bit and mulled over what had just happened.

I willingly read Apple's mind. I didn't force myself to. Abby thought.

Abby let go of Jadeine's hand. "ABBY!" Tiger yelled. "What are you doing?"

Lizzie jumped from the top of a tall tree (wow, who knew Lizzie could do that?) and landed in front of Abby with a glowing purple rope. It looked rough and sturdy. Abby didn't want to get tied up—the rope looked itchy and thick.

"Let me guess, Devil's Knot?" Abby asked, remembering Aeryn.

"No. Lizzie's Rope," Lizzie answered. "Because I made it. Get it?" She laughed.

Tiger pulled Abby away from Lizzie. Tiger kicked Lizzie as hard as she could in the stomach. Lizzie crumpled, and Jadeine yelled as loud as she could.

"STAFF!" Jadeine called out.

Jadeine's voice echoed. But…it wasn't what she had shouted.

"THE STAFF IS IN THE MEADOW OF H.E.G.R.S," Jadeine's voice echoed back.

"Meadow of H.E.G.R.S?" Abby asked, panting.

"We refer to the founder of magic as H.E.G.R.S, Headmistress of Evil and Good, Relics and Sorcery," Jadeine explained. "We have to go find it."

"AIEEE! YOU'LL PAY FOR KICKING ME, YOU INSOLENT CHILD!!!" Lizzie screeched, bent over in pain.

Lizzie tried to run after them, but Jadeine, quick as lightning, grabbed Abby's backpack and ran up to Lizzie. Abby couldn't believe Jadeine was giving up…until she realized that Jadeine wasn't. Jadeine gripped Abby's bag tight and whacked Lizzie with it. Then, she ran back to Abby.

"Let's go!" Jadeine cried.

They started running, but Lizzie caught up with them in a matter of seconds. And she was furious. Abby folded her hands into fists, then unclenched them. She thrust forward her arm and squeezed her eyes shut, concentrating hard.

"Immobilize Lizzie, immobilize Lizzie…" Abby chanted.

A bright beam of light shot out of her hand and hit Lizzie. Lizzie tried to duck, but it was too late. She stayed frozen in place, teeth gritted and eyes filled with hatred.

"Let's go, before my spell wears off!" Abby exclaimed.

They didn't need to be told twice. They ran until they found Lumi there. Lumi looked around and then gazed at Abby distastefully.

"Uh-oh. Lumi doesn't like me because I made Apple sad," Abby realized. "Actually, she only likes Apple! Oh no…"

"WATCH OUT!"

Lumi flew away, her tail slapping Abby's chest on purpose. Abby got knocked over and fell on the grass. She sat up, groaning.

"Great, there goes our only ride," Abby sighed.

"Unfortunate." Jadeine clicked her tongue against her teeth.

"Maybe, we can ask a relic for help?" Abby suggested.

"Great idea!" Tiger exclaimed.

Abby pulled out the tiara.

"Um, tiara? We could use a little help now," Abby whispered.

"A fairy godmother will come your way. Prepare," the tiara responded in an angelic voice.

"Prepare," Tiger echoed. "Huh, that sounds unsettling,"

Abby heard a flapping sound behind her and whirled around. A shimmering fairy landed on the soil. The fairy had golden wings and a matching golden dress. She also had brown skin and frizzy, black hair.

"Hello, dears, I'm Ismelda, your fairy godmother. Need anything?" the fairy asked in a sweet tone.

"We do! We need to get to Cinderella Town!" Tiger cried.

"Wait a second. Are you working with Lizzie?" Ismelda frowned.

"No! Not at all!" Abby exclaimed.

"Well! In that case, let's go!" Ismelda cheered. *Are all fairies so trusting?* Abby wondered.

Ismelda snapped her fingers, and they were back in Cinderella Town. Ismelda smiled. Abby noticed that Ismelda's dress was now half-silver, half-gold. But…hadn't it been fully golden when she had arrived?

"Your dress changed color," Abby said.

"It did!?" Ismelda yelped.

"Yeah…wait a second…" Abby murmured as she noticed more of the dress became silver. *What if she's not who she claims to be?* Abby thought. "Who are you, really?"

"Glad you asked." Ismelda smiled. Not in a happy way. But in a cruel, knowing way.

Ismelda's dress turned completely silver, and her hair turned white. She narrowed her eyes, and her smile faded altogether.

"I'm an outcast. People call me a bad fairy," Ismelda explained. "Like your mother. Except she's called *the* bad fairy."

"How do you know my mom is the bad fairy? I mean, she's not really bad, but how do you know?" Abby asked, panicked.

"I'm a mind-reader, just like you, except way more advanced. There's nothing about you that I don't know." Ismelda smiled in that cruel, knowing way again. It looked like an evil smile.

Abby now knew how horrible it felt to have all your secrets revealed to a stranger. Her heart dropped to her shoes, and her insides felt a sudden rush of coldness. With a pang of guilt, she thought about how Apple had felt. Abby felt tears in the corners of her eyes. *How could Ismelda be so cruel and do that? How?* Abby thought. Had Apple felt like that when Abby had called him a murderer? Knowing that your secret was out…and then having people use it against you…that must have felt horrible.

"Still feeling glum about your friends?" Ismelda asked, twirling her hair.

"Yeah." Abby bit her lip, and then her stomach did a backflip. Why was she telling stuff to this strange, unfriendly fairy? Her mind went back to thinking about how Apple must have felt. She regretted yelling at him and reading his mind even more now, and she wanted to throw up.

"You're regretful about reading Apple's mind and yelling at him," Ismelda noticed. "I don't get why. Me? I don't regret anything. You haven't realized the joy of mind reading."

"So, which side are you on?" Abby whispered. "Ours or Lizzie's?"

"Honey, you'll know in time." Ismelda flashed a toothy grin. "Maybe I'm on yours, maybe on Lizzie's side. Maybe I'm just neutral and don't care about this silly race for the relics at all. *Maybe.*"

"Wow, that's ominous." Tiger shuddered.

"Well, bye! See you at the final battle," Ismelda chirped. "Maybe."

Abby's eyes widened as Ismelda vanished. She turned to see Crystal standing behind them.

"AIEEE! HOW LONG WERE YOU BEHIND US?!" Abby exclaimed.

"Were you Ismelda, too?!" Tiger wanted to know.

"I wasn't," Crystal replied. "Ismelda is my cousin. Honestly, just because I tricked you, what, two times? Yes, two times. Just because I tricked you two times doesn't mean I'll *always* trick you."

"She's your cousin?! Is she evil?" Jadeine asked.

"No, but she isn't truthful most times except about who she is," Crystal explained.

"Oh, so is she a fairy godmother?" Abby queried.

"Yes, but she is the worst one," Crystal sighed.

"You remind me of someone…" Abby trailed off.

"Oh! Did Apple not tell you?" Crystal asked, dismayed.

"I can't believe you don't recognize her. She's Sleeping Beauty. The most powerful and able queen of all," Jadeine whispered.

"No need to keep anything a secret, dears," Crystal told them. Jadeine blushed.

"Um, where's the fourth relic?" Abby asked. "Do you have it?"

"Yes, as a matter of fact, I do have it for you!" Crystal exclaimed.

Crystal put her hand into a leathery orange satchel, which Abby was certain hadn't been there before. She handed them a pair of red shoes. Abby immediately recognized them.

"Are those the shoes that make people dance even if they don't want to?" Abby asked.

"Yes. Ms. Arunis is the girl in that story," Crystal explained.

"Really? I've never heard of this story before, so can you tell us?" Tiger requested.

"Sure." Crystal agreed. "Long ago, a girl named Ruby lived with her mother. She had everything she needed—food, a warm bed—but she was very ungrateful. Ruby was walking with her mother one day when she saw a pair of pretty red shoes in the window display. She wanted to have it so badly, but they were poor, so they couldn't afford it. Ruby was so upset! After her mother died, Ruby moved in with her grandmother. Her grandmother, who was rich but kind, bought her the shoes, but kept her from wearing them too much. Ruby was satisfied until her grandmother saw a homeless girl on the street who had no shoes and gave her Ruby's new red shoes. Ruby was so mad, she ran away and started her own business by stealing pears and apples from the market. Years later, she saw the same red shoes lying on the ground, so she picked them up and kept them. When she was a teenager, she was invited to go to a ball. She also wore her precious red shoes. When it was time to dance, she danced wildly. She got tired, but she wasn't able to stop dancing! She danced and danced all night, trying to take off her shoes, but to no avail. The next day, she managed to stop dancing and take off her shoes. Ruby became the laughingstock of the village for a long time, and Ruby's story was heard throughout the land."

"Wow, that's sad. Was she a nice person, though?" Abby asked.

"She aimed to be. She was a little selfish at times," Crystal replied.

"So…not a very generous lady who karate kicks people trying to arrest innocent children?" Abby asked.

"Definitely not! That's me!" Crystal laughed.

"Can I try it on?" Abby asked.

"If you are selfish or mean, you'll be cursed like Ruby," Crystal warned.

Abby realized something: now was the time to test if she was really a bad person for reading Apple's thoughts! She nodded.

Crystal handed her the red shoes. Warily, Abby slipped them on…and nothing happened. They remained normal shoes. Abby exhaled with relief.

"I bet Aeryn would have to dance. Maybe tap dancing!" Jadeine remarked. Abby giggled at the thought of Aeryn tap dancing in front of them. She took the shoes off and handed them back to Crystal.

"Now we just need one more!" Tiger chirped, trying to sound peppy.

Abby nodded. "Yup. Where to next?"

They all looked at Crystal, but Crystal shook her head. "I am sorry. I can't be of any more help." With that, she vanished.

Abby groaned. "Ugh! Is it just me, or do people always vanish when they're really needed?"

"Not just you. Why don't we go find Apple and Jill?" Jadeine suggested.

"Okay!" Tiger agreed.

So the group set off in the direction of their missing friends.

Chapter 26
It Never Gets Less Dangerous

They found Apple rather quickly.

After only a couple of minutes of walking, they heard his voice echo from within the trees.

"Abby? Is that you?" His voice sounded scratchy, like he had been crying. Which he probably had.

Abby ran around the corner, Tiger and Jadeine on her heels. Apple was sitting on a tree stump. His face was smeared with dirt, there were leaves in his hair, a new bruise on his forehead, and red-rimmed eyes. He sniffed and wiped his eyes with his sleeve.

"Apple, what happened?" Jadeine asked. "Did you fall in some dirt or meet a wild animal or…"

"I'm fine. Really. Just tripped over some branches," Apple answered, sounding the exact opposite of fine. "I'm okay."

The group all knew that while Apple said he was okay, he was definitely not okay. An awkward silence followed this, while everyone wondered whether to bring their huge fight up or just pretend like it had never happened.

Apple chose the first option. "Look, Tiger, I'm sorry I got so mad. I shouldn't have."

She smiled. "What are you even apologizing for? I'm the one who should be sorry. I shouldn't have read your mind in the first place."

"Neither should I have," Abby put in. "I'm so, so sorry."

"Hey, Apple? Did you mean that about sacrificing yourself?" Jadeine asked quietly. The mood changed, and they all got quiet.

Apple hesitated. He opened his mouth and then decided to change the subject. "Uh, speaking of Jill…"

"We weren't," Tiger pointed out.

"Where's Jill?" Apple asked.

Abby groaned. "She got mad, too. She told me I was a Snoopy McSnoop face, and she couldn't stay anymore."

"Snoopy McSnoop face?" Apple furrowed his eyebrows, then a slight smile appeared on his face.

Apple was obviously trying not to laugh. He clamped his hand over his mouth.

Tiger didn't have as good control. She burst out laughing.

Abby tried to look stern, but then she gave in. They all ended up standing there laughing. The awkwardness went away.

Then something shocking happened. Tiger stepped forward and threw her arms around Apple. "You're my best friend," she declared.

Apple was blushing so hard it looked like someone had scribbled all over his face with a red marker.

The noise of metal tapping against a tree caught their attention. Jay, the staff! He stopped banging against the tree.

"Isn't that the staff?" Apple asked.

"It is!" Abby cried. She grabbed the staff. "Traitor!"

"Wait!" the staff protested. He twisted in Abby's grip, but she held on tight. "Let me go!" he wailed.

"Talk first!" Abby warned. "Or I'll break you in half!" Of course, she couldn't *really* break him because he was a relic, but he seemed to believe it.

"I broke free from the curse Lizzie put on me–it wasn't that strong, only a simple spell–and then I flew back here, and along the way I heard some news you might want to know," he replied. "It's about your mom, Abby!"

"Mom?" Abby dropped all pretenses of being threatening.

"Yeah! This guy, Geppeto…he's mad at her for killing his son! He's out for blood! You better find her."

"How do we know you're not lying?" Abby tightened her grip on the staff.

He squirmed a bit. "Um…"

"I thought so," Abby growled.

A sound that sounded like wings flapping descended upon them. Abby whirled around and saw 5 dragons. Lumi was leading the group. There was a dragon with scales that looked like the sunset, a shimmery blue dragon, a giant green dragon and a small purple dragon. She looked like a runt.

"Hello, I'm back," Lumi said.

"How can you talk?!" Abby cried, shocked.

"I always could. You never asked," Lumi replied, shrugging.

"That's what I said, too, when they found out I could talk!" The staff cracked up.

"I'm Ambrosia," the sunset dragon introduced herself.

"And I'm Aqua," the blue dragon added.

"I'm the leader of this group. My name is Scales," the green dragon informed them in a haughty voice.

"No, you're not! I am!" Lumi exclaimed.

"I'm the biggest, though," Scales insisted.

Lumi and Scales eyed each other with menace. They circled slowly around the patch of dirt they landed in.

"Guys, fighting it out won't work," Ambrosia cooed in her angelic voice.

"Exactly! Besides, the humans are petrified!" Aqua added.

They looked down at the group that was staring up at them with eyes as big as dinner plates. Abby was standing only a few feet away from Lumi, and she looked ready to scream.

"Ok, fine, geez," Scales gave in with an eye roll. "We'll be co-leaders."

Everyone relaxed.

"Choose a dragon to ride on," Lumi ordered.

"Um, do you know where the fifth relic is?" Tiger squeaked.

"Yes," Lumi replied. "Also, I only take Apple."

Abby looked at Ambrosia. She looked pretty and nice. Abby moved towards her, but then she noticed the runt at the far end, looking left out. Abby stepped towards the runt.

"Hi. What's your name?" Abby asked. "I'm Abby."

"Primrose," she replied in a meek voice.

"Oh. Could I…ride you?" Abby asked.

"No one would dream of that," Primrose told her glumly.

"I would." Abby grinned.

"Really? Then hop on!" Primrose cried, delighted.

Abby had no trouble getting on Primrose's back, which was one plus of the dragon being so small. (Jadeine had to boost Tiger onto Scales's back.) The dragons soared into the sky. Abby laughed as Primrose twisted and turned, and screamed when she dove down.

"Thanks so much, Primrose," Abby said. "Hey, do you know what the fifth relic is?"

"It's a dragon egg. It's inside a volcano," Primrose replied.

"Hey, Primrose!" Scales called out. "You're so tiny, an ant could crush you! I can take 2 on my back! Unlike you."

"Scales! Be nice!" all the other dragons chorused.

"You wouldn't know how many times Scales teases me." Primrose sighed.

"It's ok. Lots of times, people teased me because they thought I was too smart," Abby replied.

"What?! That's so dumb! Everyone loves the wise here!" Primrose spluttered.

"Yeah, well, welcome to my world." Abby sighed. Sometimes she felt like the earth was built of jealousy and anger.

Abby spotted a massive volcano that had erupted from the ocean. In her mind, she had always imagined volcanoes like how kids made them for science fairs: perfectly symmetrical cones with bright red lava pouring down the slopes. But this volcano was gray and sprawling yet tall. A wispy plume of smoke blew from the top.

"There are fire dragons and demons in there," Primrose explained nervously.

"Sounds like a nice place to hang out," Abby muttered, taking a deep breath.

The dragons descended upon the volcano and perched on the rim, allowing Abby and the others to disembark. Abby coughed and squinted past the smoke into the volcano. She couldn't see the bottom or even the magma. How deep was this volcano?

Apple had dozed off during the ride (how??) and had woken up with a scream to see the volcano below his feet.

"Glad you're awake, buddy." Lumi nuzzled his hand and helped him climb off of her.

"So, how do we get the egg if it's in the volcano?" Tiger wondered.

"If Aeryn wasn't a traitor, it would've helped us a lot." Jadeine sighed.

"Who's Aeryn again?" Tiger asked. Abby remembered they had met Aeryn before Tiger, Apple, Cherry, and the dragons.

"The evil fairy." Abby wiggled her fingers.

"No offense, but isn't your mom the evil fairy?" Tiger asked.

"No, of course not! It's Aeryn!" Abby grunted. "My mom's just misunderstood." But even as she said it, she wondered, *WAS her mom evil?*

Abby could tell Tiger didn't believe this, but Tiger shrugged and said, "Okay, sure."

"So, about the volcano…" Jadeine trailed off. They all looked down and gulped.

"I have a serum that will make you invincible! It'll help you!" Ambrosia exclaimed. "It'll also help you move around—normally, magma is too dense to swim in."

"Okay, great!" Abby said. "Where is it?"

"It might sound gross, but it's my saliva." Ambrosia giggled.

"EW! WHY?" Apple burst out. "WHY DO I HAVE TO GET COVERED IN DRAGON SPIT TO SAVE THE WORLD?!"

"Yeah, EW!" Jadeine exclaimed. "Are you sure there's no other way?"

"Nah, not unless a fairy randomly happens to be passing by," Ambrosia said.

She stuck out her tongue over them. Apple had his eyes squeezed shut. A big drop of saliva that looked like honey fell on them. Their skin shimmered, and the honey-saliva melted into their skin. Abby shuddered.

"So do we just jump?" Tiger asked, biting her nails.

Ambrosia nodded a little too enthusiastically.

Abby stared down at the seemingly endless darkness of the volcano. Could they really fall in there and not get hurt?

Jadeine jumped first, followed by Tiger and the dragons. Apple prepared to jump, but Abby grabbed his arm. "Wait! Don't go yet! I'm not ready!"

"Just jump!" he told her.

She bit her lip. She had never liked heights.

Apple rolled his eyes. "Oh, whatever. You brought this on yourself." He pushed her from behind. "Bon voyage!"

Abby screamed as she fell. After what felt like forever, she plunged into the magma. Abby lost sight of her friends.

Abby felt heat surrounding her from all sides, but it didn't hurt her. She could barely believe she was swimming in magma!

Abby didn't see a dragon egg, so she swam deeper down. The magma was super dense, so she was forced to move slowly.

She spotted a door carved into the side of the volcano. She reached for the knob, but then the magma in front of her formed slowly into a demon! Abby screamed and frantically unzipped her backpack while awkwardly attempting to swim away. Maybe the shoes could help.

"Red shoes, help," Abby whispered.

The shoes just sat there. Why wasn't it working?

The magma demon reached for her. She dodged, feeling like she was in one of those slo-mo videos. Ugh, why was the magma so thick?

"Please, red shoes, help!" Abby tried.

The second she said 'Please', the shoes sprang into action. They kicked the magma demon, who screamed in fury.

But the shoes were no match for the demons. Abby realized there were more than the one she had fought. The demons slowly surrounded her and her friends. The biggest one hissed menacingly.

Suddenly, the magma fizzed and bubbled. *Oh, no.*

The volcano erupted, spitting Abby and her friends up into the air. They all shrieked. Abby knew the lava would carry them more than two thousand feet down the sides and into the freezing water. She flailed desperately and squeezed her eyes shut. *Please, God...*

Abby heard the flapping of wings and opened her eyes. The dragons! Primrose scooped Abby up, and she hung on tight.

The dragons escorted them to safety. Abby was glad to have her feet on solid ground.

"We can try again," Jadeine suggested half-heartedly.

"No. We almost became demon food!" Abby snapped. "Let's sleep now. It's getting late. We can try tomorrow."

Abby sat down on the grass and sighed. The sky turned a reddish hue, and she fell asleep, thinking about volcanoes, demons, and dragon eggs.

The next day, Abby woke up with a bubbly attitude. She had dreamed that she had defeated the demons and got the fifth relic. Abby shook everyone until they were awake.

"Are you ready to go get that egg?" Abby asked.

"No..." Apple groaned.

Soon they were all up, and they marched towards the volcano (Well, Abby marched—everyone else trailed behind sleepily).

Ambrosia dropped the magic saliva on them again, and they jumped in. Abby was glad Apple didn't have to push her again (bon voyage, seriously?! Did he have to say that?).

Abby fell deeper into the volcano until she hit the fiery magma. This time, she knew what was coming and was ready.

Many magma demons were surrounding the door. The demons threw a bunch of potions at the group.

Abby swam away from a green one just in time before it hit her face. She swerved to avoid a pretty blue one and was almost hit by a purple one, but Jadeine pulled her away just in time.

The potions seemed to keep coming. They were endless! Abby gently grabbed a potion and threw it back at one of the magma demons. The demon vanished into the depths. Abby grinned as she exploded another demon, and then another.

"Keep 'em coming!" Abby cried out.

"You don't need to announce it! We're doing that too, you know!" Tiger exclaimed.

"Sorry!" Abby apologized sheepishly, then screamed as a potion hit her arm. The potion sizzled…but Abby didn't feel anything! Abby remembered her temporary invincibility powers and swam ahead confidently. She reached the bottom, but was confronted by the same demons.

Abby kicked a demon, then proceeded to open the door. The door flew open, and Abby swam in. The rest of the group followed.

Abby looked around. They were standing in a circular chamber with a pedestal at its center. On the pedestal sat a dragon egg.

Suddenly, a giant dragon with a scar just below its eye curled down from the ceiling. Abby screamed.

"Hello, little thieves," the dragon hissed.

"We're not thieves!" Abby insisted.

"I find that very hard to believe," the dragon said.

The dragon snapped forward, and Abby darted around him. She leaped for the dragon egg again, but missed.

Her backpack was unzipped, and the Merqueen's tiara fell out. She seized it and desperately flung it at the dragon. He screeched when it pierced his scar and retreated, hissing.

Abby snatched the egg. It was a pretty color like the sunrise. She tucked it under her arm.

"Sayonara!" Abby called out, leaping away.

Abby shoved the egg in her backpack and zipped it properly this time.

The group swam up. When everyone was there, they hopped on the dragons who soared away.

"I think you should give the egg some air," Apple suggested.

Abby pulled the egg out and handed it to Apple, who seemed eager to hold it. He stared at it, as if dazzled by its brilliant color.

They had all five relics! Now all they needed to do was test it to see if all their relics were real (she hoped so) and find the Book of Light.

And then they could save the world.

Chapter 27
Expect the Unexpected

Cherry was still in the wolf's mouth.

By now, she had stopped squirming and complaining. She lay limply, trying not to focus too hard on the saliva droplets on her curls.

Oh, great, now she felt like she was going to throw up again! She gagged.

The wolf approached Lizzie, who was pacing around. Cherry squeaked. *OMG, it's Lizzie! THE EVIL QUEEN!* Cherry thought.

Would she kill Cherry?

"It's the princess!" Lizzie squealed. "OMG! You're amazing, wolfie!" She hugged the wolf. If it had been possible for a wolf to blush, he totally would've.

Cherry kicked. "Please, let me go!"

The wolf laughed. "Let you GO? Never."

Cherry tried not to burst into tears.

Lizzie frowned. "Where is the prince? What's his name? Orange?"

"Apple," the wolf corrected. "I don't know."

Lizzie's mood went from overjoyed to fuming in an instant. "YOU LET HIM GET AWAY? WHAT IF HE'S WITH ABBY? OR WORSE, MY CRYBABY SISTER?"

"But, my queen—" he started.

"NO! SILENCE!" Her eyes turned green, and his mouth snapped closed.

"I'm sorry, your Highness," he whimpered, tail between his legs.

"That's more like it." Lizzie sniffed.

"What do you want with me?" Cherry scowled.

"You're not the sharpest pencil in the bunch." Lizzie sighed.

"I'm not a pencil, I'm royalty," Cherry corrected.

"Think twice before correcting me," Lizzie hissed.

"I'm not afraid of you!" Cherry cried. The wolf let go of Cherry and thrust her towards Lizzie. She tried running away, but Lizzie caught her wrist and grasped it firmly.

"Well, there's a princess with a bad attitude," Lizzie smirked.

"What do you want?" Cherry asked, trying yet failing to tug her arm out.

"What else? *'Remember the death threat Mama got?'*" Lizzie mocked.

"You heard." Cherry was absolutely mortified.

"Of course I did." Lizzie frowned.

Lizzie pulled out a small vial of purple liquid and shook it.

"Wondering what this is?" Lizzie asked. "Let me show you."

Lizzie let a drop fall onto a leaf. The leaf sizzled and burned until it was nothing more than a pile of ash. Lizzie brought the vial close to Cherry's face.

"No, no, no, no, no!" Cherry shrieked. "Stop! Stop! STOP!!!"

Lizzie tilted the vial over Cherry's eyelid. The wait was almost tormenting.

Lizzie kept tilting it ever so slightly. Cherry closed her eyes, waiting for the end to come.

Just when it was about to fall on her face, someone shouted, "STOP!"

Cherry cracked an eye open. It was the wolf who had shouted! What? Why would he do that?

Lizzie stared at him with that stare that could freeze fire. "What is the matter, wolf?"

He squirmed. "I…I just…"

"Out with it!" Lizzie ordered.

"Wouldn't it be more useful if we kept her?" the wolf said in a rush. "As a bargaining chip. So then Abby will come for her, especially if Apple is with her."

Why had he saved Cherry? Cherry didn't really care, as long as she was safe.

Lizzie tilted her head. "I suppose," she replied finally. "Fine, we won't kill her."

Lizzie loosened her grip on Cherry. Cherry, seeing her opportunity, elbowed Lizzie in the stomach.

Lizzie yelped and let go. Cherry ran for it.

"Catch her, wolfie!" Lizzie yelled.

The Big Bad Wolf started chasing her. *No!* Cherry thought. She needed to escape; she could never outrun a wolf. But how?

She dashed out of the woods and entered a quaint town. By sheer luck, a woodcutter happened to be walking by, heading towards the woods, axe over his shoulder.

The wolf shrieked and skidded to a stop. Of course, he was terrified of woodcutters.

Cherry didn't look back. She kept running until her legs gave out, and she fell to the ground, shaking.

"Hey, kid, are you OK?"

Cherry sat up and looked at the man standing above her. "Yeah," she replied. "Just winded."

He shrugged and moved on. Cherry decided that maybe the middle of a sidewalk wasn't the best place to rest.

She scrambled to her feet and scanned the area. The buildings were unmistakable. She was in Cinderella Town!

She wandered around aimlessly, thinking hard. She needed to find Abby, Apple, and the others.

Cherry flopped onto a bench and wondered where they might be.

OK…so they'd had three relics when she had left. They had been looking for the fourth one.

But where was the fourth one? Cherry racked her brain. She didn't know where any of the others were either. She sighed.

"I'll never find the fourth relic," she murmured.

"Did you say relic?" someone gasped.

Cherry looked up. "Uh…"

"That's dangerous!" the lady yelped. "You shouldn't be looking for that!"

Before Cherry could say anything, the lady's eyes widened. "Wait—Princess Cherry?!"

The lady dipped into a deep bow. Then she rose. "EVERYONE! IT'S THE PRINCESS!"

Cherry bit back a groan. Most of the time, she loved being a princess. Riches, glory, what's not to like? The answer was no privacy. You could never go anywhere unnoticed. Cherry would probably make a horrible spy.

Just as she'd suspected, the townsfolk crowded around her. "Your Majesty! Take a photo of her, quick!"

Cherry glared at them. "Stop! Go mind your own beeswax!"

Slowly, the crowd dispersed. But everyone was still staring at her. No way could Cherry think now.

She stood up and walked briskly away. She ended up in an alley.

A *meow* came from her feet. Cherry looked down.

A tiny kitten mewed. It wasn't dirty, so it couldn't have been there long.

Cherry reached down to pet it, but as soon as she did, it tried to bite her!

"Ow!" Cherry yelped, jerking away.

The kitten bared its teeth and slunk away. Cherry sighed. She was getting lonely.

All her life, she'd been surrounded by people. Noise. Colors. *Movement.*

Servants offered to get her whatever she needed. People danced at the palace with the sound turned up so loud, it was like a million decibels. And now…just an alley. Silence.

The heaviness of being away from home for the first time began to sink in. She had thought this was going to be like those games she and Apple had played when they were small children. She was so wrong.

Cherry would sit, but she didn't want to get her dress dirty. She wiped her eyes. Should she go home?

But that would be like giving up. Cherry understood now. She couldn't always step back and let someone else finish what she'd started. She needed to stick through this and not be a stereotypical princess—like a damsel in distress.

But how?!

Chapter 28
Moonlight

Tiger had always loved the stars.

She tilted her head up and gazed at the vast expanse of twinkling lights in the darkness.

Tiger had never seen so many all at once before, because she lived in a town with significant light pollution. The stars made all their troubles here in H.E.A.L feel tiny and insignificant. All those other stars were out there in the universe, and she was just a tiny speck in it.

That didn't make her feel sad that she was unnoticeable in the universe. That made her feel curious about other planets and if they had any life (other than the Unknown) that faced similar problems.

"Should we go to sleep now?" Jadeine wondered.

Tiger opened her mouth, but she was interrupted by the sound of crunching leaves. Someone was here, and that someone could be Lizzie or the Big Bad Wolf. She whipped around, and so did everyone else.

A figure emerged from the trees. Tiger couldn't see who it was in the dark. "Who are you and what do you want?" she cried.

"It's me!" The person stepped forward, and her dark curtain of hair fell backward. Jill!

"Jill!" Abby smiled, and then seemed to remember their huge fight. She leaned backward, uncertain if Jill had forgiven her or not.

"What are you smiling at, Snoopy McSnoop face?" Jill grumbled. Apparently, she was still mad. "Oh, Apple's back."

Jadeine updated her on everything that had happened. Tiger looked at the dragon egg, which was cradled in Apple's arms. It was beautiful—peach and rose pink swirled together, with a hint of pale blue. It looked like a dawn sky. Stunning.

"What about you?" Jadeine finished. "Did anything interesting happen?"

Jill shook her head. "No…I wandered around for a bit. Went to town. I looked in some shops, and then came back here to find you guys when I'd cooled down."

Tiger yawned. "Let's go to sleep. We'll go relic-hunting in the morning."

Two minutes later, they were all on the forest ground. Tiger was next to Apple, who was curled up under Lumi's wing.

Tiger shifted, the leaves scratching her face. She stared up at the night sky, questions swirling in her mind.

Would Jill forgive Abby? Would they defeat Lizzie? And most importantly…did Apple mean it about sacrificing himself? I don't want him to, she thought.

Tiger finally fell asleep, but she woke up in the middle of the night. It was still dark out, so she didn't want to wake the others. The cold wind whipped her in the face as she closed her eyes in an attempt to get back to sleep.

This time, she couldn't get back to sleep. "Anyone awake?" she whispered, loud enough so awake people could hear, but soft enough so that sleeping people could sleep in peace.

No one answered, and Tiger was about to give up, but then Apple whispered, "I am."

She turned to face him. He was still under Lumi's wing.

"You think we'll find the Book of Light?" she asked.

He pressed his lips together. "I…I don't know. We should be able to, I guess. After all, we got all five relics."

Tiger sighed. "I wish Lizzie weren't doing this. Why can't she leave us all alone?"

"Same reason anyone does anything. Lizzie is selfish." In the dark, Apple's gold eye was twice as bright as the blue one.

"Not everyone's selfish…"

"Most people are."

Tiger turned over so she faced Abby's snoring form. She didn't want to talk about this anymore. "Good night."

"Good night."

Tiger must've fallen asleep, because when she woke up, the sunlight was dappling everyone's face. Apple was already getting to his feet.

He looked at Tiger. "I'm glad Jill didn't wake us up so loud like usual."

"That's because she's still asleep." Tiger nodded at Jill. That gave her an idea. "Hey…what if we do that to everyone?"

Apple considered this. A smile stretched across his face. "OK. Three, two, one…"

"WAKE UP, SLEEPYHEADS!" Apple and Tiger yelled together.

Abby shot up, her hair all messed up. Jadeine jumped to her feet, holding the staff out in front of her. Jill screamed like a little girl.

Apple and Tiger both burst out laughing. Apple laughed so hard he had to grab Tiger's shoulder to steady himself.

Jill grumbled. "I guess I deserved that. Alright…any breakfast?"

Jadeine decided they should go to town and order food from a restaurant, since they only had that disgusting tomato soup. Everyone agreed with this wholeheartedly.

As they walked out of the forest, Tiger noticed something strange. There was a weird noise coming from her left.

She turned. Apple was next to her. "Are you making that sound?" she asked.

He looked around. "No…"

Then they all heard a CRACK! Apple and Tiger both stopped in their tracks and stared at the egg, which Apple was holding.

Sure enough, there was a tiny hole in the top. Tiger watched it warily. Suddenly, an eye was peering out of the hole.

Apple shrieked and almost dropped the egg. "Be careful!" Tiger chided.

The dragon's eye was beautiful. It was huge and yellow, with a black pupil at its center. The baby dragon's scales were midnight black.

In their shock, they hadn't realized they were standing way behind the others. "What's the holdup?" Abby called, running over. Then she noticed the hole in the egg. "Oh…holy cow."

By now, everyone had crowded around Apple and Tiger. "What do we do?" Jill cried.

Jadeine pinched the bridge of her nose. "Um…why don't we just keep walking?"

"But it's going to hatch!" Apple countered.

Jadeine opened her mouth and then closed it. "Well, it hasn't made a crack for a minute now…let's hope it'll be slow."

Apple and Tiger ended up walking next to each other behind the group. Lumi lectured them about proper dragonet care:

"So, you want to keep the baby warm at all times. Normally, the mother dragon will keep it under her wing, but we don't know this dragonet's mother…" Lumi trailed off. "Oh, no."

"What?" Tiger asked, nervous.

"A dragon is like a duckling. It imprints on the first living being it sees. Since that thing is you two…"

Tiger gasped. "Yikes! It thinks we're its parents!"

Apple stared at the egg. "How do we raise a dragon?"

Lumi nuzzled his hand. "Don't worry. I'll help you!"

Thankfully, the egg didn't make another peep as they reached town. Tiger looked around. "Where should we eat?"

Abby squealed and pointed at a deli across the street. A neon yellow sign in the window proclaimed, 'BEST SOUPS AND SANDWICHES YOU'VE EVER HAD!'.

"Guys, we should go there!" Abby shrieked.

"Chill, Abby," Jill sighed. "It's just…"

Jill noticed a waiter serving a customer a bowl of delicious soup through the window. Her mouth watered, and her eyes grew wide. *That. Looks. Amazing!* Jill thought excitedly.

"Scratch that. It looks amazing!" Jill exclaimed.

"Uh…I think you're missing something. I'm a dragon. When people see me, they freak out. It's fortunate that everyone is too busy to notice me right now," Lumi pointed out.

"Oh, right. Sorry, Lumi. We'll…uh, get something for you to eat," Apple reassured Lumi.

"Meat!" Lumi cried excitedly. "Get me like a tuna sandwich or something. I'll wait here."

Apple nodded. They walked towards the restaurant, drawn to it like a moth to a flame. A bell jingled when they pushed open the glass door.

A waitress in an apron hurried towards them. "Hello! Party of…"

Jadeine quickly counted. "One, two, three, four, five people,"

The waitress showed them to a five-seater table. "My name is Maria. I'll be your server for the day."

Tiger grabbed a menu and flipped through it. "Ooh!"

Abby shrieked with excitement. "A Caprese sandwich! I'll get that!"

Jadeine ordered a salad, Jill ordered tomato soup, and Tiger ordered ginger carrot soup. And, strangely, Apple ordered…an apple. Apple remembered that Lumi wanted meat, so he also got the tuna sandwich.

Maria placed everything down in front of them. "Hope you enjoy your meal. If you need anything, I'll be happy to help."

They did enjoy, very much. Jill even licked the bottom of her bowl when she was done.

Apple handed over twenty marigolds, and they left. The bell jingled again when they walked out.

The bell was why Maria almost didn't hear the dragon egg crack. *Almost.*

"Wait!" Maria yelled. "Did you hear that?"

"Hear what?" Tiger asked innocently, her heart racing.

Maria narrowed her eyes. The dragonet chose that exact moment to split out of the egg, chirping like a baby bird.

Maria shrieked and dropped the plates she was holding. They shattered at her feet, and food was strewn all over the floor. "THERE'S A DRAGON IN THE RESTAURANT! KILL IT!"

Everyone in the deli panicked, and the people outside the deli stared at them in confusion. "Run!" Abby cried.

They all dashed for the forest again. Lumi screeched giddily when she saw Apple with the tuna sandwich. Apple tossed Lumi the sandwich and tried to catch up. Abby, Jill, and Jadeine were first inside, disappearing into the trees. Apple was slower because he was carrying the dragonet, so Tiger ran back for him.

"You go!" he panted.

"What about the dragon?" Tiger screamed.

"This way!" Apple yelled and took a sharp turn to the left. Soon, they were standing in an empty alley, panting.

Tiger groaned. "Ugh…we lost the others again."

Apple and Tiger looked at each other. Then Apple burst out laughing.

"What are you laughing at?" Tiger cried, annoyed.

"I'm…sorry. It's just that…we're alone with a dragon in an alley!"

It wasn't really funny, but Tiger laughed too. A moment later, they were both quiet again.

Tiger looked at the dragon. Apple placed it on the ground. It squirmed and flipped over for a moment, and Tiger could see it was male.

The dragon had midnight-black scales, with silver scales gleaming around his eyes. He whined and licked Apple's shoes.

"I think he's hungry," Tiger realized. "You got any food?"

Apple held up his half-eaten apple from the deli. He handed it to the dragon, but the dragon just poked it with his snout and then ignored it.

Apple facepalmed. "Oh! Dragons are carnivores, right?"

Tiger frowned. "Where are we going to get meat?"

"Right now, let's just find the others," Apple decided. "Then we can worry about the dragon."

"What will we name him?" Tiger wondered as they walked.

Apple pressed his lips together. "Uh…"

"Well, he has black scales," Tiger observed. "How about Midnight? Starry?"

None of those names really fit, though. Tiger sighed.

In time, they were back in the woods. A squirrel threw an acorn at Apple.

"Hey!" he yelped.

In a flash, the dragon had flown up there. Tiger and Apple watched in horror as the dragonet did indescribable things to the squirrel.

"Wasn't that dragon just born a minute ago?" Tiger asked Apple, eyeing the dragonet as it wrestled the squirrel.

"Most dragons gain the ability to hunt at a young age, but not this young…but he's a relic after all," Apple said.

A minute later, the dragon flew back and dropped the dead squirrel at their feet. He nudged it forward with his nose.

"Uh…that's OK," Apple told him.

The dragon lifted a wing, as if shrugging, and then gobbled the squirrel up himself in one bite.

Tiger shuddered. "Yikes."

Soon, they heard voices. Tiger ran forward.

"Tiger! Apple! We were wondering where you had gone," Abby said. "Oh, holy moly, the dragon!"

Apple told everyone how it had eaten a squirrel. Abby made the finger-down-the-throat gesture.

"What's the time?" Jill wondered.

"Uh…10:27 AM, I think," Apple replied, checking his antique-looking watch. Abby had only seen that kind of watch in olden times movies.

"Is the eggshell the relic or is it the dragon?" Tiger wondered. "Because what if the dragon dies?"

"That's a good question," Jadeine mused. "Mmm, I think it's the dragon, right, Lumi?"

Lumi was preening herself. "Sorry, what?"

Jadeine repeated the question. Lumi nodded. "Yeah, you're right."

"Have you named him?" Abby asked.

"No," Apple admitted. He sat down next to the dragonet.

Apple was good with animals, Tiger realized. The dragonet seemed to like him, and so did Lumi.

Tiger sat down next to him. She stroked the dragonet's head, and then all of a sudden, the dragonet bit her finger.

"OW!" Tiger shrieked, hopping up. She wasn't sure why she thought spinning in circles and screaming was a good idea, but she did it anyway. The dragonet swung around with her.

Apple laughed so hard, he fell over. She stopped spinning and glared at him. "You could've helped me, you know."

He stood up, still laughing, and pried the dragon's snout open. As soon as he did, the dragon fluttered to the ground and curled up, asleep.

Tiger examined her finger. The dragonet hadn't broken her skin, but he had left a series of teeth marks. She sucked her finger, not caring if it was unsanitary or not.

She looked at Apple as he played with the dragonet. They had five relics, but she couldn't get rid of the feeling that something was wrong.

But, she supposed, all was well.

Chapter 29
Trickery

Lizzie was fuming.

First of all, there was her baby sister Melissa, who had openly defied her. *Ugh!*

Then there was that useless Big Bad Wolf. He had failed in everything! He couldn't even stop that princess from getting away!

And worst of all, her beautiful, plum dress was dirty! She needed new clothes, but she had no allies! Who would get anything for her?

As Lizzie paced around in frustration, she tripped on a gnarly tree root and fell to the ground. She got a faceful of dirt all over her. The Big Bad Wolf snickered, but stopped when Lizzie glared at him.

Lizzie stood up and brushed off the dirt. She was just going to have to find Abby herself.

Lizzie confidently marched off into the trees, but didn't hear footsteps behind her. Lizzie whirled around and saw the Big Bad Wolf walking away.

"Wolfie!!! Where are you going?" Lizzie demanded.

"Well, I'm not going to stick around a person like *you*," The Big Bad Wolf said. "I don't want to be on the losing side."

Lizzie made a sound that was somewhere between a growl and an amused laugh. "You think Abby will actually let you join her pathetic group?"

"No," the wolf said calmly.

Then he trotted off.

"FINE!!! YOU'LL BE SORRY, WOLFIE!" Lizzie yelled.

She stomped her foot and continued walking. Lizzie snapped her fingers, and she appeared in Cinderella Town.

Everyone screamed and ran away when they noticed her. Lizzie smirked at everyone, then marched into a shop that said 'BEST SOUPS AND SANDWICHES YOU'VE EVER HAD!'. It was the closest to Lizzie.

Lizzie looked around and peered behind the counter. A woman in her 40s was behind it. She had pretty brown hair and tanned skin with freckles. She cowered when she saw Lizzie.

"What's your name, woman?" Lizzie asked.

"M-M-Maria," the lady answered.

"Have you seen Abby, that famous girl collecting the relics, with a wannabe group trailing behind her?" Lizzie questioned.

"I can't tell you anything," Maria stammered. "And I won't!"

"Why? Are you not *scared* of me?" Lizzie hissed.

"No, I'm not! You're a person covered with dirt, so why should I be scared of you?" Maria blurted. "And you probably want to harm them, and I don't want to give you any possibly useful information."

"Say that one more time and I'll have your tongue for dinner," Lizzie threatened.

"No, I will never tell you," Maria said, her voice wavering.

Lizzie grumbled and muttered a spell to make Maria do her bidding underneath her breath. Then she commanded, "Now, tell me what you know."

Maria squirmed. She looked solemn. She stared down at her shoes and played with her hair. It seemed like she was trying to resist the spell.

"Describe," Lizzie ordered. Maria nodded.

"Um, a girl with black hair in braids wearing farmer clothes, a woman with an emerald cloak and a staff, a girl that looked like Cinderella's stepsister, but I'm not really sure, and, uh, a boy around 13, maybe 14. They all looked tired, and their clothes were kind of dirty."

"Perfect. Anything else?" Lizzie asked.

"They had a dragon egg. It hatched by the door. Terrifying experience," Maria shuddered.

"That's all the information that will be needed," Lizzie said.

Lizzie tried to get back to her castle by snapping her fingers. She appeared in front of a lake. She stared at it in confusion, then snapped her fingers again. This time, she appeared near a tree in the woods. *Ugh!* Lizzie thought in frustration.

Why was her magic going haywire when she most needed it?

"AIEEE!" Lizzie shouted.

A low growl from the undergrowth returned her shout. Lizzie stepped towards the sound with her hands tingling with magic in case she needed to attack.

A large dragon with green scales rose from his hiding spot. The dragon bared his teeth. Lizzie sent her dark magic near the dragon, but the dragon barely flinched.

Lizzie growled. "Who are you?!"

"What's the matter?" the dragon asked smugly.

"Get away!" Lizzie exclaimed.

"I know your magic isn't working. It's because you feel powerless," the dragon taunted.

"How dare you!" Lizzie shrieked.

Again, Lizzie blasted the darkest magic she had in her towards the dragon, but only a couple of his scales loosened. Lizzie screamed in rage.

"I am Scales, the leader of the dragons, king of all!" the dragon boomed.

A rustling noise was heard beside Scales. A gleaming white dragon rose out of the bushes.

"Scales! Now is not the time to brag!" the white dragon exclaimed.

"Lumi, I suggest we focus on this…woman." Scales sighed.

Lumi rolled her eyes. "You weren't focusing on her befo–"

"This woman?! I am *Queen Lizzie,* and you can't stop me!" Lizzie yelled.

Her eyes turned neon green, and the dragons backed away. The bewitchment should have taken full effect, but the dragons' eyes were just a little glazed over. They returned to normal in a matter of seconds.

"Poor thing has had her pride crushed." Scales pouted like he was talking to a baby.

"More like crushed under my foot." Lumi grinned.

"Lumi! I crush annoying people under my foot, not you!" Scales exclaimed.

"Wanna bet?" Lumi growled.

"No! I wanna teach this coward a lesson!" Scales exclaimed.

"I. Am. Not. A. COWARD!" Lizzie boomed.

"You're right. Before you weren't. Now you are," Scales sang.

"AGHHHHHHH! STOP IT!!!" Lizzie shrieked, agitated.

"Oh, by the way, we took your necklace, crushed it, and gave it to the Sea Witch," Lumi told Lizzie.

Lizzie gasped. She had worn a black necklace all her life. It channeled her powers! Without it, it took a massive effort to do anything! Her hands flew to her neck. She hoped with all her might that the dragons were tricking her.

"You give it back!" Lizzie yelled.

Lizzie let out her most agonizing scream ever. She withdrew a pocket knife and charged the dragons. The dragons hovered above Lizzie and grinned.

"Poor Lizzie indeed." Lumi smiled.

"Would it serve her good in jail?" Scales asked.

"Yeah! Or, we could keep her near the dragonets so they can play with her!"

"Ooh, good idea!"

Lizzie huffed and turned away. She was going to have to try her luck. Lizzie vanished and was brought to Liquid Sunlight Ocean. She pumped her fist. Yes! Her powers were finally working!

The waves reached her ankles. Lizzie pinched her nose and dove in. The cold water felt like a thousand needles stinging her face. She swam towards a jagged rock formation.

She almost reached the bottom when she realized she didn't have enough air! Lizzie frantically swam to the top. She gasped for breath. She needed magic *now*.

"Sea Witch! Uh, I need to trade!" Lizzie called.

No response came.

"Please!" Lizzie begged.

Lizzie began talking to herself.

"Gosh, Lizzie! You're cold-hearted! The Evil Queen! Why are you begging right now? And why are you so afraid?" She thought to herself. "How could I let a dragon with a name like Lumi destroy my necklace?! I know it's ironic, but now I remember my parents calling me an angel, and I'm not that at all. At least I'm not like the fairies. Ugh! They're so merry all the time and—"

"Hello." Lizzie was cut off.

"Sea Witch?" Lizzie asked hopefully.

"Yes," the Sea Witch replied.

The Sea Witch emerged. Lizzie smiled.

"What do you wish?" the Sea Witch asked.

"I want my precious necklace back in one piece!" Lizzie demanded.

"Oh…" the Sea Witch frowned. "That depends on what you have to give."

"I have a dragon, but it's, uh, not here," Lizzie hazarded. She could probably kidnap a dragon somewhere, right? Hopefully, Scales or Lumi.

"I can't trust you, Lizzie, Queen of Deceit and Evil," the Sea Witch said.

"Tell you what," Lizzie prompted. "I'll give you my earrings now and the dragon later. Deal?"

Lizzie took off her earrings. They were rubies carved into the shape of a swan. She placed them in the Sea Witch's palms. The Sea Witch examined them with great interest.

"Astounding," the Sea Witch gasped. "I'll take them. But by the end of the month, I want the dragon."

The Sea Witch extended her palm, revealing a brand-new necklace. Lizzie giddily put it on.

"I promise I'll come back," Lizzie vowed.

Then, with a grin, Lizzie vanished. The Sea Witch was so gullible! After all, Lizzie was known for taking things and not giving anything in return.

And now, she had her necklace back.

Chapter 30
Trying to Not Be A Brat

"Hey, hon, you OK?"

Cherry blinked her eyes open. She groaned. Had she fallen asleep in the *alley*?!

Yup, she had. *Gross,* Cherry thought. She rose, her neck aching.

An old lady was standing there, with so many wrinkles that her face looked like a raisin. Ew.

Wait, no, that was mean. Cherry put on a fake smile. "Hi. Yeah, I'm good. I'm…going home now."

The lady started to walk away, but hesitated. "You sure? Want me to walk you home?"

"No, thank you," Cherry replied. Wow, being polite and demure was *hard*. "I'll be fine. I live pretty close by." She didn't lie…If you counted a kingdom and a forest away as *close*.

The lady shrugged and left. Cherry scrambled to her feet and wandered around. Her stomach grumbled hungrily. Cherry felt the sudden craving for a tasty snack. She imagined the cloud pie she always had at her birthday party, and imagined eating it now. Cloud pie tasted SO GOOD.

Cherry noticed a restaurant and entered it. She smelled fish and wrinkled her nose. As she looked around, she noticed a baby that looked like an old lady. The baby looked weird. Cherry shook her head. She wasn't going to be mean.

Cherry walked to the counter. "Um, hi. Can I have a sandwich? Any sandwich is fine."

"Sure–wait! Princess Cherry, is that you?! What are you doing all alone?" the man behind the counter asked.

Everyone looked her way. Cherry put on a confident, princess-like smile, except she didn't really feel confident. How could she? Cherry didn't even know where she was.

"Um, I'm just visiting here," Cherry said.

"Are you looking for a restaurant that is for…royalty?" the man asked her.

Cherry blushed a dark shade of red. "Um, no. I was hoping I could…eat here?"

Everyone stared at her. No one answered. *This is ridiculous. I mean, me going to a restaurant for locals?* Cherry thought. She wanted to say that out loud, but that might hurt their feelings.

"Um…please?" Cherry tried.

"Oh, um, yes, Princess Cherry! You can take our finest dish: a salmon sandwich!" the man said quickly.

The man called for a person named Johanne, and a woman came running out from the kitchen. Johanne handed the man a salmon sandwich, and he gave it to Cherry. Cherry looked down at it and instinctively wrinkled her nose. The sandwich looked disgusting! The salmon wasn't properly cooked; it looked watery. And the bread was cold and soggy. Still, Cherry had to be polite.

"Um, thank you. It looks…delicious," Cherry fibbed.

Well, maybe it could still taste good, Cherry hopefully thought as she took a small bite and swallowed. Except it was NOT good, not even close! Her taste buds had grown used to 5-star food, and this was not even close to 5-star food. In fact, it tasted *horrible. It is the worst thing I've ever tasted! This restaurant needs to hire a new chef! Disgusting!* Cherry thought. Except she wasn't going to say that, even though she really wanted to. That would be mean.

Cherry suddenly felt like her stomach was filled with worms. She desperately needed to vomit. And she knew she couldn't hold it in for long. She clutched her sides.

"Um, this tastes great!" Cherry weakly grinned. "And, uh, I gotta go! See you, maybe!"

She ran out of the restaurant and threw the salmon sandwich into the trash can outside. Cherry desperately wanted to see Apple, and Abby, and, well, anyone she knew. But as Cherry ran into the streets, hoping to find a familiar face, she only saw strangers.

Would she ever find Apple?

Chapter 31
Searching for Abby

Melissa lay on her bed, staring at the ceiling.

Where was Abby? Was she safe? Melissa thought. Melissa rolled on her side and stared at the clock on her nightstand. It was 7:14 AM.

Melissa sat up. Ugh! She couldn't just be idle. Abby wouldn't just randomly appear in front of her, like she had been hoping for the past couple of hours. If she wanted to know where Abby was, she would have to go find her.

Melissa marched out of the cottage that she had made using her magic. With her head held high, she started towards the road.

That was when someone jumped in front of Melissa. Startled, she screamed and lurched backward.

"I demand you turn Pinocchio back, you evil fairy!" Geppeto yelled. He was holding a rake in his hand.

"Sorry, Gep," Melissa apologized.

"Don't you *dare* call me Gep," Geppeto warned. "And what do you mean by you're sorry? Do you mean you can't? You have to turn him back! I don't care if you say you can't! People like you are always lying!"

"Like Pinocchio," Melissa couldn't help but point out. "He lies a ton."

"HE WOULD NEVER…Well, he does lie, but that's okay, because he's my son!" Geppeto remarked. "Now TURN HIM BACK!"

"Okay, I'm going to. Just hold on for a second," Melissa said.

Geppeto blinked in confusion. This was evidently not what he had expected.

Melissa walked over to the Pinocchio tree and snapped her fingers. The tree slowly started to disappear until Pinocchio was standing there, where the tree had been a few seconds ago.

"Father!" Pinocchio cried joyfully.

Geppeto embraced him and twirled him around. As she watched Geppeto and Pinocchio hug, a pang of loneliness hit her. She missed Abby and wanted to see her again so badly. Melissa stepped away and kept going.

Soon, reality hit her. She stopped and sighed.

She had no money, no sense of direction…nothing. How could she ever find Abby?

Melissa didn't know what to do. She knew Lizzie was still strong, and she needed to do *something*... but what?!

Melissa stared at the shops across the street—a pet shop, a bakery, and a potions shop.

That gave her an idea! She raced to Eleanor's house and banged on Eleanor's door. Melissa had met Eleanor a couple of times and knew that she had plenty of potions stocked up in her house.

Cyrus opened the door, still in his pajamas. "Hi. How can I—"

Melissa shoved past him. "Eleanor!" she yelled. "Come here!"

Eleanor appeared from her room and sucked in her breath. "Melissa?"

"I need a potion," Melissa explained. "I want to get a portal potion that will take me to where Abby is."

Eleanor's eyes softened. "I'm sorry, I don't have that," Eleanor apologized. "But I do have a potion that will help you know where she is."

"Thank you, Eleanor," Melissa said with a grateful smile.

Eleanor brought Melissa into the kitchen and rummaged in a cabinet. She pulled out a small bottle of bright blue elixir.

"It's the last one," Eleanor told Melissa. "Use it well."

Melissa poured the shimmery purple liquid in a circle on the floor and focused on the image of Abby in her mind. A bubble popped up, and she saw Abby and her friends in the woods.

They were playing with a dragonet. Melissa blinked. *Is it a relic?* Melissa wondered.

Melissa cleared her throat. "So they're in the woods. Okay, uh…thanks, Eleanor. Now I should go find a transporter." She took one last glance at Abby before she waved her hand and the image disappeared.

"Bye," Eleanor said. "Good luck."

Melissa smiled awkwardly and left. "TRANSPORTER!" she yelled, not caring that people were staring at her.

A transporter appeared. "Hello, my name is Ms. Everly. Where would you like to go today?" She smiled perkily.

"To the woods where my daughter, Abby, is," Melissa requested, then thought to add, "Please."

The transporter opened her mouth, but then blinked. "Oh, it looks like someone else is calling. Would you mind coming along?"

"Sure," Melissa said, trying to be nice and helpful. Ms. Everly snapped her fingers, and they were standing in an alley. *Ew,* Melissa thought.

Then her eyes caught on the person who had called. This girl was so dirty she could barely tell who it was—and then she realized. She was Princess Cherry!

Princess Cherry looked at Melissa warily. "You're the bad fairy!"

Melissa sniffed, offended, even though she was the bad fairy. "And you're a spoiled brat!"

"No, I'm not!" Princess Cherry insisted. "I am just looking for my brother! You're probably, what, off to go eat children?"

Melissa rolled her eyes. *That's the gingerbread witch. Elyse,* Melissa thought. Ms. Everly changed the subject. "Where would you like to go, majesty?"

Princess Cherry brightened at the princess-y term. "Where Apple is. He's with Abby and the group."

"Wait!" Melissa cried. "That's where I'm going!"

Cherry wrinkled her nose. "Why? Are you stalking my brother?"

"What?? No! Of course not! I…"

Ms. Everly cleared her throat hastily. "Let's just go. She snapped her fingers, and they appeared in the woods."

"...and the dragonet is so cute!" Jill said. Then she looked up and gasped. "Princess Cherry! And...Abby, your mom!"

Prince Apple ran into his sister's arms. "Cherry! You're here! How'd you get free from the wolf?"

"Tell you later," she said. She looked up. "And I brought someone." She said this with a tone of disdain.

"You didn't bring me," Melissa informed her. "I brought myself." She and Abby looked at each other awkwardly.

Then Abby broke the trance. She dashed towards Melissa and hugged her so hard she almost knocked her over. "Mom!"

Melissa embraced her, not caring that they were both super dirty since they hadn't taken a shower in about a week. She stroked Abby's hair. "Honey, are you okay?"

"Yeah," Abby replied, pulling away. "Are you? Do you know where Lizzie is?"

"No." Melissa dropped her gaze. "It doesn't matter, though."

"What? Why not?"

"We're going home, aren't we?"

"No!" Abby cried. She stared at her mom, aghast. "We're going to find the Book of Light and defeat Lizzie! Don't you–don't you want her gone? She's been the cruelest to you out of anyone!"

Melissa's eyes brimmed with tears. "I know, but...I don't want you to get hurt."

Abby's eyes hardened. "I'm 12. I can take care of myself. We need to save H.E.A.L before we can go back home. I care about these people, Mom. I'm not leaving until they're safe."

Melissa was about to drag Abby back home. She grasped Abby's hand, then let go. She realized that Abby wasn't a little girl anymore. Abby was strong and determined. Melissa thought of all the times she'd held Abby back because she was afraid that what happened to Jay would happen to her…but Abby was a capable girl, and Melissa knew it would be unfair to hold her back yet again. "Alright…but I'll come with you." She hugged Abby fiercely.

Princess Cherry was smiling. "Oh, how cute!" she cooed.

Abby glared at Cherry and stepped back from her mom, thinking Cherry was calling Abby's mom hugging her cute. Cherry blinked. "What? The dragonet *is* cute…"

"Oh, I thought…never mind!" Abby said, changing the subject. "We have some relic-testing to do!"

Chapter 32
Relic-Testing

"So, which of the relics are real?" Apple asked.

"Well, we know that Jadeine's staff is real, Nadine's tiara is real because Ismelda came out of it, and when we were getting the dragonet, the red shoes helped us beat the demons. We don't know about the ice scepter or the dragonet yet," Abby said. "OK, Tiger, give me the ice scepter."

Tiger held out the ice scepter, and Abby took it. She pointed it at a tree covered in moss and tried to get ice to shoot out. Try as she might, no ice or snow or even a slight chill came out of it. Nothing. Tiger took it from Abby and tried again. Abby hoped with all her might that nothing was coming out because Tiger wasn't using it right, but Abby had a feeling that wasn't the case…

"Abby, I'm sorry, but I think this one is a fake." Tiger grimaced.

Abby's face clouded over. "Oh no…"

"It's alright, Abby. There's still hope that the fifth one is a real relic," Jill said, squeezing Abby's hand.

"Yeah." Cherry gave her an encouraging smile. "Let's test the dragonet now."

"Wait! How do we test a dragon?" Apple cried.

"Um…oh! We need to get him to breathe fire! If the dragonet's not real, it won't breathe fire!" Cherry realized.

"How?" Abby's mom wondered.

"Come here, Apple and Tiger," Jadeine told them. "You're his *parents*."

Apple and Tiger came to the dragonet's side. "Uh, breathe fire!" Tiger commanded.

The dragon did not.

"Is it fake, then?" Apple asked. "Or just stubborn?"

"I have an idea," Tiger announced.

Tiger scooped up sand and threw it at the dragon. The dragon squealed in anger, which made everyone cover their ears, because the squeal sounded like a squeaky violin. He tried to see who threw it, but couldn't. He tried to scratch the sand out, but he only bruised his eye. In frustration, the dragon breathed fire.

It wasn't normal fire, though. It was a purplish-black color, and the fire extended far out, scorching a couple of trees. Melissa put the fire out quickly with her magic.

"Whoa. That's a real dragon, for sure." Apple nodded.

"It's a Nightshade dragon! It has the most destructive flames!" Abby's mom exclaimed, gleeful.

"Are you a dragon expert or what?" Jill asked.

"I just read about it in a book," Abby's mom replied with a shrug. "What can I say? I grew up with books. Well, for a while anyway." Melissa's face fell.

"What's wrong, Mom?" Abby asked, concerned.

"It's because of me…" Melissa muttered.

"Maybe we can name this dragon Nightshade!" Apple exclaimed. He had seen the hurt on Melissa's face and decided to change the subject to spare her an explanation quickly. He knew what it was like, telling people about your saddest days.

"Ugh, that's the most unimaginative name ever! Can't we do something cool like Sparky? Naming it Nightshade is like if you got a pet bird and named it Bird," Jill groaned.

"Hey, Nightshade is a cool name," Tiger protested.

Jill rolled her eyes. "Ugh, whatever. Name him Nightshade."

They all beamed. Nightshade trotted around in the dirt.

"So…we still need to get the real third relic," Abby said, downcast again.

"Hey, we still have 4 real relics! It's going to be fine, Abby," Jill soothed.

"We need to steal them from her," Apple decided.

"Right. If we want to get that third relic, we'd better get a move on!" Jadeine declared

Chapter 33
So Many Questions And No Answers

"We should go find Lizzie and get the real third relic—the ice scepter—back," Abby said.

Everyone nodded, except for Cherry. "No! We're not ready!" Cherry argued.

"What makes you say that?" Jill asked.

"Because…because…" Cherry was at a loss for words.

"We have to go, Cherry, even if we're not ready!" Jill exclaimed.

"I…it's Lizzie, actually Lizzie. Everything we did before, well, we didn't have to steal from Lizzie or go near her. But now…we'll really face her again. And considering what she did to me before…" Cherry explained.

"Oh. Well, we'll have to do it, whether you like it or not," Jill said.

"Jill, that's not how you give a pep talk," Abby said, then turned to Cherry. "It's okay to be scared, but this is the only way to rid this world of Lizzie. You will never have to face her again after we get rid of her. Please, Cherry, we have to go."

"Okay…thanks for the pep talk, Abby," Cherry said and smiled. Then she hugged Abby.

Abby blinked. Cherry had never acted like this before. Abby had half-expected Cherry to snap at Abby that she was fine. Cherry had never been like this before. Abby hugged Cherry back, then let go.

"Where is Lizzie, anyway?" Tiger wondered.

Jadeine opened her mouth to answer Tiger's question, but just then Lumi came fluttering down from the sky, followed by Scales.

"There's news about Lizzie!" Scales gasped. "And—ooh, new people. Who are they?"

Abby cleared her throat. "This is Cherry, and my mom, Melissa."

"Anyways, I smashed Lizzie's power source," Lumi announced.

"And dropped it off to the Sea Witch," Scales grunted. "And now Lizzie has it back because she made a deal with the Sea Witch!!!"

"Hey, I didn't know the Sea Witch would help Lizzie! Aren't they supposed to fight over power or something like that?" Lumi protested.

"Yeah, if you're wondering, Lumi got 0% on life skills class," Scales explained. "Actually."

"Scales!" Lumi erupted, blushing with embarrassment.

"What? It's true!" Scales insisted.

"Wait, so Lizzie got her power source back?" Abby asked.

"In tip-top shape!" Lumi nodded vigorously.

"Where was Lizzie when you last saw her?" Jadeine asked them.

"Um, she was near Snow White's kingdom?" Lumi answered, unsure.

"Ok, let's search from the sky," Abby decided. "Guys, pick a dragon."

Melissa hopped onto Lumi's back, sandwiched between Apple and Abby. She loved Lumi's pearly white scales. She held on tight as Lumi soared into the clouds.

Melissa felt like the clouds were cotton candy. She remembered a faint memory of her eating cotton candy with Jay. The cotton candy was bliss.

Melissa wished Jay were here. He would have loved this.

"Are you scared?" Apple asked.

"Scared?" Melissa looked at him. "Why would I be scared?"

"Because someone has to sacrifice themself," Apple explained.

"Who do you think will do it?" Melissa asked.

"Me," Apple whispered.

"You?!" Melissa exclaimed, bewildered.

Everyone turned to look at them.

"Shh." Apple put his finger to his lips. "I don't want them to know."

Melissa nodded slowly. She wondered why Apple wanted to sacrifice himself. Was he just a good person? Or was there more to his story…

Lumi descended slowly. Melissa saw who Lumi was following. It was a woman with a hood over her face and a plum dress. It was Lizzie!

Lumi's claws zeroed in on the items in a duffel bag that Lizzie was carrying. The real third relic would be in there! Lumi tried to reach for it silently, but Lumi's wings made too much noise. Lizzie looked up and grinned wickedly.

"Well, well, well, if it isn't Abby and her pathetic little group," Lizzie smirked. "Have you found out about my precious jewel?"

"Yes," Lumi gritted her teeth. "Charge, Scales!"

Scales charged forward, but Lizzie put her hand up, and Scales froze. Lumi let out an angered screech and also charged at Lizzie. Abby saw Lizzie slowly reach for the ice scepter—the real one!—and slowly point it at Lumi. Abby knew they would all freeze if they didn't get off.

"Guys, get off! JUMP NOW!" Abby yelled, jumping off Lumi. Everyone followed Abby.

They watched as Lumi froze. Lumi's mouth was open, and her eyes were widened. Abby turned to face Lizzie.

Apple was the first one to talk. "How dare you! TURN LUMI BACK!"

"Be afraid, Orange. I have…this," Lizzie said, holding up the ice scepter.

"My name is not Orange! It's Apple!" Apple protested.

Melissa took a deep breath. She kicked Lizzie in the shins. Lizzie shrieked. "OW!" She dropped the ice scepter.

Melissa, quick as lightning, grabbed the ice scepter and replaced it with the fake relic. Lizzie sat up, groaning. She, thankfully, didn't realize her relic was stolen.

"Come on, let's go!" Melissa urged everyone.

"YOU WILL SUFFER!" Lizzie declared.

Apple darted to Lumi. He must have forgotten that Lumi couldn't fly them because she was frozen. But then, as Apple put a hand on Lumi, Lumi's eyes opened.

"Let's go!" Lumi roared.

"Apple, how did you do that?" Abby asked, leaping onto Lumi.

"I don't know!" Apple exclaimed gleefully. "Actually, I do know! I read somewhere that if a person and an animal have a strong connection, the person can help the animal in ways that seem like magic."

Everyone was on Lumi's back except Apple. He raced to free Scales. At first, Scales stayed frozen, but he slowly thawed. Then Apple joined them on Lumi's back.

Lumi took off into the air while Scales stopped Lizzie from reaching them. Lizzie had no idea her only real relic had been stolen and replaced.

Abby smiled at Melissa. "Mom, that was amazing!"

Lumi landed back on the island. Melissa put the scepter in Apple's hand, who handed it over to Abby.

"Hey, guys, should we take a break?" Cherry asked. "We collected all five relics!"

"Okay," Jill agreed.

"I am so hungry!" Abby exclaimed.

"We should eat that tomato soup and then figure out our next move," Jill said.

"And, um, should Scales and I go?" Lumi asked. "We're done here."

"We really should. Ambrosia said she was making a volcanic slew, mixed with Antarctic ice." Scales smiled.

"Volcano slew?! I'm in!" Lumi exclaimed.

"What is a volcanic slew?" Abby asked.

"Ah, lava and lava dragons," Lumi chuckled nervously.

"You eat other dragons?! That's cannibalism!" Apple shrieked.

"Yes, but only evil ones," Scales explained. "Bye, Apple! Bye, weird humans!"

As the dragons left, Melissa shuddered. Cannibalism?

"Who's hungry?" Abby asked.

A chorus of hungry voices rang out. "I AM!"

Melissa hadn't eaten actual food since Lizzie had cursed her. She slurped up the tomato soup.

"Bleh! You like this stuff?" Abby asked.

"I haven't eaten a proper meal in a week! It's hard finding food when you're hated by almost everyone here!" Melissa explained.

"You call *this* a proper meal?" Jill asked, wrinkling her nose.

Abby had little appetite. She didn't eat any of her tomato soup and handed it over to her mom, who devoured it.

"Where is the Book of Light anyway?" Jill asked when they were all done eating.

"I don't know. The best bet is the Sunshine Realm—Brightshine," Jadeine answered.

"Sounds sunny," Apple mused.

"Duh! It's the Sunshine Realm!" Abby exclaimed.

Jill squeaked, probably because Abby said 'duh' to a prince. Was Jill still not over the fact that Apple was royalty? Because now, they all seemed like friends.

"But…how do we get there?" Tiger asked.

Jadeine frowned. "That's the thing. Brightshine only brings worthy people into their realm."

"So, a golden phoenix would appear?" Melissa asked. "That's what I heard."

"Exactly! But it's not appearing," Jadeine grumbled.

"What about my magic?" Abby asked.

"The phoenix is the only possible way to get to Brightshine," Jadeine explained.

They stared at the bright sun for a while, then looked back down, eyes watery. Abby thought she might go blind after all that direct sunlight!

"We *have* to get the Book of Light," Jadeine declared.

"Wait!" Abby yelped. "What's the witch's hour?"

They all turned to Melissa. She glared at all of them, then fixed her facial expression and smiled.

"I really don't know," Melissa replied.

"But you're her sister!" Abby cried.

"I'm guessing it's 3:00 a.m.," Melissa said.

The sky was turning dark, and twinkling stars began to appear. Melissa wasn't feeling tired until Jill yawned.

"Let's sleep on it," Cherry suggested.

"But what about the Book of Light?" Abby argued.

"The Sunshine Realm can only be accessed in the daytime," Jadeine explained. "So it'll be fine if we sleep."

Melissa sighed. She didn't think she would be able to sleep, even though she was exhausted.

But what else was there to do? She curled up along with everyone else.

Where is the Book of Light? When is the witch's hour? Will Prince Apple really sacrifice himself?

How can I defeat Lizzie—my powerful, evil sister—with a book, four random objects, and a dragon? Will we all survive?

So many questions. No answers.

Melissa looked up at the night sky.

She could make out a couple of constellations.

Melissa bit her lip as another thought popped into her mind.

The biggest question of all: How could this ragtag group ever defeat the Evil Queen?

Chapter 34
To The World Of Happiness

Apple woke up around 6:00 AM.

It was so early. Apple guessed he was just used to Jill yelling for them to wake up, but she was still asleep, too. Apple considered employing the same prank that he and Tiger had done before, but then he decided against it.

Instead, Apple went around and gently shook everyone awake.

Tiger groaned. "I was awake until, like, 3:00 AM. There was this loud noise all night."

"Same!" Abby cried. "I couldn't sleep because *someone* snores like a chainsaw." She looked at Cherry accusingly.

Apple laughed. "I know, right? You're so lucky you don't share a room with her."

"Not. A. Word," Cherry hissed.

"So!" Jadeine chirped. "Let's find the Sunshine Realm!"

"We need the phoenix," Jill mumbled. She was the only one still lying down.

"That's right!" Jadeine exclaimed.

"No…a ghost…stealing my tomato." Jill snored softly. Oh. So she was still asleep.

Apple considered waking her up, but it was fun to watch Jill sleep-talk.

"And…UGH…I'll kick you all! Who is the…ghost?" Jill asked, still very much asleep.

Jill continued.

"And…why is Apple an actual…apple? Why did someone…eat Apple?"

Apple's cheeks flushed a deep red. Tiger snickered, and Cherry burst out laughing. Apple decided it was better to wake Jill up. He shook Jill hard, and she opened her eyes.

"Oh wait…there's no ghost…it's—oh…Apple! Hey!" Jill rubbed her eyes. "Look up at that sky with that phoenix…wait, A PHOENIX?!" She sat up.

Everyone looked up and saw a beautiful golden and fiery red bird land on the ground. It was as big as Scales and looked like it weighed a gajillion pounds. It squawked impatiently at them.

"It's the phoenix, y'all!" Jill exclaimed.

"Come on, let's go on the phoenix!" Abby said.

"Wait…we need permission. Do we have permission?" Jadeine asked. She directed the question to the phoenix.

The phoenix gave a swift nod. Everyone smiled.

They all climbed on the bird, which was very hard to do because it was so large. When they all boarded the phoenix, it took off into the sun.

Apple shielded his eyes. The phoenix went through a beam of sunlight, and suddenly, they were in Brightshine. They were right above it. Strangely, the air felt cool.

Light filled the skies, and a ginormous golden palace twinkled like a star. There were strange folk roaming the streets. They looked solid, but transparent if you looked at them hard. It appeared that they were made out of sunshine.

The phoenix landed, and everyone slid off. Apple bumped his head on the ground, and the phoenix made strange, shrill sounds, which sounded like laughing. *Rude,* thought Apple.

"That was rough," Cherry groaned.

"Okay, group. We need to split up!" Melissa announced.

"Why?" Jadeine asked.

"So we can find the Book of Light!" Melissa replied. "It'll be easier if we split up."

Abby immediately clung to her mom. They all slowly shifted into groups. Jadeine and Cherry were in a group (because Cherry claimed she needed a break from her brother). Apple, Tiger and Jill were in a group of trio.

"Let's meet up right here?" Jadeine suggested. "We can meet up when one of us finds a good lead, and if you don't, just come back here."

Everyone agreed.

They set off in different directions. Apple, Tiger and Jill wandered down an abandoned street. Apple saw a rat skitter across the path and cringed.

Apple looked at a dusty library. It looked abandoned, but it was still a library! And they were searching for a book. *The* Book.

"Guys, let's go in there," Apple suggested.

"Oh, let's not. The ghost is in there," Tiger replied, biting a hangnail.

"What ghost? And how do you know?" Jill and Apple asked at the same time.

"The ghost of Mr. Lollyding!" Tiger exclaimed. "He was the founder of this library!"

"Lollyding?" Jill laughed. "What a weird name! Although I'm talking to two kids named Tiger and Apple…"

Tiger shoved her gently. "Whatever. Be nice. Let's search somewhere else."

"We can't," Apple said. "It's a library, and we're looking for a book!"

"Do you think the Book of Light would be in some random library?" Tiger argued.

"Well, maybe they put it somewhere unassuming so we would go past it."

"'They?' Who's 'they?'"

"Guys!" Jill interrupted. "Who's afraid of some silly old ghost named Lollyding? Not me. You can stay outside if you'd like. But I'm going in."

Jill marched to the door. Apple followed Jill into the library. Tiger hung back at first, but then she sighed and came in after them.

Old books lined the shelves, which stretched almost all the way to the ceiling. Apple realized the library was bigger than he had originally thought.

"You guys think it's on one of the shelves?" Jill wondered.

"No…" Tiger bit her nail again. "Probably in some back room."

"I'll check the children's section," Jill announced. "Tiger, you can take YA books, and Apple can do adults'."

Apple nodded. He strolled off to the adults' section. He skimmed through mystery/thriller, romance, sci-fi, and stopped at a section labeled 'Spells and Other Magical Things'.

Most of the books on the shelf were dusty, but one of them was clean and shiny. Apple craned his neck sideways to read the title, but there was no title. Was this the Book of Light?

"JILL! TIGER!" he called. "I found a book!"

"*The* Book?" Jill yelled back. "Or *a* book?"

"*A* book—but it might be *the* Book."

Jill and Tiger came running towards him. "That looks way different than the others," Tiger remarked.

Jill pulled it off the shelf. "Should I open it?"

Apple nodded. Jill pulled it open to a random page.

Chapter 35
Fatal Curses

Many curses can be fatal or chronic, such as the ones I am a fan of, but one stands out among them all…

The words disappeared suddenly. "What's happening?" Tiger yelped. Jill dropped the book.

Painfully bright red lights started sweeping the interior of the library. A siren sounded. Apple covered his ears. "RUN!"

Apple, Tiger and Jill ran out of the library. When they were in the alley, the sirens and lights were still sounding, which they could barely hear. Apple noticed a new sign on the door—RESTRICTED. He was sure it hadn't been there before.

"What's happening?" Apple gasped.

"I knew this was a bad idea!" Tiger groaned, rubbing the back of her neck.

"Well, you should've hung back outside," Jill told her.

"But you told me to come!" Tiger pointed out.

Jill pinched the bridge of her nose. Tiger was staring at the library through the windows, her hands pressed against the glass, then screamed and stumbled back.

"Tiger? What's wrong?" Apple asked.

"Guys…look." Tiger whimpered.

"Where?" Jill inquired.

"In the windows," Tiger whispered, pointing at it.

Apple peered at the windows of the library. All he saw was dust and books and darkness inside (of course, with a faint touch of light).

Then something shifted in the darkness. Apple startled and took a couple of steps back from the window when he realized it was a ghost.

The ghost didn't look like a scary ghost, like a haunted clown. Just a transparent version of a grumpy-looking old man.

"I suggest you leave right this instant," huffed the ghost from inside the library. Somehow, his voice was clear, not muffled.

Tiger's hands flew to her mouth. She screamed and ran away.

"Tiger, wait–" Apple started, but she was already gone. He looked back at the ghost helplessly.

"Well, that's a way. Would you mind moving a bit?" the ghost asked.

"No. We need the Book of Light," Apple said.

The ghost went from calm to raging in a millisecond. The ghost flew out of the library and stared down at Apple.

"Look, I don't care if you think I'm some feeble old ghost, but I'm serious right now," the ghost spat. "Go NOW."

"And I don't care either," Jill replied, raising her chin. "My name is Jill, and nothing scares me."

"Except falling off a hill. Childish, really." The ghost sighed.

"Hey, how do you know that? Creepy stalker ghost!" Jill hissed.

"We can see anyone doing anything, no matter where you are," the ghost explained.

"Isn't that invading people's privacy?" Apple asked.

"I'm a ghost! What do you think I do in my free time?!" the ghost exclaimed.

"Um, say 'BOO' and haunt people?" Apple guessed.

"Look, Apple, you're here for a limited time."

"You mean, my life? I know." Apple lowered his head.

Jill stared at him. "Huh? What do you—"

"No, in the Sunshine Realm," the ghost interrupted. "It only allows perfectly good people. In truth, no one is completely perfect. But, well, you'll be gone before Jill and Tiger go."

Apple looked down at his shoes. He knew why he wasn't staying long.

"The only person with a shorter stay time is the bad fairy. I know she's here. I can feel her presence. The bad fairy has a negative aura, yet it's not that negative. Curious, her aura isn't all bad, since she's evil," the ghost went on.

"You just insulted Abby," Jill muttered. "Way to go, Lollyding."

The ghost glared at Jill and opened his mouth to speak, then closed it. Footsteps were heard behind them. Apple and Jill turned around. The ghost suddenly vanished.

"Hello, Apple and Jill," a voice said.

Apple panicked. How did this woman know his name? A woman with blue hair and a black cloak concealing the rest of her face stepped forward.

"Who are you?" Apple asked.

"You really don't recognize me? Such a shame," The woman clicked her tongue.

"I mean, you're not showing your face, so of course I'm not able to recognize you." Apple had a sickening feeling growing in his stomach.

Why did this lady expect him to recognize her? He only knew his mother, Nadine, and Lizzie were after them. But his mother wouldn't wear a cloak. Either Lizzie or Nadine. But Lizzie didn't have blue hair. Apple realized who she was with a start.

The woman removed her hood and smiled at them. It was Nadine! Her smile quickly disappeared, and she roared, "GIVE ME BACK MY TIARA!!!"

"RUN!" Jill yelled. She turned around and fled.

Apple followed Jill. He risked a look back. Nadine was right behind them! Apple's heart beat faster with fear. Soon, his legs were on fire, and his breath was fast and short. Nadine hadn't given up.

Apple and Jill gained more ground and saw a wall with a slippery ladder in front of them. "Climb!" Jill hissed.

Apple clambered up after Jill. Nadine set her foot on the bottom rung, but as soon as she did, the ladder disappeared and she fell to the ground. "Curses!" Nadine yelled. "Oh, whatever. You don't have the relics anyway. I'll find that cursed Abby Palmer, then!"

Nadine vanished. Apple shivered. "Yikes."

Just then, Tiger came running to them. She jumped from the building next to the one they were standing on and stopped, panting. "Watch out! Nadine is coming for you!"

"A little late for the warning." Jill sighed. They all climbed down the ladder.

Apple told Tiger the whole story. Tiger replied, "Wow. Nothing much happened to me. I saw Cherry. She seemed fine, so I didn't talk to her."

"Oh." Apple stared at the wall. "Ugh…Abby has the tiara, right? Will Nadine go for her next?"

"Yeah, she said so," Jill answered.

"Let's go back to the meeting spot," Apple decided. "We found a possible lead, and we can warn the others about Nadine."

The three of them walked back to the meeting spot. Apple's stomach growled. It was almost lunchtime by now.

Apple sighed. He wondered if someone had found the Book of Light. Probably not.

And did he even really want them to find the Book?

Because every second they didn't was a second Apple stayed alive.

Chapter 36
Searching

Abby was frustrated. Every moment she didn't find a lead made her feel angrier and more disappointed in herself. *Surely the others would have found some possible leads by now. And I'm the only one who hasn't,* Abby thought.

How hard is it to find a book? Maybe it was in the castle…no, then everyone would know. Or would they? What if it is hidden in a secret room? Or the queen keeps it a secret.

The sunray people looked like ghosts, and a bit scary too. Abby couldn't decipher their faces, or even tell a man apart from a woman!

Melissa stepped a bit closer to Abby, then spoke in a low voice. "Do you know the story of the Book of Light?"

"No. And I'm not in the mood to hear it," Abby replied, frowning.

"Well, too bad. Guess you won't know the connection between the book and the fairies." Melissa shrugged nonchalantly.

"I'll guess," Abby grunted. "The fairies came from the book."

"Wrong! The first fairies wrote the Book of Light," Melissa told her.

"Cool! But how—Wait." Abby frowned. "You're trying to get me to listen to your story."

"It's a good tale, my sandwich! Listen to it!" Melissa exclaimed.

"Well…it does sound pretty cool." Abby gave in, smiling.

"Well, before the Book of Light, there were fairies, obviously," Melissa started.

"Well, you said there were! You don't need to repeat yourself," Abby said.

"Sandwich, let me talk." Melissa asserted, "A girl named Fair lived below Brightshine, and she loved happiness." She wanted to create a realm where darkness didn't exist. So, she captured a wild phoenix and asked it to create a realm for her, with only light. Fair and the phoenix created Brightshine, and then, Fair created people so *good*, they looked like the sun! And she ruled wonderfully. But darkness got in, and half the kingdom was poisoned with darkness."

She continued, "Fair was in distress. She asked the North Star, whose brightness is visible in the Unknown as well, and asked it to create a book of light. The North Star poured its light into Fair's favorite fairy tale, and The Book was created. It's worshipped everywhere."

Abby looked at the palace with newfound respect. She smiled up at it.

"Can we ask Fair?" Abby asked.

"Sadly, she died centuries ago, but her great-great-great-great-granddaughter, Fair the 7th, is ruling over," Abby's mom responded.

"Maybe we can go in?" Abby suggested.

"Abby, there's a spe…"

"Mom, I'm going to go knock on the door. Don't worry about me, I'll be fine," Abby said.

Abby walked towards the castle. At one point, she passed right through the sunray people (whoops!) because she had a sudden urge to turn around and go back to her mom, but she didn't want to do that. So she put so much effort into concentrating on going forward that she didn't notice any of the sunray people and continued to pass through them.

Abby started to doubt herself as she neared the door. *Should I do it?* Maybe there were rules in Brightshine about going up to the doors of the palace. And maybe those rules made it illegal to march up to the palace doors and knock. *What if I need a permission slip or something to go to the palace?* Abby thought worriedly. She wanted to try, so she pushed on.

But suddenly, she screeched to a halt, as if she wasn't in control of herself. Abby was just ten yards away from the castle, but couldn't move ahead, no matter how much she wanted to. She grunted and jerked backwards, then forward. Abby slowly fell into a daze, and when she snapped out of it, she realized she was facing away from the castle. She begrudgingly walked back to Melissa against her own free will.

"Right. As I was *trying* to tell you, the castle has a powerful spell to stop intruders." Melissa smiled weakly. "You should've listened, my dear sandwich."

"But that's…ugh!" Abby groaned. "And, yeah, I *guess* I could've listened to you first."

"I know, I know. Be patient, Ab—". Melissa got cut off by Abby.

"Mom, I know it sounds weird, but I feel it's hard to be patient!" Abby complained. "We're so close to defeating Lizzie—we have all the relics. We just need to find the book, but that's the one thing we can't find!"

Melissa sighed, and her skin looked a little…hazy? "Mom…are you OK?"

Melissa nodded shakily. "It's nothing, just—ugh, I don't want Lizzie to be evil, sandwich."

Normally, Abby would've been annoyed that her mom was calling her 'sandwich' so many times, but her mom didn't look well, so Abby decided not to complain. She tilted her head. "What do you mean?"

"What if I turned out to be evil to you? Wouldn't you wish that I would change? I don't want her to be the Evil Queen. Just my sister Lizzie," Melissa explained, tears in her eyes.

Abby got it now. "Maybe there's still hope for her."

Melissa laughed dryly. "Yeah, right."

"What now?" Abby asked. She felt exhausted. Maybe she had lost a lot of energy when she had been in a daze.

"Oh, I don't know…should we go back to the meeting spot?"

"Already?"

"Well, it's been quite some time."

"We haven't even done anything, Mom."

"What do you suggest we do, then?" Melissa pursed her lips and looked down at Abby with an 'I'm very fed up with this, so DON'T YOU DARE pester me' look. And Abby knew what would happen if her mom got annoyed, and she knew it wouldn't be anything good.

"Let's go ask someone. I'm sure someone around here will know," Abby suggested, trying to make sure her mom didn't get too annoyed. She quickly pulled her mother toward a woman selling incense outside of a hardware store. Melissa quickly transformed their faces to resemble those of other people.

"Hello," the woman greeted them. "What incense would you like? I have floral, woody, spicy, resinous, citrus and herbal scents. These are all guaranteed to have a strong smell even after you light them. "

"We have a question," Melissa told the woman. "But first, what's your name?"

The woman's smile grew even bigger. "Most people don't ask that. I'm Jackie!"

"Nice to meet you, Jackie," Melissa replied. "I'm…Lauren, and this is my daughter…Ava. We were wondering where the Book of Light is?"

Jackie gasped. Her smile disappeared. She leaned in and lowered her voice. "Don't talk about that here! You're holding up the line. Shoo, shoo!"

Melissa walked away. "What do you think happened, sandwich?"

Abby shrugged. "I think they don't like talking about that. Why did you lie about our names and change our appearances?"

"They know my face, Abby, and they'll call the police on me. They know your face, too, and they'll all flock around you. They know our names. Being infamous for me and being world-famous for you…it isn't easy," Melissa explained. She snapped her fingers and turned their faces back.

"Okay…"Abby sighed. "Ugh! How will we ever find it?"

Abby and Melissa began to wander without a clear plan in mind. They passed parfumeries, a whole street filled with nothing but theaters, and some bakeries. And now Abby was craving a donut with rainbow sprinkles.

They ended up on an empty street. There was an old library there, with a sign on the door proclaiming "RESTRICTED."

"Should we go in?" Melissa wondered. "I mean, it's a library and what better place than a library to find a book?"

Just then, Tiger, Jill, and Apple came running around the corner. "Don't!" Tiger yelped. "There's a ghost!"

"What?" Abby stared at her.

"Apple, Jill, and I were here, and there was this ghost that kicked us out. We found an interesting book, but I think that was why the ghost got angry."

"What kind of ghost?" Abby wanted to know.

"An old librarian ghost," Apple replied.

Abby nodded slowly. "Weird. But it could be the Book of Light...did you read it?"

"It was about curses."

"Curses?! But they don't allow curse books in Brightshine!" Melissa exclaimed in shock.

"So, tell me, why was it there?" Jill wondered.

"Maybe..." Abby bit her lip, trying to think of a logical explanation. Then it clicked. "Maybe it's a library full of illegal books!"

"Yeah! That would explain it," Apple replied. "Also, why was the ghost so angry at us? He probably thought we would take his books away or something."

"I forgot to tell you, Nadine's here!" Tiger yelped suddenly.

"Wait, what?" Abby gasped.

"She wants her relic back," Jill supplied. "She's persistent. Too persistent."

Melissa frowned. "Ugh…"

"Maybe we should go check out the market," Abby pointed to an especially bright area, out of the abandoned street.

"Not me! The sunray people are creepy!" Apple said.

Jill shuddered. "Yeah. Here, why don't Apple and I go to the meeting spot and see if Jadeine and Cherry are there? You three can go to the market."

So Abby, Melissa, and Tiger walked to the sunny market. Abby looked among some weird-looking lemons and rainbow candy. Abby's mouth was watering by the time she saw purple pudding that swirled out of its cup sometimes and into the air, morphing into a tiny human figure and dancing—she learned it was called Dancer's Pudding.

Her mom wasn't any more focused than Abby. She kept stealing bites of everything, stuffing them in her mouth.

Tiger was actually paying attention. First of all, she had smelled more scrumptious foods before. Second of all, she had learned to stay attentive so that she would never accidentally reveal that she was Cinderella's stepsister. People hated her.

Tiger noticed an alleyway that was shining brightly, almost *too* brightly. It was as if the sun itself had squeezed in there.

Meanwhile, Abby walked over to a stand with bright, spiky purple fruits. She grabbed one and pulled at it. Were you supposed to eat the spikes or peel them? And how would you even go about peeling it?

"Guys?" Tiger called. Abby turned. Tiger was standing in the narrow alley behind the market, staring into the alley.

"What?" Abby started to run over, Melissa on her heels.

Tiger just pointed. Abby looked.

At the end of the alley, in a gray bin, something was glowing eerily. "What is that?" Melissa whispered.

"Let's go check it out. I didn't want to go near it until you guys came here," Tiger suggested. She jogged towards it.

Abby and Melissa followed. When they were closer, Abby could see that it was actually a bottle—with light inside. "Huh?" she asked.

"It's liquid sunlight!" Melissa yelled in surprise. Then she lowered her voice. "You know the Liquid Sunlight Ocean? It's near here. The ocean used to be filled with this stuff, but then evil things moved in, and the ocean turned to regular water. This bottle is probably one of the last drops of the thing."

"Does it have anything to do with the Book of Light?" Tiger wondered.

Melissa shrugged. "Who knows? Maybe. We should take it just in case."

"Oh, no, you won't. Not until you give me my relic back!"

Abby yelped and spun around. Nadine was standing behind them.

"Not again!" Tiger groaned. "I am getting *so* tired of this."

Nadine stepped towards them threateningly. "You're not leaving here until you give me my relic."

"No way!" Abby cried. "It's ours!"

"What?! It's mine!" Nadine insisted. "You stole it from me!"

Abby blushed. "Well…"

"And then you broke my second deal, too!" Nadine went on.

"That was a trick!" Tiger erupted.

"Fine!" Nadine waved her hands in the air. "Forget about that. After you failed to bring me the Sea Witch, that was fine by me, and I wasn't mad or anything because I didn't think you could do it anyway—and I was right—but then you took the tiara anyway! Which is *so* unfair! That! Relic! Is! MINE!!!"

Abby turned and started running. But then Nadine tackled her and shoved her to the ground. Abby yelped and held the straps of her bag tightly. A small scrape formed on her cheek.

Nadine climbed off Abby and unzipped Abby's bag. She grabbed the tiara and vanished.

"NO!" Tiger yelled. "It's gone!"

Melissa helped Abby up. "You OK?"

Abby started to nod, then shook her head. "Ugh! Now we have to get back the tiara and get the Book of Light!"

Abby's eyes were brimming with tears. They had been so close!

Abby stared up at the sky, touching her bruised cheek lightly so as not to hurt the wound. *Please, God, let us defeat Lizzie.*

Chapter 37
Ghost

Jadeine flipped through the pamphlet.

A random old woman had accosted her and practically shoved it at her. There was nothing useful in it, just 'Your best vacation ever! Go to Brightshine.'

"Nothing helpful here," Jadeine sighed and turned to Cherry. "What should we do?"

"We can't go back to the meeting spot yet…" Cherry trailed off.

"Oh, why not? We've been out here for like two hours!"

"But we haven't found anything yet," Cherry argued.

Jadeine groaned, for it was true.

"Come on." Cherry dragged her into a parfumerie. Jadeine sneezed when she accidentally sniffed a strong scent; it was cedarwood, she decided.

"Why are we here?" she asked, waving her hand in front of her nose.

Cherry pointed to a man in the back. He was hunched over, whispering into the ear of another man. They were both wearing hoods. "Suspicious, aren't they?"

Jadeine nodded. She shoved the pamphlet into Cherry's hands. "Here. I'll go check them out."

She walked over to them and pretended to look at the aisle filled with lavender and vanilla perfumes. But really, she was eavesdropping.

"You know we can't, Kevin," the first guy whispered.

"What makes you say that?"

"A million reasons! The casino…"

Jadeine walked back to Cherry. "They're just gamblers," she reported. "That's why they're acting strange."

Cherry sighed. "C'mon, then."

Jadeine and Cherry walked back outside. "Look, a market!" Jadeine suggested.

They wandered through the market. Then Jadeine saw Tiger, Abby, and Melissa in the crowd. "TIGER! ABBY! MELISSA!" she yelled.

Tiger, Abby, and Melissa weaved through the crowd. "Jadeine! Cherry!" Tiger smiled. "Any leads?"

"No." Cherry sighed. "You?"

"Lots!" Abby chirped. "Tiger and the others found a weird curse book in a haunted library, and then we found liquid sunlight, and then…" she trailed off. Her shoulders slumped. "We lost the second relic."

"What?!" Jadeine gasped. "How?"

"Nadine!" Melissa groaned. "She was angry and she came and stole it!"

Jadeine suppressed a scream. *NOOO*! They were *so* close! Jadeine felt like just lying down on the ground and sleeping through this whole mess. But she had to help.

"But the other relics are accounted for, right?" Jadeine asked with a weak smile.

Abby riffled through her bag. "The staff...the scepter...the shoes...What about the dragon?"

"Nightshade is with Apple," Tiger reported.

"Hello, my dears. Having a good time in the market? I've always dreamed of coming here," someone suddenly said.

Jadeine didn't even whirl around this time; she was so used to people appearing behind them, like Aeryn. She turned around... ...and there was Lizzie. Jadeine's breath caught in her throat.

"Melissa?" Lizzie gasped.

Melissa raised her chin. "Yes." Her voice was the slightest bit wobbly.

Lizzie stared for a second and then burst out laughing. "Wow! My little crybaby sister is working with her itty-bitty daughter! How sweet."

"I'm not itty bitty, I'm 4'11! How did you get in here? Brightshine only allows people with good hearts, but you..." Abby trailed off.

"The phoenix. All it took was a simple perfume that smells like dandelions." Lizzie snorted. "They go crazy over dandelions."

"What do you want?" Jadeine snapped, annoyed.

"I want the relics!" Lizzie replied, as if it was obvious. Which it was. "Mmm, which one should I pick?"

Abby pulled the backpack closer to her. "No way. You can never take them."

Lizzie lunged for the backpack, but Abby quickly stepped to the side. Lizzie's eyes narrowed, and she managed to grab hold of Abby's backpack. Jadeine quickly cast an invisibility spell on Abby, and Abby disappeared from view. Lizzie looked confused, and then her cheeks flushed with anger.

Lizzie grabbed Cherry's arm. Cherry tried to free herself, but Lizzie was too strong. Lizzie squeezed Cherry's arm hard, and Cherry winced in pain.

"I'll keep the tiny princess," Lizzie informed them. "And if you try anything, I'll kill her. Bring me the relics by tomorrow."

"I'm not tiny!!! I'm taller than a 14-year-old!" Cherry huffed.

Jadine, invisible Abby, Melissa, and Tiger tried tugging at Cherry. Lizzie swiftly kicked all of them in the shins, and everyone fell down in pain. With a snap of her fingers, Lizzie vanished along with Cherry.

Now, Jadeine did scream. She ran forward and tripped on the uneven cobblestones. Jadeine clawed at the air. "NO! NO, NO, NO! CHERRY!!!"

Abby became visible again and moaned. Melissa sat down on the ground, her face unreadable. Tiger just stared at the spot where Cherry had been.

For a moment, they were quiet. Then Abby piped up, "She won't kill her, will she?"

"I don't think she'll change her mind," Tiger said gloomily.

Melissa gave a dry laugh. "Agreed. Once Lizzie wants to do something, it is set in stone."

"Guys, Cherry will be killed if we don't give Lizzie the relics. But we need the relics at the same time…" Abby trailed off.

"If we don't give Lizzie the relics…Cherry will be gone," Melissa concluded.

Jadeine slumped her shoulders so far down, she thought she might be permanently hunched over. She didn't want Cherry to die. But she didn't want to give up the relics.

"We *need* to get both Cherry and the tiara back," Jadeine declared.

"Yes, we know that," Abby groaned.

Jadeine glanced at the bottle of…liquid sunlight in Tiger's hand. When Jadeine squinted, she thought she saw a piece of paper inside it.

"Tiger, give me that," Jadeine requested.

Jadeine practically snatched it from Tiger and opened the bottle. The corkscrew popped open and fell to the ground. When she looked through the hole, she saw a piece of paper in it, clear as day. Jadeine pulled out the letter and unfolded it. It read:

To whomever it may concern:

My name is Fair the 1st. If you are reading this note, that means I am dead.

There are monsters everywhere, literally and metaphorically. This liquid sunlight can help you a little way.

Merely drink a drop, and you can defeat them. Remember, kill them with kindness. Show them what it means to be sweet.

Always,

Fair the 1st

Melissa gasped. "A letter written by Fair!"

"Who's Fair?" Tiger asked.

"This girl who made the Book of Light," Abby responded.

"*She* made the Book of Light?! That's amazing!" Tiger smiled—a genuine smile. Maybe this letter could turn things around for them!

The others read it. "Does Fair know about us getting the Book of Light?" Abby asked.

Jadeine massaged her forehead. "Maybe…"

Melissa smiled. "I can already tell this is a strong woman."

"Back to the problem!" Tiger interrupted. "We're missing one relic, and Cherry might die. What should we do?"

Jadeine took a deep breath. "Okay. Jill and Apple are at the meeting spot. We can discuss how to go about getting Cherry back."

"And the tiara," Abby added.

"Sure. And the tiara," Jadeine sighed.

The four of them started walking back to the meeting spot.

"Where's the meeting spot again?" Tiger asked.

"It's just a few blocks away," Melissa replied.

Jadeine heard someone yell her name. She looked behind her, but there was no one there. So she kept walking.

"That was odd. I thought someone called my name," Jadeine said.

Melissa opened her mouth, but then there was a bright flash of light. She vanished.

"Where did she go?" Abby yelped. "Mom?"

"Oh!" Jadeine facepalmed. "You can only stay in Brightshine for a certain amount of time, depending on whether you've done evil things before. Since Melissa cursed Sleeping Beauty and all that, she's gone."

"Will she be OK?" Abby asked.

"Oh, sure!" Jadeine replied, even though she didn't really know.

"Will Apple be going, too, then?" Tiger asked.

Abby bit her lip. "Probably."

Five minutes later, they were at the meeting spot. Jill and Apple were standing there. When they saw the group, they smiled and waved, but then noticed their downcast faces.

"What's wrong?" Apple asked.

"We lost Cherry!" Jadeine cried.

Jill gasped. "Oh, no! I just noticed that! Where is she?"

Jadeine quickly explained about Lizzie taking Cherry.

"I hope she's okay," Apple moaned. "This is bad. This is really, really, bad."

"We know," Abby informed him. She pursed her lips, then sighed and shook her head.

Jadeine was relieved. She hated fights. Arguing wasn't going to solve anything. In her opinion, teamwork was the answer, which was becoming increasingly difficult due to all this tension. Jadeine tried hard to hold the team together.

"So now what?" Tiger asked.

The letter from the sunlight bottle glowed in Abby's hands. She opened it, and they all gasped. There was new writing on it:

Hello, Collector of the Relics.

I am Fair, the 1st. I can give you a clue where the Book of Light is. The only librarian in Brightshine knows—he is a ghost and very grouchy. Be cautious not to anger him.

Good luck,

Fair the 1st

"I cannot believe this! Fair the 1st wrote to us!" Jill shrieked.

"That's cool, but we need to go back to the library to see the old ghost," Apple declared.

As soon as he said that, Apple vanished in a burst of light. Nightshade screeched and dropped to the floor, since Apple had been holding Nightshade. Abby picked Nightshade up and put him in her bag, leaving the top part open so Nightshade could stick his head through the hole to breathe. She hoped he wouldn't bite her.

Jill looked around. "Where'd he go?" Jill asked.

"You know Apple's done some bad things before, so he has a limited stay," Abby explained.

Jill nodded, taking it in. Jadeine walked towards the library where the ghost was. She knocked on the door. *Knock knock.* Nothing. *Knock knock.* Nothing. *Knock knock.* Still nothing. Jadeine gave up and sighed, resting on the door.

"It's no use," Jadeine sighed.

Jill's face grew angry. "Well, if we ask politely, he'll never open up! You've got to make him mad!"

"But Fair—" Jadeine got cut off.

"This is the only way, Jadeine! Hey, MR. UGLY WRINKLES! OPEN UP!!!" Jill yelled.

They all flinched. Mr. Ugly Wrinkles was way over the top, in their opinions.

The ghost flew out the door. He was mad. Very, *very* mad. Jill gave them a look as if to say, *See? Told ya so!*

Everyone else backed away from the mad ghost. *Didn't Fair tell us not to make him mad?* Abby thought.

"How *dare* you?! I am Mr. Lollyding, and you will face my wrath!!!" the ghost yelled.

"Lollyding," Tiger chuckled under her breath. "Funny name."

"We need to know where the Book of Light is," Abby demanded.

The ghost thought for a second.

"Do you have permission from Fair?" the ghost asked.

"Um, yes?" Abby pulled out the letter and handed it to him. She thought it was a bit odd that she had received a clue and permission from Fair, and that the ghost had also asked for permission from Fair.

The ghost examined it, then sighed.

"Forgive me if I was a bit harsh," the ghost apologized. "Since Fair said you have permission to know this…she was very wise. And so I shall tell you."

"Where's the Book?" Abby asked.

"At the place where all joy stands, and darkness dare not enter, if you seek the book, you must let out all your joy and happiness; this you must remember," the ghost recited.

Abby nodded. "Thank you so much."

"My pleasure," the ghost said. Then, the ghost vanished.

Jadeine looked down at her pamphlet and flipped to the next page, bored. What she saw made her eyes grow wide.

"Look, guys!" Jadeine exclaimed.

The pamphlet stated:

Come to the heart of the city, where all joy takes place! Visit the Fair Fountain and the Heart of Joy sculpture! These amazing places won't cost you any money!

"Well, that was easy." Jill laughed. "After all that…"

Tiger laughed, too. "Yeah. We were searching for so long."

"Let's go to the Heart of Joy, then!" Abby cried.

"Wait!" Jadeine frowned as a thought came to her mind. "Who's going to let out all their joy and light?"

"I don't know. Maybe Abby, because she's the prophecy girl," Jill suggested. (Abby did not look very happy at this option.) "Come on! Let's go!"

"What about Cherry?" Tiger interrupted. "Lizzie's going to kill her! We need to save her!"

"Yeah!" Jadeine agreed. "Exactly! Let's come back to the Book of Light later."

"Or we can get the tiara," Tiger said. "Nadine is definitely weaker than Lizzie."

Jill nodded. "She's right."

"But you can't kill a tiara," Jadeine pointed out. "Cherry, however, is very much mortal."

"That's a good point," Tiger agreed.

"Let's vote," Jill suggested. "All in favor of going to find the Book?"

Abby and Jill raised their hands, then smiled at each other.

"All in favor of finding Cherry?" Jill went on.

Jadeine and Tiger raised their hands.

"So, it looks like no one says tiara," Jill concluded with a sigh. "It's a two-way tie."

"We could split up," Tiger offered.

"We did that before, and look where that got us!" Abby exclaimed. "Also, horror movies, hello?"

"We need the tiara, guys. Besides, we have 'til tomorrow to go save Cherry and even more time to find the Book," Jill decided.

"But Cherry is in danger!" Jadeine exclaimed.

"I know. But what if Lizzie gets the tiara first?" Abby asked. "Then she'll have two relics."

"Um. Ok, I guess we should get back the tiara," Jadeine declared. "Then we can find Cherry, and then get to the book."

"Ok…let's go back to Nadine's castle. We'll bring back The Little Mermaid in exchange for the tiara," Abby declared.

"Abby, have you lost your mind? The Little Mermaid is sea foam right now!" Jill exclaimed.

"I mean…" Abby curled her fingers and glanced at them. "You can do a lot with magic."

Chapter 38
Returning What Was Lost

Abby was really nervous. Like, 'drowning in a lake, being eaten by piranhas,' nervous. Did piranhas live in lakes?

Jadeine, Tiger and Jill all looked at the lake warily. Abby took a step towards it, then waded into ankle-deep water. The others followed her.

They kept going until the water reached their shoulders. There was no swan in sight, just a lot of algae and murky pond water. It didn't look as clean as before.

"Hello?" Jadeine yelled. "You there?"

"Nadine?" Abby called.

Tiger gasped and pointed at some bubbles at Abby's feet. Not bubbles, *sea foam!*

The foam took a strange pattern, gurgling and churning, until it looked like a young mermaid's face. The foam gurgled louder, and Abby strained her ear to listen to the faint voice of the sea foam.

The sea foam, of course, wasn't actually talking, but it was more like a voice in Abby's head.

I am the Little Mermaid, the foam whispered. *And I suggest you refrain from trying to turn me back into what I once was.*

"Why?" Abby asked. "Don't you want to be free? And how did you know what I wanted to do?"

It's nice being foam, the foam replied. *Except I cannot speak to many people. I mean, they can't hear me. You must be very powerful if you can. And since I'm sea foam, I slip into people's thoughts very easily. Don't ask.*

"Not really. I can barely hear you," Abby replied.

Good enough. The foam churned more. *It takes strong magic to change me back, more powerful than the Book of Light. You must be willing to give up your magic for me.*

"Sure," Abby replied. "That's acceptable."

Are you sure? Because once one has experienced the feeling of magic at their fingertips, they never, ever want that feeling to leave, the foam warned.

"But you were willing to give up being a mermaid and risk the chance of never being one again," Abby protested.

However, I deeply regret that choice to this day. Please, I beg you, do not try.

"I will try."

Ugh. The willingness of humans. Your attitude is both stubborn and admirable, given how much you're willing to give up.

Abby channeled her magic from within. She concentrated on freeing the foam and restoring it to its mermaid form. She started sweating, and she almost collapsed in on herself, but Jadeine caught her.

"Are you ok, Abby?" Jadeine yelled. She put a hand to Abby's forehead. "Your forehead is warm! You're really sick! Just stop!"

"I…I got this, Jadeine. I…can…do it," Abby muttered.

Abby felt a surge of magic coming from within her. Finally! Abby didn't feel too good, but she decided that once her magic was gone, everything would be fine.

Everyone watched her with amazement as purple light shot out of her fingertips. She pointed it towards the foam. The foam tried to form words, but Abby couldn't hear it. She angled her palms towards the foam, and the beam of light hit it.

Abby Palmer, you have made a grave mistake…

Abby watched as the calm water turned into a maelstrom. Abby felt like throwing up. A figure rose out of it, and when the figure was on its feet, the maelstrom dissipated.

Abby was mesmerized as the watery form transformed into a woman with red, sopping-wet hair and pale, wrinkled skin. Her blue eyes bored into the water and stared at her own reflection. She was wearing a ragged blue dress with cuts in her hem.

Suddenly, Abby felt like she had been dipped in lava. Her ears started to buzz, and her vision began to blur. She said something, but she couldn't hear it. Her eyes fluttered closed. Abby went limp in Jadeine's arms.

"Get her an ice pack or water or a bandaid—ugh, why would she need a bandaid—get whatever!!!" Jill yelled frantically.

"Wait! I can help heal her," The Little Mermaid said.

The Little Mermaid held out her hands like she was expecting Jadeine to give her something. Then, blue sand formed in her hands. The Little Mermaid dumped the sand over Abby's face, and Abby instantly came back to consciousness. She coughed and swiped the sand away from her eyes.

"Sand…don't feel good…" Abby coughed.

Abby fell face-first into the water. For a second, Abby fell unconscious, then her eyes widened and she sat up. She coughed up water. Abby still didn't feel too good, but she had enough strength to plant her hands in the sand below the water to steady herself. Her face was almost touching the water.

"Abby! Are you ok? You said, 'Is it her? Did I…? Then, you fainted!" Jadeine yelped.

"I…ugh, dizzy…fine…maybe I'll die…" Abby spluttered.

"Abby, you're not dying! The Little Mermaid said that…" Jill trailed off.

"I…" Abby suddenly snapped straight up and shot out of the water, *hovering* above it. Her eyes glowed blue, and she gasped. Abby creepily hovered for some time before splashing back into the water. She was alert now.

"What happened to me?!" Abby exclaimed. "Am I in heaven? Have I died?"

"No, but let's put that aside. I told you not to free me!" The Little Mermaid cried.

"But…you're free." Abby frowned, confused. "You can roam the land and seas. Don't you want that?"

"Yes, but you've lost all your magic! You're defenseless, powerless, heartbroken! Change me back and reclaim your powers!" The Little Mermaid begged.

"I'm not heartbroken," Abby said.

"But-IT'S JUST SO HORRIBLE NOT TO HAVE POWERS!!! IT'S TRAGEDY!!!"

The Little Mermaid burst into tears while Abby watched her with eyes that conveyed, *Um, what's happening?*

The Little Mermaid wiped her tears away. "Sorry." She sniffled. "It's just that I get so sad when someone loses their special gift."

"It happened to you," Abby argued. "I get it. You don't want someone to suffer. But I've had my powers for barely a week!"

"Oh." The Little Mermaid stared at her.

"So, Little Mermaid, we need the second relic to defeat The Evil Queen," Tiger told her.

"Who? An evil queen?" The Little Mermaid asked.

"You've been cursed a long time, haven't you?" Abby sighed.

"Oh! Is it a woman named Lizzie?" the Little Mermaid asked. "Wait, she hasn't been overthrown yet?"

Abby nodded solemnly. The Little Mermaid silently fumed.

"My sister won't give it to you unless I go to her," The Little Mermaid replied. "But..."

"But what?" Abby asked.

"Nadine is a horrible sister! She ordered me around like a servant and gave me only leftovers when we were kids. She always took duties away from me and chided my 'poor dress choices.' Can you believe her? This dress is made of ultramarine dragonfly silk and mashed fairy pearls for the laces! It's fabulous—well, it used to be, before I became sea foam."

"Oh, my mom's sister is like that too!"

"Really? Who is she?"

"Lizzie."

The Little Mermaid backed away from Abby hastily.

"It's okay, I'm not evil," Abby assured her. "That's why we're going to defeat her."

The Little Mermaid sighed. "For the greater good, I'll return to my sister. To defeat the greater evil."

She produced a key from a hidden pocket and opened the invisible door. They were standing in Nadine's palace in seconds. And right in front of Nadine.

"Ah! You—oh, you nasty little thieves!" Nadine scowled.

"Hello, Nadine," The Little Mermaid sighed.

"Oh, servant girl! Wonderful to see you!" Nadine pasted on a fake, bright smile without looking at The Little Mermaid at all.

"Ahem. I'm your sister. I'm Nedora?"

Nadine looked at the Little Mermaid, and her eyes grew huge. Nadine stared for a second, then hugged her sister in a tight embrace and let go in about a second. Abby could see the displeasure in her eyes when she thought Abby and her friends weren't looking. *She must really hate Nedora,* Abby thought.

"Nedora! Is that really you?" Nadine gasped. Her gasp was very pretentious.

"Of course it is," Nedora grunted. Then she added, "I've also got some defense tactics up my sleeve, too."

Nadine let the slightest trace of worry show on her face. Then the worry was gone.

"Who brought you to life?" Nadine asked.

"A girl named Abby," Nedora replied.

"ABBY PALMER?!" Nadine yelled.

Abby held her breath. Was Nadine merciful at least? They had done her a big favor by returning her sister. Well, maybe minus some bonus points because they were rivals. But Nadine had to keep up the lie of loving her sister.

The seconds felt like hours. Jadeine's eyes were fixed on a coral masterpiece. Jill was eyeing Nadine with a look that said, *I will punch you and tear you to shreds if you try to do anything to any of us* and Tiger was looking down at her shoes.

Abby wondered when anyone would speak. The silence was too much. Abby hated awkward silences.

Nadine adjusted her tiara a bit. Abby examined it and gasped. It was the relic!

"So," Nadine piped up finally. "I guess you're expecting the relic in exchange for my sister, aren't you?"

"Yes," Abby replied. "And if you don't give us the relic, we'll take Nedora far, far away. And I'm *sure* you love your sister…*don't you?*"

What Abby said caught Nadine's attention. Abby knew Nadine didn't want to say she didn't care about the Little Mermaid. It was because the castle was bustling with servants, and she didn't want anyone to hear that she didn't care, for fear that her reputation would crumble like a house of cards. She reluctantly pulled Nedora over and clutched her. Then she took off her tiara and handed it to Abby.

Abby was about to accept it when she realized it might be a copy of the real item. Abby snatched it and started muttering the words to bring Ismelda here.

When she finished, Ismelda appeared in front of Abby. She looked at Nadine, then at Abby, and then back at Nadine.

"The relic Abby's holding is real," Ismelda announced. "If that's what you were wondering."

"Now, Ismelda, please stop pestering us," Nadine huffed.

"I was called here! By Abby! You-you can't just call me a pest!" Ismelda spluttered.

Nadine snapped her fingers, and Ismelda vanished. Abby swallowed a lump in her throat and gazed at Nadine.

When they had first met, Nadine seemed like a joyful and smart person. She seemed like the perfect queen. But now Abby could clearly see that Nadine was selfish, demanding and mean.

Abby glared at Nadine. "Why did you call Ismelda a pest?"

"Because, honey, she is." Nadine shrugged.

"But she's *your* fairy! Treat her with respect!" Abby exclaimed.

"The girl's right, Nadine," Nedora chimed in.

Nadine furrowed her eyebrows. She stared into Abby's eyes, trying to find a weakness.

"I'm this close to taking back my relic." Nadine put her thumb and pointer finger so close together, Abby could barely see the gap.

Abby nodded, and the group left without saying a word. Abby felt horrible for leaving Nedora behind with that awful Nadine. At least they had the tiara back.

Abby smelled of lake water as she plopped down on the shore.

"Where's Apple?" Jill wondered.

"They're probably back on the island." Abby groaned.

They looked at the clouds and saw Lumi flying down, worried. Only, her flying wasn't normal. She was spiraling down. When she landed, Abby could see that her wing was bruised and scorched. Abby even saw a bone jutting out.

"Are you OK?! You look hurt!" Abby cried.

Lumi winced. "I…ugh. I'll be fine, but I can't fly…"

"We understand!" Tiger assured her. "We'll figure something out."

"Anyway. Lizzie is on the same island as Melissa and Apple," Lumi announced. She shuffled her feet.

"Are Apple and Melissa all right?" Abby asked.

"For now…" Lumi said darkly. "Oh, and Cherry is with them. They were all in a cage."

"That's…this is all your fault!" Jill yelled suddenly, pointing at Abby.

"What do you mean?" Abby asked.

"I mean, *you* dragged us into this mess! It was all you!" Jill exploded.

"You could have chosen not to come, you know," Abby replied softly. She knew fights weren't worth it.

Jill calmed down and sighed. She shook her head. "You're right. Sorry, Abby."

"It's fine, Jill," Abby said with a wide smile.

They were successful in getting back the tiara, but they still needed to find Melissa, Apple, Cherry, and the Book of Light. Additionally, their group was now down to four people.

Abby looked up at the sky. It was getting dark, and the pretty sunset colors were fading away. Patches of sky were a restless black that seemed to move unsteadily. It was how Abby felt. Uneasy and unsteady.

"We don't have much time," Abby declared. "We need to get Cherry back...and Apple and my mom."

"Oh, please don't tell me we have to call my aunt here again," Jadeine groaned.

"You don't," Abby replied. "But I seriously don't get what you have against her."

She pulled out the tiara and muttered the words to summon Ismelda. The beautiful fairy appeared again, but she was frowning deeply.

"Oh, please, don't waste your time by torturing me," Ismelda sighed heavily.

"We need your help. Actually," Abby replied. "We would never tease you just for the sake of it."

"Well then, what can I do?" Ismelda asked, smiling.

"Can you take us to the island below Brightshine?" Abby requested.

"I don't know…" Ismelda hesitated. "There's a strong aura of dark magic coming from there."

"We need to free our friends," Jadeine pleaded. "Abby's mom, Cherry, and Apple. *Prince* Apple. So technically, you'd be rescuing someone important."

Ismelda blew her bangs out of her face. "Fine. Make a circle holding hands."

Abby held Jill's hand, who grabbed Jadeine's hand, who grabbed Ismelda's hand, who grabbed Tiger's hand, who grabbed Abby's free hand.

Ismelda flew into the sky. Abby screamed at the unexpected takeoff. They flew over a tiny sea, and finally, the island came into view.

As they neared, storm clouds swarmed around them, obscuring their view. A purplish figure, laughing, could be seen through the massive clouds. It was definitely Lizzie.

Lizzie held up a hand, and an invisible force pulled Ismelda downwards. They crash-landed in some shallow waters. Abby sat up and realized a cage had been put around them. Water sloshed inside her shoes, and her feet became itchy.

Cherry, Apple and Melissa had also been caged. They were on land. Melissa's eyes widened when she saw them. Then her face fell. Apple groaned. Cherry was full-on wailing.

"Now, Abby, let's play fair. Hand over the relics and I'll hand over your friends," Lizzie vowed.

"The relics are all fakes!" Abby lied.

"They aren't, and I know that," Lizzie replied.

Lizzie drew out a pole crackling with electricity from within her dress. She brought it close to Cherry's arm.

"Now, would you like to see a spectacular light show?" Lizzie leered.

Lizzie inched it closer and closer to Cherry. Cherry squeezed her eyes shut when it was only an inch away from her.

"You can't do this," Abby rasped, her throat dry.

"Abby Palmer, you see, I am the Evil Queen. And I, being the Evil Queen, can do whatever I want," Lizzie responded, not looking at Abby, but at Cherry with a wicked grin.

Lizzie was about to make the pole touch Cherry when Abby couldn't take it anymore. She had to stop this.

"STOP!" Abby screamed.

Jadeine suddenly picked up her staff and made a hole in the cage. She broke free and raced towards Lizzie, determined to stop the pole from touching Cherry.

Jadeine grabbed Lizzie's arm and stopped it from moving forward.

"Let go of me," Lizzie growled.

"Never!" Jadeine exclaimed. Lizzie tried to pull her arm out of Jadeine's firm grasp.

Abby, having an idea, took out the ice scepter and pointed it at Lizzie. "Jadeine, let go!" Abby exclaimed.

Jadeine did. Lizzie surged forward, the pole making Cherry's hair stand up on one end…but then ice shot out of the scepter and Lizzie was frozen in an instant.

Abby stepped out through the hole in the cage. Abby darted to the others' cage.

"I'm so glad you're not hurt, Abby!" Abby's mom exclaimed when she was freed. She squeezed Abby in a tight hug.

Jadeine helped Cherry get to her feet. "You're free! I'm so happy you're safe!" Jadeine squealed and hugged her.

Cherry shot her a strange look. "OK. You seem very enthusiastic to save me, but I guess that's the perks of being a princess." Cherry flipped her hair.

Jadeine let go of Cherry and stared at her disapprovingly. "Wow. You really have a way of making someone regret hugging you."

Melissa's face darkened. "Remember when I told you I wish Lizzie were just my sister, and not the Evil Queen? Today…I wish that more than ever."

"It's fine, Mom, it really is," Abby reassured her. "Besides, Lizzie won't die. She'll just be trapped."

Abby's mom nodded and pasted on a bright, fake smile, like the smiles that people have in those free photos from photo frames in Walmart.

They all formed a circle and began to chat. They began discussing the Book of Light.

"We have all the relics. We just need to go to Brightshine." Abby bit her lip.

"Yeah, but we keep disappearing," Apple pointed out.

"Then, we'll…" Abby trailed off.

"We could just leave Apple and Melissa here," Jill suggested.

Jadeine shook her head adamantly. "No way. If someone disappears, they disappear. Let's see…Melissa got to stay for three hours. Apple got about half an hour more than that. That's more than enough time to be in and out with the Book."

Everyone slowly nodded. Abby gazed at the sea's waves crashing against the shore.

Abby walked to the shore and put her feet in the water. The sun was high in the sky. The wind was calm. It felt like the moment Abby had been desperately waiting for: a bit of peace. But it didn't last long.

A phoenix swooped down from the sky, talons open and aimed right at them. Abby shrieked like Calista (in case you forgot, she's the baby Abby babysits) and ran under a palm tree to avoid its sharp claws. It was useless, though, because they all got swooped up.

"Ow…" Abby moaned because the phoenix had dug its claws into her back before tossing her onto its back.

"Well, here goes nothing! Off to Brightshine!" Apple exclaimed.

To their surprise, the phoenix answered.

"Yes, off to Brightshine," the phoenix repeated.

Abby's stomach felt queasy, and she wanted to throw up, but the phoenix seemed like it would be really mad if she did.

"How can you, um, talk?" Abby asked.

"I'm a reincarnation of my former self," the phoenix replied.

"So a spirit?" Tiger concluded. "Like the Little Mermaid."

"Yes. I used to be Fair-the-1st."

"WAIT, YOU'RE HER?!" Jill squealed.

They arrived in Brightshine again. Fair-the-1st's talking phoenix dropped them on the ground.

"Wow, it's really you," Tiger breathed, staring up at the phoenix.

"If you wish to vanquish darkness, you must know the Song of Joy," Fair told them.

"Song of Joy…yes, my sister used to sing it to me," Jadeine commented.

"Is Jocelyn a good singer?" Jill asked.

"Yes. The best."

"Well! On with your mission! Good luck!" Fair squawked.

Fair took off to the skies. They watched her go, then rushed into the touristy area of Brightshine. Families were strolling around and taking pictures of the gigantic metal heart in the middle.

"Uh, excuse me!" Jill yelled, pushing through the crowd.

"Jill, wait!" Abby called. "There are too many people! We gotta do it at night!"

"But…" Jill trailed off. "I thought Jadeine said we'd be in and out in less than three hours!"

Jadeine shrugged. "I guess I was wrong. Abby's right. Let's wait until the crowd goes away."

Jill sighed. "Ugh! It's only midday! It'll take hours!"

"I guess we could probably just check the place out," Apple suggested. "I saw some pretty interesting places earlier."

"OK…we could go to the palace!" Jill offered.

"I…also forgot the lyrics to the Song of Joy. We'll ask for help," Jadeine decided.

"No chance. There's magic protecting it, and I don't have magic anymore," Abby moaned.

"Abby, did you not realize this? We can just ask to go!" Jill laughed.

"That won't work."

They all turned around and saw a guy wearing a black hoodie standing behind them.

"Hey…aren't you one of those gambler guys that I, um, saw yesterday in the parfumerie?" Jadeine asked.

"How did you know?!" the guy sounded surprised.

"She thought you were fishy, so she spied on you," Cherry explained.

"That's…unnerving." The guy laughed. Then he glared at Cherry. "Wait, are you guys the Queen's secret guards?"

"She has secret guards?" Cherry yelped.

"Whoa, that's totally my gig," Melissa replied, grinning.

"Mom!" Abby hissed. "Now it's going to take forever to change his theory!"

"Actually, I just realized you were clueless about how to get into the castle. You must be rebels too. *New* ones," the guy decided, smiling.

"You're a rebel?" Abby asked, taking a step back. "Rebelling against what?"

"So…not a rebel. Tourist then?" His smile faded.

"No, actually, we need the Book of Light," Jill deadpanned.

"JILL!" everyone yelled in unison.

Jill rolled her eyes. "What? We need help, don't we?" she asked, batting her eyelashes innocently.

"You must be…collecting the relics!" the guy realized, sounding awed and afraid at the same time.

"Yeah," Abby confirmed.

"Um, yeah. You have to have strong magic, *really* strong magic," the guy explained. "To get the Book of Light, I mean. Plus the sacrifice thing…"

"Oh," Abby looked at her shoes and frowned. "I don't have magic. Not anymore."

"But I do," Jadeine announced.

"Of course! We forgot that Jadeine has magic!" Tiger exclaimed. Then she looked at Melissa. "And Abby's mom does, too!"

The guy looked at them with interest.

"Anyways, I'm Kevin. I'd like to come with you," he chirped.

"To do what, exactly?" Abby asked.

"Um…" Kevin tugged at his hair. "To…bring in some surprise decorations! Yes, that's it. The servants said that the queen is *dying* for this new dress, and they're having me bring it."

"That's a lie," Melissa blurted out. "If you want to tell a lie, you've gotta think of a lie before you lie so you won't stammer. Also, you literally said 'That's it!'"

"Mom, that's so creepy how you know he's lying," Abby said.

"What? It's so obvious, it's impossible not to know," Melissa said.

"Yeah…I want to overthrow Fair-the-7ᵗʰ," Kevin confessed.

"Why would you do that?" Jadeine gasped.

"Because, Fair-the-7ᵗʰ isn't like Fair-the-1ˢᵗ," Kevin responded. "She's really awful! Last week, she…she…" he looked at the ground and gulped.

"Why should we help you?" Apple narrowed his eyes. "You're just a random guy."

"A random guy who knows how to get the Book!"

"How do you know that, anyway?" Tiger asked suspiciously.

Kevin shrugged. "I'm shady—I know stuff the average person doesn't."

That seemed like a reason *not* to trust him, in Abby's opinion. She was about to point that out, but then Jill spoke up.

"Fine, we'll go together," Jill said, squinting at him. "Deal?"

"Deal," Kevin replied, beaming.

They all walked to the castle together. After a while, they met the defensive barrier.

"Right." Jadeine rubbed her hands together.

She lifted the staff and channeled her powers through it. It hit the defensive barrier, but had no effect. Another wave of magic hit it, but the barrier wouldn't budge.

Jadeine started panting, then slumped over…before collapsing on the ground.

"Jadeine! Are you all right?" Abby shrieked, running to Jadeine's side. The others crowded around her.

"Is she alive?!" Cherry gasped. "Check her pulse!"

Jadeine's eyes were closed. Abby looked at the palace with newfound anger. She dashed towards it and, surprisingly, slammed into the barrier. It took all of her strength to resist the magic.

Abby suddenly felt very angry. Why did Fair-the-7th have to keep a magical barrier anyway? Did she not have any guards? Or was it because of the Book? Many people didn't know that the Book was there! Abby had one pet peeve, and that was *failing*. It felt a lot like failing. And that made Abby mad. No, not mad. Furious.

Abby felt a tingling sensation surge up her fingertips until it burst out.

Abby looked down, afraid that her fingers would be gone, but instead saw bright violet light streaming out of them.

Abby pressed the magic against the barrier. The barrier shimmered…then burst. Abby stumbled forward, but caught herself before she fell.

Jadeine, right on cue, opened her eyes. "Huh? What happened?"

"You just collapsed," Tiger explained. "You OK?" She helped Jadeine up.

"I…my magic…it's back!" Abby cheered.

"That's…amazing! Abby, you're as powerful as I am!" Melissa exclaimed.

"It only works when I'm really angry or sad," Abby admitted. "But…why is it back?"

"Probably because your magic is really strong," Jadeine surmised. "You have Lizzie's *and* Melissa's magic flowing through your veins. That's a lot of magic."

"Yay, but there's no time to celebrate. Hurry, the guards will come any moment." Kevin ushered them to the palace.

Kevin showed the others a giant bush by the doors, and they all hid behind it. As soon as the doors flung open, and the last guard came out, they sneaked inside.

Abby was stunned by all the light pouring into the castle. It had vibes that made her feel at home.

"This is amazing," Abby whispered.

"It is," Kevin replied. "But I'm sure you can admire the palace later. C'mon!"

Kevin helped them get near the Queen's chambers and then ran off into a thin hallway. Abby hoped Kevin wasn't doing anything illegal. Then again, they all had just broken into a palace without permission. *That* was definitely illegal. Abby felt a squirming in her gut. Jadeine stepped up and knocked on the door.

"Daughter, is that you?" a voice came from inside. "Fair the 8th, I'm busy, hold on."

"Do these people have no imagination when it comes to names?" Jill muttered.

"It's so people know that they're Fair the 1st's descendants," Jadeine whispered back.

The doors swung open. As soon as it did, Fair-the-7th screamed. "Intruders! I shall have you beheaded!"

"We only need to talk to you," Abby pleaded.

"I'll have you publicly executed!" Fair-the-7th shrieked.

"Why is there a barrier, anyway?" Jill asked. "Just a drawbridge or even a big wall could suffice."

"I see… you're tourists from afar." Fair-the-7th nodded slowly.

"Also, we need to know the Song of Joy," Jill put in.

Fair-the-7th's eyes grew wide. "The Song of Joy is forbidden! I'll never teach you the lyrics!"

"But this is the land of brightness and happiness! The Song of Joy is supposed to be, like, your national anthem or something!" Abby protested.

"What's an anthem?" Jadeine asked.

"Guys. I'll use my mind-reading skills instead," Tiger suggested.

Tiger stared at Fair-the-7th as she tried to run, but Melissa froze her in place. Abby looked at Tiger, waiting for good news. Tiger stopped staring after a couple of moments. She grabbed Abby's hand and started running. Melissa unfroze on Fair-the-7th, and she (Fair-the-7th) let out a scream filled with anger.

"Let's go, I got the song!" Tiger exclaimed.

Kevin joined them as they ran. "What about her being a horrible ruler? Did you fix that?"

"What were we supposed to do about that?" Abby half-wailed. "We'll help you later!"

They ran down the hallway until they were in the garden. Guards were standing there…knitting? Abby wondered why until she saw the barrier start to form from the thread.

They dashed out of the garden and back to the town. They stopped and looked at Tiger.

"Ok, the song." Tiger rolled her shoulders back.

Tiger took a deep breath and sang quietly.

"Brighter than the sun

And the stars combined

We're gonna get the world, oh yeah

The whole world is mine

Oh, I could lift off the ground

I could touch the clouds, that's right

I won't come down

No, I won't come down tonight

Oh, oh, oh, oh, oh, oh, oh

Oh, oh, oh, oh, oh, oh, oh

Oh, oh, oh, oh, oh, oh, oh

Oh, oh, oh, oh, oh, oh, oh

Joy and happiness warm

My heart inside and out

Ecstatic laughter

Bubbles from my mouth

Oh, I could lift off the ground

I could touch the clouds, that's right

I won't come down

No, I won't come down tonight

Oh, oh, oh, oh, oh, oh, oh

Oh, oh, oh, oh, oh, oh, oh

Oh, oh, oh, oh, oh, oh, oh

Oh, oh, oh, oh, oh, oh, oh."

Tiger let out her breath in a long whoosh. "Then it basically repeats again and again…and that's it."

There was a moment of silence. Then Jill started clapping, albeit slowly.

Tiger rolled her eyes. "I sound like an injured dog."

"No!" Cherry argued. "Don't say *that*!"

She did sound kind of awful. Abby wasn't going to tell her that, though. "Uh…you sounded unique."

Tiger snorted. "Yeah, right. Unique!"

"Anyway!" Apple clapped for attention. "What do we do now? Just go to that Heart and sing the song?"

"And how do we sacrifice someone?" Abby wondered. She didn't want anyone to die.

"Oh, my little sweeties, clueless as ever," a voice came from behind them.

Abby whipped around. Her breath caught in her throat.

Standing there was the Fairy Godfather.

Chapter 39
Fairy Godfathers Are Mean

Abby stared at The Fairy Godfather, stunned.

"Your Supreme Highness!" Jadeine exclaimed, flustered.

Jadeine dipped into a deep curtsy along with everyone else except Abby, because Abby figured that she didn't really need to curtsy since she wasn't from here. Also, they weren't fairies, so they technically weren't his subjects. *Wait, will he get mad at me if I don't curtsy?* Abby thought nervously. Fortunately, the Fairy Godfather didn't look mad.

"No need for that." The Fairy Godfather chuckled. Abby felt a bit uneasy standing before the Fairy Godfather. That didn't make sense, especially since he was one of the most famous do-gooders in the fairy tale world. But, there was a sort of…ambience around him, and it just didn't feel good.

"Oh. I'm very deeply sorry, Your Majesty," Jadeine replied, blushing with shame.

"What I mean by 'no need for that' is that there is no need for all this bowing and calling me Majesty. Simply 'Fairy Godfather' will do," The Fairy Godfather said.

"Oh. I'm very, truly—uh, I mean, I'm sorry," Jadeine corrected herself before she went all formal again.

The Fairy Godfather cleared his throat and narrowed his eyes at Abby. "I see, you have the blond girl from the Unknown. Take this advice, dears. Don't sacrifice anyone."

"Why?" Apple asked. "It will be done for the greater good."

"Prince Apple, I know that you want to sacrifice yourself. But your life is so… valuable, my dear. Don't waste your life for this… stranger." The Fairy Godfather gestured to Abby.

"Me?! A STRANGER?!" Abby exclaimed with frustration. "I'm trying to save your world!"

The Fairy Godfather guffawed. "Oh, sure. That's what they all say. You know, I went on a tour of the prison once! There was an inmate— I asked him what he had done to get in there. He said, 'I was just trying to save the world!' Ha, how pathetic!"

"HEY! Are you comparing me to a prisoner? Because I'm *not* a prisoner!" Abby spluttered. "I thought you would be better than this. I thought you were amazing. Well, apparently, I was wrong." Abby's voice dripped with ice.

The Fairy Godfather just rolled his eyes. "Ugh, the nerve of you. You're missing the point."

"What *is* the point?" Jill cried, annoyed. "In my opinion, we were doing just fine without you!"

"Yeah, right." The Fairy Godfather snorted. "Like how Cinderella was doing just fine on her own, getting to the ball."

"That's *different*," Abby suppressed a scream. "Just tell us how to get the Book of Light already!"

"OK…" The Fairy Godfather sighed as if Abby had asked for a huge favor. "So-o-o, to get the Book is to sing the Song of Joy to the heart, in a voice deemed beautiful by an angel. Then, a door will appear somewhere in Brightshine containing the Book, and the angel will guide you to it."

Everyone was quiet for a moment. That was easier than Abby had thought! Or was it harder? Where would they find an angel, anyway? Would the angel just come to them?

"And there's only one way to banish Lizzie," the Fairy Godfather said.

"Is it easy?" Abby asked.

"I guess…" the Fairy Godfather trailed off. "But…"

"But what?" Abby asked.

"But it's not ideal…"

"Just tell us what it is!"

"You put the relic's magic into the Book of Light, and then, to trigger the ultimate magic required to banish Lizzie, someone has to sacrifice themselves. So, you don't kill Lizzie. The powerful magic will just send her to the Badlands."

"Great. We'll do that," Abby decided.

"Sure, but where *are* the Badlands?!" Cherry cried.

The Fairy Godfather shrugged. "Figure it out. And it won't matter anyway."

"Why not?" Abby asked. A sickening feeling grew in her stomach.

The Fairy Godfather leaned in close. His breath smelled like cough drops. "Your precious tiara can make any man rich. So I'll be taking that!"

Before any of them could react, the Fairy Godfather snapped his fingers. The tiara appeared in his hands. Just like that, he was gone. They all stood there, shock frozen on their faces. Cherry was the first to move.

Cherry crumbled to the ground. "I give up. I give up. I give up."

"Don't say that!" Abby cried. "We'll find a way. We always do, right, team?"

She looked at her team, which at that time didn't look very promising. Everyone looked worried and terrified. Abby sighed.

She noticed that all the tourists were gone. Had that been the Fairy Godfather's doing?

Abby didn't really care. The truth was, she felt just as miserable as the rest of them.

Everyone deals with bad things in different ways. For Abby, it was just too much. All the bad feelings she had been feeling built up into anger. *Why did I actually think this would work? WHY?!* Abby thought furiously. She was mostly mad at herself for thinking that she could *actually* save an entire world. She couldn't even save…save…*I can't think about that right now.* A load of angry words formed in the back of her throat. Abby tried to hold them down, but they slowly advanced upward until they came flying out of her mouth.

"WHAT'S WRONG WITH YOU ALL?!" she exploded. "WE'RE SUPPOSED TO FIND THE RELICS! COME ON, COME ON!"

No one made a move to leave. Cherry was still curled up on the ground. Her eyes were open, but she seemed lifeless. Everyone was sort of like Cherry, except they were standing and staring off into space.

Abby spun around and started running, to where she didn't know. *Anywhere but here*, she thought while running. *Anywhere but this miserable place.* Her feet pounded the cobblestones as she ran…somewhere.

She was aware of the others calling her name, but she didn't stop. Not until she reached the woods.

TWEET! TWEET!

Abby sat up, groaning. Her shoulder ached. Had she fallen asleep in the woods?

Yup, she had. Songbirds were chirping in the trees above. She checked her watch. It was 5:00 in the morning.

She wondered if she should go back to the others. Abby was embarrassed that she had run away. But saving the world was so hard! And…the Fairy Godfather was not the type of guy who would help Cinderella go to the ball. He seemed like the type of guy who would make her believe she was wearing a pretty dress, but really, she had gotten an ugly one. And he would have a good laugh at her expense.

Abby looked up and saw fresh apples dangling from a low tree branch. Looking at them made her think about Apple, how he wanted to be sacrificed. Abby sulked in the shade.

A songbird flew in front of her face and landed on her shoulder. It tweeted merrily.

"I guess songbirds have everything easy, huh?" Abby sighed wistfully.

The songbird surprised Abby by speaking.

"Yup. We never shed a tear!" the songbird tweeted.

Abby felt worse. She should have stopped her mom from going to H.E.A.L., and never come here at all. Abby wept, and her tears soaked the songbird's feathers.

"Great! Now I have *tears* on me!" the songbird wailed in disdain, as if tears were the worst thing in the world.

The songbird took off. Abby stood and walked towards a clearing. When she was out of the forest, she was in the city again. All this happiness seemed phony and extra…

She looked around for a place without happiness. She needed to feel sad and not so confident for some time. Abby spotted a guy in a black hoodie, jet black hair and dark brown eyes. Kevin!

"Kevin!" Abby called. "Over here!"

Kevin looked up and then screamed.

"FUGITIVE!" Kevin yelled, pointing at her.

Abby looked around to see if someone else was near her, then realized she was being blamed. *Why?*

"This is extreme! What are you doing?" Abby looked at Kevin frantically.

"The Fairy Godfather!" Kevin squeaked. "Sorry, Abby."

Abby's mood sank to depression. "Oh, no. What did he do now?"

Kevin gazed at her sadly. "He popped back around in the middle of the night and put a curse on us. Every time we see you, we have to scream, 'FUGITIVE!'"

Abby groaned. "No!"

He nodded. "Anyway, come quick!"

Kevin tugged Abby back into the town square. The group was there. Well, really only Jill, Jadeine, Tiger and Cherry. Abby realized that Apple and her mom were long gone.

"FUGITIVE!" they all screamed in unison. Then Tiger clapped her hands over her mouth.

"I'm so sorry, Abby!" Tiger yelped. "The Fairy…"

"Yeah, Kevin told me." Abby sighed.

Abby pursed her lips and stared at her battered, mud-stained shoes. She wished that fairy godfathers weren't so mean. She had thought fairy godfathers weren't selfish. That's what led Abby to become mad and run into the woods. *I hate that guy,* Abby thought.

"OK. Moving on. We need to get the Book of Light. Now!" Jill declared.

"Ok, team." Abby rubbed her hands together. "Let's do this."

They rushed back to the statue of a heart and began singing.

"Brighter than the sun

And stars combined

We're gonna get the world, oh yeah

This world is mine

Oh, I could lift off the ground

I could touch the clou…"

A scream cut through their singing.

"FUGITIVE!" Someone yelled.

Abby sighed. She started singing again.

"Brighter than the sun

And the stars combined

We're gonna get the world, oh yeah

The whole world is mine

Oh, I could lift off the ground

I could touch the clouds, that's right

I won't come down

No, I won't come down t'night

Oh, oh, oh, oh, oh, oh, oh

Oh, oh, oh, oh, oh, oh, oh

Oh, oh, oh, oh, oh, oh, oh

Oh, oh, oh, oh, oh, oh, oh

Joy and happiness warm

Abby looked at everyone. She was surprised to find their eyes wide open, mouths agape.

"What? What's wrong?" Abby asked.

"Nothing's wrong. Sorry. Your singing, though…it's beautiful," Jadeine said.

"That was amazing!" Cherry commented. "You have a lovely voice."

"Oh, glad you like it," Abby replied. "I've never sung in front of anyone before."

She looked up at the bright blue sky, hoping to see an angel descending. The weather was cloudy. The sun was barely visible, and the sky was dark blue. After a while, Abby dropped her gaze, disappointed, when she heard a gasp.

"Oh my," Jadeine gasped. "Look up."

Abby looked up to see that the clouds had vanished. The sky was getting bluer. It changed from navy blue to blue, then to sky blue. The sun shone brighter than it ever had before, and Abby immediately looked down. They all heard a flapping sound and a thump next to them. They looked up and gaped when they saw what had to be an angel.

The angel had dark brown skin and black, inky eyes that blinked innocently at them. She had a couple of freckles. Her hair was also black. The angel was wearing a white dress. The dress was billowing in…the breeze? But there was no breeze. There must have been some kind of angel-like power that made her dress billow like that.

"Hey!" the angel greeted her. "I'm Isha.."

"Uh, hi! I'm Abby." Abby wasn't sure how to phrase this next sentence. "Is my voice…beautiful?"

The angel smiled. "Very!"

Abby pumped her fists in the air. "Yay!"

"Yeah…wait a second…I feel the presence of…the Book of Light!" Isha exclaimed. "It's what you wanted, yes? That's why you called me here?"

"Yeah!" Abby exclaimed.

"That's great! It's somewhere in the Fairy Godfather's castle," Isha reported.

Jill groaned. "Ugh, *him*?"

"So! How has your day been going so far?" Isha asked politely. That made sense to Abby. *Angels should be polite,* she thought.

Abby exchanged glances with her friends. "Uh, not that great, but I'm glad you care about how my day has been going so far. And—oh no!"

"What's wrong? Is there anything I can do to help you?"

"I just remembered! The Fairy Godfather—he took our relic!"

"You're searching for the relics? Wow. You must be brave," Isha said, then took in the part where Abby had said their relic was missing. Isha frowned. "That rotten Fairy Godfather. I hate that guy, even though that's against the law where I come from. But which relic did he take?"

"The tiara from the Merqueen's palace!"

Isha gasped. "The tiara?! From the Merqueen's palace?! It's expensive and *so* valuable, he'd definitely keep it!"

Abby groaned. "This is bad."

Kevin nodded in agreement. "It *is*."

"Do you guys want me to help you find the tiara?" Isha cut in. "I mean, that's also where the Book of Light is, so I guess I'd have to go anyway."

Abby, Kevin, and Jill looked at each other. "Of course! You're our angel guide after all!"

"Um, can I stay here? I do *not* like that Fairy Godfather. He scares me," Jadeine piped up.

"Sure, you can stay, but this is coming from the person who immediately bowed the minute she saw The Fairy Godfather?" Abby waggled her eyebrows.

"I didn't know that he was so cruel!" Jadeine protested.

"And, also, I feel a bad vibe around the guy. And, I can stay to keep Jadeine company," Tiger put in. "And to guard the relics."

"Me too," Cherry agreed. "I think I would just slow you guys down."

"Sure, Tiger. How about Kevin, Jill, Isha, and I go find Apple and my mom and get that tiara?" Abby suggested.

"OK," Kevin agreed. "My time is almost up anyway."

Abby blinked. Then she realized he meant Brightshine time. "Why, what have you done?"

Kevin laughed. "What haven't I?"

Abby stared at him.

Kevin, seeing her look, shook his head. "Real talk: I gambled a little because I…" he stared off into space.

"Kevin?" Abby nudged him. "You OK?"

He nodded, but he didn't look OK. "I…yeah. Let's go! What are we waiting for?" He gave a wobbly smile.

Isha stuck two fingers in her mouth and whistled. Fair-the-1st swooped down from the sky and squawked, "Where do you need to go?"

Abby looked at the others. "Uh…could you take us to the Fairy Godfather's castle?"

Fair nodded. Abby, Isha, Kevin, and Jill climbed on the phoenix. They made small talk as the phoenix flew.

"So, how old are you, Abby?" Isha asked cheerfully.

"Twelve," Abby replied. "I'm starting seventh grade in August. What about you?"

"I'm fifteen. Kevin?"

Kevin blinked. "Sorry?"

Isha repeated the question. "Seventeen going on eighteen," Kevin answered.

Abby figured that Isha was really into knowing how old everyone was.

"Ok, as much as I'd love to know how old everyone is, and ride a phoenix, we don't have time. We need to find the Fairy Godfather right *now*," Jill declared.

Isha nodded. "Sure. Bye, Fair!"

She snapped her fingers, and they arrived in front of a palace with rainbow windows. Fairies guarded heavy, golden doors. Isha smiled at the guards.

"I need to come in," Isha requested, very politely.

"What's your business here?" a guard queried. He shot a glare at Abby. "I think I recognize the blond one, but I'm not sure from where. No doubt you guys are up to something."

"Hey! I'm not up to something bad! Seriously, are all of the people who stay here so mean?" Abby complained.

"Are you hinting that his Majesty, his Excellency, Ruler of Fairies, The Fairy Godfather, is *mean*?" the guard asked, raising a bushy eyebrow.

"Uh…*no*? Isha, tell him why we're here," Abby said.

"We need to talk to the Fairy Godfather," Isha replied.

The guard's cheeks turned red with anger. "NO. Now SCRAM!" The guard made a shooing motion.

Isha dug her feet into the cobblestone and looked at the guard with a peppy smile.

"Sorry, but isn't there a code against being mean to angels?" Isha asked, her white wings raised. "Like, there *actually* is. We only want to give people the best things, and at least, treat us *nicely* in return."

"You're just a fairy. Or maybe a human in a clever disguise. Angels look like heaven. Perfect. And you, missy-who-is-very-much-not-an-angel, have acne," the guard huffed.

"So?" Isha asked, gritting her teeth. "Angels can have acne."

Abby finally noticed the giant red spot in the center of Isha's forehead. She felt bad that the guard didn't think Isha was an angel just because of one red spot, just because of one imperfection.

"Yeah, but to me, you look like a descendant of a mean ol' witch." The guard laughed.

Isha's eyes flickered from peaceful to angry. She pressed her lips together and clenched her fists. Isha's wings flapped faster.

"I don't want to cause trouble," Isha said carefully after a while.

"Yeah, right," the guard snorted.

Isha squeezed her eyes shut, then opened them, except her eyes were glowing yellow. The sky turned from a calm blue to a blinding shade of yellow, the same color as her eyes. White feathers fell from the sky and landed on the ground. The guard backed away.

"I'm sorry, go in!" the guard yelped, holding the door open for them.

Isha's eyes returned to their normal color. Isha led the others in and followed behind them. The inside of the palace wasn't as bright and sunny as the exterior.

The Fairy Godfather turned the corner and froze in his tracks. His eyes widened when he saw Isha's white, fluffy wings and halo.

"Y-you're here." The Fairy Godfather squirmed. "But, of course, I blocked your angel magic. The door never appeared, did it?"

"You!" Abby exclaimed. Abby's eyes glowed a bright purple. "YOU!"

Abby floated above the rest and angled her eyes at The Fairy Godfather's crown. The Fairy Godfather ran, but Abby simply followed.

The Fairy Godfather decided to fight. He turned around and held out his hand, like he was expecting a high-five. A blinding blue light streamed from his hand and struck Abby. Abby got knocked down and she crashed hard on the marble floor. She heard shouts of 'Are you ok?' and 'Did you get hurt?' and 'Come on, Abby, you can do this!'.

Abby got up and rubbed her aching back. Then, she jumped to her feet and dashed after the Fairy Godfather, before realizing it was pretty much an impossible chase. The Fairy Godfather easily zipped in front of Abby. Abby boosted herself up using her magic, although she sometimes plunged a couple of feet before rising again, and then almost hit her head on a chandelier.

Then, Abby knew what to do. She squeezed her eyes shut, and when she opened them, her eyes were glowing a deep purple. A lasso erupted from her, and she threw it at the Fairy Godfather's head. The Fairy Godfather kept swerving to avoid it.

"AGHHHHH!" Abby screamed in agitation. "Just GIVE UP ALREADY!"

"Ha! You're so foolish! Never!" The Fairy Godfather chuckled.

"No!" Abby yelled. "You're the foolish one! Don't you realize that the Evil Queen is rising right under your nose, and you're not lifting a finger to stop it? You're jeopardizing the world! You are truly evil."

The Fairy Godfather had the nerve to look shocked. "What do you mean? I'm a great king!"

Abby snorted. The Fairy Godfather looked at everyone else. "I…I am, right?"

Now was the time. Abby swooped down, snatched the crown, and flew back to the others. The Fairy Godfather zipped after her, but a quick blast of magic and the Fairy Godfather got blown back by a couple of yards.

She placed it in her bag and grinned at them.

"How did I do?" Abby asked.

"That was awesome, Ab!" Jill cheered.

"Yeah. Isha, where's the Book of Light?" Abby asked.

"In here," Isha frowned. "Somewhere. Sorry, I'm not good at this."

Abby sighed. "I don't think the Book is here exactly. Maybe somewhere else, really deep into the castle."

"Or maybe it's right here," Kevin stared at the wall.

She looked at the wall where Kevin was staring. A shining door that Abby hadn't seen before had appeared. Abby stretched her hand out and twisted the knob. The door creaked open to reveal a glowing book sitting open on an altar.

Abby leaned forward and grabbed the book. The Book of Light. The cover was pure gold. Abby felt happiness surging into her. She walked back to the group and smiled at them.

"Guys," Abby breathed. "We did it. We really did it." Abby smiled.

"Woohoo! Anyway, can I go now?" Isha asked.

"Sure, Isha." Abby smiled.

Isha vanished, and Abby smiled again.

"Guys, we gotta go, because THE FAIRY GODFATHER AND HIS ANGRY GUARDS ARE COMING!" Jill screeched.

They turned and ran. Abby's feet thumped against the cobblestone, and she drew in short breaths. Her lungs felt like they were on fire, but Abby forced herself to keep running.

"Guys!" Abby panted. "We have to get out of Brightshine! Call a phoenix!"

Jill whistled, and a phoenix swooped down. It was Fair again. Fair picked them up using her claws and tossed them onto her back.

"Thanks, Fair!" Jill exclaimed. "Take us to the island below Brightshine, please!"

"Whoa, whoa, whoa. Why did you call the bird Fair?" Kevin asked, confused.

"It's her reincarnation!" Jill explained.

"Really? That's AMAZING!" Kevin exclaimed.

"We're here!" Fair announced. Fair dropped them off on the island, where Melissa was waiting for them. Apple was using a stick to draw figures in the sand.

"Hi, sweetie!" Melissa exclaimed.

"Hey, Mom!" Abby exclaimed. "And, hi, Apple!"

"Oh. Hi, Abby. Hi, Jill, Kevin," Apple greeted.

"So," Melissa prompted. "We have to banish Lizzie to the Badlands."

"Right…our adventure is close to over." Abby sighed, surprised to feel a pang of sadness.

"What's wrong, Abby?" Jill asked.

"Nothing. I'm fine," Abby fibbed.

Fair dropped them off by the heart statue. Jadeine and Tiger waved from below.

"Hello, you," Jadeine huffed. "Took you long enough."

"Sorry…we got the book!" Abby exclaimed.

"You did?!" Tiger jumped up and down. "Let me see, let me see!"

Abby looked around. Barely anyone was in the town square, just an old lady and a young couple gazing into each other's eyes.

Abby pulled out the Book of Light. The pages shone brighter than before. Abby leafed through the book and attempted to read the words, but she didn't see any. It was probably just the light. Abby shoved it back in her backpack when she noticed the old lady looking at her in the eye.

"Ummmm…ok, first we need to find Lizzie," Abby said.

"Then why did we even get back up here in the *first* place?" Jill asked.

Abby thumped Jill's head. "To get our friends!" Abby exclaimed.

"Right, right," Jill said.

"Hi, Abby! I'm glad you're back!" Tiger chirped.

"Hey, we got the tiara!" Abby exclaimed.

"Cool. But there's something else…" Tiger narrowed her eyes.

"What?" Abby asked.

"I know it takes a long time to get the tiara from the Fairy Godfather, but for how long did you think you were gone?" Tiger asked.

"Um…an hour? Maybe two?" Abby guessed.

"Then what were you doing for 6 whole hours, Abby?!" Tiger burst out. "You made me worry! I thought the Fairy Godfather had imprisoned you or something!'

"Wait, we were gone that long?" Abby asked, panicked.

"Well…the Fairy Godfather might've warped time or something before we left," Jill suggested.

"Maybe…but we never saw him after I snatched the tiara," Abby argued.

"I did. I wanted to see the look on the Fairy Godfather's face. He was casting a spell, and light came out. Only a sliver hit us. I didn't think anything would happen," Jill explained.

"Well, the important thing is that you're here now," Jadeine sighed.

"Yeah, that's something," Tiger nodded in agreement.

They all stood around awkwardly for some time. Abby realized this felt like the first time she had ever just stood silent.

Then, to their surprise, Apple whistled and a phoenix—not Fair, just a regular one—swooped down and grabbed them with its claws. It tossed them onto its back (not very gently, unlike Fair) and soared down.

"APPLE, WHAT?!" Jill screamed. "YOU ALMOST GAVE ME A HEART ATTACK!"

"Sorry!" Apple looked sheepish. "Um, take us to the beach!"

The phoenix dumped them onto the beach. Again, not at all gently! Tiger opened her mouth to say something when she spotted a figure running towards them in the distance. They all squinted.

"Cherry!" Apple yelled. "What are you doing here?"

She shrugged. "I had this really bad dream that…something bad would happen to you. And then, I just couldn't shake the feeling, so I came." She brushed some sand off her leg. "Ugh, how do you stand all this sand?"

They all rolled their eyes. "So. What now?" Tiger asked.

"Well, I could give us a lift," Abby's mom decided.

Abby's mom snapped her fingers, and a strong wind blew them upwards, then carried them forward.

"Mom?" Abby asked. "THIS IS AMAZING!"

"I know," Abby's mom responded with a smile.

The winds dropped them off at a familiar place…Cinderella's summer palace! Abby beamed up at the sky, then at her group. Cherry landed on the ground a bit too hard, and a scrape appeared on her cheek.

"OW! SOMEONE HELP, I AM DYING!" Cherry screamed.

"We'll have to meet Lizzie and use what we have to banish her," Abby said.

"But…Abby, I never thought it would come to this. I'm scared, Ab." Jill whispered. "I…I don't think I can do this."

"Look…we *can* do it. There's no can't, okay? We have to keep going." Abby said.

"We will keep going," Jill said, resting her hand on top of Abby's.

"Yeah," Jadeine smiled, and kept her hand on top of Jill's.

Everyone placed their hands on top of each other.

"Ok, guys. We can do this. We have the brains, the strength, the relics—and most importantly, we have each other. Let's go fight Lizzie, guys."

Chapter 40
Meltdown

Lizzie was having a meltdown. A really bad one. And Lizzie's regular meltdowns are terrifying, so you can imagine how terrible this one was.

Lizzie's eyes were green and had been so for the past hour. She had amassed an army of thousands. Still, she was angry.

Lizzie stomped her foot on the ground one, two, three times. The ground shook, and a couple of small buildings collapsed. A radio lay beside Lizzie's feet. Lizzie kicked it and then clutched her foot in pain. The radio started playing, and Lizzie could hear a distorted voice coming from it.

"…and Abby Palmer has managed to get all the relics! We're all so happy! All of us are hoping she manages to get the Book of Light and save us from the wrath of Lizzie…"

Lizzie clenched her fists. Abby Palmer had everything. Everything. She had taken away Lizzie's pride and her subjects. People were less afraid. All because of her crybaby sister, Melissa.

Lizzie screamed so loud that the surrounding buildings collapsed. Lizzie roared more and more until all she could see was dust. Dust got into her eyes, and she swiped the dust away.

"Abby Palmer…UGH!" Lizzie shrieked.

Lizzie picked up some dirt and threw it at her bewitched people. It hit a little girl's shoulder, and she started wailing.

"Shut up," Lizzie muttered.

The girl stopped crying, and her chin began to tremble. All of a sudden, Lizzie felt like a rock had been put inside her throat. Her eyes burned, not with rage, but with tears. And when a tear managed to get out, more followed.

And then Lizzie cried. She had never cried before. Lizzie felt humiliated.

"I HATE MELISSA! I HATE ABBY! I HATE JESSICA DAVIDS! I HATE SNOW WHITE! I HATE SNOW WHITE'S FRUIT KIDS! I HATE...*I absolutely hate...**EVERYTHING IN EXISTENCE!***" Lizzie screamed.

Lizzie was out of breath. She took a deep breath. Lizzie decided then and there that she would face Abby. Whether Abby liked it or not, *this was the final battle.*

Lizzie snapped her fingers. *Take me and my most loyal servants to Abby Palmer*, she thought. Lizzie and her bewitched army arrived in a small town. The aura of the town was way too cheerful. *Ugh*, Lizzie thought, *Sunshine and rainbows every day.* Lizzie snapped her fingers again, and a map appeared in her hand. She unfolded it.

Lizzie made tiny circles with her fingers across the map until she landed it on a big chunk of the map.

"Cinderella Town...Happy Boulevard?! Ugh, you gotta be kidding me!" Lizzie groaned.

A friendly-looking baker ran up to Lizzie with loaves of bread in each hand. His apron and face were covered with flour.

"Hey, miss, you must be new here! I saw you looking at the map!" he announced cheerfully.

"New?" Lizzie snorted.

"What?" the baker asked.

"It's just that…don't you know me?" Lizzie asked.

That's when Lizzie saw her hair. Curly black hair. And her skin! Her skin was very, very pale, like…Snow White. She was wearing a luxurious orange sweater and diamond earrings, but underneath, she wore a yellow and blue dress. Rats. She looked like Snow White.

The baker studied Lizzie for a second, then bowed.

"Oh, forgive me, your majesty," the baker said, "I didn't recognize you with that…new look."

Lizzie's first instinct was to laugh at him and then shove him aside, but she realized that Snow White would never dream of doing that.

"Ah, it's ok. No worries." Lizzie sighed.

"Oh, you must come for tea!" the baker cried.

"Well…I'm on a tight schedule." Lizzie fibbed.

"It'll only take 15 minutes!" he begged.

"15 MINUTES! I-OH FORGET IT!" Lizzie screamed.

"I'm sorry, your majesty."

"SO- I mean…no, I'm sorry. I'm a bit anxious about getting everywhere on time, as you must know."

"D-do you still have time for tea?"

"Well…if that includes t-…" Lizzie caught herself before she said, 'traumatizing you.' "Um, if that includes the bread, then yes."

"Oh, thank you, thank you, thank you!"

The baker danced a bit before dragging Lizzie into his shop. But Lizzie caught a glint in the baker's eye that was very familiar…gray eyes that twinkled like it was telling a secret.

The baker spun around and tackled Lizzie to the ground. Lizzie squirmed, but a rope had been secured around her.

"Who are you?!" Lizzie shrieked.

"Eleanor Queen," the man replied.

Eleanor's disguise wore off. Lizzie wormed out of Eleanor's grasp and glared at her.

"I gave you your son back!" Lizzie spat.

"Liar." Eleanor glared at her. "You made him your servant, *then* gave him back."

"What?!" Lizzie sputtered. "You're lying!"

"I'm not."

"Yes, you are."

"Nope. Also, can I mention this—before, I was never on your side."

"Of course you weren't."

"Well, now I *am* on your side."

"You just said that you weren't!"

"Now I am. And if you keep calm, then I'll stay on your side."

"No. I can't…can't…."

"Trust me? You can bewitch me if you'd like."

"Really?"

"No."

Eleanor grimaced at Lizzie's cheeks and red, rimmed eyes. "C'mon, Liz. Let's go get Abby," Eleanor said.

"Sure. But quit calling me Liz!" Lizzie exclaimed.

"Sure, Liz," Eleanor smirked.

"You just—!"

"I just what?"

"I plead with you not to call me Liz."

"Hmmm, soft now, are you?"

"What do you mean by 'soft'?"

"You're as soft as a squished marshmallow that just got squished again under a foot."

"I. Am. Not. Okay…Ellie? And that was a weird example."

"Sure. If you say so!"

"Well," Lizzie said. "Onwards."

Eleanor and Lizzie marched out of the shop. Lizzie scanned the area until her eyes found a woman in a green cloak. A group of kids surrounded her, and one of them was wearing a bulging backpack, with a dragon in their arms. It *had* to be Abby and the group. Lizzie dashed forward. She skidded to a stop right in front of them.

"Stop!" Lizzie shouted.

The group turned around. And Lizzie locked her gaze with Abby Palmer's.

"Lizzie!" Abby yelped.

Abby had not expected that Lizzie would find them first. She had expected that they would find Lizzie first. And now, Lizzie had found them unprepared.

"Yes, it's me," Lizzie smiled.

Abby took a deep breath. "It's too late. You're going to the Badlands."

Abby dug through her backpack and took out the relics. She pointed the ice staff at Lizzie.

"Surrender or freeze," Abby threatened.

Lizzie threw her head back and laughed. She looked Abby in the eye.

"Oh, Abby, you're so young and clueless." Lizzie snickered.

"I'm 12, for heaven's sake! That's not young. Now—do you surrender?" Abby asked.

"Never!" Lizzie cackled.

The sky turned a brownish hue, and the ground became barren. Abby looked at Eleanor in fright.

"You're still—what?" Abby was shocked.

"Abby, I'm pretending," Eleanor mouthed.

Lizzie suddenly sent a wave of dark magic towards them. The battle had begun. Abby pointed the scepter at Lizzie, but Lizzie skillfully dodged it. Abby sent another shard of ice directly at Lizzie's eye, but Lizzie broke the ice in half with her hand.

Jadeine used her staff to send electrifying shocks at Lizzie, but hit Jill instead after Lizzie deflected it.

"Jadeine!!!" Abby yelled.

"Sorry!" Jadeine gasped. "I didn't know that would happen!"

Tiger dashed to Jill, who had fallen to the ground. Lizzie kept defending herself against the attacks, but then switched to offense.

Lizzie cackled as she tried to wrestle Jay (the staff) from Jadeine. Apple threw a couple of sticks at Lizzie, and they hit her head. Lizzie flinched, which allowed Jadeine to back away.

"Guys, we have to put the relics together and use their powers at the same time," Jadeine said. "But first someone has to…sacrifice themself."

"I'm scared. Are you?" Abby asked.

Jadeine opened her mouth to say something, but before she could, she held up her staff to deflect some dark magic.

Abby stood next to Jadeine and pulled out all the relics and the Book of Light from her backpack. A wave of dark magic made Abby put the relics back in the bag. Abby's heart was pulsing, and she was sweating. She felt like napping and letting the world happen around her. Abby closed her eyes, but was then awakened by Jadeine.

"Abby, that was Lizzie's magic! Come on, get up!" Jadeine exclaimed.

"Ughhhhh," Abby replied. "Ok." She dragged out the 'k' part of 'ok'.

"We have to weaken her," Jadeine said.

"But how?" Abby asked.

"Abby!" Tiger exclaimed. "Can you make a fountain?"

"Um…I'll try," Abby replied.

Abby opened her hands. She felt her magic tingling inside of her, but it refused to get out. Abby needed to let it out, but her fear held it in. Abby thought back to when she first discovered her magic. She had been angry. What if she was angry now? Would that work?

So Abby tried to remember the times when she had been angry. She thought of when she had seen her mom following Lizzie's orders in a daze. She thought of Jadeine's story of how she was trapped in the forest. An unexpected thought came to Abby's mind.

She remembered one day in school when she was walking with her friend, Hailey, in the hallway. They hadn't been friends, actually. They had been best friends.

But then, these mean kids told lies about Abby. One day, they framed Abby for stealing Hailey's things. Hailey didn't want to be friends with her after that.

Abby thought about how the mean kids had laughed at her. Hailey had looked at her, disgusted. Those kids ruined Abby's life! They made sure that wherever Abby went, no one liked her! They had *targeted* her! *They made sure I never felt happy again, and I hate it. I HATE THEM! I HATE THEM SO MUCH BECAUSE **THEY RUINED MY LIFE**!* Abby thought.

A storm swirled around Abby, and a fountain streamed out of Abby's hands. The storm dissipated, but Abby still had a couple of clouds drawing near her.

Lizzie gazed at the fountain. What would happen? Lizzie felt uneasy and turned to face Abby, but instead saw Jill's outstretched hands. Lizzie screeched as Jill pushed her into the fountain.

Lizzie screamed. She tried to get out, but she was trapped!

Lizzie focused her energy on freeing herself, but this magic was powerful. It would take some time…WHICH SHE DIDN'T HAVE!

Abby tugged open the Book of Light. "C'mon, guys!"

"What are we supposed to do? I forgot!" Jill yelled, running over. She was limping a little.

That was when the Big Bad Wolf slunk onto the scene.

"Wolfie!" Lizzie exclaimed gleefully.

"Hello! I will kill them!" the Big Bad Wolf said with the same enthusiasm.

He ran for Abby. "Not her!" Lizzie yelped. "She's mine! I give you permission to kill any of them EXCEPT Abby! Or Melissa!"

"Who first?"

"I don't care, you illiterate wolf!" Lizzie screeched.

Apple reached for the Book.

Cherry screamed and ran even though the Big Bad Wolf wasn't running at her (actually, he was 12 yards away).

Lizzie finally broke out of the fountain and directed all her dark magic at Melissa, who crumpled.

Basically, chaos was ensuing (like, you couldn't waste a second without using a ton of brain power and energy).

"MOM!" Abby yelled, rushing to her side.

Lizzie cackled.

The wolf pounced at Tiger, who somehow staggered to her feet. She grabbed the staff, which Jadeine had dropped when she had grabbed Cherry, and flung it at the wolf. It pierced the wolf's leg. The wolf howled in pain and lay there, quivering.

Lizzie raised her arm, ready to kill Abby.

Someone threw a punch that drilled Lizzie right under the eye. She whipped around it was Eleanor Queen.

Tiger grabbed Lizzie's hand.

"What are you going to do to me?" Lizzie taunted.

Tiger calmly twisted Lizzie's pinkie and ring finger backwards until there was a crack. Lizzie screamed.

"What are we supposed to do now?" Abby yelled, scrambling up. Cherry was now sobbing, standing in the middle of the chaos, with Tiger making sure nobody harmed Cherry.

"The relic's magic!" Jadeine called. "To banish Lizzie!" Jadeine pulled out the relics.

Tiger was still twisting Lizzie's hand backwards. She looked kinda wobbly from the wolf's strike, though.

Lizzie used that to her advantage. She shoved Tiger back. She tumbled to the ground and lay there, not moving.

"Tiger!" Jadeine cried.

"No time!" Jill reminded them.

"Yes, no time at all!" Lizzie agreed gleefully. She raised her hand.

And this time there was no one to stop her...

Chapter 41
Prophecies Are Never Wrong

They were about to die. And fail H.E.A.L. It had been Abby's job to save H.E.A.L, and yet she couldn't. She hadn't known it was possible to do anything other than the prophecy!

Abby glanced at Cherry. Jill was trying to calm her down, but Cherry was sobbing..

Abby wished that no one had to sacrifice themselves.

The deadliest magic of all was aimed at them. And as Abby slowly watched the deadly magic, she realized that you couldn't do the exact opposite of the prophecy, no matter how hard you tried (Abby didn't want to do that, of course).

I can do this.

Abby summoned all of her magic and pushed it out of her body, enforcing a shield around her friends. The shield trembled. She needed more magic.

Jadeine used her staff and sent power through the shield.

It wasn't enough. Abby thought about what was at risk. Her mom. Her dad. Jill. Jadeine. Cherry. Tiger. Kevin. Ismelda. Crystal. Heck, even Aeryn and Nadine!

She needed to save them all. So she thought about everything she loved.

I love walks on a sunny afternoon. I love ice cream, especially chocolate. I love books. I love fairy tales. I love how Mom reads me fairy tales every day. I love her eyes. I love my dad. I like all my friends.

I like riding on dragons. I like using my magic. I like inhaling the scent of the earth. I like having a personal fairy godmother. I like being called a mad scientist. I like biking. I like roller coasters.

I like sleeping under the stars.

Then Abby imagined having it all gone. Every single thing she valued in this world, gone. Abby couldn't let that happen.

"Abby! We need more magic!" Jadeine yelled.

"Abby! Your mom woke up!" Jill cried.

"Abby! Look! The wolf!"

"Abby! LOOK!"

"Abby, the dark magic is coming through!"

"ABBY, DO SOMETHING!"

Abby's hair flapped wildly like it was windy, and her insides did feel stormy. What would others say if she let down the shield?

Abby Palmer was supposed to be our hero. But she's our failure.

Abby hated being a failure, even when it was just the wrong answer on a pop quiz. Or a burnt edge on a grilled cheese.

Abby thought of Caprese sandwiches, and the shield became a tiny bit stronger. She thought of all the hard work she had put herself and her friends through.

Abby took deep breaths. She couldn't keep the shield up forever. She needed the strongest power source for magic. But…what?

"Abby! It almost touched me!" Jill shrieked.

Abby thought harder. Then she realized. It was *her*. She had to sacrifice herself as well. She could be a hero, right? Just…a dead one.

Abby shook off the thought. No, there had to be another way. However, in situations like this, options were quite limited.

"I'm sorry, guys," Abby breathed.

"WHAT DO YOU MEAN, SORRY?!" Tiger cried.

"I-I-I'll turn into the shield," Abby explained.

"ABBY, NO!" Abby's mom yelled.

"Sorry," Abby shrugged.

"You can't just say sorry! GET BACK RIGHT NOW!" her mom ordered. "You have to do what I say! I AM YOUR MOTHER!"

Abby shook her head. *I, Abby Palmer, will turn into a shield and become magic itself.*

Abby focused her magic so hard that the shield faltered a bit. Jadeine reinforced it quickly. Abby's hands slowly vanished. It was a tingling sensation. Abby was relieved that vanishing permanently didn't hurt.

Abby had imagined it would be like a chainsaw. Ouch. Luckily, it wasn't. Abby's arms disappeared.

The missing arms became magic and made the shield a tiny bit stronger. Abby slowly, very, very slowly vanished.

"Abby. You. Cannot. Do. This." Jill glared at Abby, but her lip was trembling.

"Yes, I can, if you want to live," Abby replied.

"But I don't *want* to survive without you!" Jill wailed.

"I thought I was just a mere companion to you," Abby replied, growing sad.

"But you weren't!" Jill protested. "ABBY!"

Abby was almost gone. Her head only remained. It was probably creepy to the others. Or maybe not.

Lizzie's laugh grew louder and louder.

"You can't run from me!" she cackled.

"We're not doing that!" Tiger exclaimed.

"But you're not on the upper hand, are you?" Lizzie asked sweetly.

Jadeine let the shield drop a bit and blasted some magic towards Lizzie. Lizzie screeched and then fell on her back.

Abby's team took out all the relics. The dark magic grew so strong that Abby knew this was her moment.

Jill scrubbed her hands down her face.

"I won't let you go. Your sacrifice won't be needed," Jill declared.

The dark magic became stronger, and Jill's eyebrows creased. Then, Abby's hair began vanishing.

"Abby! No!" Abby's mom exclaimed.

"Yes."

"No." Abby's mom grunted.

"Yes," Abby replied.

"No."

"Yes."

"No."

"Yes."

"No."

"Yes, Mom, yes."

"NO!"

Abby's mom was hysterical when Abby's neck vanished. And then her eyelashes.

"I'm sorry, everyone. This is for H.E.A.L," Abby whispered.

And with that, the girl known as Abby Palmer, age 12, disappeared into purple sparks.

And it didn't look like she was coming back.

Chapter 42
Poisonous Berries

Jill watched in horror as Abby disappeared. She swung at the air frantically and saw purple sparks fly up and shield them.

Was it too much to hope that Abby was still there?

Was it?

"Okay, guys!" Jadeine commanded. "I know that we need to…" Jadeine looked at Cherry. "Well, you know. Uh, sacrifice someone, but first, we have to try our magic and the relics' magic. Maybe we won't have to sacrifice someone then."

Melissa nodded. "Okay. Jadeine and I can use our magic."

"Me too!" Tiger chimed in.

"Tiger, not your mind-reading magic. Sorry," Jadeine explained.

Everybody aimed the relics towards the Book. The relics sent a rainbow light towards the Book of Light. Then, Melissa and Jadeine directed their magic into the book. Purple and green light flew into the Book. The Book of Light grew brighter, brighter still.

Jill held her breath. Would it work? Lizzie was still standing there. She was obviously in pain because her face was stressed, but she wasn't disappearing.

"Ugh, AGAIN!" Jadeine shouted. "Pour all your magic into it! Well, not all, but as much as you can!"

They tried again. Magic shot into the Book. The Book grew brighter, but their magic still wasn't working!

"MELISSA, WHEN I SAY USE AS MUCH MAGIC AS YOU CAN, I MEAN USE AS MUCH MAGIC AS YOU CAN!" Jadeine screamed.

"Abby's mom is doing her best!" Apple exclaimed. "But we need something more! We need…me."

"What?" Cherry asked, bewildered. "Apple, no!"

"I have to, Cherry," Apple said. "I want to die with honor and grace."

"NO, APPLE, NO!" Cherry screamed. "DON'T DO THIS! PLEASE!"

Cherry reached forward to grab Apple, when Jadeine pulled her close to her and whispered something into her ear.

Whatever it was, it made Cherry howl. Her howl didn't contain any exact words. It was a howl of a sister who was about to lose her beloved brother forever.

The Big Bad Wolf tried to get to them, but the shield contained powerful magic.

For a second, everyone's attention was on the Big Bad Wolf. But those couple of seconds were enough for Apple. A big flash of blinding light came from the Book of Light's direction. Cherry froze. She knew without looking that Apple was gone. Cherry could soon see tears on everyone's stricken faces. But she didn't look. Looking would mean that Apple was gone, and she wanted to believe he wasn't.

"Guys, stop," Cherry did her best to laugh, but it came out as a strangled cry. "It's not funny. Stop pretending that he sacrificed himself."

"Cherry…I'm so sorry," Jill whispered.

Cherry's eyes flashed with rage as she spun around. She instantly regretted it. Cherry looked up at the purple sparks that seemed to look…sad? It was Abby, sort of. But Cherry didn't care.

"I DON'T CARE IF YOU CAN'T HEAR ME OR NOT! I! WILL! KILL! YOU! FOR GOOD!" Cherry screamed.

She tried to run, but instead, she fell to the ground, sobbing. Tears fell from her eyes and onto the ground.

"No…Apple…you can't be gone…no…" Cherry mumbled, tears falling from her face.

Everyone stared at Cherry sympathetically, but a stream of light from the Book made them look away from Cherry. The light soared in an arc towards Lizzie. Lizzie screamed and crumpled…but didn't fade.

It hadn't worked. But the only thing that mattered to Cherry was that Apple was dead, and she felt even worse now that his sacrifice went in vain. She screamed at the top of her lungs and pounded the ground. Everyone's eyes became blurry with tears, and for a second, they all cried together. But then, Jadeine realized why it hadn't worked, and she wiped away her tears.

"Apple's sacrifice wasn't in vain!" Jadeine exclaimed. "Remember, we need to 'kill' her at the witch's hour!"

"Um…we can go forward in time!" Jill suggested, wiping away a tear.

"It won't be that easy. We need magical thyme and a transportation potion." Jadeine said. "Abby's mom might have some transportation potions in her pocket."

Tiger ran over to Abby's mom and checked her pockets. Tiger triumphantly pulled out a vial of purple transportation potion.

"Amazing. Jill, can you get the thyme? It's located in the Elven Forest," Jadeine requested.

"But…elves!" Jill cried.

"Yes, we know, elves. JUST GO!" Tiger ordered.

Jill snatched the transportation potion and held it, thinking, '*I want to go to Elven Forest—even though I really, really, really, don't want to.*' Jill opened her eyes and saw a pine tree in front of her face.

Jill scoured her surroundings for thyme, but she only saw blackberries. Mmm. Tempted, Jill grabbed a bushel and promptly ate it. Suddenly, her stomach churned and she became nauseated. She had eaten poisonous berries. It was only a matter of time before she died!

Jill raced through the woods, refusing to throw up. Jill had learned that she'd throw up her heart if she did! She crouched down and searched for thyme. Jill's eyes landed on a single thyme leaf. She plucked it from the ground.

Then Jill saw a person. No, not a person. An elf. The elf looked at her, and the elf's eyes widened. Jill needed to get back to the battleground, and fast. Elves and humans never mixed very well…but that was a story for another time.

Please, please, let me go back to the battleground within the shield, PLEASE! Jill prayed. With a pop, Jill returned to the battlefield. The defense looked weaker. Jill handed the transportation potion and the thyme leaf to Jadeine, out of breath.

Jadeine muttered something to herself. She put the thyme leaf in the transportation potion. The liquid swelled like a hurricane, and without even noticing it, the sky had turned dark. It was 3:00 a.m.

The Book sent an even brighter light towards Lizzie. Lizzie capsized like a sinking boat. She shriveled to the ground, like a dead plant. Then…

Then, Lizzie disappeared for good. And she wasn't coming back.

"OH MY GOD. I CAN'T BELIEVE WE DID THIS," Jill said what was on all their minds.

The sky turned blue again, and they reappeared in Cinderella Town. The villagers looked at them, mouths agape.

"Everyone," Jadeine announced. "We have defeated Lizzie!"

The crowd erupted into loud, happy cheers. Lots of them laughed in happiness. A few cried with tears of joy.

Cherry looked up. She obviously couldn't handle all this happiness, not when she had just lost Apple. She got to her feet, wiped away her tears, and ran away somewhere.

"You did it!" A little girl clapped her hands in approval.

Jill smiled so wide that she thought her ears would fall off. Jill searched the sky for purple sparks…*there!*

Jill felt like shrieking with excitement as the sparks swirled closer to the ground. A jar formed, and the sparks went inside. Jill picked it up and unscrewed the lid. The sparks flew out, and slowly but surely, Abby started to take shape.

And in a minute, standing before Jill was Abby Palmer. Abby hugged Jill briefly, then raced to her mom and leaped into her arms. A chorus of 'awwww' came from the crowd.

It wasn't long before a huge crowd amassed. Jill watched as they all flocked around Abby. Melissa turned invisible. Jill got it. Everyone hated Melissa.

"Yes, yes, yes…it was scary," Abby told them.

"Abby! What is it like to have the bad fairy as your mom? She must have deserted you long ago, because, well, she's evil!" a person with a 'Go Abby!' shirt asked.

Jill winced as Abby's happy face turned to stone. "You don't know anything about her. She's the best mom in the world, and you all are so wrong about her!"

Jill smirked as the person with the 'Go Abby!' shirt backed away.

Jill noticed everyone seemed to ignore her. Jill was fine with that. She didn't like too much attention anyway.

Jill looked at Jadeine as her stomach began churning again.

"Um, you look…OH NO, DID YOU EAT POISONOUS BERRIES?!" Jadeine shrieked.

Jill's eyes bulged, and she nodded. Jadeine muttered a spell, and Jill felt much better. She wrapped her arms around Jadeine.

"Thank you so, so much," Jill said.

"You're welcome," Jadeine replied, smiling.

"Hey, Jadeine. Can I see Jack now?" Jill asked.

"Yeah…we can tell Abby and go," Jadeine replied.

"Oh, please! I can't wait!" Jill exclaimed. "We'll see Abby later!"

"Well…all right." Jadeine sighed.

Jadeine lifted her staff and grabbed Jill's hand. They soared into the blue skies and dove when they saw Jadeine's forest. Jill jumped off the staff and landed with a 'thump!' on the ground.

Jill raced to the castle and saw Amelia sitting on the steps.

"Amelia!" Jill gasped. "Is that you?"

Amelia looked up and gasped.

"What? How many relics did you find?" Amelia asked.

"All of them! And the book! AND we defeated Lizzie!" Jill yelled. She squealed. The excitement finally surged through her. She felt light-headed.

"REALLY?!" Amelia exclaimed.

"Yeah, it's amazing! Wait, how did you escape?" Jill asked.

"I…it's complicated," Amelia grinned,

"Well, ok. By the way, is Jack still here?" Jill asked.

"No, he felt better yesterday, and I took him back home," Amelia replied.

"Well, to town it is," Jill decided. "Bye, Amelia! Have fun in the castle!"

"Seriously? *Have fun in the castle?*" Amelia grumbled.

Jill skipped off into the forest, then ran. When she saw the town, her heart raced with thrill. She splashed in the fountain and laughed. She was starting to think splashing in the fountain was becoming a ritual here.

Jill turned and saw Jack! She rushed to him and hugged her brother tightly.

"Jill!" Jack exclaimed. "You survived!"

"Everyone did!" Jill replied. "Well…not everyone…"

"What?! Did Lizzie kill someone?!" Jack asked.

"No. But…" Jill trailed off.

"Tell me! WHO DIED?" Jack asked with anticipation.

"Uh, just…Prince Apple," Jill replied, rubbing her forehead. She knew her brother wasn't going to take this news well.

"That's not good," Jack whispered.

Jill nodded solemnly as Jack began to go delusional. His eyes bulged and his face went pale. Jill waved her hand in front of his face, but Jack took no notice.

"Uh…Jack, are you okay?" Jill asked.

"The prince…gone…" Jack gasped.

"Yeah, uh, let's not talk about that," Jill decided hastily. "Where's Mom?"

Jack opened his mouth to say something, but a delighted scream behind him cut him off. Jill slowly turned around and faced their mom.

"Jill! You're back, alive, and in one piece!" Jill's mom exclaimed.

She rushed to hug Jill. When Jill buried her head in her mother's hair, she smelled raindrops and…brownies?

"Mom, what were you making?" Jill asked, drawing back.

"Just a little 'goodbye Lizzie' treat!" Jill's mom giggled.

Jill stared at her mom. Her mom grabbed their hands and pulled them inside their house.

As she walked into the kitchen, she remembered standing on a step stool, making bakery items alongside her mother.

On the table, a big blob of brownie sat in a foil tin. There were three pieces cut out—presumably for Jack, her mom, and her dad. Jill took a seat and stuffed one brownie into her mouth while reaching for another one.

"Mmmm, so good." Jill moaned with delight.

"Really? It's that good?" Jack asked.

Jill glared at him. "Hey, you didn't survive for a week on a disgusting can of watery tomatoes."

"I guess I didn't."

Jack ate a bit of his brownie and then looked at the walls of the kitchen. Jill also stared at the walls…until she saw something strange. A blue flicker of light. And then a hologram of Abby appeared. Jill jumped out of her seat.

"Hi, Jill. I…have to leave now, so…will you come?" the hologram asked.

"Um…sure," Jill agreed.

Jill walked out of the doorway without a backward glance. After she was out the door, she ran to the mermaid fountain, where Abby, her mom, and her dad were waiting.

Jill threw her arms around Abby.

"Don't leave!" Jill exclaimed.

"I want to stay, I really do. But my mom…" Abby trailed off.

Abby's mom was tapping her foot impatiently beside her.

"She hates this place. Everybody hates her, too. And…I can't stay." Abby sighed.

"But you have to!" Jill moaned.

"Jill…I don't want to leave, but I have to." Abby's voice cracked a bit.

"You can't!" Jill protested.

"You don't get it! Now, Abby, we have to go!" Abby's mom snapped, looking around.

"Mom…just some final words," Abby pleaded.

"Yes, Melissa. Abby may never be able to see them again," Jay said.

Abby's mom nodded reluctantly. Jill hugged Abby.

"Jill, you're my best friend," Abby whispered.

"Thank you. Promise me we'll always be best friends, forever, no matter what," Jill whispered back.

"I promise," Abby vowed.

Jill squeezed Abby as hard as she could. When Jill let go, she saw that Tiger and Jadeine had arrived.

"I'm going to miss you all." Abby smiled sadly. "This is goodbye."

"Bye, Abby," they all chorused.

Jill felt dust in her eyes and blinked two times, before looking at Abby…or where she had been standing. Jill frantically looked around, but she didn't see Abby.

Jill wiped her eyes and, with her head down, headed back home.

Chapter 43
Looking to the Night Sky

Abby was ecstatic the minute she stepped into the house with her dad.

Abby's dad picked her up and tossed her into the air, as if she were still 6 years old. But Abby didn't mind. Sunshine and smiles filled the house, and warmth filled Abby. Her dad slowly lowered her to the ground, and Abby jumped out of his arms.

Then, her mom's eyes filled with tears, and she hugged Abby's dad.

"Why did you leave without telling me?" Abby's mom asked him.

"I knew you wouldn't let me. I didn't think I'd be stuck there forever," he replied.

"I'm just so glad you're back," Abby's mom whispered, squeezing him tighter.

Abby cringed at every word. She hated it when her parents got mushy, which was pretty much all the time.

"Mom! Please stop getting all mushy! It's torture!" Abby exclaimed.

"All right, all right," Abby's mom laughed. "Maybe your dad can make his famed Caprese sandwich!"

"YES!" Abby exclaimed a little too loudly.

Abby's dad chuckled, shook his head, and went into the kitchen to get the ingredients.

Abby watched in wonder as her dad skillfully sprinkled mozzarella cheese, basil, and sliced tomatoes on top of a slice of bread. How did he so effortlessly manage to keep all the cheese from spilling? How did he make the tomato look so juicy? Abby's dad put a second slice of bread on top of it, then put it inside their panini maker. After some time, three delicious-looking Caprese sandwiches sat on their plates.

Abby gulped her sandwich down in no time. Flavors swirled through her mouth. She felt the crunch of the tomato and the cheesiness of the cheese.

"Mmm," Abby moaned blissfully. "This is the best sandwich I've ever had!"

"You always say that," Abby's dad said with a laugh.

"True," Abby said. "That's because you're the best at making Caprese sandwiches."

Abby's dad tipped his imaginary hat to her. "Yes, I am."

Even though nothing was funny, they laughed. After Abby licked the entire plate, she put her dish in the sink.

Abby checked the clock on the wall to see if it was past her bedtime. Unfortunately, it was past 9:00, which was Abby's bedtime. She never broke her mom's rules.

Abby rushed upstairs and flung herself onto her bed. She sank into her mattress and stared up at the blank white wall.

She reminisced about her adventure at H.E.A.L. A tiny ball of anger formed inside her when she remembered how she couldn't say goodbye properly because her mom had dragged her out of there. And Abby's eyes gradually filled with tears when she remembered how Apple had sacrificed himself. She hadn't been in her regular human form, but she had seen everything.

Cherry's cries and screams filled her mind, and Abby choked out a sob. Cherry's screams made her want to cry. Tears trickled down her cheeks. Abby tried to forget the screams and cries, but they haunted her mind. Abby covered her ears with her pillow, but the screams only seemed to grow louder.

Her mind quickly thought up all the good memories, like when she had met Snow White, and when she had tried the Caprese sandwich in the restaurant where Maria had served them, even if Nightshade the dragon had broken out.

The screams floated away. A smile slowly crept across Abby's face as she remembered the crowd cheering when the news that Lizzie was sent away to the Badlands.

Her story was like a fairy tale. There had been many hardships, betrayals and tears along the road to defeat Lizzie. But she had met good people, and that had led to their success. In the end, they had defeated the villain.

Abby thought about how her story was over. And how her story had a happy ending, like all fairy tales. She wasn't sad that she wouldn't be able to go back to H.E.A.L, but at least she had a memory.

Her eyelids grew heavy as she drifted off into her dream world yet again.

But little did she know that her story had just begun.

Epilogue
For Better Or For Worse

Apple wasn't the only one dead.

A part of Cherry had died along with him—the part of her that loved and felt joy. The part of her with the moral compass.

Cherry gazed at Apple's empty bed, still neat with the sheets made, waiting for Apple to come back and sleep in the bed again. *Well, that's not going to happen now,* Cherry thought.

Tears pricked Cherry's eyes. Cherry didn't want to cry, but she couldn't stop herself. Tears fell out of her eyes for the millionth time, rolling down her cheeks. A whimper escaped from her mouth.

The door swung open, and a maid stood outside her room.

"Your mother wishes to see you," the maid reported.

"Ok, now *go away!*" Cherry exploded, embarrassed that the maid had caught her crying. How DARE the maid come in at a time like this?

"Sorry, miss," the maid bowed her head in shame.

"I JUST SAID GO AWAY!" Cherry yelled.

The terrified maid scampered away.

Cherry walked to her mom's room. When Cherry saw Snow's black dress, she knew what was happening.

"Apple's funeral," Cherry guessed, with no emotion in her voice.

"Yes. We have to go now, Cherry," her mom whispered.

"Well, I don't want to!" Cherry yelled. She didn't want to see her brother officially declared dead.

"You have to." Her mom glared at her. "It won't be respectful otherwise."

"Apple knows me! He knows I'm not respectful, and he'll know why I didn't come!" Cherry exclaimed. Her eyes were once again brimming with tears. But her mom wasn't having it.

"Cherry, no excuses," her mom hissed.

Cherry crossed her arms, but nodded.

Snow handed Cherry a black dress, and Cherry went to her room. She slipped it on and gazed at herself in the large mirror before going out of the palace. Her tears had stopped. She felt in a trance. Here, but not here.

Snow White held the door of the royal carriage open for her, and Cherry took a seat inside. The inside of the carriage had white plush seats and a velvet carpet. The top was curved and covered with golden streaks.

The carriage rolled along the uneven cobblestones. The palace gates opened, and Cherry closed her eyes. Too many memories.

When they arrived at the funeral site, Cherry was slightly comforted by the fact that it was situated in a lush garden, rather than a gloomy field.

Apple's many portraits rested on an altar. An empty casket was just behind it. Ode to Joy played in the background. *Seriously? Couldn't they have picked a sadder song?*

Cherry took a seat in a black folding chair and tried not to look at the casket. She looked at the mortician, but when the mortician moved in front of the casket, Cherry saw baby breath and lavender resting on top of it. Tears pricked at her eyes again.

"Welcome," the mortician greeted them. He was also dressed in black. "Let us take this moment of silence and respect."

Everyone bowed their heads in unison. After that, it was time to pray.

Cherry closed her eyes and touched her hands together in a prayer position. What she thought during the thirty seconds was:

This is all Abby Palmer's fault. Why couldn't she sacrifice herself, huh? I bet she made Apple do it! I bet he would still be here today if it weren't for her! They were all lucky she was gone, and good riddance!

"Let us all open our eyes and have a moment of clarity."

That was the mortician. Cherry's eyes flew open.

He was starting the eulogy: "Apple White was a son, brother, and a prince. We here are: his grieving sister and mother, and his loyal subjects, in death and life. He was beloved, and he was on track to be a wonderful king one day. His death was not in vain. May his soul rest in peace."

"Amen," everyone chorused.

"Now, we shall each have a turn at the altar to speak about his life. Your Majesty?"

Snow rose and walked shakily to the altar. She cleared her throat. "Apple was the best son you could ask for." Her voice cracked. "He always beat me at chess, and—and—" She got too choked up to speak. The mortician asked her to take a seat.

"Now, Princess Cherry, would you be so kind as to grace us with your pre—Princess Cherry, where are you going?"

Cherry was already out the door. She couldn't listen to this anymore.

"Cherry!" Snow called after her. "Cherry, come back!"

Cherry didn't.

The next day, it was sunny. Too sunny. It was as if the sky had forgotten what had happened to Apple and moved on already.

Cherry moved robotically through her daily routine. Snow White hadn't left her room since the funeral.

A maid holding out an envelope (the same maid from before) walked tentatively into the dining hall, where Cherry was having breakfast. "Your Majesty, someone's sent a letter for you."

Cherry snatched the envelope and opened it. She dismissed the maid, and the maid scurried away. Inside was a letter which read:

Dear Princess Cherry,

A lot's happened since we last saw each other.

Abby and Melissa went back to their home in the Unknown. That rotten Fairy Godfather bribed us into letting him get off easy by freeing Jay Palmer, Abby's father. He (Jay) went home with his family.

Jack and Jill also went back to their town. Their mother is overjoyed. She even made everyone brownies—Jill gave some to me. They were delicious. You should really try the brownies.

Jadeine moved in with her sister, out of that creepy castle in the middle of nowhere. Speaking of Jadeine's creepy castle, Amelia apparently likes that castle. So she lives there now.

Eleanor has her son Cyrus back, as you know. It's a little awkward between them, 'cause they've spent so many years apart, but I'm sure it'll get better eventually. All things take time.

The Sea Witch AND Nadine are being thrown into Mermaid Jail because it turns out that The Little Mermaid was originally supposed to take the throne. However, even before the seafoam incident, Nadine had already become Merqueen! Nedora has now claimed her rightful position as Merqueen.

Kevin the gambler! I'm actually not sure what happened to him. He disappeared shortly after Abby did. His last words to me were: 'Stay safe and don't do anything I would do.'

Lizzie's gone for good, I think. Unfortunately, the same cannot be said for the Big Bad Wolf. He ran off into the forest after his queen disappeared, but he has apparently been sighted once in Jill's village and once by a random person (although that person was related to the Boy Who Cried Wolf, so I'm not sure how credible their account is).

As for me, well, I'm still living with my dad. Back to my old life. I'm helping with the search for the Big Bad Wolf. I visit Jill, Jadeine, Amelia, and Eleanor occasionally. I tried to visit you once, but the maid said you were busy.

OK. Enough rambling. Let me say what I started this letter to say:

Cherry noticed that from this point on, the letter was splotched with wetness. Teardrops.

I'm so sorry about Apple.

I miss him so much. His smile. His eyes. How he loved Nightshade the dragon.

Cherry, believe me, I would've stopped him if I could've. But that doesn't help, does it?

I'm so, so, sorry. If there's anything I can do for you, I'm here.

Always,

Tiger Canterwood

Cherry crumpled up the letter and threw it into the corner. *TIGER is sorry?! TIGER misses Apple?! She doesn't know anything about Apple! How could she, of all people, MISS him?!* Cherry thought.

Cherry marched to the door and walked down the long hallway. At the end of the hall, there was a display chamber.

At the end of the chamber was Marianne, the magic mirror. Cherry walked into the room and knocked twice on Marianne's glass. She wanted *power*. Power to save herself from misery. To make Abby pay.

And most importantly, to get Apple back. That kind of power would only come if she were a queen. No, the ONLY queen.

The mirror glowed pink and red. "Yes, Your Majesty?"

Cherry smiled coyly. "Give me magic, give me all, make me queen of them all."

Cherry's eyes were turning green, a hideous neon green.

Just. Like. Lizzie.

Acknowledgements:

We've had a wonderful time creating this story. It started with an idea, and then it grew into so much more.

We would like to thank all the people who gave us their full support throughout the creation of this book. We're grateful to all the people who took the time to read this book.

Buckets of sunshine and brightness to Shambhavi Pophale, one of our best friends, for her initial contributions.

Thank you to our parents who reviewed our drafts. Our story would have been very dull without you.

Thank you to our wonderful teachers, who made us better and smarter students.

www.ingramcontent.com/pod-product-compliance
Lightning Source LLC
Chambersburg PA
CBHW031153010826
48971CB00012B/115